# BOLEYN
*Traitor*

# Also by Philippa Gregory

**THE PLANTAGENET AND TUDOR NOVELS**
*The Lady of the Rivers*
*The Red Queen*
*The White Queen*
*The White Princess*
*The Kingmaker's Daughter*
*The Constant Princess*
*The King's Curse*
*Three Sisters, Three Queens*
*The Other Boleyn Girl*
*The Boleyn Inheritance*
*The Taming of the Queen*
*The Queen's Fool*
*The Virgin's Lover*
*The Last Tudor*
*The Other Queen*

**ORDER OF DARKNESS SERIES**
*Changeling*
*Stormbringers*
*Fools' Gold*
*Dark Tracks*

**THE FAIRMILE SERIES**
*Tidelands*
*Dark Tides*
*Dawnlands*

**THE WIDEACRE TRILOGY**
*Wideacre*
*The Favoured Child*
*Meridon*

**TRADESCANT NOVELS**
*Earthly Joys*
*Virgin Earth*

**MODERN NOVELS**
*Alice Hartley's Happiness*
*Perfectly Correct*
*The Little House*
*Zelda's Cut*

**SHORT STORIES**
*Bread and Chocolate*

**OTHER HISTORICAL NOVELS**
*The Wise Woman*
*Fallen Skies*
*A Respectable Trade*

**NON-FICTION**
*The Women of the Cousins' War*
*Normal Women*
*Normal Women Teen Edition*

# PHILIPPA GREGORY
# BOLEYN TRAITOR

WILLIAM MORROW
*An Imprint of HarperCollinsPublishers*

Without limiting the exclusive rights of any author, contributor or the publisher of this publication, any unauthorized use of this publication to train generative artificial intelligence (AI) technologies is expressly prohibited. HarperCollins also exercise their rights under Article 4(3) of the Digital Single Market Directive 2019/790 and expressly reserve this publication from the text and data mining exception.

This is a work of fiction. Names, characters, places, and incidents are products of the author's imagination or are used fictitiously and are not to be construed as real. Any resemblance to actual events, locales, organizations, or persons, living or dead, is entirely coincidental.

BOLEYN TRAITOR. Copyright © 2025 by Philippa Gregory. All rights reserved. Printed in the United States of America. No part of this book may be used or reproduced in any manner whatsoever without written permission except in the case of brief quotations embodied in critical articles and reviews. For information, address HarperCollins Publishers, 195 Broadway, New York, NY 10007. In Europe, HarperCollins Publishers, Macken House, 39/40 Mayor Street Upper, Dublin 1, D01 C9W8, Ireland.

HarperCollins books may be purchased for educational, business, or sales promotional use. For information, please email the Special Markets Department at SPsales@harpercollins.com.

hc.com

Originally published in the United Kingdom in 2025 by HarperCollins Publishers.

FIRST US EDITION

Library of Congress Cataloging-in-Publication Data has been applied for.

ISBN 978-0-06-343968-9

25 26 27 28 29 LBC 5 4 3 2 1

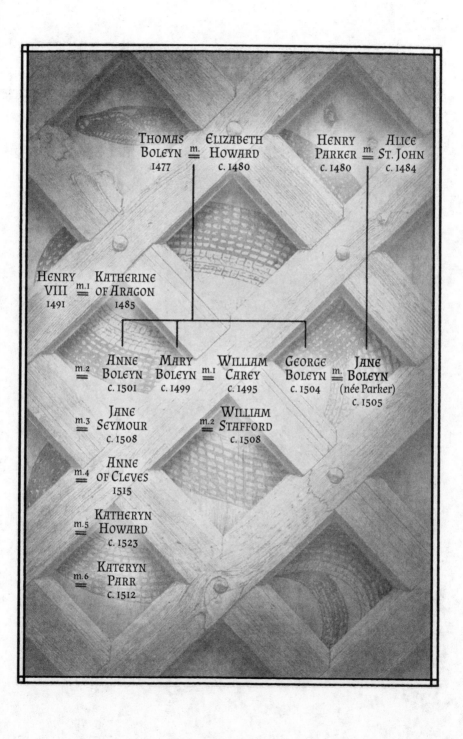

# GREENWICH PALACE, SUMMER

## 1534

In the hammered silver of the mirror, we look like two headless ghosts – our black hoods hiding our faces. I throw back the thick veil to reveal the mask of a golden falcon. The sharp beak is enamelled gold, the flaring eyebrows brass. The feathers of head and throat are cloth of gold: they shift and settle like plumage, speckled like peregrine feathers, as if a free bird has been cursed into gold by *Midas*.

I push up my mask over my light brown hair to show my creamy skin, my secretive smile.

'And you can take that look off your face,' Anne says, throwing back her own hood, raising her head for me to raise her veil and free her of her mask.

'What look?'

'Your false face – your two-faced face. What are you thinking?'

A courtier's mouth is always full of unspoken words. 'I was thinking: it's going to be hard to dance in this,' I lie. 'It's going to be hard to see.'

'We're here to be seen, not to see.'

She gets up and spreads her arms for me to unlace her stomacher, her sleeves, the skirt of her gown. She scratches her rounded belly through the fine linen shift. Five months into her second pregnancy, she is more tired than with her first. She says this is a sign of a son. Her daughter, Princess Elizabeth, was easier to carry. She rests on her bed every afternoon before dinner when the king is bathing and changing his clothes after his afternoon sports.

'What's the masque called?' she asks, climbing into the great golden bed.

'*The Falconers.* We dance as birds, and then . . .'

'Let me guess,' she interrupts. 'The king and his friends come in disguised as falconers, and they catch us, and we dance with them? And then we all unmask, and I discover I am dancing with the king! I am amazed! I had no idea! I thought he was a handsome stranger.'

I give a trill of false laughter. 'You're so funny!'

I take off her embroidered shoes and peel down her fine silk stockings. This is honourable work for a lady-in-waiting to a queen, and the duty of a beloved sister-in-law. I am proud to be both.

She closes her eyes. 'Surely, not even he can believe I don't know my own husband?'

Of course, the king does not think that we believe a group of strange Savoy princes or unknown Russian lords in thick furs have burst into the queen's presence chamber. This is a game at court that we all play knowingly, and the prize is that the king shines. Among all the playacting is a single truth: the second son, the second-rate, second choice has been transmuted into gold; he is heir. Over and over again, we re-enact this miracle, as if it were the greatest luck that Arthur, the firstborn, died, and Henry became heir and then king. Twenty years ago, someone named him the 'handsomest prince in Christendom', and we have had to keep it up ever since.

When I first came to court as a maid-of-honour I was a lonely bookish little girl of eleven and he was the twenty-six-year-old dazzling young husband to the beautiful queen: Katherine of Aragon. I fell in love with him, with her, with the glamour and beauty of the young royal couple. Then I fell in love with the whole Boleyn family: Anne, her ambitious brother George, her sweet-natured sister Mary, their parents, and the noble House of Howard – all professional courtiers as I wanted to be, in service to the most beautiful powerful court in the world.

Now, I am a Boleyn myself, married to George for almost half my life, rising with him to the title of Lady Rochford, nearly thirty years old. The queen I first loved and served is long gone, and the handsome king is in his prime. I have watched his need for praise grow from a young man's joy to a mature man's vanity, and I have learned – we all have – to fatten the compliments to match his hunger.

'Masking and revealing is a game to him,' I say soothingly. 'He just wants the world to see that you choose him, even when he is disguised. You fall in love all over again.'

'Well, I do,' she says, with a sudden wide false smile. 'I am Anne, "The Most Happy".'

I tuck the lambswool blanket around her. Thanks to Anne, I am first lady at court, and I will be aunt to her baby, the next king of England, and first in the procession to carry him to his baptism. It will be a victory parade for us beautiful, clever women – we will have defeated the old lords and won the king from them.

'When will you announce you're with child? You announced Elizabeth much earlier.'

She shrugs. 'When I choose.'

Only the favoured few know that she is expecting a baby this autumn. She is right to delay sounding the starting bell for a new race of eager young women to the king's bed; every slut at court will snatch at the king's attention when they know the queen is pregnant.

'Do something for me, Jane,' she says as I warm lavender and juniper berry oil in my palms to rub on her swollen feet and ankles. 'Speak to that Agnes girl. She's not respectful.'

Agnes is a young maid-of-honour, blonde, and agreeable. Dark-haired Anne dislikes blonde, smiling women, but still, they flock to court in their best gowns.

'What's she done?'

'Her curtsey is too shallow; she bobs up and down as if I am nothing more than a viscountess.'

This is my title. I was born Jane Parker, won the name Boleyn through marriage, and now I am Lady Rochford. I pinch her toes, smiling. 'It's very grand to be a viscountess,' I tell her.

'It's good enough for now,' she agrees. 'But when I give birth to a prince, I'll have George named as a duke!'

This is the dizzying Boleyn ambition. My father's plan was for me to be a mid-rank courtier, expert in this new trade for educated men and women. He sent me to court speaking French and English and reading Latin. He advised me to learn German, as the Protestant thinkers write in German, and hide my Spanish from the Spanish queen.

But Anne never had any interest in discreet courtier work; she went straight to the fount of power and seduced and married the king. She has all the courage of her mother's grand house, the Howards, and all the ambition of the self-made Boleyns. If she wants a dukedom for George, she will get it, and I will be a duchess. Anne, and all of us, Boleyns and Howards, are on the rise – we cannot be distracted by a girl like Agnes.

'She curtseyed properly to the old queen. She used to sink down as if Katherine of Aragon was the Virgin Mary,' Anne complains.

We all did. But that was three years ago and courtiers' memories are as short-lived as mayflies.

'Dowager princess now,' I remind her.

'And she was talking to the Spanish ambassador,' Anne says fretfully. 'What can a fool like her have to say to a fool like him?'

I make a mental note to tell my patron that Agnes has been recruited into the Spanish ambassador's network of friends and spies. 'Oh, he talks to everyone,' I say reassuringly. 'What else can he do?'

'He can go home to Spain. He can lock himself up in Kimbolton Castle with the queen.'

'Dowager princess,' I prompt again.

'But who else does she talk to?' she asks. 'To the Papist lords? The Courtenays? The friends of the old queen and Princess Mary?'

'Lady Mary,' I remind her.

Queen Katherine is to be called dowager princess, and her

daughter is newly named as Lady Mary; but those who served and loved them refuse to miscall them, and the rest of us have to learn a new habit.

'None of them matter to you. You've won. It's only old people, childhood friends of the king! Doddering Papists! Looking back to the old days. Not us – not us of the new court, the new religion, the new world. Time is on our side. They'll die of old age or just give up. If your baby is a boy, it will prove that your marriage is God's will, and the old queen, her daughter, and the Spanish ambassador and all the faithful will just fade away.'

'Where's George?' she demands. 'He's late.'

I never complain of George being late; but I am his wife of ten years, and she is his queen.

'Go and fetch him, Jane.'

I am saved from looking like a needy wife hunting for her husband by a tap on the door that connects the queen's bedroom to the king's private gallery. George slips in, breathtakingly handsome in a new hose and jerkin of rich brown velvet. He carries a mask and a hat with a long sweeping heron's feather in his hand. He is like his sister: dark-eyed and dark-haired, as if they are twins, carved from mellow polished wood into the same hard intelligent features and darkly promising eyes.

'Behold a rustic falconer!' he announces and comes to the bed and takes Anne's hand to kiss. He looks at her keenly. 'You're pale.' He turns to me. 'You've not let her get overtired?'

'She only tried on her costume and ran through the dance – since then, she's been resting.'

I step towards him for a kiss of greeting; but he turns to sit beside her and unpins her hair. I hand him her silver hair brushes, and he sweeps the long dark heap of hair from her forehead and plaits it.

'I'm troubled,' Anne complains.

'Don't be,' he says instantly. 'You must think of holy things, joyous things to make the baby grow. You have to be Anne, "The Most Happy".'

'Agnes Trent,' I explain, and see his quick nod of thanks.

'She has to show respect,' Anne says.

George fastens two ivory pins in the plaits at the nape of her neck, so loosely that the king can release a tumble of her scented hair and bury his face in it when they are alone.

Anne gestures for me to slide on fresh stockings, and winces at the tightness of the red silk shoes. 'I've told Jane to speak to her.'

'She's a new favourite,' George warns me. 'Speak tactfully.'

'But clearly,' Anne insists. 'I'll have nothing less than complete loyalty. I didn't send the queen—'

'Dowager princess—' George and I say together.

'The dowager princess to Kimbolton Castle, Cardinal Wolsey to hell, and Bishop Fisher and Thomas More to the Tower, only to have enemies under my own roof. The old lords speak against me in council; their old wives gossip behind their hands. All the old people want everything back the way it was. They want the old queen back.'

'Well, you can't put them all in the Tower!' I joke; but nobody laughs. At once, I am grave. 'Of course, I'll speak to Agnes.'

Anne stands up in her tight shoes. 'Fetch her now; she can dress me.'

George drops a kiss on her shoulder and throws a salute to me 'Thank you!' he mouths, hidden by the door.

I see the door is safely closed behind him before I cross to the opposite door to the queen's privy chamber. 'Her Grace is ready for dressing,' I say, and three maids of honour obediently rise. Agnes swings past me, not a care in her world.

I touch her arm. 'Is there any reason that you don't make a proper curtsey to the queen?' I ask her pleasantly. 'I'm sure there must be some mistake.'

'No mistake but hers,' she says rudely. 'I curtsey low enough for her.'

'Curtsey low enough for a crowned queen. And let the matter end here.'

'It'll end where it started: with her.'

I tighten my grip. 'Mistress Agnes, when I was first at court, I minded my manners. That's how I rose to be first lady-in-waiting.'

'And I mind mine! There's no need for you to pinch me, Lady Rochford. Your sister has a Tower full of torturers to do that.'

'I wasn't pinching you,' I lie.

'And I curtsey just right,' she lies in reply, and goes into the queen's bedchamber.

I watch her through the open door, and I see that she does not.

NEXT DAY, AFTER prayers in the royal chapel, the king stays kneeling on the great embroidered cushion of his prie-dieu, with his hands steepled, his eyes closed, conferring directly with God. Nobody can move until he comes to himself. He beckons Anne to join him on his side of the chapel, and I follow her, carrying our prayer books and her pearl and coral rosary. The king's secretary, Thomas Cromwell, stands silently behind him, young Francis Weston and my husband George behind Cromwell. George winks as we join them. Francis gives a little bow.

'My lord husband,' Anne curtseys to the king, smiles at the courtiers, and acknowledges Thomas Cromwell with a small nod, as if he were a visiting tradesman, come with a bolt of worsted cloth.

'Cromwell has a question about the visit to France,' the king says, still on his knees, his hands clasped in prayer. Apparently, God is attending this meeting, too.

'I did not know if Your Grace wishes to visit France this summer?' Cromwell asks Anne, circling the obvious question: *are you with child?* 'Should His Majesty go to France alone?'

We have to persuade France to make an anti-Papist alliance, join us against the pope and Katherine of Aragon's nephew: the Emperor of Spain. But Anne cannot travel while she is pregnant, and she won't let the king out of her sight. Master Cromwell's inquiring brown eyes meet my grey ones.

'Oh! I shall need you at my side!' Anne cries to the king. She clasps her hands around his, as if he is swearing fealty. Henry holds the pose, like a knight errant kneeling to his lady. 'You can't leave me when I'm nearing my time!'

Of course, she is not due until the autumn and perfectly safe to travel; but Anne would rather die than go to France too broad-beamed to dance, and she would never allow the king alone with the notoriously beautiful women of the French court. We are staying home this summer, and so – as he is about to decide – is the king.

'What d'you think, Sire?' George asks the king, in a pretty masque of consultation.

'I ought to go.' The king is so cheered at the thought of a woman longing for him that he forgets about God and gets up. 'Lady Rochford, d'you think your lady would be able to sustain a separation from me? Very briefly?'

I don't need a look from Anne to prompt me. I know this playscript backwards. This is no ordinary love: this is *Tristan and Iseult* – a great Romance; they can never be parted. 'I wouldn't advise it,' I say gently. 'She would pine for you, Sire. But could your meeting with the King of France be delayed until after the birth? And then the visit could be a celebration? Part of the announcement and rejoicings?'

The king beams as he imagines his triumphant visit to France with the young wife who has given him the son, in place of the old one who did not.

Cromwell takes my hint and joins in. 'We could send a messenger to suggest a delay. Someone of importance – so they know there's no disrespect.'

The Duke of Norfolk, George's uncle, the head of the House of Howard, is the obvious choice; but he and Anne are barely speaking since he pulled off the brilliant trick of marrying his daughter to a royal bastard: the king's illegitimate son. And almost all the other noblemen are secretly on the side of the old queen.

'Oh, not one of the old lords!' Anne exclaims. 'Not one of the ancients!'

The king taps her cheek. 'Old friends,' he says. 'Faithful friends.'

'Exactly so! Old friends, old men!' She smiles at him. 'Stuck in their old ways – not like you!'

'Viscount Rochford?' Cromwell suddenly exclaims, as if my husband George were not standing right in front of him.

The king laughs. 'Perfect! But can you spare him, Lady Rochford? Or are you with child, too, and won't let him go?'

It is my hidden grief that we have been married ten years with no sign of a child. But I laugh as merrily as if I have never cried in George's arms. 'Ah, Sire, we can't all have our first child in the first year of marriage and a second in the second year! We are not all as happy as you and the queen!'

'"The Most Happy",' George confirms. We never allow anyone to forget Anne's motto.

The king takes Anne's hand and kisses it again. 'She has done all that she promised me,' he says dotingly. 'And I have done more than anyone thought possible. I am making a new England, for a new royal family. And my newborn son will prove that God blesses me and my bride.'

Anne glows at him and spreads her hand on the slight curve of her belly to make it look bigger.

'George shall go to France and tell them the meeting must be delayed until after the birth of my son,' the king declares. 'We'll visit in the autumn.'

'I'm honoured by your trust,' George says, as if he was going out to kill dragons. 'I'll not fail you.'

The heroic note is exactly right. Henry takes George's lower arm in a knight's grip. 'I know it, George. You are my brother.'

'We would have confidence in no other.' Anne smiles. She slides her hand on the king's arm and invites him to walk in the cool of the garden before we go to breakfast, just the two of them. I know that she wants to be rid of her ladies, trailing behind to distract him; but he imagines a young handsome king with a beautiful queen leaning on his arm, walking on grass speckled with flowers as bright as a new-woven tapestry.

Master Cromwell bows and goes out. George and I are left alone with Francis Weston.

'See how we rise!' George exclaims. 'Thank you, my love. You steered us right, as always – and now I can tell the King of France that I am to have a royal nephew!'

'Just my duty,' I say modestly.

He beams. 'You know, there were times when I thought I'd always be here, running love notes between Anne and the king, a diplomat in the maids' chamber, an ambassador in the sewing rooms, never getting to the source of power, always bobbing around in the froth.'

'Lord, I wish I could come with you,' Francis says, who has years of bobbing around ahead of him. 'But I shall guard your lady while you are gone, if she will accept my service.' He puts his hand on his heart and bows low to me.

'Oh yes, yes.' George waves away the game of courtly love as pointless without an audience. 'Jane – send a message to the stables. I'll need my horses reshod before we start. I'll take two spare. I'm famous for how fast I make this journey.' He kisses my outstretched hands. 'I'll come home quickly to you.'

I make sure I do not cling. 'I shall miss you,' I tell him.

'I'll be back inside a month,' he promises.

THE QUEEN'S ROOMS are dull without George to suggest a theme for a masque, a new way to wear a French hood, or a round of games. We are visited by an old lady of the former royal family: Margaret Pole, kinswoman to the king. Years ago, she used to come to hear our lessons in the royal schoolroom and praised me for being the cleverest of the old queen's little maids. She has never said one word against the tragedy of the divorce, or the humiliations that Anne heaped upon the old queen and her daughter. She begged for permission to serve Lady Mary or Queen

Katherine, and even offered to serve for free, but Anne insists that she is always refused.

Lady Margaret Pole wears a serene mask over her heartache. Today, she is accompanied by another royal kinswoman, Gertrude Courtenay. They curtsey to Anne to exactly the right depth, but somehow, they look as if they are doing her a favour. We sense their unspoken opinion that we are too noisy, too playful and young. Gertrude learned her manners from a strictly raised Spanish queen; we learned ours from the fashionable French. They think us too flirtatious, too witty. We read theology; we question too much for these unswervingly faithful Papists. Lady Margaret Pole's favourite son is a scholar at Rome, and has been writing a book about the errors of reform for all his life. It may be very fine – my father the scholar says it will be brilliant – but I think it would be better for Reginald Pole, and better for his old mother, if he were to accept that Anne has persuaded the king to become Protestant, and all of England must be Protestant, too.

Lady Margaret Pole and all her noble family are supporters of the old queen's daughter, Lady Mary, and nobody knows how far they will go to get her returned to court, acknowledged as a princess and royal heir, and restored to her lands and titles. They hate our Princess Elizabeth who has replaced her, and our queen who has replaced theirs; but you would never know it from their fine courtly manners. From the sharp pinnacle of their old-fashioned gable hoods to their elegant plain leather shoes, these are noble ladies condescending to their inferiors. In return, we do everything we can to make them feel outdated and out of place in our fashion-mad court.

Lady Margaret Pole greets the king's niece Margaret Douglas with affection and asks after her mother, who was Queen Regent of Scotland and still advises her son King James of Scotland. The old lady quietly remarks on Margaret's French hood and the raised hem of her gown that shows the embroidery on her silk stockings. Margaret blushes at this mild rebuke from her former governess, and Anne laughs aloud and says this is what they are wearing in

Paris – and even the countess must surely remember what it was like to be a pretty young girl, however long ago it was?

Anne is reckless in her power. She won't tolerate Lady Margaret Pole coming into her rooms and making her look like an upstart but Lady Margaret never wavers in her quiet dignity. No one but George could smooth Anne's ruffled feathers. He's so well read that he can argue like Martin Luther himself, and his love for Anne turns the vapid games of courtly love in her rooms into something tender and true.

Without him, the love-talk grinds on by rote; and more than one young man is reduced to stammering silence, strolling into the queen's room in a new silk cape, with a spray of roses in his hand, signifying true love, but no witty words ready-prepared. The lute player Mark breaks off his song and does a little twang to draw everyone's attention to his embarrassment, and we laugh unkindly at the young nobleman's shyness.

Anne needs me and George for she has no friends of her own. A self-made queen relies on self-made courtiers; everyone wants the chance to ride on this new queen's coattails. Anne's sister Mary is little use: more rival than supporter, as she was once the king's lover. She is at the Boleyn family home, Hever Castle, this summer, and Anne is in no hurry to bring her back to court. We are a court of upstarts, soaring without firm foundations, so, everyone is relieved when George comes home early, making the journey from the Queen of Navarre and her brother King Francis in three weeks, bringing gifts and messages of goodwill from the French court.

He has brought back a new tennis racquet from Paris and swears that he will challenge all comers. Anne promises a prize to the winner, and the master of revels draws up a tournament with all the noblemen of court on the list. They start in the early morning, and we ladies sit through the heat of the day on the queen's balcony, under the wooden roof that gets hotter and hotter as the day goes on. We watch the players sweat and lunge for difficult shots, enduring the nagging bang of the ball against the back of the court and the loud rolling on the roof above our heads.

'Shall I get you a tisane?' I whisper to Anne.

'You can tell your husband to hurry up and finish,' she says sourly.

He is playing the final match against the king, who is flushed and strong, dressed in white linen. The king has played two matches before this one, and his red-gold hair is dark with sweat, his damp shirt clinging to his muscled chest. When he stretches to hit a high ball or races to the net, he is as graceful as a bounding dancer.

George loses by a few points; he misses the last shot with a desperate lunge and goes off court laughing to Francis Weston, who wraps him in a drying sheet. The king, beaming with triumph, comes to stand below the queen's balcony, excited by his victory and laughing at George's Parisian racquet – demanding it as his prize as well as the gift from the queen.

George hands it over without hesitation, though it cost us a small fortune, and says that the king is by far the better player; but he will have his revenge next week. The ladies chime in, their voices like bells in full peal; everyone agrees that the king is as strong and as quick as a youth of twenty.

Not Agnes. She spent the entire tournament in the cool draught at the back of the queen's box, out of the burning sunshine. While we lean over the edge of the box to praise the king and tease his opponents, she says nothing; but drifts forward to stand beside me, and when the king rubs his red sweating face on the sleeve of his shirt, she drops her handkerchief – like a floating petal – down to him. He snatches it out of the air as if it were a thistle seed and puts it against his flushed cheek. He looks up at her and presses it to his mouth.

Anne's smile never wavers. She hands down the prize for the tournament – a gold hat pin – and she leads the way back to the queen's side of the palace. She sets her ladies to sewing shirts for the poor – it is always shirts for the poor when she is in a rage.

She waves George and me into her bedchamber, and I close the door quickly so that no one else can hear the storm break the moment we are alone.

'You saw that. She insults me.'

George is hot from the tennis court, with the sheet around his neck and his muslin shirt sticking to his back. 'I have to go and wash.'

'No, stay. You saw what she did. She insults me.'

'I smell like a horse.'

'It doesn't matter. Tell me what I should do. She's throwing herself at him!'

'At least let me wash!'

She flicks her hand in dismissal, and he goes into the grand stool room that adjoins her bedroom. We hear him splashing the big ewers of water over himself and lathering up her fine soap, and finally he comes out, his hair curly from the water, one bath sheet embroidered with her crowned initial wrapped around his waist and another thrown over his shoulders. She pays no attention to his nakedness.

'You saw her. She's doing everything but swive him under my nose.'

'Did this start while I was away in France?'

'Not that I've seen,' I say.

George rubs water from his ear with the sheet. 'Jane misses nothing. If Jane didn't see it, it's only just started. So, it's nothing: it's the game – the courtly love game. We all play it, all the time. You can't object . . . in your condition . . .'

'My condition's supposed to be my saviour!'

George looks at me to intervene.

'Your condition is your saviour,' I agree. 'It means you're above challenge. Even if he flirts with someone else, even if he falls in love . . .'

'He's already in love!' she shrieks. 'Unending love! Not like you, married by arrangement!'

'All marriages are arranged,' George says quickly. 'It's just that you arranged your own. And all marriages are of love. I didn't choose Jane, but I was glad to have the daughter of Lord Morley as my wife, and she's been as loyal as a . . .' He breaks off, trying to imagine a simile for loyalty in this false court.

'As a dog!' she snaps.

George puts his arm around my waist. 'Well, anyway, loving and loyal – and right! Jane's always right. As she says: you're above challenge. But while you're pregnant and he can't swive you, he's bound to have other women. He's not going to live like a monk for five or six months until your son's born and you're churched and can come back to your place – he's going to have someone! He always did before.'

'Before!' she repeats. 'Of course he had other women when he was married to an old queen constantly losing her babies! She was old and sick, and their marriage was cursed. But he's not going to have anyone other than me! I held him at arm's length for six years! Six years!'

'You didn't hold him at arm's length,' George points out. 'There was all sorts of kissing and pleasuring. Sortilèges. French tricks.'

I didn't know of this perverse and sinful behaviour. I had truly believed it was all courtly love. I hide my shock, and Anne doesn't thank George for the reminder.

'Next to nothing, and I could do it again now! Why shouldn't I hold him for another six months?'

The marriage is less than two years old, and it was made – uniquely – for love. Anne has made herself into a new sort of queen, a new sort of wife: a beloved-wife, a love-queen. She has made a new age for women – recognised for our beauty and brains. Is such a queen, married for love, as secure on her throne as one pledged in a cold-hearted international alliance? Or should a marriage made for love, last only as long as love? Does a husband, married for love, have to be seduced and won over and over again?

Of course, we know the answer to that! The king tells us in every joust he wins and every masque where he plays the hero. He must be courted and fall in love daily. He never tires of the game of courtly love. Every day he has to fall in love again. Every day: fresh and new and passionate. And this was all very well when Anne was a honeymoon wife, and we, ambitious courtiers, played the music and danced him into her arms. But how can a wife heavy with child dance like a seductive girl? What can she do when he is strictly forbidden by the Church from coming to her bed?

'He's never going to stop playing at courtship,' George says gently. 'He has to be adored. It's going to be "declare I dare not" to someone new every time you're with child. He has to be the great lover – desired above all others. You know that! You'll have to look the other way and know that when your son is born, you're back in the game. Until then, look the other way.'

'The queen looked the other way!' she exclaims bitterly. 'Never said a word against me until it was too late! See where that got her? Dowager princess in Kimbolton Castle and a household of half a dozen? Her daughter named "Lady Mary" – never to command as a princess again? If the queen had nipped it in the bud, I'd not be here today – and she'd not be there!'

George laughs – it is a masterstroke; only he would dare to laugh at her in her rage – and take her in his arms, half-naked. 'Nobody could ever have nipped you in the bud,' he assures her. He wraps his arms around her, sways her from side to side, and she closes her eyes and puts her hot angry face against his cool bare skin. 'Anne, sweetheart. Wait – what did he call you? Lady of my heart!'

Reluctantly, she giggles, remembering the king's laborious poetry. 'Never let us be apart.'

'Storm-tossed maiden!' he reminds her, and she laughs outright, leaning back in his arms. 'I can't blame him for that,' she says. 'That was one of my lesser lines.'

'It was brilliant,' he assures her. 'And you'll always be the love of his life. Agnes doesn't matter. You don't stoop to complain of a girl like her. Don't bring her to the court's attention; ignore her, and he'll court her and have her, and then he'll get bored and find another Agnes. He'll find dozens of Agneses during your reign. You won't care. We've won. You're queen, and once you have a prince and heir, you don't even need him in your bed.'

I think he has soothed her, and the storm has passed.

'He promised he would love me forever,' she says resentfully.

George shrugs. 'He married you. That's forever.'

Of course, Katherine of Aragon exiled in a cold castle, shows us all: it is not.

'Agnes shall leave court if she upsets you,' I suggest. 'Your mother can speak to her parents.'

'That's right.' George gentles Anne; he presses her into a chair and takes off her heavy hood. 'Rest,' he urges her. 'Rest and be calm for the baby. This baby's going to make everything all right.'

'Jane can get rid of Agnes.'

'I don't know how . . .' I begin, looking to George.

They laugh, their eyes bright as weasel kits. 'Oh, Jane, don't pretend!' George exclaims. 'You've been at court long enough.'

'Spill ink on her gown or wine on her linen, loosen her girth so her saddle slips and she falls from her horse.' Anne laughs.

'I can't loosen her girth!'

'No, don't kill her!' George agrees.

'Put a forbidden book in her chest and report her,' Anne suggests. 'Rub her shoes in dog shit. Or just tell the girls that you don't like her, and they'll do the rest for you.'

'I'm supposed to keep them orderly, not bully them – they'll hate me!'

'It doesn't matter who hates you, if we love you!' Anne knows the note to strike with me. 'We love you! George will protect his clever wife; the earl my father will protect his daughter-in-law; my uncle the duke will protect his niece! Remember, you're a Boleyn, of the House of Howard. You belong to us, and nobody can do anything against you.' She stops and laughs at me. 'Dear Jane! Look how she melts at the thought of being loved!'

George steps across to me and cups my face in his palms. 'Dearest Jane,' he says sweetly. 'Little wife. Get rid of Agnes for us. Do it for love?'

THAT EVENING, THE king calls for a circle dance: gentlemen in an outer circle, ladies on the inside. The king starts with Anne as his partner and works around the circle, dancing with each lady until he returns to his wife again. Each girl blushes as soon as he takes her hand: a king causes desire with his touch, just as he cures sickness. I feel the heat in my own face at his whispered: 'Ah, Jane! Pretty Jane! I danced my way all around just to reach you!'

He is nearly forty-three years old now, but, like everyone else at court, I cannot see his age. He is still handsome: his brown beard curling around his sensual mouth, his dark blue eyes smiling down at me as his warm hand takes mine. For me, for all of us, he will always be the stunningly handsome young boy-king who came to the throne at seventeen, married a Spanish princess for love and swore he would make his kingdom the finest in Europe. He is as light on his feet as he was then. He turns me in the steps of the dance and draws me close. 'Jane, I swear, if you were not my sister-in-law . . .'

I feel a blush in my own cheeks. The king has been the lover of sisters before, he was bedding Mary Boleyn when he fell in love with Anne.

'The queen would have me beheaded!' I whisper, and he laughs and squeezes my hand, and moves on in the dance.

Mark Smeaton, the lute player, should be standing with the musicians, but he dances around the outside of the circle and lingers beside Anne, never missing a note.

The dance takes the king from me to Agnes, and suddenly, she stumbles on her hem, and pitches into his arms. It's a shameless move from a maid-of-honour, she must be quite determined to capture his attention. Mark slows the cadence of his playing for a moment, and the king whispers something in her ear. She blushes like an innocent girl, recovers her balance, and Mark picks up the tune, and it is as if no one hesitated. The dance moves the king on to his next partner but I see him glance back, as Agnes shakes her head and mouths: 'I dare not!' – the very motto of courtly love that he once used about Anne.

It is evidence enough. When the dance ends with curtseys and bows, I slip from the hall to the queen's rooms, picking up a jug of warm creamy milk from her serving table as I go past. I tap on the door of the room for the maids-of-honour; but there is no reply. Ten of them sleep here in five comfortable beds. Agnes shares the bed by the door, her prayer book on a little prie-dieu by her bedside, her rosary beside it. Her clothes are in a chest at the bottom of the bed. I pull back the covers and pour milk on the sheets where it will soak through to the bedding and the wool-stuffed mattress beneath. It will smell of sour milk even after they have washed the sheets three times. Her bedfellows will say she pisses the bed and refuse to share with her, their maids will say she smells. She will be horribly shamed.

That night, I climb into the huge carved bed beside Anne. 'Did you see her?' she demands. 'Did you see him with her?'

I nod.

'Did you warn her?'

'Milk in her bed.'

Anne laughs like a young girl. 'Jane, you are the best of sisters.'

I laugh, too. This is what it is to be a great courtier – I can stoop to the pettiest of spites or undertake the greatest of embassies. No one but George and I can do both great and small acts for our queen.

Anne and I sleep curled up together, like loving sisters, and I think: this is the life I wanted – to serve with love and to be treasured for it. This is the family I wanted, when I was sent away from home in childhood. This is the love that I missed then, raised as a courtier and not as a beloved daughter. This is the woman I wanted to be: at the centre of power, serving a woman of power.

I AM WAKENED BY the clutch of her hand like a vice on my wrist. 'What?' I demand, half asleep.

'Get George.'

'What?' I say stupidly. 'What?'

'Get up, light the candles and get George, you damned fool,' Anne says through her teeth, biting back a moan of pain.

I feel the sheets are wet beneath me; for a moment, in sleepy confusion, I think Agnes has poured milk into our bed in an instant revenge, but when I touch it, my fingers are black in the darkness.

I light a candle from the embers of the fire and throw back the sheets. Anne is lying in a spreading pool of red.

'Get George!'

I don't argue. I throw a robe around my shoulders and dive out through the connecting door to the king's rooms, run barefoot through the gallery. Our door is unlocked. I cross our hall to our bedroom and shake George's naked shoulder.

He rolls over at once. 'Jane? What is it?'

With a jolt of horror, I see my hand has left a bloodstain on our sheets. George looks down at it. 'That's Anne's blood,' I tell him. 'She's losing the baby.'

In one swift movement, he is out of bed, pulling on his shirt, heaving up his breeches. I want him to hold me, but he fends me off.

'Get the midwife,' he says.

'I don't know where she lives!'

'Then wake my mother,' he says. 'Just her. Don't say a word to anyone else.'

'Wait for me . . . you can't go to Anne's bedroom—'

But he has already lit a candle and gone through the door so quickly that the flame streams back and shows his handsome face like a mask of fear.

The Boleyn family rooms are beside ours. I tap on the bright new shield of the three black bulls and the blood red inverted $V$, and I go in. Beyond the hall is a presence chamber, the privy chamber, and the master bedroom. I tiptoe through the rooms, my bare feet shrinking from the strewing rushes. I tap on the bedroom door and hear the rumbling snore of my father-in-law.

No one hears my knock. I open the door and peer in.

My mother-in-law, the Countess of Wiltshire, is lying on her side, facing the door, her eyes closed. Beside her is the mound of my father-in-law, heaped with furs.

Gently, I touch her shoulder with my clean hand, my bloody fingers behind my back. 'It's Anne,' I whisper. 'She's ill.'

She wakes at once and slips out of bed without disturbing her sleeping husband. Her robe is at the foot of her bed with her Turkey leather slippers.

'The baby?'

'I don't know.'

I do know; but I dare not say. 'George sent me to wake you and to fetch a midwife.'

'My woman knows where she lives,' she says. 'Wake her and tell her to fetch Emily la Leche from her house in Duck Lane. Tell her that it's you that's sick, that I said to bring her to you in the queen's rooms.'

I see that the Boleyns will give me a dead baby before I get a live one. Elizabeth Boleyn does not wait for me to agree but hurries out. One outflung hand points to the women servants' door, and then she is gone. She does not take my candle; she goes down the shadowy gallery without a light, as if she can see in darkness like a cat.

I order the servant, and then I walk on, down the king's gallery, my candle flame bobbing in the warm draught. Next door to the Boleyns is the bigger suite of rooms allocated to the Duke of Norfolk. Thomas Howard is here alone – estranged from his wife, who stayed faithful to Katherine of Aragon when the rest of us did not. Late as it is, the door opens at once to my quiet tap.

A servant waits for me to speak.

'Is my lord here?' I whisper.

He bows and gestures for me to come inside, closing the great door behind me with a noiseless click. He crosses the big hall to the double doors of a grand bedroom and scratches against the oak panel. It, too, opens at once, and there is Thomas Howard the Duke of Norfolk, in a heavily embroidered night robe, wide awake, his long face grooved with lines, showing no surprise.

'Yes? Jane?'

I have been his eyes and ears ever since I first arrived at court as a lonely little girl. Thomas Howard was the only one to notice me. He said I was a clever little poppet, and he gave me ribbons when I brought him news. He praised my learning and asked me what the queen had said in Spanish when she was alone with her ambassador, what she whispered in Latin to her confessor. Who came and went through the private door to her rooms? Who was her secret doctor, and why did she summons him?

When I married George, the duke became my uncle and the head of my house and said I was to think of him as a father, that I must go to him with all my little troubles, with any little secrets. Especially, I must tell him about the queen as the king turned against her and fell in love with my sisters-in-law: first Mary and then Anne.

I brought him news from the queen's rooms, trivial gossip at first, and then I learned the number code that the Spanish diplomats used for writing secrets – and I copied her letters. I warned him when his own wife, Elizabeth, the young Duchess of Norfolk, hid a message to the queen in a basket of Seville oranges. The duke took my word against hers and locked her up far from her home and her children. At first, I was horrified that one word from me had destroyed a woman's life: separated her from her children and made her home into a prison. But I felt proud that a great man like the duke trusted me, a child, more than her. He prized my whispered word above his wife's denial. I learned a secret, I gave the secret to my patron, and he acted with power. It was as if the power was mine, as if I earned my own power with my secret.

After that, he trusted me completely. Together, we watched the growth of a Spanish party – a traitorous group formed deep inside the court, with adherents all over the country, financed by Spain and the Roman Catholic Church, linked to many of the old lords, many of the old royal family, sworn to defend the old queen against the king, sworn to restore England to the Papist faith, sworn to restore Lady Mary as the king's only heir, sworn to the death and destruction of Anne, of all of us.

'What news?' the duke asks me, knowing it must be terrible news for me to come to him, barefoot in my night robe.

'Anne's losing the baby,' I whisper. 'Her mother, your sister, told me to fetch a midwife.'

'Did she tell you to wake me?'

'No. It's to be kept secret. Nobody knows I'm here.'

'Well done. Go back to Anne. Tell me when it's all over. Either way.'

He shows no sign of distress, though this is the end of a royal Howard baby. But of course it's not the only chance for him. His daughter is married to the king's bastard son; he might get a royal Howard baby from them.

'Thank you for coming to me, Jane. I rely on you.'

I curtsey and turn to the door. The silent servant opens it for me, and I hear the quiet click as it closes behind me. I hurry back through the king's private door into the queen's bedroom.

THE SCENE IN the queen's bedroom is familiar and vile. I have attended more than one death here, in exactly these rooms, with exactly this sense of unstoppable despair. Then it was Queen Katherine, lying flat on the bed with her legs raised high on a stack of pillows, white as her sheets, mouthing prayers, her rosary clutched in her hand, her eyes on a crucifix. Now it is Anne, holding the newly translated English Bible, her eyes fixed on her brother's face, both of them whispering the psalm for courage in the valley of death.

Her mother has Anne swaddled tight, as if bedding stuffed between her legs can hold the baby in place. The blood seeps through the whiteness as George mutters in English: 'Why, though I shall go in the midst of the shadow of death, I shall not dread evils, for thou art with me, thou art with me, in the midst of the shadow of death, I shall not dread. I shall not dread. Though I shall go in the midst of the shadow of death, I shall not dread evils, for thou art with me.'

For a long time, there is no sound but the muttered psalm. Light seeps around the joints of the shutters. Then I can hear birdsong, the bubbling, rippling joy of a blackbird. Now, it is so light that the candle flames look yellow and tawdry, and I blow them out. The spreading stain on the sheets is not black in the darkness any more but red as jam; soon the servants will be waking, and someone will try the door and know there has been a night-time vigil over the queen's bloodstained bed.

Still, Anne says nothing; her eyes are fixed on George's dark face as he prays like a priest, and her mother tightens the sheets between her legs.

I want to hold them both; I want to hold Time itself, so that this dreadful day never dawns, instead I clutch at the bedpost and whisper 'Amen, Amen,' to their prayers.

A mouse-like scratch at the door interrupts us. A servant, half-dressed, whispers: 'One of the Boleyn servants said this woman was wanted for Lady Rochford . . .'

'Yes,' I say, opening the door a crack. 'Come in.' I pull the midwife into the room and close the door on the waiting woman and the Boleyn servant.

'This is Lady Rochford,' Anne's mother points to Anne. 'Is she losing her baby?'

The woman takes off her shawl, pulls back the bedding, unwraps the bloodied sheets. There is a sweaty smell of blood and juices.

'She's not losing it,' the woman says, and we all look at her, with disbelieving hope in a miracle, as if she has come to save us, to save England itself. Even Anne lifts her head from George's shoulder.

'Not losing it?' I whisper.

'She's lost it already,' she says with brutal honesty. 'It's done.

It's all come away. This here' – she unwraps the sheet to show a little mess of bloody clots. 'This was it. Not much to see, and it's all done. The blood is just the rest of it. She'll likely stop bleeding in a few weeks.'

Anne drops her face into the crook of George's shoulder and neck. He bends around her so they are like one strange creature with two dark heads – an *Orthus* – sprouting from a tangle of bloodied sheets and one pair of forked naked legs.

'I'm cursed,' Anne whispers. 'The queen has cursed me.'

'It's gone?' Elizabeth Boleyn confirms coldly. This is not the first time she has sat beside a queen birthing a dead prince. More than once, she has rolled up bloodied sheets with a crowned monogram and burned little messes and thrown the ashes down the jakes.

'Long gone,' the midwife says.

'But she can get another child?'

'Nothing to stop her if the husband can do his part,' the woman says agreeably.

'Then stay and clean her up. She has to be up and riding and dancing as soon as she can.'

'Women's work,' is all the old woman says, smiling grimly, as if women's work is well-known to be dancing and riding and conceiving and cleaning up bloodstained sheets and broken hearts. She takes the bloody linen out to the stool room.

'Pay the woman when she's finished,' my mother-in-law says to me. 'And tell her to keep her mouth shut.'

She turns to go, and sees George and Anne, still entwined. 'Oh, go to your room, George,' she orders him with sudden irritability. 'You shouldn't be here at all.'

'But what are we to say?' I ask.

She pauses in the doorway. 'We say nothing. We never announced a baby. There was no baby; we never said there was.'

'She told the king.' I point out quietly, when George and Anne are silent.

'She admits to him that she made a mistake; she missed a course or two, and she hoped . . . We never say "miscarry". Nor "dead-birth". We never say "dead".'

'I went to France, Lady Mother,' George points out quietly. 'I told the King of France that Anne was with child and that we'd visit when he was born.'

'The King of France isn't going to complain, is he? He'll be merry as May Day at our grief. But it doesn't matter what he thinks. What matters is what our king thinks. What matters is that our king never hears the word "miscarry" again. Never hears anyone say his baby was "dead-born". He heard it enough times from the first wife. He's never to hear it from Anne.'

O
VER THE NEXT few days, I watch us Boleyns and Howards tell a bold-faced lie and dare anyone to contradict us. I am the key to the cypher of lies, as people whisper questions to me that they would not dare ask Anne's mother Elizabeth Boleyn, or her uncle Thomas Howard. Again and again, I confide – in strictest confidence – that Anne thought she was with child, but her course was just late, by a month or so: a little mistake, natural to a new wife. The quickest way to spread a story in this court is to swear secrecy.

The only person with a right to know is the king; and he asks nothing. His court, the reformation of his religion, the revolution in his country – his entire life – is based on the belief that his first wife could not bear him a son because their marriage was invalid and so not blessed by God. His new marriage is valid, *ergo* it is blessed by God, *ergo* he will have a son. It is a matter of logic: the king's own brand of logic that cannot be denied. Whatever happened to Anne (and we all stoutly maintain that nothing happened), the king's seed cannot fail. Since the perfect king has a perfect wife, he is bound to get a perfect son on her.

Gertrude Courtenay pays us another unwanted visit, and I manage to talk for half an hour without deviating from our lie. Everything

I say will be on the desk of the Spanish ambassador within an hour and read in Toledo within the month. She tries to make me admit it was a deadbirth, and I widen my limpid grey eyes and say that a young wife, a young mother, is apt to make mistakes and that next time there will be no mistake and there will be a boy. Gertrude Courtenay can take that back to the Spanish ambassador, the old lords, and the hidden Papists. She can tell it to the West Country that her family commands as if it were their fiefdom; she can whisper it to the Lady Mary and write it to the old queen. It makes no difference if the Spanish party believe our lie or not. There is a new law of England – Anne's law, passed by Anne's parliament – that says that Anne is queen and her son will be the next king. Whether her son comes this year or next, that is still the law.

Anne rises up from her bed in days. She dines with the court, keeps the king in a ripple of laughter, dances with him, smiling into his warm face, and praises him for the reforms he is proposing for the Church, and no one remarks that her belly was rounded and now it is flat.

Only the Duke of Norfolk, Anne's uncle, speaks of it. But never to his niece the queen, nor to her mother – his sister. It is me, that he follows to the edge of the great hall after dinner, as they take away the tables to make space for dancing.

'Is she quite well now?' His dark eyes sweep my face; his hard lean face is turned towards me.

'She is, Your Grace.'

Anne is laughing with the king, leading him to the card table to play whist with George and the king's brother-in-law, Charles Brandon.

'Is she able to get another child? She got Elizabeth easily, didn't she? My sister tells me nothing but lies.'

'Do you trust anyone, Your Grace?' I ask curiously.

'I trust you,' he tells me. 'You've never coined the truth to me, nor clipped it. You keep your eyes open, and you're not squeamish. That's why I prefer you to any other, my little poppet. Will she get another?'

'The midwife said she can, if the husband could do his part.'

'God's breath! The midwife said that? And everyone heard her? She questioned the king's potency?'

'Oh – she didn't know she was speaking of the king. They gave her my name. She thought she was speaking about George. She thought it was my dead-birth.'

He makes a little grimace of sympathy. 'No reason for you to give up hope, anyway. You're not yet thirty – plenty of time.'

I nod. A child will bind me even closer into this family. I want them to think me a true Boleyn, mother to a boy of the House of Howard, loyal by blood.

'Now, Jane, I'll want to know the moment that Anne conceives. You tell me at the very first sign. Not when Anne wants it given out. You tell me the moment you know anything – anything.'

A good courtier needs a patron, and a man of power needs information. We are paired, like a falcon and the falconer. I hunt for him; he protects me.

'I hear Anne's pressing for another new law in which everyone swears loyalty?' he asks me. 'Is it not enough for her that her children: Elizabeth and all the ones to come, are named as the only heirs?'

'It's not enough,' I say. 'She wants all the hidden Spanish party forced to a public oath. Too many bow their head to Anne as queen and her children as heirs, but are secretly loyal to the old queen and Lady Mary.'

'Face-value was always good enough before.'

'No, this is an end to false faces.'

'They have to swear loyalty to a babe unborn?'

'Or face a charge of treason.'

'It's clever,' he says begrudgingly. 'I give you that – it's clever. And it'll expose the Spanish party. But it doesn't suit me – it disinherits my son-in-law.'

The king's bastard son Henry Fitzroy has been married to the duke's daughter for nearly a year. It's not a full marriage, it has not been consummated, and now the great triumph of the wedding might come to nothing. Under Anne's new law – the young man will only ever be an acknowledged royal bastard, never a royal heir.

'D'you regret the wedding?' I ask curiously. Mary Howard does, for sure. She is cold as ice when she and her husband meet publicly. Most of the time they are apart.

'The king's like a wet nurse over the precious boy,' the duke grumbles. 'Says he's still too young to bed his own wife.' He scowls for a moment. 'Can't you get Anne to drop a word for me? She's no friend of mine these days, but we're still family, for God's sake!'

'She's at work on her own account,' I warn. 'The king didn't like her taking to her bed. And now, there's Agnes Trent.'

'That little slut?' The duke drops his voice to a bad-tempered growl. 'You can tell Anne I'm with her against Agnes. We can't have a Spanish party favourite slipping into the king's bed. We can't have the king distracted from Anne. Get rid, Jane. Do whatever you have to do. Just make sure she goes.'

A NOTHER NIGHT, AND though Anne could not have been more charming through a long day of amusements and entertainments, the king does not send word that he is coming to her bedroom. 'You can be my bedfellow tonight, Jane,' she says, pretending to be cheerful as the ladies plait her hair and I hand her her white cap.

'His Grace said that he will rise early for prayer,' I say.

She nods. 'There is no king more devout than ours.'

All the ladies agree, and curtsey and leave us.

'Did he?' Anne asks abruptly.

'No.'

'Is he with Agnes?'

'I don't know. I really don't,' I say, though I do.

'He doesn't want me as he used to do,' she says restlessly. She sits by the fireside and puts out her hand for the posset of herbs that she takes every night to make her womb rich and ready for his seed.

'He's one of those problems where the solution is the problem itself.'

'*Aporia.*'

'For Christ's sake!' she snaps. 'Your endless learning! Who cares?'

We are silent for a moment. 'So, what's the question?' I ask patiently. 'What's the question that contains its own answer?'

'The king can't desire a willing woman,' she says simply.

'He's never forced anyone!'

She shows me a bitter smile. 'No. But he desires refusal. He likes the old Romances – a mistress that flees from desire, a beautiful woman who refuses the finest of knights. He's all *Lancelot* and *Guinevere* – forbidden love. So that's what I did – I was a heroine in a Romance. I gave him the challenge: throw down the queen, and then throw down the pope, if you want to win me. As big a quest as killing any dragon. He did it. Just like in the Romances, he triumphed and won his reward – the fair lady: me.'

She looks deep into the fire as if she is telling fortunes. 'And now the virgin is on his knee. The storm-tossed maiden has made it into port and tied up. So, what now? What can a knight errant do with a woman who is wooed and won? Wedded and bedded? Of course – nothing. The story's ended. Satisfaction is no joy for him – when the disguises come off, there I am! His wife: bound to him. By law, I can't refuse him, and he cannot desire a woman who does not refuse him.'

'He loves the chase . . .'

She shakes her head. 'No, it's worse than that. Normal men love the chase and the capture. But for him, there is nothing but chase. He doesn't want capture; he doesn't want satisfaction. He wants to seek, forever seek, and never find. He likes to see himself bravely seeking, he likes pursuit more than he likes me, found and taken.'

'He got Elizabeth on you . . .' I protest.

'Before we were married!' she exclaims impatiently. 'Don't you see? That was still part of the quest? Don't you remember the fuss I made about swiving him? I refused him for six years and drove him half mad – I only let him into my bed when he made me a marquess and promised we would marry. I only agreed to marry him when he had defied the pope himself. But there's only ever one first time.' She glares at me as if I should have a solution. 'Jane, I was the greatest quest of his life, and now I am the one woman in the world that he cannot desire. He can swive a smiling slut who doesn't matter, he can long for an unobtainable maiden with all his heart, but he can't stand up for an honest loving wife.'

THREE NIGHTS LATER, long after midnight, the king sends Francis Weston to say that he is coming to Anne's bed. They have been drinking all night, and the king leans on the door frame as they bring him in. I leave the king and queen, side by side in bed, like effigies on a tomb, and go through the darkened galleries to our Rochford rooms.

George is in his night robe, blinking at the flames of our fireplace. He raises his head, pours me a drink and pulls up a chair for me. 'Have a drink. God knows I've had enough. He's in bed?'

'He is, but I don't know if it'll do any good.'

He raises a scornful eyebrow. 'Christ knows, we've done all that we can. We sent him to her pot-valiant. We swear he's the greatest lover since Sir Gawain. We tell him we all desire her; we're all panting like dogs for her, but she'll stoop to no one but him. It excites him to think that we all want her but only he can have her. We've lit the fuse tonight – she'll just have to jump on him before he fizzles out.'

'She's his wife! She can't play the whore.'

He shrugs. 'She's got to do something to get another baby off him. Anything that works. French tricks . . . anything.'

I hesitate, standing behind his chair as he gazes into the fire. 'But, George, as a wife she can't provoke lust. It has to be a holy act to make a prince. The king's conscience won't allow French tricks, and it's against church law for her to mount him. She shouldn't stoop to whorish games; it's . . . it's not queenly.'

George snorts derisively. 'She won't get fucked being queenly.'

I lean forward and wind my arms around him. After a moment, he tips his head back against me with a sigh, and I kiss his temples and his frowning forehead. 'And what about us?' I whisper. 'Shall we go to bed?'

'To sleep,' he says. 'I've drunk so much that I'm less use than the king himself.'

## GREENWICH PALACE, AUTUMN

### 1534

George is master of the buckhounds, and it is his task to make sure that the hunt goes off perfectly for all the court. The king and all his friends are magnificent horsemen, trained for a cavalry charge, and they come out into the yard laughing and shouting bets on the day's sport. They will hunt stags and bucks this late in the season, and they make crude jokes about being bucks and stags themselves.

They jump up on the mounting blocks as the grooms bring the horses, who are sidling and pulling at their reins in eagerness. The king rides heavier every year; his horse is a big Chapman horse, well-muscled with strong shoulders and huge haunches. George is at his side on his new chestnut mare.

'She'll never last the day,' the king says to George.

'Would you put a guinea on it, Sire?'

The king laughs, and the bet is laid.

Agnes is riding a neat grey, and I see her mount and gather up the reins. My groom brings me my roan, a gift from the Duke of Norfolk, and I get into the saddle and bring her up alongside Agnes.

'Don't crowd the king,' I tell her. 'He's riding with my husband the viscount.'

'If he asks for me, I'll have to ride beside him.' She smiles at me from under her green velvet cap. 'Or d'you want me to tell him that you forbid it?'

'I want you to behave like a young woman who knows her place,' I snap. 'It is an honour to be in the queen's rooms; it is an art to be a courtier. It is not jostling for favours like a fishwife in a marketplace.'

'Of course,' she says simply. 'But the queen was a maid-of-honour just as I am now. Her sister Mary too. Didn't they jostle?'

My reprimand is drowned out by the baying of the hounds and the blast of the horns as the dogs pour out of the kennel yard into the great park, across the public highway, where the common people wait and cheer as we go by. Agnes shows me a small triumphant smile and loosens her reins to let her horse go forward with the others.

We ride deep into the forest of the great park and then wait, while the hounds cast about for a scent and the huntsmen shout their names and watch them trace the ground and turn and cast again. Then, suddenly, the first hound bays, a great excited roar, and all the hounds peel away after him, the whippers-in behind them and the king ahead of George and behind him, everyone else at full gallop, wherever the dogs lead, through streams, over fallen trees, and bursting out into the park over hedges and ditches. I ride cautiously at the back of the hunt, going round hedges rather than jumping them, finding my way along grassy lanes rather than tearing across rough ground. But the men ride as if their lives depend on it, and some of the ladies recklessly keep up with them.

The kill comes quickly with the stag at bay, and the huntsman hold off the hounds, and three of them get hold of the poor beast, hauling its head upwards for the king to strike the murderous slash across his throat. It is the perfect end to a long, exciting chase – the creature defeated, helpless before the king, and then the spurt of pumping blood. Excited by the chase, wiping his bloodstained dagger, seeing that Anne has not yet arrived in her litter, the king beckons Agnes to ride beside him to the little city of tents the servants have set up for us in a forest clearing.

The horses halt, and the king swings heavily down from his saddle and reaches up for her. She drops her reins and puts her hands on his shoulders, as if he were her groom, and he lifts her down from the saddle. He slides her down his body, holding her close even though half the court is watching and half of them will report to their patrons that the king has a new favourite. The Spanish party will celebrate putting their spy in the royal bed to supplant the Protestant queen.

'Stop her,' George hisses in my ear. 'Anne'll be here any moment.'

I can hear the hoofbeats of a dozen horses, Anne's guard around her mule litter, her mother riding on one side. The king hears it too, and abruptly releases Agnes and turns to greet his wife. He helps Anne out of her litter, tells her that he has had a great day's sport, and escorts her to dinner.

She is looking her best, in a dark-red riding jacket with a gold net over her black hair, as if she has ridden here on a high-bred palfrey. She asks the king if George's new mare kept up; she turns and laughs with George and Nicholas Carew; she strips off her red leather gloves and washes her hands in the golden basin. She is at her best at these informal events. She glows so brightly that she makes the king shine beside her, boosting his pride, making him feel equally beautiful, equally clever, equally beloved in a court of lovers.

The cooks have set up charcoal burners to roast meat, and ovens to bake bread, and the sweet-smelling smoke hangs in the dappled sunshine and makes everyone hurry to their places at the rustic tables. There are crocks of thick creamy butter to go with three sorts of bread, huge wheels of cheeses, fish in crisp skins, and crayfish and oysters in their shells.

Anne throws back her head to swallow an oyster from the shell, looks at the king and licks her lips, sensual as a cat. The king flushes and waves the silver platter away from her. 'They're not fit for you in your condition.'

Smilingly, she agrees; but she misunderstands. He does not mean her fertility; he means her condition as a queen. He does not like to see Anne sucking on oyster shells like a woman with earthly desires and a healthy appetite. Now that they are married, he does not want a real woman. He wants a wife who is above other women: a saintly wife and a remote queen.

They bring roasted game, pheasant and woodcock, and pies of beef and lamb, honey puddings and mead cakes and pond-pudding with a ball of spiced butter at its sweet heart. The king drinks deeply of strong red wine; his server refills his glass again and again, and he toasts the huntsmen and the deer, the day and the ladies. Anne, at his side, is drinking water with a splash of wine, stone-cold sober while the king laughs more and more loudly at his own jokes. He repeats a story about hunting in France that he told at the beginning of the meal, and his men roar with laughter as if they are hearing it for the very first time; the ladies echo the false merriment but cast a nervous look towards his stone-faced wife.

Anne won her place in this court as the young woman who would stay and drink with the men and laugh with the king. She refused to withdraw with Queen Katherine, who always left as soon as her young husband became rowdy. No one ever told a bawdy jest to the Spanish queen, but Anne was the first to tell a joke, the first to challenge the king to a riddle or a poem or a game. She made herself the heart of the laughing, lovemaking, singing, noisy court. No one was over thirty years old; no one cared for the rules in Anne's court as it undermined the sombre dignity of the older queen.

But now Anne is the queen, her rival court is now the only court, and no one quite knows what to do as this new Anne: sober, pale, and quiet, sits beside her hard-drinking husband while he starts making toasts to her ladies.

'To the beautiful Lady Rochford!' he bellows, and the court raises their gold cups to me, and I have to stand and smile and drink a toast in reply to the king.

'To the beautiful countess, Elizabeth Somerset!' the king declares. 'Our favourite county!'

Somebody shouts that he has been in Somerset often, and Elizabeth's brother, Anthony Browne, slams down his gold cup and glares at her. But the king sees nothing; he is working his way through the ladies. I can see at once where this is going and what is going to happen next; but I am powerless to stop it.

'To Lady Margaret Douglas, my dear niece,' he says.

All the men cheer, and Lord Thom Howard – the Duke of Norfolk's baby-faced half-brother – raises his cup to Margaret in a silent pledge. She rises to her feet and takes the toast, her eyes on Lord Thom, and then the king shouts loudly: 'To the most beautiful lady of your heart! And you must each drink to your own choice!'

The men roar with laughter, and the women flutter and smile. Some wives shoot cautionary glances at their husbands, the men rise to their feet and raise their cups to their favourite flirts. Some old lords leer at their second wives, young enough to be their daughters. Charles Brandon's pretty ward is now his duchess, and young Catherine Brandon stands up to drink in reply to her husband – old enough to be her grandfather.

This is all part of the game of courtly love that the king likes to play; but the dividing line between his prudishness and his rowdy joy is always hard to guess. The old queen drew a clean line – her ladies were strictly raised and modestly behaved. But Anne is trapped in the paradox of mistress turned wife, poacher turned gamekeeper. She has to play the part of a Spanish duenna and yet be as exciting and promising as a new lover. She must be both lascivious favourite and dignified queen: it is a *paradoxos*. It can't be done.

George looks straight past me, his wife, and raises his cup to Anne. So does William Brereton – in a sober reproach to the king; so does Francis Bryan, with a twisted smile on his masked face, as if he is winking under his black eye patch. Surprisingly, so does Charles Brandon, up on his unsteady legs for the second time. He has always been our enemy, a staunch friend to the old queen, a loyal member of the Spanish party, and for a moment I hope that his courtesy to Anne means that he has changed sides. But then I understand that both Francis Bryan and Charles Brandon are giving the king cover for his own game, as he gets to his feet, staggering a little, and points his cup directly at Agnes and whispers her name.

She looks back at him intently and she rises to her feet to reply to his toast, but he does not sit down, so as everyone else subsides, the two of them are left standing as if they are alone. She raises her cup to him then throws off her drink with an upraised arm so that her sleeve slides back to give him a forbidden glimpse of the crook of her elbow and the hidden pale flesh of her rounded upper arm. She smiles at the king, a long smile, sweet as a promise, and she sits down again, among the maidens, as modest as a primrose.

The court is stunned into silence, it is the end of the dinner. I wish to God it were the end of the day, but we all have to ride home together. George and I sweep Anne into her litter and ride beside her, ahead of everyone, so she cannot see the king, lingering behind with Agnes. She draws the curtains, and we ride on either side in stony silence.

When we are nearly home, we hear the king canter up behind us with Francis Bryan and Charles Brandon on either side, and I give up my place so that he can ride beside Anne's litter. I mutter quickly: 'The king!' so she knows he's there, but she does not draw back the curtain to greet him.

'I think the queen is sleeping,' George volunteers to explain the silence and the drawn curtains.

The king chuckles; he is still drunk. 'We'll let sleeping dogs lie, shall we?'

Charles Brandon laughs out loud. 'Sleeping bitches bite.'

Anne tears the curtain open, and Charles Brandon bows his head and turns his horse to one side.

'Are you tired, my lady?' the king says, with the careful politeness of a drunk husband.

She shoots him a furious look and says nothing in reply. George drops back to give them some privacy; but everyone can see Anne's hand gripping the silk curtain against the gold-leaf frame and hear her low-voiced stream of complaints.

'Stop her,' George says to me.

'You stop her,' I reply, for we both know I cannot push my way between the king and the litter, and anyway, the grooms have pulled the mules to a halt, and the whole court can hear the king's furious bellow.

'Madam, I tell you this, and I will only tell you once. You will shut your eyes and endure, as your betters have done—'

I look around to see the blank horror on Anne's mother's face.

'Betters,' I repeat in a whisper.

Anne spits a venomous reply; but the king raises his voice and goes on: 'You should know . . .' He is drunk, but his speech is clear; they will hear every word even at the very back. 'You should know that it is in my power to humble you again, in a moment – in a moment! Just as I have raised you.'

She does not meet his bulging-eyed stare. She looks straight ahead, white-faced. The king gives a harsh, wild laugh and beckons his men friends to follow him, and they take off past the litter at a gallop back to the palace. The beautiful French mules harnessed to the litter shift restlessly and rock Anne in her seat.

George tips his head to me to stay with Anne as he puts his heels on his horse and thunders after the king. Their mother, Elizabeth Boleyn, comes up on the other side of the litter but says nothing. We ride back to the palace in silence, the dust from the king's gallop settling on the silver white curtains.

Anne gets out as soon as the litter halts before the wide front doors, and she and her mother go inside while I am dismounting from my horse. Slowly, I follow them to the queen's rooms, the ladies-in-waiting ahead of me. For a moment, I hesitate, remembering all the times I have gone through this door to hear someone reading from the Bible or the buzz of laughing conversation and Queen Katherine presiding over a peaceful busy room. Now, I walk into a frosty privy chamber, the ladies sulking after a scold.

Elizabeth Somerset nods her head towards the bedchamber. 'You're to go in. We're all in disgrace. I don't know why. It's not as if it's our fault!'

In the bedchamber, George is leaning on the mantelpiece; the fire is out. Anne's mother has made her escape to her own rooms through the king's door. Anne is in the window seat, still in her red-velvet riding dress, glaring down into the garden below.

I close the door and wait.

'You saw what he did,' she says tightly. 'You heard him rage at me.'

'You'll make up,' I say. 'You always rage and make up.'

'We will. But that's the last toast he'll drink to her.'

I glance at George; his beautiful face is stony, sculpted like the limestone fireplace.

'Tell Agnes to go,' Anne orders. 'Tell her that she can't stay at court.'

I hesitate. 'Better not today,' I say. 'Not after that scene. Better to leave it, when she can leave quietly?'

'No,' George says decisively. 'As an example for others. You can bed the king but not advise him. You don't put words in his mouth. We do that: only us. She's to leave – not because she's his flirt but because she's told him that Katherine of Aragon was a better woman than Anne. Because he said that Anne should put up with what had been done to her betters.'

Anne spits an oath and looks out of the window.

'The duke, our uncle, wants her gone,' I confirm.

'So, what are you waiting for?' George asks me with forced cheer. 'Go to it! Cast off, my falcon!'

'It's my command,' Anne rules.

I WALK INTO THE sullen privy chamber. 'Where's Agnes?' I ask one of the maids-of-honour.

'Changing her dress,' she says. 'The king has sent her some beautiful sleeves. They were on her bed when she came in.' She simpers. 'With a poem! He's written her a love song!'

I enter the bedroom that Agnes shares with the other maids-of-honour without knocking. Three girls, cooing over a handwritten page, drop it as they see me, and whisk out of the door. Agnes stands by her bed with the new sleeves spread before her. I pick them up and fold them over my arm; she makes a tiny movement as if to snatch them back, and then she holds herself still.

'I warned you,' I say kindly, for she looks like a frightened child, standing by her bed. 'I warned you, but you have continued to behave—'

'The king!' she whispers.

'The king's behaviour is beyond comment. He is the king. You serve the queen, and it is her good opinion you should be seeking. You have lost that. So, you have lost your place. You should write to your parents to take you from court at once.'

'The Marquess of Exeter assured my father and mother that I should have a place in the queen's rooms.'

Fool that she is: she has revealed her patron is Henry Courtenay Marquess of Exeter, Gertrude's husband, of the old royal family, leader of the Spanish party. A novice spy, she has confirmed that they brought her to court and placed her into the queen's rooms in the hopes of stealing the king from Anne. They must be delighted with her progress. The king has never spoken to Anne like this before, never told her to endure as her betters had done: he never thought that there was anyone better than Anne! This is not a lovers' tiff; it is a masterstroke against us. The Poles, the Courtenays, all the royal cousins and kin know that the king has to be surrounded by the best – the best jousters, the best dancers, the best poets, the most beautiful women. A second son himself, he cannot tolerate second place in anything. They know this, they have known him from childhood. Agnes, their mouth to his ear, has suggested Anne is second best. With them writing her lines she is a real danger to us. She has to go.

'That was kind of the Marquess of Exeter; but the queen has a right to choose her own household. You are not suitable. So, pack your belongings and leave. Her Grace does not want to see you again.'

She opens her mouth to speak, but she has nothing to say. She hesitates, stammers; she suddenly looks much younger, as if she is about to cry.

'I will take these,' I say, showing her the beautifully embroidered sleeves in my arms. Her eyes linger on the luminous mother-of-pearl buttons, on the rich silk slashing. 'They came to you by accident. The king intended them for the queen. It will be better – far better for you – if I tell her that. But I shall see that you are invited back to court within a year or two. You can come back then, and no one will know that I ordered you to go.'

'You order!' she finds the courage to say, with a little quaver in her voice. 'Who are you to give orders to me?'

'I am a Howard,' I say simply. 'His Grace, Thomas Howard the Duke of Norfolk is head of my house, and the queen is my sister-in-law. Who are you to question me?'

She gives a sulky little curtsey. 'I'll return the sleeves to the royal wardrobe myself,' she says.

It is her surrender, and I give them to her and go out of the room, closing the door behind me. As I walk through the presence chamber, I hear the sound of her running feet and a little breathless sob. She is looking for a friend to have a good cry and rail against me, and someone to take a letter to her parents, and someone to take the sleeves back to the royal wardrobe.

We are rid of her. My work – my spiteful courtier work – is done.

Half an hour later, the king stalks into the queen's presence chamber, ignoring all of us ladies-in-waiting, though we are dressed to perfection and waiting for him. He tells Anne he will speak with her privately.

Her face lights up; she thinks he has come for a passionate quarrel and reconciliation, as they used to do. She leads the way into her privy chamber and closes the door on us. She thinks she will fly at him and slap his face, and he will grab at her and kiss her into submission. Perhaps they will whirl from anger to lust, from privy chamber to bedchamber, and we will all be late to dinner.

But she is wrong. She is the queen now; the days of fighting and lovemaking are gone.

I stand close to the privy-chamber door to prevent anyone eavesdropping, and I hear the low heated mutter of the king's banked-down rage and the quick staccato reply of Anne denying whatever he is saying.

Then he says one thing loudly: 'If she is causing this much trouble between us, then she must go.'

The door jerks open, and he comes out to the presence chamber.

I think: at any rate, we have won. He has named Agnes as trouble and insisted that she must go. But at that very moment, from the gallery end of the presence chamber, the king's friends stroll in, merry as ever, George among them, and – to my utter amazement – on George's arm is Agnes – not tear-stained and shamed; but rosy and chattering, smiling as if she walks into court every day with my husband at her side . . . and she is wearing the new sleeves.

Anne Parr, one of the ladies, touches my hand and says: 'The queen wants you.'

I cannot tear my eyes from Agnes' triumph. 'What?'

'The queen. In her privy chamber.'

I curtsey to the king; but he does not see me. George does not acknowledge me. Suddenly, I am invisible; everyone is smiling at

Agnes, who is spreading her arms and pirouetting to show off her new sleeves.

I go into the privy chamber, and Anne is bleached white with rage.

'Agnes just walked in,' I tell her. 'On George's arm. In the new sleeves.'

'The king says she's to stay at court,' she says, through gritted teeth. 'He says you're not to torment her. He says that if you cause this much trouble, you are to go.'

I can hardly hear her. 'I?'

George opens the door and closes it quickly behind him. 'Get out there,' he says to Anne. 'Go quick – don't give her another moment to show off. And smile: for God's sake, look as if it's nothing to you. It was a catfight between your ladies: Jane and Agnes. Nothing to do with you at all.'

'After what he said to me at the hunt?'

'Because of that!' George says urgently. 'You must be more queenly than ever. She's nothing beside you – a passing fancy. Put her out of his head. Shine her down. You can do it! You've always done it before. He has to forget that he said he raised you from nothing; he has to forget that he said Katherine was your better. We make it a petty quarrel between two women. It's not about him seeing you for real: it's Jane. It's Jane's fault. It's Jane being a scold and bullying Agnes.'

'It's not!' I find my voice. 'Agnes knows I was obeying Anne's order, and she'll have told the king.'

'Anne'll deny it,' George says briskly. He gently pinches her cheeks to bring the colour to them, and then he kisses her swiftly on the lips to give her courage and pushes her towards the door. 'Go on,' he says. 'I'll come as soon as I've got Jane out of the way.'

She raises her chin and sets her shoulders back. She breathes in, like an actor preparing to walk on a stage, and she goes without another glance at me.

'Out of the way?' I demand. 'What d'you mean?'

'My love – you've got to take the blame for quarrelling with Agnes.'

'There was no quarrel! How could there be a quarrel between a maid-of-honour and the senior lady-in-waiting? I dismissed her, as you told me to! The duke told me to! Anne told me to! I didn't loosen the saddle girth and kill the girl! I've done far less than Anne wanted! I'm not taking the blame for this.'

'You are,' he says shortly. 'Agnes stays at court, and you retire. The king says he won't have you causing trouble.' He throws up his hand to stop me arguing. 'I know! We know! These are Courtenay's words in His Majesty's mouth. But better for us all if you just go. We'll get you back within weeks, and Courtenay will be sorry he put up a girl against us. Of course. But you've got to leave tonight. I've got your horse saddled and a guard ready to ride with you.'

'But I did it for Anne!' I protest. 'For you! For the Boleyns! For the Howards! You can't repay me by throwing the blame on me.'

'We don't blame you,' he says quickly. 'We love you as always. It's just a setback. The Spanish party win this round: we'll win the king back.'

'I want to see the duke.'

'He'll be at dinner.'

'I won't go without seeing him.'

George sighs. 'Don't get upset. Go and change into your travelling clothes. I'll ask His Grace to meet you in the stable-yard.'

Thomas Howard the Duke of Norfolk will intervene for me. He will invite me to stay at his great London house at Lambeth for a few days while it all blows over. He has as much influence as the Courtenays. He is my patron; I am under the shield of his name; he loves me. He trusted my word against his own wife.

I tumble my books and my jewel case into a little box. I tell the man at the door of our chambers to carry it down to the stable-yard and put it in the cart with the rest of my things; but this is packing for show: pretend goods into a pretend box, like a play. I am not really leaving. I change into my riding gown, and I pull on my hat and cape, and then I run down the stairs and into the stable-yard, where the Boleyn guard is mounted and waiting, and my horse saddled and ready. I try to smile at my waiting maid. 'We're going nowhere,' I tell her, and then Thomas Howard the Duke of Norfolk comes out of one of the doors from the king's side of the palace, and I know I am safe.

'You ordered Agnes Trent from court?' he asks, with no preamble, his face more hawklike than ever.

'As you told me.'

'The girl went straight to Courtenay and complained of you, and he went to the king.'

'But you will intervene for me,' I say.

He shrugs; his black eyes are set deep, the eyelids drooping down. 'Anne won't defend you; your own husband doesn't speak up for you. Why should I?'

'Because I've worked for you since I was a girl!' I exclaim. 'You're my patron! You're promised to me – and I to you. Who will serve you when I'm gone? Who will be your eyes and ears in the queen's rooms?'

He laughs with genuine amusement. 'Oh, don't you worry about that. There's Mary Shelton, or my sister, or my daughter Mary; there's half a dozen Howards in the queen's rooms, and half a dozen more I could buy with pennies. But you – you're too visible now – you're of no use to me.'

'You said you would protect me! You promised me . . .' I am as shocked as a child.

'You were my spy,' he concedes. 'And if you had been born in the sex of that handsome fool your husband, I would have made you into a great diplomat, an ambassador – far better than him. If you had the allure of your sister-in-law Anne, you'd have made a better queen than her – far better. But you're just a very pretty, over-educated young woman, Jane. There's nothing for you to do at court but quarrel with other pretty girls.'

'You know it was not a quarrel! You know it was not pretty girls quarrelling!'

He turns away as if he is leaving. I have to make him turn back. 'I know something about your half-brother Thom,' I hiss. 'He has proposed to Margaret Douglas, the king's niece. They say they will marry in secret.'

He pauses and nods. 'Not much of a secret – I knew that.'

'I know more,' I gabble. 'Something about Anne. Something serious!'

He waits.

'The king isn't potent with her! He's lost desire.'

He is silent for a moment. 'That's a great secret – a grave secret, and it's a disaster for Anne – but who can tell it? Anything that detracts from the majesty of the king is treason. You're a traitor to even say it. I did not hear it. Go to the country, Jane, and study silence.' He turns on his heel and leaves me, as if there is nothing more to be said, as if he will never speak to me again.

I am stunned. I let him go without a word of complaint.

The groom brings my horse, and George returns and silently helps me up the stone steps of the mounting block. He squeezes my hand in sympathy. 'I'll get you back as soon as I can.'

'I'm no traitor!'

'No, of course not. It's just that you're no use right now.'

'I thought he would protect me?'

He shakes his head. 'Not him! He's got a heart of stone, that man. But Anne and I love you. We'll bring you back.'

'He said I have to study silence.'

'Well, you're going to the right place for that,' he says cheerfully.

'Beaulieu? I'll have a hundred things to do.'

'You're not going to Beaulieu.'

I stare down at him from the height of the mounting block. 'Not going home? Then where am I going?' I can hear the sharp note of panic in my voice. 'I'm not going to Hever with Mary Boleyn!'

'No, you're going home to your father.'

I am as cold as if I were entering the Tower by the water gate. 'George, are you divorcing me? Putting me aside like Queen Katherine? Putting me out of my house like our uncle did to his wife?'

'No! No! Not I!' He laughs at my consternation. 'We're not to be parted forever! But if the king commands you leave court – what can I do?' His charming smile is so like Anne's. 'We're too finely balanced. We can't carry the weight of the king's dislike. The Spanish party have got Agnes in his bed. She whispers their words in his ear; she's turned him against us. And we're blaming all that on you. If the king doesn't want you here, then you're no use to us. We've dropped you.'

## MORLEY HALLINGBURY, NORFOLK, WINTER

## 1534

I HAVE NEARLY A year, a long year, to learn what my husband means when he says that they have dropped me. It is a fall; it is a fall so terrible that I lose all sense of who I am. It is like the steep fall from the gates of paradise down to earth: the fall of the angel from heaven to a hell of nothingness. I was a star of the morning at court, and now I am eclipsed. From childhood, I have been a courtier, raised and schooled to be indispensable in the complex dance of a royal court, to know the masks on show and the faces hidden beneath them. Now, there are no false smiles, no pretend compliments, and my mother and father share the same look of shuttered disappointment.

I have no spymaster and nothing to spy on, no work but the drudgery of a spinster-daughter in a manor house: sewing, polishing, work in the still room, in the spice room, and in the herb garden, duty to the poor, and service to the church. I make ink for my father from oak galls boiled in wine and stirred with gum arabica. I order the gamekeeper to trap crows, and pluck feathers from their left wings, for me to trim into quills, so the curve of the feather suits my father's right hand.

I cling to my name and insist on being addressed as Lady Rochford, but here, I have no parade of husband, royal sister-in-law, no panoply of cousins, no uncle the duke. My homes, my childhood homes, are lost to me: royal palaces of Greenwich, of Westminster, of Windsor Castle or Hampton Court. I am confined to a house which is grand in Norfolk but is little more than a new-built manor. Everything seems impossibly small, and I am a nobody, wondering at my father's pride in his house at Morley Hallingbury that I left at eleven years old, thinking I would never return.

I look around the empty nursery and wonder where that child has gone, and what she has become? She was a serious little girl with her hair in a plait, indifferent to her mother but adoring her father, the scholar. He encouraged her learning, letting her waste expensive paper scribbling Latin and French verbs. He taught her to shelve his books, hundreds of books, some inherited from his patron, the king's grandmother, some sent to him by scholarly friends, some written by himself and richly bound for him by the nuns of Syon Abbey. He taught his little girl languages: Italian, so she could read the great writers of Florence; Greek and Latin, so she could transcribe classical authors.

I thought there was no higher calling than to be his clerk. I wanted to stay home all my life – his little shadow. I was the only one of his children allowed to study with him. My brother cared only for hunting, my sister was too young and noisy for the library. But I might be the equal to the clever daughters of Sir Thomas More in faraway London.

But now Sir Thomas is in the Tower – and all Margaret More's famous education cannot save him, and I am dropped. My father must think a woman's education is of no use: an experiment that has failed. My mother once told him that my tender heart would betray my clever head, and now he thinks she is proved right.

They never ask me what happened at court. My mother imagines me sobbing the heartbroken reproaches of a jealous wife and offers me the silent sympathy of a fellow weakling in damp glances. I ignore her. I don't know what my father thinks. I feel his measuring gaze on me, silently reviewing me, as if I am an essay returned from a fellow scholar, half unread. He is confident that I was not dismissed from court for a failure of manly intelligence – he taught me too well – so it must be the fault of womanly weaknesses, the curse of Eve: oversensitivity, imaginary ailments, hysteria.

I cannot bring myself to tell my father that it was not my weakness that caused my exile – but George's. It was George who lacked decision, firmness of will, strength of purpose and manly loyalty. But I will not betray George. I will never betray George.

My father spends his days in his study, but I am not invited to write his letters. I don't even ask to read his books: they have been no help to me. I studied his translations of Niccolò Machiavelli and Baldassare Castiglione, and I understood their cold calculations on how a king usurps power from his lords, as courtiers steal power from other courtiers. But this was no help when courtier work was degraded into slavish charm for only one man.

There is no subtle work of politics and persuasion at Henry's court; it has become nothing more than pleasing a difficult man in a court of weakened men. Anne and the Howards and the reformers whistled the king to their side, as you might train a dog: they petted him, they seduced him, they lulled him, and they inflamed him, until he abandoned both Church and wife.

Then, I thought we had won a great victory for reform and for Anne. Now, I see that it was just as Machiavelli describes – as one power rises, another falls, and as soon as a power falls, it will try to rise again. Nothing ever changes: there is rise and fall, flood tide and ebb, but it is the same river. We beat the queen and the Spanish party by stealing the king away with Anne. Now, they hope to steal him back with Agnes.

I only see my father once a day when we dine in the great hall, and by the silence that falls on the household as I walk past the servants' tables, I know that everyone thinks me shamed to be returned to Morley Hallingbury from my palace of Beaulieu. Exiled from my father's library, I sit beside the fire in my mother's private room in the evening, and we sew by candlelight, and sometimes I read aloud to her – Romances in English or lives of saints.

There is nothing of interest in her room; she has no papers on the reform of the Church or books on the new learning. Her confessor, the priest who served in our chapel, silently moved to the parish church in the village when the Church reformed and the pope was dishonoured. Now, the chapel in our house is cold and quiet and closed, and the priest preaches from the pulpit in the village church that the king is Supreme Head of the Church. His theology is a mash of old faith and reform. He omits all prayers for the Holy Father, but still serves the mass in the old way, drones on in Latin, and absent-mindedly keeps all the feasts and holy days as if they are not forbidden. My mother does not notice, and since my father is the owner of the church and pays the priest, no one will know, unless there is an inspection from the bishop. I don't even care. The heated discussions about the reform of religion that I had with Anne and George seem far away and pointless. I can barely remember them. Perhaps I will never argue with George again; perhaps I will never agree with him again. I am dropped – I don't know if I will ever be picked up.

When I hear nothing from any of them, not from Thomas Howard my patron, not from my mother-in-law, not from Anne, not even from the husband who promised to cleave to me until death parted us, I realise that the Boleyns, Anne and George, and the Howards are like Machiavelli's courtiers, only true to themselves. All their talk is courtier-talk: the glazed smile, the false face, the sweet word – always a means to an end. George writes love poetry for its wit – not for love. He is master of the buckhounds – not to hunt but so he can ride beside the king. He married me – not for love; but because our lands ran alongside each other, because my dowry was good, because my father was an influential scholar in the days when the king prized scholarship. He told me that he was glad to be my husband, because anything else would have been impolite, and George has beautiful manners. But none of the Boleyns or Howards or the royal court itself ever cared for me – for myself. I was dear to them when I served them well. When I failed: they dropped me.

I know this – but I have to repeat it over and over again in order to fix it in my mind. My father did not love me more than any lord cares for his children in their distant nursery. It amused him that a little girl would run from her mother to be his clerk in his library, and then he was proud to claim his daughter was as clever as Margaret More.

Thomas Howard did not love me; I was his spy in miniature, a weapon hidden by childhood. My innocence, my trust in him, made me a powerful tool. Nobody has ever wanted my happiness, nobody has ever thought of it.

As the days go on, I walk through the woods and in the meadows of the park, now enclosed in a huge wall to preserve the game: nothing can run free in Tudor England, not even deer. As I kick the fallen leaves in a swirl of colour around my feet, I mutter like a madwoman, speaking hard truths to myself. I have to teach the little girl I once was, that to be used is not the same as to be loved. When I know that, when it is clear to me, like a theorem becomes clear on the page, I think I have completed my education in heartbreak.

Then I have another thought. I did not come to George as a bride wanting love, to Anne as a girl wanting a sister. By then, I was a knowing child. I had worked as a courtier and a spy in a suspicious court for years. My love for them was a mixture of need and ambition. What I really wanted from Anne, from George, from the duke, was to be one of them, inside the Howard family and a viscountess by marriage. I was not so much married into their family as recruited into a faction, protected from the Spanish party; but when we were in trouble, I was faithless to them as they were to me.

I walk on muddy paths that grow hard with winter frost and think that I am not an innocent victim. I, too, spoke words of love but preferred secrets. I said that I loved them, but I sold them out: my aunt the duchess to my uncle, Anne's dead baby to him, Anne's inability to seduce the king to George, the king's impotency to my uncle. I have never been true to any one of them. For a moment, I pride myself that I have never betrayed George; but then I realise that in the ten years of marriage, he has never trusted me with any secret. But even so . . . even so . . . still, it gives me a small comfort to think that I have never been a traitor to George.

First thing when I wake in the morning and last thing after my bedtime prayers at night, I am back in the stable-yard, my hands cold on the reins, George beside the mounting block, looking up at me with Anne's dark eyes in the long lean Howard face as he says: *We're too finely balanced. We can't carry the weight of the king's dislike. The Spanish party have got Agnes in his bed. She whispers their words in his ear; she's turned him against us. And we're blaming all that on you. If the king doesn't want you here, then you're no use to us. We've dropped you.* And then again, I see him smile so regretfully and say: *We've dropped you.*

I talk to George as if he is beside me on my long daily walks, and I see him again in my dreams. I am racked with shameful one-sided desire for him who does not desire me now, and perhaps never did. In my dreams, his touch is light, insubstantial, and I wake up feeling dry and cold, and I know it is a sinful dream, and there is no getting a baby alone in dry dreams, any more than there is getting a baby alone in a marital bed. I am an untouched field; I am an empty nest; I am a barren bitch. Neither George nor Anne, nor my uncle the duke, nor anyone in the queen's rooms, nor anyone in the whole court, loves me for my true self. And then I think: nobody knows my true self. Not even me.

It gets colder, and the thick greyness of the countryside in November closes on the folded valleys and bare trees around Morley Hall. I have not been in the countryside in winter for nearly twenty years; I had forgotten how dreary it is. I don't know how my mother can endure months of lighting candles in the mornings to write up her rent books, huddling over a fire in her private rooms in the evening. Winter at court is a blaze of feasts and entertainments, all lit by sconces of beeswax candles and warmed by roaring fires in every room. I miss the light and the warmth as much as the music and the chatter. I miss the sense of importance, of knowing everything at the heart of the kingdom – life is passing me by here, and I am doing nothing.

My father goes to London, summoned to his seat in the House of Lords to pass two new laws composed by Anne. I am sure they are her work – I can almost see her handwriting, I hear her voice in the words. Everyone in the country is ordered to swear a public oath that Anne is queen and her children royal heirs, and that Katherine of Aragon and Lady Mary are neither queen nor princess. The second law is that the king is the Supreme Head of the Church in England – not the pope. Anne has already won court, king, parliament, and country, and now she stamps her seal on the next king, who will be her son, and the Church, which will be his treasury. I long to see her revelling in her triumph; but I know she will not send for me – she does not need me in this moment of victory. She has defeated the Spanish party and her other enemies with nothing but her own quick wits and the sword-like thrust of her will.

My father comes home in December, riding on frozen roads in a mood as dark as the afternoon. He has done his duty to the king and sworn his oath; but he fears that the old queen and Princess Mary will never be brought to swear that one is a whore and the other a whore's bastard daughter. And the old queen's confessor, John Fisher, and the old Lord Chancellor, Sir Thomas More, will never swear that the king is Head of the Church. How can they? They bound themselves to a Church founded by a pope chosen by God, and confirmed by his cardinals, based on the rock of St Peter – how can they suddenly say that the papal crown can be picked up by a Tudor from a hawthorn hedge?

'And then I suppose I shall have to sit on their trial,' my father says heavily as he dismounts in the stable-yard.

I am wrapped up against the cold, waiting for him, hoping that he will pour out what is happening in London in the first moments of his relief at returning home. 'Could you refuse to judge? If it comes to trial? Could you not say your conscience . . .?'

He scowls at me, pulls off his thick riding gauntlets and rubs his cold hands together. 'This is no season for a man to have a conscience. I am loyal to your sister-in-law, Queen Anne, as is any man who wants to rise. And anyway – she's made it a treason to deny her.'

'Anne was fighting for the king's favour when I left court,' I whisper. 'The Spanish party had put a new mistress in his bed and she was speaking for Lady Mary.'

'Well, she must have beaten the girl and beaten the Spanish party. Here you see the fruits of her victory. She's going to have the monasteries and convents and abbeys valued and all their riches and lands assessed for tax, to be paid to the king. She's persuaded the king that there can be no other ruler in England but himself, she his queen and chief advisor, and Cromwell his tax master to bank the profits for him. Here,' my father remembers. 'I saw him – Master Secretary. He spoke of you.'

'Of me?' I cannot imagine that Thomas Cromwell has remembered me when my own husband has dropped me, and they have won all the power they need without me.

'Aye. He thinks of everything that man, forgets nothing. He gave me a note for you.' My father plunges his hand into his inner pocket and hands me a folded sealed note. 'You can open it,' he says. 'Go in. I'm coming out of the cold as soon as I've seen the horses into their stables.'

I take the letter to the kitchen, the only room in the Hall where the fire is always kept in, and I sit beside the warm belly-curve of the bread oven and ignore the irritated bustle of the cook. The letter is intricately folded to prevent it being opened and resealed. The single page is turned back, pushed through a slit at the bottom of the page, and sealed with a wax seal. It can only be opened by breaking the seal and slicing open the letterlock, which cuts off the bottom corner of the page. Nobody can open and read it without cutting off the corner, betraying themselves. I have seen such letters but never received one of my own.

I borrow a knife from the cook, slice it open and break the seal, and there is Cromwell's signature: the C like a half-moon rising over the slit in the page. He hopes I am well and asks if I have many visitors? He reminds me to send a new year gift to the king and queen, and to the Princess Elizabeth, and to Lady Mary. The court will be at Greenwich for Christmas, and he regrets that I am not the only face missing. My sister-in-law Mary Boleyn has married in secret, and the Boleyns have cast her off, too. She will have to live in some country farmhouse with her farmer husband. She has asked Thomas Cromwell for help, and he will get her husband posted to Calais Castle.

I rest the single page with the sliced corner in my lap. I have no idea why he is sharing these family secrets with me; but then I understand:

*Mary Boleyn – Mrs Stafford (as she now is) – cannot return to court, and this will leave Her Grace the queen without a sister in her rooms. I can invite you back to court, if that would be your wish.*

An invitation to serve at court is an incredible favour, usually bought by half a dozen begging letters accompanied by rich gifts. Nobody ever gets a place without a long campaign and calling-in of favours. An invitation from Thomas Cromwell is like a comet, blazing across a dark sky: extraordinary in its own self, and a portent of something else.

I take a lot of care with my reply, and I write in Latin:

*Dear Master Secretary,*
*I greet you well and thank you for your enquiry after the health of my father and mother who are (praise God) both well this Christmas season.*

*I am grateful for the invitation to return to court. If there be any service that I may do you, I shall not fail you.*
    *Jane Boleyn*

I fold and double-fold the page, and I spend an hour on making a letterlock and sealing it with wax. It does not hurt to show him that my father has taught me Italian spy-craft as well as Italian courtier skills. Whatever Thomas Cromwell wants from me, he will not be offering me a rescue for nothing in return. No one in Thomas Cromwell's service is idle.

## MORLEY HALLINGBURY, NORFOLK, SPRING

# 1535

THE SNOWDROPS COME out like little fingernails of green and white, pushing through the dead leaves as if they will never grow tall and droop their pretty heads like bells. I think the winter has been long for them, but still they rise. The people in the cottages at Hallingbury have eaten up all their winter stores, and Mother says they must go to the abbeys for charity: the king's new church must take care of the king's poor as the old one did. Someone breaches the wall of the park and kills a deer; my father says that he will hang him. The game in our park is for sport – the king might want to come and kill our stags one day – it is not meat for stew pots of hungry people.

It has been a long cold winter for the traitors in the Tower, too: four monks, a priest, and Sir Thomas More and Bishop Fisher have gone all season without fires or hot food. I suppose that the king is leaving them there to die of cold and hunger, but Father says no: Master Secretary Cromwell is wrestling with them.

'Wrestling?' I ask, as if they have a booth on Tower Green.

'Entrapping them,' he says. 'But I don't think even Thomas Cromwell will trick Thomas More. He's a learned man, and he loves his family. He's not going to make a slip of the tongue that could cost him his head. He's going to want to get home to that funny little wife of his and his great library in that beautiful house by the river.'

'But who wants the house by the river?' my mother asks, coming in at the end of the conversation and getting the wrong idea, as usual. 'Who gets the library?'

Slowly, the dawn comes earlier and earlier each morning, and the birds start to sing at seven by the church bell, and then six and then five, and the woods turn green; but still, I wait for an invitation to return to court. At church on Sunday, the sunshine streams through the stained-glass window, and when I enter, early, for mass, I find our priest working on his missal with a knife and glue like a spy on a letter. He is sticking a piece of paper over the name of the pope every time it occurs in the prayers for blessings.

'What are you doing, Father Pierce?'

'Obeying an instruction from my bishop.' His pale face is flushed with irritation. 'I am to cut out the name of the . . . of the Bishop of Rome . . .' The title sounds oddly in this church that has prayed for our Holy Father since it was built five hundred years ago. 'Cut it out of my prayer book! And we are no longer to pray for . . . him. See—'

He shows me the bishop's letter. It says that instead of the pope and the cardinals, the prayers are to be for the whole Catholic Church and for the Catholic Church of Rome, for the king – only Supreme Head of the Catholic Church of England – for Queen Anne and the princess, Lady Elizabeth, for the whole clergy and temporality.

He looks at me, indignant. 'What will your father say to this, Lady Rochford? What would he have me do? For my bishop commands it – but the people won't like it, and I . . .' He breaks off.

'He'd want you to obey the law. The king's will,' I say firmly.

'But is it the king's own will?' the vicar asks me in an undertone. 'For it's not what he swore at his coronation, and it's not what I swore when I was ordained? Is it the king's will or that of bad advisors?'

I shake my head. We both know this is Anne's will, and the law is written at her bidding. Who but Anne would command the people of England to pray for her and order every priest to name her in royal prayers in every parish instead of the pope?

'My father obeys the law,' I say shortly. 'As do we all.'

He bows his head; he turns away, as if he is disappointed in me, and he goes back to defacing his missal. We both know it is the vandalising of the books that will upset my father more than anything.

## MORLEY HALLINGBURY, NORFOLK, SUMMER

# 1535

Just before midsummer day, Father is summoned to London on royal business.

'They don't ask for me?' I check.

He shakes his head. 'You don't want to come to court this summer, Jane, and I wish I didn't have to. It's a bad business. The trials of Bishop Fisher and the king's dearest friend, Thomas More.'

Mother and I stand on the great steps of the new hall to wave him goodbye, the bright oak double doors behind us, open to the summer sunshine.

'I'll be back in a sennight,' my father promises dourly. 'This won't take long.'

I go down the steps to his horse's head to ask him quietly, so that no one else can hear: 'What if they plead not guilty? What if Bishop Fisher and Sir Thomas refuse to swear the oath and refuse to say anything at all? You can't be guilty of treasonous words if you don't speak – can you? You can't find them guilty if won't take the oath; but don't say why?'

My father makes a grimace. 'I'm not riding up to London in the heat of summer to find them not guilty,' he says shortly. 'This is a treason trial organised by Master Cromwell for the benefit of the Boleyns. The verdict is as secure as that man's grasp of the law – which is to say clawlike – *unguibus*. I'm going to show loyalty to the king and to enforce his will – not to judge guilt or innocence.'

I bend my head for his blessing, and he puts his heavy hand on my hood.

'Anyway,' he says more cheerfully. 'Cromwell has promised me the pick of the books from Thomas More's library – I'd go for that alone. Your husband's already got More's lands.'

'Before the verdict?' I ask, shocked, though I also want to know: what lands? And how much?

'Aye,' my father says. 'Before the verdict. Before us judges even arrive, before we're sworn in. So that tells you there's no doubt, doesn't it? Thomas More isn't going to go home and find his furniture gone and his books missing. He's never going home at all.'

He wheels his horse, and his men form up around him, two before, two on either side, and two behind; the roads have become dangerous in Anne's England. He waves to my mother and pats his pocket to show her that he has the list of things that she needs from the London merchants. He throws a salute to me, and he sets off down the long drive between the fresh green beech trees, to sentence the Bishop of Rochester and the Lord High Chancellor of England to death – because these two good men, great men, refused to obey Anne's new law.

WHEN HE COMES home, a pack horse behind him laden with books from Thomas More's library, he brings the news – that is no news – that Thomas More and Bishop John

Fisher – and five holy men were all sentenced to death, for refusing to acknowledge that there is a new pope and he is Henry. Thomas More and John Fisher have gone to the scaffold, true to the faith of their childhoods.

'There's no greater power than the King of England in England,' my father says shortly. '*Ergo*, the king is pope and emperor in England.'

I open my mouth to ask that – since there is only one church – if the king is pope in England, is he also pope in Italy, where the other pope sits on his throne at Rome? Is he an emperor in Spain, where the emperor is Charles?

But my father shakes his head, draws me very close, and whispers in my ear: 'Seven better scholars than I answered that question, and they are dead for it. A wise man or woman does not ask it. A good courtier does not think it. Prepare yourself to return to court, Jane, and don't think of things where the king has been advised, parliament has enacted, and the executioner has confirmed – most finally as only he can do.'

AFTER THE DEATHS of Bishop Fisher and Thomas More, the court goes on summer progress without a care in the world. Protestants and Papists, enemies and friends leave the crowded, diseased capital city for weeks, and Church and people are forgotten by the man who demanded complete power over them.

'Nobody is going to invite you back to court while they are on progress.' My mother states the obvious.

'I know,' I say patiently. 'I don't expect it.'

'So, when do you expect to go? If you know everything?'

'I don't know,' I say, gritting my teeth on my irritation. 'Master Secretary will send for me, when the queen needs me.'

'She gets everything she wants,' she says with mild spite.

'Of course,' I say. 'She's queen.'

It is not until the end of summer that another letter comes for me, with the Cromwell seal on the outside and the loopy round initials of *T* for Thomas and *C* for Cromwell at the foot of the page. Again, it is letterlocked: folded over and over and spliced on itself, though again, there is nothing in it to interest any spy.

Cromwell writes the usual courtesies: he tells me of the summer progress the court made to the West Country; they chose not to stay at Margaret Pole's great palace at Bisham – which I read as a snub to the lady of the old royal family and a blow to the Spanish party, who are reeling with the death of their champions, Fisher and More – and their majesties are so merry that progress is to be prolonged into autumn.

Only at the very end of the letter do I find the invitation.

*The queen's rooms have missed your good sense, and her ladies have missed your supervision. Her Majesty will need the ladies of her family at her next confinement, and her sister, Mary Boleyn – now Mary Stafford – will never return to court. You may come back to your former place as senior lady-in-waiting in the queen's rooms, living with your husband on the king's side, on the usual terms. The queen commands me to say that you may come at once, and I trust you will consider me as your friend.*

I note that Anne – now the wife of a pope and an emperor – is now 'Her Majesty'. I don't care. I will call her Holy Father if she wants.

I tap on the door of the library, and enter, confident of my welcome. My father is seated at his great carved table, parchment unrolled and weighted down around him, writing on a great folio of paper, with one of the many quills I trimmed for him. I see the scribbled versions of different translations and the blotted tries at rhyming words.

He looks up as I come in, and he smiles at me. 'Master Secretary told me he would invite you back to court after the summer progress. Has he done so?'

I lay the letter before him, and I see his satisfied smile as he reads it.

'You could not have a better man for your sponsor,' my father says. 'He's not noble blood; but don't despise him on that account, Jane. He's a man of great abilities and a favourite of the king. In him, you see how a common man rises through work and education. His Italian is better than mine; I envy him his years in Florence.'

'He says I am to consider him as my friend.' I point to the looping words.

'Yes, he means you're to tell him all that passes in the queen's rooms.' My father picks up his pen and corrects an error in spelling, just for his own satisfaction, because he cannot help but improve a line, even from another author.

'I'll never interfere in royal business again,' I say hotly. 'I shan't fight Anne's battles for her!'

'You'll do your duty,' he corrects me. 'He's not invited you back to court to be idle. You'll observe her, and her ladies, and tell him what you see. He's putting you in the queen's rooms to give him forewarning. He'll want to know everything before it gets out – that the pregnancy is going as it should, that her ladies are fit for their posts, that no one's speaking against the new laws, who's in favour of the old queen – that sort of thing. More than anything, he'll want to know what Anne is thinking, before he hears from the king that he has had a new idea – quite his own – and it must be law tomorrow.'

'As the queen's senior lady, it is my duty to keep the king's principal secretary informed,' I say carefully.

'Warn him what she's thinking,' he tells me. 'If you can, tell him what she's going to say, before she puts it into the king's mind as his own idea. Get ahead of her, and you're ahead of the king, and so – more to the point – is Cromwell.'

I hesitate. 'But Father, is this not to make a tyrant? To do his will before he's asked it? If the king is first among equals, should he not speak his wishes and his peers debate it in parliament? And now, as Head of the Church – should he not put his ideas to the bishops and scholars for them to test against the Bible and the philosophers? Otherwise, he is the only power in England? Is that not tyranny instead of monarchy? Wasn't that the dilemma of Rome?'

My father puts a gentle hand on mine. 'Yes,' he says very quietly. 'But I have just come from the execution of a man who warned of this. Think, Jane, as I have trained you to think. Machiavelli says that all kings have to become tyrants or be overthrown. This is the rise of the Tudors to tyranny; this is the rise of Anne to tyranny. Make sure you rise with them.'

## GREENWICH PALACE, AUTUMN

### 1535

GEORGE IS NOT waiting for me in the stable-yard at Greenwich when I ride in, at the head of a small train of my father's servants. He is not in our rooms when I go to change from my travelling clothes. I understand at once, that I am restored to court, but not to a true wife's place. The tidy well-swept room is cool, indifferent. I am not returning to a loving home. I make my way to the other side of the great hall, to the queen's rooms. The guards open the doors with a bow, and I go in.

Anne barely looks up at my reverent curtsey. She is seated on a decorated chair, wearing a gown as big as a tent, as if to emphasise that she cannot bear tight lacing over the baby in her belly. This pregnancy is to be no secret. This baby, announced in the first month, cannot come soon enough. Her dark hair is loose, hanging down over her shoulders; she is crowned with a circlet of wheat.

The ladies are practising tonight's dance – the court is celebrating harvest – and Anne is seated at the centre of it.

She nods at me and says grimly: 'I am *Ceres*. Fertility.'

'Not *Demeter*?'

She scowls and says: 'For God's sake! I see you've been in your father's library all year.'

'I didn't mean to correct you . . . It's just that *Demeter* is the Greek goddess, and your gown is Greek style, so I thought . . .'

'The gown's called *Demeter*, then. And I am *Ceres* inside it. Does that satisfy you?'

I giggle, and she finally smiles.

'Anyway, welcome back,' she says.

She may not have missed me, but she needs me. She is surrounded by kinswomen and companions but no friends. I can tell at a glance that the new favourite flirt must be our kinswoman Mary Shelton – the second Shelton girl to come to court. She leads the ladies in the dance, and beside her is an empty place for her partner, the lord of the harvest. Who else would play lord of the harvest but the king? He's not going to sit beside a pregnant wife for the next seven months. Mary Shelton has the long Boleyn face, but her grey eyes are sparkling with excitement, and she is always smiling. She's a younger, merrier version of Anne. If Anne had ever been carefree, this is what she would have looked like.

One glance at Mary, and at the beautiful sleeves laced onto her ordinary gown, tells me everything: that our family has put one of our own in the king's path, so that the place of the Boleyn wife will be held by a Boleyn mistress for the duration of the pregnancy. Someone has managed to persuade Anne that she cannot demand the king's fidelity for the next seven months. Someone chose Mary Shelton as a girl whose loyalty to family means she will step forward and then step back again, and someone has persuaded Anne to turn a blind eye. It can only have been my husband. Only George could have persuaded Anne to tolerate Mary Shelton, her own cousin, as the new favourite, and only George could have persuaded Anne that it is better to be a ruling queen in power for life, than a mistress beloved for months and then forgotten.

I smile at Mary Shelton so she knows this is well understood by me: she is the new herald of the king's supremacy, and there will be no milk in her sheets or pinching. I look at her bright, flushed face and think it a shame that all this liveliness and prettiness should be devoted to a man who will use her only to boast of his virility.

'Do I have to learn the steps?' I ask Anne.

She nods. 'They saved a place for you. Edward Seymour's your partner.'

'Who is George's partner?' I ask. My voice sounds strained, I assume he has taken a mistress.

'He sits out with me.'

Margery Horsman points out where I am to stand, and I take my place in the rows of young women and look around. Nan Zouche and Jane Ashley smile at me; Margaret Shelton gives me the confident wave of a kinswoman; Lady Anne Cobham curtseys; Jane Seymour, who was a maid with me in Queen Katherine's rooms, is too shy to greet me – Lord knows why Anne has brought her back to court. Anne Parr, my old schoolfellow, gives me a wry smile; her younger sister Kateryn is beside her, visiting court. Elizabeth Somerset introduces a young kinswoman. The Queen of England needs a defensive camp of women around her, whatever name she goes by: *Demeter* or *Ceres*, Katherine or Anne.

I learn the choreography of the dance, and we run through it three times. Then Anne says: 'That's fine, that's fine – you can do it again tomorrow,' as if she is bored of watching from her ceremonial throne. 'I'm going to rest; you can sew. Margery, read to the maids from the gospels, and the rest of you, listen.'

There is a muffled murmur of dissent from the maids – something I have never heard before in a queen's rooms – but Anne ignores them and nods to me to follow her to her privy chamber.

'They complain at sewing?' I demand. 'We sewed every day for Queen Katherine, and we went to chapel three times a day as well!'

'They're so idle.' She shrugs. 'They only come to court to catch husbands, not to serve as we did. That Mary Shelton writes poetry to Thomas Wyatt and love notes to Francis Weston, but since she's writing songs with the king himself, I can't reprimand her! Scribbles in her prayer book and passes it over in the very chapel! Anyway, how did you like the country? I take it you don't prefer it, like my sister? You'll have heard: she's gone to live with a farmer and won't be coming back?'

'Yes, I heard.' I don't tell her who told me.

'She came to court with a great belly on her, quite shameless! I told her – we have to be above question. I can't have the king doubt the virtue of any Boleyn. You'll have to be without fault, Jane.'

'I will be,' I promise. 'Nobody shall say anything against me or you, or any of us. Is he happy now that you have a baby on the way?'

She makes a face. 'We had a good summer on progress,' she says. 'Sometimes we were merry, and he forgot I was his wife and queen, and we were lovers like the old days. But the moment we were back in Westminster, and I told him I was with child, I was transfigured into the Virgin Mary.'

I giggle; I can't stop myself. For a moment, Anne bristles, but then she laughs with me. 'I know! I know. Now I am carrying the heir to the throne, I am blessed among women. I have to be as holy as Our Lady.'

'And what's his part? John the Baptist?'

'St Peter,' she says gloomily. 'Rock of the church. First pope ever. Infallible as the pope. As powerful as an emperor since now he commands both the Church and the people. Of course, he's rich beyond his dreams thanks to me – he needs no other taxes but what I have won him from the Church, he'll never need parliament's agreement ever again. He can fine every religious house that he says is failing, he can close them down and take everything if they refuse to pay. Heaven grant that he never works out what power I have given him! But see what an inheritance I have provided for my son? He will be the world's first reformed prince, a truly godly English pope, owning the wealth of the king and the wealth of the Church.' She grins at me. 'And his mother a saint.'

'"The Most Happy".'

'If I birth a son, I rule the king, and the king rules everything,' she says grimly. 'See? Everything I have done, everything I have planned, and in the end it all comes down to a labour, like a peasant woman under a hedge. If I can get a boy, then I'll have made a godly country with a tyrant king who is in my thrall. No woman in the world will have held more power.'

'Well, why shouldn't you have a boy? As you say, any peasant woman in a field can do it. Why not you?'

'The king thinks princes are given by God,' she says restlessly. 'Since God didn't bless his marriage with Katherine, they had no living sons. He's got the idea of a God-given son stuck in his head. You tell me what fool put it in there?'

'Wasn't it George's chaplain? The Greek scholar?'

She laughs, a harsh laugh with no humour. 'No! It was me. I told George's chaplain, and he told the king. Of the many moves I made against Katherine, it was the most brilliant: I said that she could never give him a son because she was no wife. It turned him against her more than anything else could have done. And – *voila!* The lesson comes back to haunt me. Who will the king blame if I lose this baby? Or if it's another useless girl?'

'Well, he can't say your marriage was invalid!' I protest. 'You weren't married to his brother and she was!'

'He bedded my sister,' she points out. 'Some say he lay with my mother.'

'God no!' I exclaim.

'Oh – they say he had yours, too!' Anne laughs at my shocked face. 'So you needn't act so Seymour.'

'So what?'

'So Seymour – so achingly virtuous-pious-virgin-shocked-modesty-nun-face. It's a whole new fashion. But it won't matter who he bedded, as long as I have a boy. If I have a boy, then I'm a queen blessed by God. The most powerful woman in the world.'

'You can't lose it.' I cross myself at the thought. 'You won't lose it.'

'I'm ill-wished,' she broods darkly. 'That old witch Katherine and her daughter Mary are praying for me to die in childbed and my baby with me.'

'They are not,' I say instantly. I remember the queen's meticulous devotions, wrestling with her selfish desires and her determined, unflinching love of her enemies, even Anne. 'She'd never pray for a baby's death. She just never would.'

'She is my death, and I am hers,' Anne says darkly. 'And God knows I pray for her death every night.'

I look at my sister-in-law with something like despair. I've only been away from court for a year, and I thought to come back to *Anna Vincit Omnia*, but it seems that the stakes are higher, the fears darker, the risks greater . . . and where will this end?

'She's ill you know; she might be dying even now,' Anne says quietly. For a moment, we are both silent at the thought of the queen we both served, dying in a cold, faraway castle. 'And if she does not die, I will kill her. I will trap her with my law, name her for treason and behead her.'

At my aghast face, she laughs harshly. 'Jane, if she will not swear that she was never queen, then she has to die. She has to deny herself or kill herself – I don't care which. But she can't live there, refusing to answer if they don't call her "Queen Katherine". If she and Mary won't acknowledge the king as supreme and me as his only queen, then they're as guilty as Thomas More of treason. As guilty as Bishop Fisher. And see what I did to them! They'll both have to die – like More and Fisher – under the axe.'

O N MY FIRST night home, I don't dine with the court but privately, with Anne, in her rooms. I don't sleep with my husband but with her. This makes it clear to me why I have returned – and for sure, it's not for a second honeymoon. I don't even see George until he comes into her bedroom through the private door, to say goodnight to her as we are getting ready for bed. He looks so different that for a moment I don't recognise him, and I am startled by this bullet-headed, hard-faced man who comes in as quietly as a servant. His hair is close-cropped to his skull; he has a dark beard around his jaw. He has the face of an older man, a common man. The forelock that he used to toss carelessly from his dark eyes is gone; the clean lines of his face are turned hard.

'Oh! George! You look so different!'

He passes his hand over his stubbled head. 'Oh, it's the new fashion. The king cropped his head and grew his beard. Told us all to do the same.'

'D'you like it?' I ask Anne.

She makes a little face. 'I'm not complaining. D'you remember the fuss the old queen made when the king first grew a beard? I say nothing.'

'But George – your beautiful hair!'

'No courtier can have beautiful hair at the court of a balding king.' George sits on a stool at the fireside and watches Anne drink the midwife's posset of herbs. He has a jar of honey from the beehives at Hever, and he gives her a spoonful when she forces the hot drink down.

'Very good,' George says indulgently. 'Good girl. Sleep well.'

'Are you going to bed now?' she asks.

He shakes his head. 'I've got to go back to the king's rooms – they're dancing.'

Anne stirs restlessly. 'Who's he dancing with?'

'Jane Seymour.'

'Then who's Mary Shelton dancing with?'

'Henry Norris.'

They are dancing without me tonight, as they have danced without me for more than a year even though I have come back. Clearly, only Thomas Cromwell wanted me back at court, and only Anne has any need of me.

'It's always a circle dance,' I say. 'Round and round. Where's Agnes?'

'Agnes who?' George asks, straight-faced, and then he winks at me. 'Long gone.'

'So she hardly mattered,' I say quietly – thinking, you dropped me for someone who hardly mattered. I broke my heart for more than a year over something that hardly mattered to anyone.

'Norris will be wishing he was dancing with me,' Anne gleams. 'He's still in love with me, he has been for years. He's not gone mad for Mary Shelton like the rest of the court.'

'We're all in love with you,' George says lightly. 'Now go to bed.'

He takes her hand and leads her to bed. She gets in, obedient to her brother, and he kisses her on the mouth as if she were his daughter.

'Sleep,' he says, with his familiar charming smile. 'None of this matters to the mother of a prince. The king will get nowhere with Seymour the Virgin, and he'll tire of Mary Shelton as soon as he's allowed to come back to you.' He glances over to me, as I tie my nightcap. 'Goodnight, Jane. I'm glad you're back at court.'

'Oh, did you miss me so very much?' I ask bitterly.

'Hush,' Anne says. 'I can't be bothered with you two squabbling.'

He throws a smiling salute and disappears to the king's private rooms without another word.

MASTER SECRETARY CROMWELL, my new patron, is with the king at the service of Prime in the royal chapel, sliding letters for signature, one after another across the prie-dieu. Everything is the same but the king, who is shockingly different. He has grown his beard from ear to ear and his hair is cropped short. I see that this harsh shearing is to hide the thinning of his hair, and the new beard conceals his thickening neck. I would not have recognised the handsome prince of my girlhood in this middle-aged man, whose scalp shines pink through a greying fuzz, whose shoulders, broadened by pads and embroidery, cannot mask the huge belly he carries. He looks more like one of the old lords, running to fat, with a red-veined nose, than like one of the handsome young men of court – his juniors. He can order that they cut their hair to match his thinning scalp, he can order that they pad their doublets to mirror his weight, but he still looks old enough to be their father – he will never again be the first among equals. His leg, stiff from a boyhood jousting injury, is resting on a stool. He raises his head to watch the priest, repeats 'Amen' without conviction, and bows again to sign and sign, glancing over his orders, nodding approval.

I am afraid that he will glance across at me, and I will see the terrifying scowl of royal displeasure. But he does not seem to notice me at all. Master Cromwell scatters sand on the wet ink, hands each document to his clerk to hold until it is completely dry and put into his walnut writing box. The whole of the country is ruled from this box, and Master Cromwell has the only key. The king can express the smallest wish – that a rich monastery is inspected, a new ship designed, a wing on a palace rebuilt, or a poor widow paid a pension – and Master Cromwell will write the instructions, the king will sign it, and it is done. The supreme ruler has a supremely efficient machine to make his will into reality without delay and without question.

Master Cromwell glances across at the queen and her ladies on our side of the chapel, our heads devoutly bowed over our prayer books, following the service in Latin, singing the responses, listening to the sermon. He sees me watching him and inclines his head.

We follow the king to breakfast, Thomas Cromwell shadowing the king as he limps heavily into the great hall. The moment the king is seated before his court, the secretary steps back and becomes almost invisible. Now the king is free to over-eat, joke, swear that he will outride every man today, and roll his eyes around the ladies as if taking his pick as to who will be his flirt and his flatterer-in-chief.

Master Cromwell will take all the work away in his walnut box and send out the letters in his own code, letterlocked by his own clerks, to his agents all around the country: those he has made sheriffs, those he has made mayors, the justices of the peace that he has appointed, his tax inspectors and customs officers and spies. This short, strong-backed, ugly man, dark as a gypsy, without great title, without great family, has made himself the most important man in the kingdom, second only to the king. Other men have greater titles or fortunes, but no one else has a network of authority like this. The king's word is law – but it is Master Cromwell who writes the words of the law and it is his men who enforce it.

He bows low to the queen, who barely acknowledges him as usual, and he walks past the ladies' table, greeting us all in the correct order of precedence with a little bow. 'Welcome back to court, Lady Rochford.'

'Thank you,' I say. 'I am very glad to be here.'

He makes a little deprecating gesture with his broad calloused hands. 'And is your father well? Do you have a letter for me from him?'

I realise this is how we will meet. 'Yes, Master Cromwell. He gave me his new translation for you.'

'Will you bring it to His Majesty's presence chamber later?' he asks and goes quietly from the dining hall, standing back to allow the servers pass with their heavy trays, as if he were not a great man and they bound to give way to him.

I TAKE ONE OF my father's latest poems in my hand to make my way through the usual press of petitioners in the gallery outside the king's presence chamber. There is a little rush towards Master Cromwell as he walks through, sober as a clerk in his dark jacket and white linen. He smiles and nods to each anxious man and promises to come back and hear every one of them, after he has seen the king. He offers his arm to me and draws me into a quiet corner.

'Thank you for bringing me back to court,' I say. 'I thank you very deeply, Master Cromwell. I'm very grateful.'

He nods, wasting no time on my gratitude. 'Is the queen truly with child? Not pretending? She says she's two months into her time? Is that so?'

'She really is. She would not lie about such a matter.'

The wry upward turn of his mouth tells me that he thinks Anne would lie about this, and anything else if she thought she could get away with it.

'And Mary Shelton – is she in play to distract the king from straying to another lover? Does she know this is her task? Did your family agree on a candidate?'

He makes us sound like the dog-keepers in a bear pit, choosing one bitch after another to go into the bear. 'It's not like that,' I say quickly. 'Mary Shelton knows that a courtier's task is to entertain the king and enhance the life of the court.'

'The queen accepts this . . . cousinly entertainment?'

I cannot explain to this plainly dressed common-born man that Howard ladies are raised to be both poets and muses, to inspire love and perform it. The youngest girl in the schoolroom at Norfolk House, Lambeth, knows that it is her task in life to win the favour of the king and get a good marriage. The youngest boy knows the only route to fame and fortune is in the king's service.

'The queen is mistress of her rooms; her ladies are a reflection of her,' I say. 'Her rooms are rightly the heart of the court. A king should be royally served.'

He gives a short laugh. 'Aye – I know you all do that. And Mistress Shelton herself? Did she seek this post?'

The rapid questions make me feel like one of his sheets of paper, slid quickly across a desk for signing.

'She makes no objection. She has come to a court that everyone knows is the centre of courtly love and poetry. She writes poetry herself – love poetry.'

'To the king?'

'To the king and to other poets: Thomas Wyatt and Henry Howard. To my husband George and to Henry Norris.'

'In Venice, a woman with half a dozen men would be called a courtesan?'

I flush with irritation at his crassness. 'It's a game,' I say. 'As I think you know well enough, Master Cromwell. It's the game of courtly love, and nobody takes it seriously. All the ladies are in love with the king, all the noblemen are in love with the queen.'

He shakes his head. 'Far beyond a simple lawyer like me. Do you have a lover, Lady Rochford?'

I turn my head from his dark-eyed scrutiny. 'I've been at court too long,' I say quietly. 'I came as a little girl, and I've seen too much.' I resist the temptation to confess that I am tired of the constant play of courtly love and more and more afraid that there is no real love at all.

For a moment, his calculating gaze softens. 'I should think you have seen too much, poor child. Does the queen favour anyone?'

'Henry Norris, I suppose. And Francis. Thomas Wyatt has been devoted to her since she was a girl.'

'Weston or Bryan?'

'What?'

'Her favourite: Francis Weston or Francis Bryan?'

I give my false courtier laugh to hide my discomfort. 'Oh, both of them! That's what I am saying. This is a court of flirtation!'

'And do they advise her? These lovers? Do they talk of the dowager princess, of the alliance with France? Do they talk of the pope and the need for the reform of the Church? She reads forbidden books, doesn't she? Does she read with them? With her brother? They're both keen reformers? He is her chief advisor? What do they speak of?'

'Of course, George has the full confidence of both the king and queen—'

He makes a noise, an irritated little *tsk*. 'Lady Rochford, do you not trust me?'

'Of course I do! I said I am so grateful—'

'Please do trust me. Half of what you tell me, I know already. I know, for instance, that the queen has forbidden books in her private library and that half of them have been given her by her brother. That they are both so determined on the reform of the Church that they swear there will be no monastery standing in ten years—'

'Only those that are corrupt—'

'And who d'you think inspects them for corruption? Me! I'm on your side, Lady Rochford. We're all on the same side. I'm for reform, and for the queen, and for her son and for a Tudor England at peace.'

'George advises Anne,' I volunteer. 'And all of our inner circle are for reform, enemies of the Spanish party and of Spain, and the old queen.'

'And what d'you think of Jane Seymour?' he says casually. 'Does she put herself forward?'

He changes the subject so quickly that he surprises me into honesty. 'Jane Seymour? She's a nothing! She has her place as a favour to her brothers. I'm surprised she came back to Anne's court. She was so fond of the que . . . of the dowager princess.'

'She, too, has a train of admirers?'

I smile at his shot in the dark. 'You can't know everything if you think that, Master Secretary. She is famously modest; she is notoriously modest; she's embarrassingly modest. She doesn't encourage anyone.'

He pats my hand. 'Please notice her in future, Lady Rochford. And tell me what you think of her. She certainly has great friends at court – important friends, if not admirers.'

'I've never seen her talking with anyone,' I warn him. 'But then, she rarely speaks. She'll never attract the king that way.'

His smile widens. 'Just as I thought! You are a scholar of the court, Lady Rochford. When we next meet, you must tell me: what is the meaning of Jane Seymour – and who has taught her silence?'

O**UR HARVEST DANCE** with Anne as *Ceres* turns into the sort of romp the king loves, which Anne used to stage for him every other night during their courtship, when her glittering rooms at Whitehall rivalled and outshone the dignified grace of the old queen at Westminster. It is as if those times have come again when the master of ceremonies announces that the dance of the ladies bringing in the harvest must be interrupted because some strange country men have demanded the return of their wheat sheaves. All the gentlemen come in, dressed in homespun like rustics. The king, head and shoulders above everyone else, fatter than anyone else, and with a halting stride, is easily spotted; but the rest of them are hidden in baggy smocks, with hats pulled down over their eyes. Mary Shelton screams in delicious alarm, and our dance breaks up in confusion. The king's choristers march in, dressed as peasants, singing harvest songs and leaping around us, and we all snatch up the sheaves of wheat and pile them around Anne's throne like a little makeshift castle, and swear to defend the harvest against this raid.

Anne laughs with apparent delight as the king lunges for Mary Shelton, who screams and ducks, holding tight to her sheaf of wheat. Jane Seymour runs away altogether, as if it is too rowdy for her, but her brother Edward, a handsome, fair-haired man of about thirty-five, sweeps me off my feet by lifting me bodily from the ground, and as I gasp, his brother, Thomas, snatches the sheaf of wheat from me and throws it across the room. It's caught in a high leap by the king's fool – who gives me a merry wave and runs towards Anne to return it to her, the queen of the harvest.

Edward Seymour yells at the fool for betraying the cause of the peasant men, and the fool pretends to be confused by the shouting, flees towards the king, and flings himself under his feet. The king nearly falls over him and snatches up a sheaf and gives it back to me as a gesture of chivalry. I run with it to Anne and am greeted by her most insincere peal of laughter.

We are all tumbled and tousled and breathless and laughing; Elizabeth Somerset is holding a torn sleeve that shows her naked shoulder, Margaret Shelton has disappeared altogether with someone; Anne Parr is tussling over a sheaf with William Herbert, when the master of ceremonies announces that the harvest has made it home and the lady harvesters have won. Anne, as *Ceres*, holds out the crown for the harvester who was first to get her sheaf of wheat home, and her gracious smile never wavers as Mary Shelton emerges, rumpled, from a dark corner, curtseys and bows her dark head for the crown of woven corn.

A harvest supper is laid out in the great hall, and we eat country style – no French forks, no elegant napkins, no silver salters, just great loaves of bread on the table, whole roasted hams and chickens, and the servers bring in great mugs of ale and cider. Anne is queen of the feast at the foot of the table; but Mary Shelton as queen of the harvest is seated beside the king at the head. The king has captured Jane Seymour and forced her to sit, blushing, on his left. Her brother Edward sits beside her to monitor any word she might dare to whisper. Lady-harvesters and pretend-peasants sit side by side at the same table, without precedence in a celebration of misrule: the world turned upside-down.

The old lords and their wives are nowhere to be seen – they knew it would be the sort of romp that they despise but cannot condemn while the king is in the heart of the fun, fooling like a man half his age. It could not be more successful in creating light-hearted laughter in the queen's court and showing the old guard that they are out of time and out of place and that the king is like us – young and daring and merry.

Anne has George on one side of her, making her laugh and drawing all eyes away from the king and Mary Shelton, and Henry Norris is on her left, whispering in her ear and giving her the best cuts of meat. I see her toss her head at some impertinent whisper and she glances down the table to see if the king is watching her. Margaret Douglas is beside the baby-faced Lord Thom and Anne Parr beside William Herbert.

Thomas Cromwell should make a map of this table like his maps of church lands, showing the family connections and the secrets that join one place to another. He would have a *carte* of the courtly loves that he pretends to find so bemusing, and he could judge if they, like the church houses, are also corrupt.

'You're new,' says a voice at my elbow, and the king's fool, still dressed in a white smock like a harvester, shows me his empty hands, palms and then the backs of his hands.

'I've been at court since I was a little girl,' I tell him. 'It's you who are new.'

'No, I've been a fool since I was born,' he replies. 'I was a fool in my cradle.'

'I think everyone is a fool in the cradle,' I say.

'D'you think we are fools to be born?' he asks, as if he is interested in my opinion. He turns both his palms upwards, and now he has a cherry in each hand.

I clap my hands at the trick. 'Are the cherries for me?'

'Can you make them disappear?'

I take them from his hand, and I put them in my mouth.

He claps his hands just as I did, with the same insincere smile. 'See? You can be a fool like me.'

'I'm the king's sister-in-law, a Boleyn,' I tell him, thinking he does not know me. 'I'm no fool.'

'Bless you!' he says with his friendly grin. 'The Boleyns are the greatest fools of all.'

The king's eyes are on us; he nods to me to come towards him. My belly sinks with fear as I rise to my feet, step away from my stool, and curtsey to him. 'Your Majesty,' I say – using the new title, knowing he prefers it.

'Majesty' suits him: he is no longer the informal prince that they called the handsomest in Christendom; he has aged in the year I have been away, thickened, lost his hair. His neck, his shoulders, his chest have grown bullish, the skin on his face coarsened by weather and hard drinking. His thick neck and chin are hidden by the beard, his forehead broadened by the new hair cut. But he is still the greatest man in England, one of the richest men in the world, the brightest star in my childhood skies. I think I will die of shame if he says one word against me or refuses my return in front of everyone. He has become majestic, to suit his new title.

His smile is like sunshine breaking through thunderclouds. He beckons me towards him. 'Why it's pretty Jane come back to us!' he exclaims. 'Why have you been so long away, Jane, my sweetheart?'

There's no time to glance at Anne for a prompt; George is blandly smiling.

I give my courtier laugh and declare: 'Madness, Your Majesty. I must have been mad to be away from you for so long!'

And he gives a great bellow of laughter, throws open his arms, and wraps me in a hug like a bear, like a baited bear in a pit will crush a silly little bitch in his great arms.

## ELTHAM PALACE, CHRISTMAS

### 1535

I REMEMBER THAT THE fool called the Boleyns fools like himself when the head of our house, my uncle Thomas Howard Duke of Norfolk, brings his daughter Mary to court for Christmas hoping that she will finally be allowed to bed the king's bastard son Henry Fitzroy. Surely, this year, at sixteen years old, Fitzroy must be thought strong enough to be a husband? He's strong enough to ride all day with his kinsman Lord Thom; they're strong enough to forever hang around the ladies at court, both of them poets, both of them courtly lovers, exchanging sonnets with Mary Shelton and the king's niece, Margaret Douglas – brimming with youthful lust and rhymes.

My uncle the duke has been grinding his yellow teeth for two years, waiting for the king to allow his precious only son to confirm the marriage. Without a bedding, the wedding can be cancelled and denied, and my uncle's hopes for a Tudor-Howard grandson destroyed. But Thomas Howard is the only one in a hurry for this consummation, not the king – whose favour to the duke is always half-hearted, unless he needs him to kill somebody – and not Anne, who regrets agreeing to the marriage.

Thomas Howard would not know a *hypothetical syllogism* if it curtseyed to him, but he must be haunted by the one that runs: *if, if, then* . . . *If* Anne fails to get a son, *if* Princess Elizabeth is disqualified from the throne for her sex, *if* Lady Mary – both woman and named bastard – is disqualified too, *if* the bastard Fitzroy gets a boy on Mary Howard, *then* there is a Tudor-Howard baby son and royal heir!

But the young couple are in no hurry to serve the Howard ambition. Young Henry Fitzroy is in love with a different girl every time he walks into the queen's rooms. He does not need a wife to slake his thirst; there are plenty of girls at the riverside inns where the young men go in the evening. Mary Howard, the bride, does nothing to encourage the husband she married at her father's command. She is a cold-hearted young woman, coolly obedient to her father, and completely estranged from her mother since the woman was locked up on my information.

She's no great friend to me for that. She probably knows I betrayed her mother for plotting with the Spanish party, and she barely smiles at me when I greet her and my uncle in the huge Eltham Palace presence chamber. The duke kisses me on the forehead as if I had never been disgraced and sent away from court. He acts as if he has forgotten that he failed me; but I have not forgotten.

'Ah, my dear friend Jane! You're welcome back to court,' he tells me. 'Your sister-in-law will need you in her confinement. When does she go into confinement?'

'I don't know,' I say unhelpfully. 'She has not announced a date.'

'Because she does not want to raise false hopes?' he asks acutely. 'You can tell me, Jane. I cannot be her friend, or a good uncle to you or your husband, if I don't know what is needed.'

I will never trust him again. 'You're very kind, Your Grace. But I don't think the queen, nor my husband, need your help? The queen is carrying a prince, and my husband is high in the favour of the king on his own merit. He is to be awarded the Order of the Garter at the next ceremony in April.'

His mouth twists into a smile. 'I shall be glad to welcome him into his stall at Windsor,' he says. 'Such a pity he was overlooked last time. But of course, he'll get my vote.'

My smile is as insincere as his own. 'We are grateful, my lord.'

'HE PROMISED HIS vote?' George asks me. We are standing either side of Anne, who is seated to watch the bringing in of the Yule log. The servants are dragging in an enormous trunk of wood, seasoned for a year in the woodyard outside the palace. Will the fool is dancing around them with a little handaxe, swiping at it as they drag it in and curse him for threatening their fingers. The choristers are singing a carol and the ladies are dancing in procession. The gentlemen are laughing and singing with wassail cups in their hands. Everyone is here to see the Yule log come in, even the old queen's friends: Henry Courtenay Marquess of Exeter and his wife Gertrude, and Lady Margaret Pole's son Henry Lord Montagu, and his brother Sir Geoffrey. They stand together, smiling, as if they are not privately thinking that it was all done better in the time of Queen Katherine. Sir Geoffrey does not even have the sense to pretend to seasonal joy but looks around, as sulky as a boy.

'He promised you his vote.' I raise my voice over the carols and the laughter. 'But I told him you would get the Garter anyway.'

Anne laughs. 'Well said! He needs our favour now; it's not the other way round.'

'He'll always be in favour when the king wants dirty work done,' George says. 'When the king needs an army to break up a riot against taxes, when some poor women are protesting against their fields being stolen.'

'He's welcome to dirty work,' Anne says. 'But soon, he'll have none to do. There'll be no parish taxes on the poor when I make the king give the monastery fines to poor people. When Cromwell closes an ill-living monastery, it will reopen as a centre for the new learning, as a school or as a hospital. The villages will become wealthy on the Church fortunes.'

'Thomas Cromwell thinks that, too,' I remark.

'Well, he would,' George says dismissively. 'It's his sort of people who are breaking down the fences; it's his sort of people leading the riots.'

Anne laughs at George's contempt for Cromwell's breeding.

The fool leaps onto the moving log as it is dragged towards the red-hot embers in the fireplace. 'Take care!' I cry out to him. He does a little running dance along the length of the tree as they haul it onto the hearthstone and then leaps clear as they roll it deep into the grate onto the glowing ashes.

'You take care!' he says nonsensically.

'I don't find him funny at all,' Anne says, watching him dance around the court, threatening the ladies' gowns with his sooty hands. 'I've never heard him say anything witty.'

'He's not a witty fool,' George says. 'He's a wise one. He tells the king things that nobody else would dare to say.'

'We've come to that?' she demands. 'The king's wisest advisor is his fool?'

'Everyone knows that it's you,' I say.

'Yes, with the two of you behind me,' she says quietly.

I have regained my place as the third point of this triangle, the *trigono* named by the Greek philosophers as the strongest shape for bearing a load. Anne's influence over the king is a heavy load to carry and I do it as my courtier work. I no longer imagine I am bound to the Boleyns by love. There is love between the two of them; but it excludes everyone else. I hardened my heart in my long exile, I dropped my longing for love, as they dropped me and I came back to court for ambition – not for love.

The fool chases people into a chain dance; he starts the dance with hands black with soot from the chimney, and as they go hand to hand, they pass chimney soot to each other and recoil laughing. Jane Seymour fends him off with both hands outstretched, like a little child trying to keep her dress clean, and she runs to hide behind the king, who takes his own silk handkerchief to wipe her fingers, scolding the fool for teasing her.

'Fools seem to be in fashion,' I say sourly.

Like the rest of court, I attend the Christmas gift-giving in the king's presence chamber. It's more a forced tribute than a joyful exchange. Everyone lines up to hand over their gift to the king's clerk, who guesses the value and jots it down so the neighbouring clerk can see. In turn, he chooses a gift from the nearby table, worth a little less, and passes it to the king, who hands it to the kneeling courtier with a word of Christmas cheer. Nothing could be further from loving, spontaneous giving; it is a well-organised exchange where value is leached from the courtiers to the king, and they pretend they are glad. In an effort to curry favour and offer something that is difficult to value, I usually give something that I have made: a box of collars for the king's shirts embroidered with gold thread. It has taken longer to sew than usual this year – his neck is thicker: a fat eighteen inches.

'I hear your father has given Lady Mary one of his translations,' Thomas Cromwell remarks to me, as people file in and present gifts to His Majesty and receive his gifts to them in reply.

'Yes, Thomas Aquinas' *Angelical Salutation*,' I say. 'The first part.'

'Her mother, the dowager princess, is said to be gravely ill,' Thomas Cromwell remarks. 'Would your father advise Lady Mary to visit her for the last time? Would he advise her to take the oath, acknowledge the king as Supreme Head of the Church, so that she can say goodbye to her mother?'

I make no comment at the cruelty of making a young woman

declare her mother a whore as the price of attending her deathbed. Instead, I emphasise my father's loyalty to the king. 'He would always advise her to obey her father.'

Unnoticed by the other people, receiving and giving royal gifts, Thomas Cromwell leans closer to ask: 'Is it true that Lady Mary is to be invited to visit court? Is the queen trying kindness?'

'Only as a bribe – she has to take the oath.'

'I am sure they would be friends! The queen can be enchanting. She made herself beloved of the king through enchantment, didn't she? Sortilèges? Magic in her smiles?'

I hesitate. 'It was magical in the sense that they fell in love. She is enchanting in that sense.'

'Why? What other sense is there?' he asks, as if he is ignorant of the other meanings of sortilèges: sorcery and dark arts. 'If only your father could persuade Lady Mary to take the oath and come to court, the queen could cast her spell. And Lady Mary will have to obey her father in the end – won't she?'

I think of the blaze of martyrdom in the princess' eyes. 'She certainly ought to,' I say cautiously.

'Does your father love Lady Mary?'

'Courtly love,' I tell him. 'Fatherly love. You know that means nothing.'

He looks intently. 'Fatherly love means nothing, Lady Rochford?'

'My father is a philosopher,' I tell him. 'The head rules the heart.'

He nods. 'Please tell him to advise Lady Mary that she must take the oath,' he says gently. 'Sooner, rather than late. And mention it to Lady Margaret Pole. Even to Gertrude Courtenay. Tell them that she should take the oath now, when it is offered in kindness, and not risk the queen's disfavour. Thomas More risked the queen's disfavour. We don't want any more martyrs.'

'Anne would never—' I start, but I remember her saying: *She is my death, or I am hers.*

'Exactly,' he says. 'The Spanish party should consider what will happen to Lady Mary when her mother is no longer here to protect her? Lady Mary's friends might wish her safe – might wish her far away.'

Thomas Cromwell never says a word that is not full of meaning. Is he now suggesting that Lady Mary should run away? 'I suppose she can't just leave!'

'I would have thought she has friends enough, clever enough and rich enough to get her to a Spanish ship in some unwatched port.'

'Are there any unwatched ports?' I ask.

'There could be.'

'She would not get captured, trying to run away? That would be the worst thing that could happen. They would have advised her to go to her death?'

'She would not be captured,' he reassures me. 'If she made the attempt, I am sure she would get away. If anyone were caught, it would be her assistants – the Spanish party. I imagine you Boleyns wouldn't mind the Spanish party being caught in treason? In the very treasonous act that got Lady Mary safely out of the country?'

He does not wait for me to answer, but makes his bow to the king and withdraws from the room, his clerk silently following behind. The queue for people waiting to offer gifts to the king is long, but I wait for Lady Margaret Pole to step forward, and her servant bows and puts down a handsome Spanish-made saddle. The clerk notes the value, Lady Margaret curtseys to the king, her cousin, and he rises from his throne and kisses her on both cheeks. His groom of the chamber passes him a small, jewelled box as his gift for her, as if she – born a princess – is honoured by a second-hand piece of rubbish. She curtseys and steps backwards deferentially, only turning her back on the king when she gets to the door of his presence chamber. I curtsey, too, and follow her down the gallery to the Pole rooms, where she stays with her sons: Lord Henry Montague and Sir Geoffrey Pole.

'My lady?' I catch her up.

'Lady Rochford.' She smiles at me as if she wants to see me as her clever little pupil in Queen Katherine's rooms, and not the skilled courtier that I have become.

'My father will visit Lady Mary after Twelfth Night,' I say. 'Shall I ask him to take your good wishes?'

She is too cautious to trust me. 'Thank you,' she says. 'Please send her my blessings. Your father was always a good friend. Lady Mary and I used to have much pleasure in reading his translations.'

I lower my voice. 'He will advise her to take the oath of loyalty.'

'I'm sure she will be glad of his advice.' This woman has survived four kings; she is not going to be surprised into an indiscretion.

'Lady Mary should understand – as Sir Thomas More did not – that there is no choice. If she is to live in England, she will have to declare her obedience to the King of England as Supreme Head of the Church, married to his first and only wife, Queen Anne. She must name herself as his bastard daughter . . .' I pause. 'If she is to remain in England,' I add, to let her think of exile.

Her hands are trembling; she tucks them into her sleeves. 'I thank you for your advice.' She speaks slowly, as if weighing every individual word. 'I know that you loved Lady Mary when you were together in the schoolroom.'

I laugh, my false laugh. 'Oh, we were little rivals! I used to say to her: "*Vaya a Esapña!*"'

She speaks Spanish as well as I do. She understands: *Go to Spain!* But she does not betray herself. 'Oh yes, I had forgotten that,' she says, smiling.

I curtsey and leave her at the door of Pole rooms. She's an intelligent woman; I don't need to say more. I have the heady sense of power like a loosed falcon. I have done something very good for Lady Mary today, while leading the Spanish party into disaster. I stretch out my fingers like the talons of a hawk. I feel as if I could grasp anything.

## GREENWICH PALACE, JANUARY

## 1536

I MIGHT HAVE GOT Lady Mary safely out of the country and the Spanish party destroyed for their part in her escape, but they freeze into inaction, horrified by the decline of the old queen, in the dark days of the new year. Even I – sister to the woman who so brutally replaced her – am waiting, on edge for the daily arrival of bad news from Kimbolton Castle. I fear she is feeling the cold of the hard winter of the eastern fenlands. She was raised as a princess of Spain in the Alhambra Palace in Granada, she has always felt the cold in England. I think of her, solitary, confined to one tower of an uncomfortable castle, separated from her beloved daughter, nothing to leave her servants after a lifetime of wearing a queen's jewels, knowing that her very name is denied, no certainty left but her faith. I imagine her shrinking from the cold wind from the east bringing more snow, knowing that none of us who once loved her can visit her, not even on her deathbed.

I cross myself, half-hidden in the corner of the queen's presence chamber, and I pray for the soul of the woman who Anne and I, and almost everyone here, served as if we truly loved, and then turned against, like traitors. I name her daughter as 'Princess Mary' in my prayers, and think of her, waiting for the news of her mother's death, bitterly aware that she can only say goodbye to her mother, if she takes the oath to deny her. To Princess Mary, swearing an oath that her mother is neither wife nor queen, must be worse than death itself.

Anne bursts into the presence chamber, handfast with the king, looking as radiant as if we have won a great victory in a war. 'Thank God, thank God, she is gone, and we are safe!'

All Anne's ladies leap to their feet and mime surprise and joy;

I turn from the cold garden, smiling brilliantly to greet the royal couple.

'And free from the danger of war with Spain!' the king exclaims. 'No one's going to invade us with no cause! And the pope will never publish my excommunication – we have outwitted him!' He puffs up his broad chest. 'We were too quick for him! Ha!'

Anne does not blink at the claim that the old queen's death is a credit to our quick-wittedness. The king's friends trail in behind the joyful couple, all laughing and talking like a chorus enacting victory in a masque. The Spanish party – the queen's old courtiers and her closest friends – mouth the words, nodding their heads like puppets in agreement, but they cannot make their lips smile. Gertrude Courtenay is as pale as the pearls she wears for mourning, and her husband, the Marquess of Exeter, is grim.

'And now we can meet with the pope and with the emperor as friends.' My uncle, Thomas Howard the Duke of Norfolk, arrives smoothly at the king's elbow. 'They have no cause against us. We can make agreements with them, step back into Christendom. We don't have to dance around the French any more. We can get back to the old ways.'

'We won't befriend Spain!' Anne snaps back. 'They've been our enemy for years. Why should we trust them just because their old queen is dead?'

Her uncle gives her his slow smile, his thin mouth like a trap. 'For sure, they'd never trust you,' he says. 'Already, the gossips are saying that the queen was poisoned and that it was your famous soup.'

The king hears none of this, turning to be congratulated by his friends, but the colour flames into Anne's cheeks and George silences her, grabbing her arm. 'Dowager princess,' he corrects steadily. 'There is only one queen. And Spain has no cause against us. They're not going to listen to gossip against the only queen of England when they need our alliance against France.'

Henry Courtenay and Henry Pole – leaders of the Spanish party – studiously ignore each other.

'Thank God!' Thomas Howard turns away from Anne and George

to clasp the king's hand as if to congratulate him. 'Thank God that the woman who wrongly claimed you is dead.'

The woman who claims him right now narrows her dark eyes at her uncle but says nothing. The realisation that Henry will now be seen by the pope – by the whole Roman Catholic world – as a widower, free to marry again in the true church, gives her pause.

But we have choreographed a joyful masque, and we cannot admit to doubts. We have dancing and drinking, and the king's friends toast to his freedom, and next day, the king and queen process to church for a thanksgiving mass, with the little Princess Elizabeth dressed in bright yellow, carried before them as the undeniable heiress of their undeniable marriage. Anne wears a flowing dress with her belt tied high and tight to show her three-months pregnancy – as if to declare she is far past the losing time and marching on to certainty.

If this baby is a boy, he will wear the royal christening gown, and this time, there will be no exiled queen to claim that it was her family gown, brought from Spain, and that Anne's baby is a bastard and unworthy. This baby will have the title Duke of Cornwall and be named Henry, and everyone will forget that there was ever another little Henry Duke of Cornwall who lived only fifty-two days and died in Queen Katherine's arms. By the time this one is born in midsummer, that first queen will have been forgotten; like a May Day queen – gone by midnight and replaced the next year.

'WRITE TO MY sister, Mary,' Anne commands me, as she is resting in the afternoon.

'Mary? Why?' I would not have thought Anne would want her sister – a former mistress of the king with two children to her credit in the nursery at Hever – ever at court again.

She gleams. 'She can see my triumph. She doubted me, and now she will see I am queen – the only queen. And I need her; I need my family around me; I need loyal family around me. I can trust no one but those who depend on me.'

'Mary doesn't depend on you,' I point out. 'She chose poverty with the farmer rather than depend on you?'

'Just write and tell her,' Anne repeats.

'But will she come? You didn't part on the best of terms, did you? You called her a whoring slut, didn't you?'

The great scandal of Mary's dismissal from court took place while I was away at Morley Hall. Apparently, Mary said she was married for love and showed her broad belly. I don't know which annoyed Anne the more, since I missed the shouting and the screaming and the tears.

'She'll come if I tell her,' Anne says simply. 'She has to.'

Mary Boleyn arrives, sulky as a serf, in time for the great joust – it has no title, but everyone knows it is to celebrate the death of the queen, and those of us who loved her – like Mary and me – hide our secret grief. We waste no time on mutual sympathy: Mary despises me as a woman who has given my life to ambition, and I am comforted when I see that though she chose love, she cannot escape the tyranny of the Boleyns: she still has to serve.

The king rides in the joust himself, revelling in his youth and vitality now that his old wife is dead. You would think he was a dozen years her junior. He plays the part of a young husband to a young pregnant wife.

The tiltyard is Henry's stage; he designed it as a viewing ground for his performance of himself. Either side of the yard are two matching octagonal towers with open galleries – one for the ladies of the court, one for the noblemen – so that we can sit up high and see every detail of the king's brilliant horsemanship and his unfailing courage. Opposite the towers are spectator stands for the people of London to admire their king, riding under his own standard, wearing his own colours. Even when the joust is in costume, everyone knows who he is. He was a great jouster when he was younger, and even now, he does not spare himself. Of course, he almost always wins.

Today is no different. Anne is in the great octagonal tower at the side of the tiltyard, at the forefront of the ladies overlooking the yard, all of us avid with admiration all morning. Mary Boleyn – now Mistress Stafford, as she reminds everyone – stands at the back: returned to court but not to favour. George rides well and wins his round with Anne's glove on his lance. The king takes one tilt, breaks his lance against his opponent's chest, and is the victor over a younger man. Everyone says loudly that he rides like a twenty-year-old.

He will rest, as others ride in the next bouts, and then he will ride at the ring at the end of the afternoon, so the huge audience of courtiers and the wealthy merchants and citizens who have come from London can see their king excel.

Anne goes back to the palace to rest for an hour in the cool while the other men are jousting. She takes Mary Shelton with her, and Jane Seymour, the king's former and current flirt, and leaves us ladies to stay behind to watch the other jousts.

One knight withdraws a lame horse from the contest, and another joust is finished quickly in one pass, so the king is due to ride earlier than was planned. He decides to ride at once; he does not want anyone to think he needs to rest. I send a page running to the queen's rooms to tell Anne that the king is riding now – she must come at once.

Henry strides out of his tent and waits for them to bring up his great horse. It too is carrying heavy armour, its head and shoulders burdened with forged plates: a shell of steel encloses the great warhorse of flesh and blood. One groom makes it halt; the other goes on his hands and knees on the ground beside the huge hooves. The king steps heavily on the man's back, puts one boot into the stirrup and heaves himself into the saddle. The big charger sidles as the weight comes down, and the king gathers up his reins. He drops the visor on his helmet with a clang, and now he is a mythical being, a faceless monster of enamelled steel, high on a huge metalled creature. His squire mounts his own horse and rides before the king to announce him: his motto for this joust is Anne's own, 'The Most Happy', as a compliment to Anne and a final jibe to his dead queen – he is the most happy, and she is not even buried yet.

He is going to tilt at the ring, a display of horsemanship and quickness of eye and hand: a crowd-pleasing show before he rides at full tilt in the final joust. There are three rings, dangling from arches, one after another on the long ground between the two viewing towers; he will gallop beneath them and catch them on his lance. The king parades around the arena; the crowd cheers him – but they are subdued: too many remember the old queen, and some point to the empty throne in the ladies' viewing box and say that no woman will ever be fit to take her place.

The king raises his lance to encourage applause, gallops round a second time to make sure that everyone is watching him and then crams his spurs into the sides of the horse. It leaps forward and thunders down the arches where the rings hang. The king raises his lance, strikes one, and pulls it free in one smooth movement, strikes the second, and then there is a clang and a shriek as he misjudges the third and his lance gets stuck on the arch, stopping dead, striking a terrible blow, to the galloping horse.

Henry is thrown from the saddle, falling towards the ground, his weight pulls the frightened horse down with him so that it staggers and, with a terrible clatter, falls on him, armoured king beneath armoured horse, and he is crushed beneath its dreadful weight.

Everyone screams; all the grooms and squires sprint onto the tiltyard towards the horse struggling on the ground. But they cannot get to it – the huge front hooves are blindly clawing the air; its back legs are kicking out. It is blinded by the head armour and weighed down by the iron plates. While it struggles, trying to roll over and pull itself up, trapped beneath it is the armoured body of the king, terribly still, as his horse rolls up and falls back and rolls again.

One groom dares to fling himself at the horse's head, pulls off the armoured headpiece so the creature can see, and hauls on the reins to make it rise. I hear him scream: 'Up, Thunder! Up! For the love of God! Get off him!'

At last, it gets its front hooves squarely on the ground and raises its big head; but its body, the terrible weight of the big body and muscled haunches grind down on the unmoving rider. Then it heaves itself to all four feet. It shakes – a terrible clatter of bent and loosened armour – and steps away from the fallen man, who lies still as death.

My hands are clamped over my mouth; I am not breathing. I take a shuddering gasp and cling to the front of the balcony. The king's physician Dr Butts comes running from the viewing tower, stumbling through the churned sand of the tiltyard. He throws himself on his knees beside the still body and, tenderly, with infinite care, lifts the visor on the helmet and puts down his ear to listen for a breath. He nods – perhaps the king is breathing? He puts his hand tenderly inside the helmet, feeling for a pulse. He nods more certainly and gets to his feet.

'He lives,' he says quietly to the waiting arena, and then the king's pages come running up with a table top snatched from someone's tent. They put it on the ground beside the king and, slowly, with Dr Butts guiding them, dig the board into the sand beneath the inert body from feet to helmet, as if they are lifting a forged iron effigy of a king.

They raise the board in one movement, straining under the weight, and shuffle cautiously out of the tiltyard. The sand pours off the board like water, as if they were carrying a drowned iron statue from the seabed. There is a long sigh, like a groan of pain, from the hundreds watching, as the King of England, our only king, our king without an heir, is carried like a shipwreck from the tiltyard to the palace.

Saying nothing, I lead the ladies in a silent procession which forms behind the pages with their terrible burden. Even at this moment of horror, we fall into the orders of precedence. Dukes first: my uncle, Thomas Howard the Duke of Norfolk, closely behind the king's still body; Charles Brandon the Duke of Suffolk, beside him; Robert Radcliffe the Earl of Sussex alongside. Then lords and knights. We ladies come behind them, men with lesser titles behind us. It is as if we were going to a great banquet or about to dance – we are all in order. But it is as if we were ranked ghosts, for we are completely silent, and when it is my turn to step into the great hall of the palace, I shiver in the sudden cool – blinking in the shadow after the bright sunshine. Everyone's face is as white as if we are underwater.

They put the board carrying the king on a set of trestles, and he is as still as a wreck at the bottom of the sea. We gather round in moving schools like gulping fishes.

'Step back – give him air,' Dr Butts commands firmly, but I hear the tremble of fear in his voice.

George is at his side. 'Should I take off his helmet?'

Dr Butts hesitates and I have a sudden, nightmarish vision that George will lift off the helmet and the head will come off inside it, and George will have beheaded our king.

'Gently, very gently,' Dr Butts advises, and he supports the bullish neck with both hands, as George takes a grip on the helmet.

It does not yield. George exchanges one aghast look with the doctor, and then he pulls, and then pulls harder. I imagine the broken bones of the neck parting, and I see my husband grit his teeth, and then the helmet yields and comes away, and the horribly shaved head, round as a bald ball, lolls back, limp as death, in the doctor's hands. The king's eyes are closed, his face greenish white like a drowned corpse. Dr Butts feels again for the pulse in the neck, bends again to feel the slight sour breath against his cheek.

'Shall we take him to his rooms?' George asks, milk-white with shock himself.

'Yes, yes.'

Charles Brandon goes ahead, shooing people out of the way, shouting to the yeomen of the guard to fling open the double doors wide to admit the table top. The pages at the head of the board have to go backwards, shuffling their feet and glancing over their shoulders, desperate to be steady. The king's men walk alongside them, a hand on each shoulder, muttering: 'Careful, straight now, step in, you're through the door . . .'

The huge presence chamber opens off the watching chamber. Nobody is going to try to take the dead weight up the stairs to his private rooms and his bed chamber. The double pairs of big doors are thrown open, to admit the procession like the maw of hell, and the gentlemen of the bedchamber rush in. The doors close on them, and we are left outside in complete silence.

I look at the other ladies-in-waiting. 'The queen,' I say apprehensively. 'We have to tell the queen.'

'You tell her,' Gertrude Courtenay says. 'You go in. We'll wait outside.'

We go in our formal procession to the queen's rooms at the rear of the palace, and there are Jane Seymour and Mary Shelton, idling in the presence chamber, gazing out of the window that overlooks the river, seeing nothing, like the fools they are.

'What's happening?' Mary demands. 'The Duke of Norfolk just came in like a charging bull, threw us out of the privy chamber, and told us to wait out here.'

'Is he with the queen?'

They nod.

'His Majesty has had an accident,' I say shortly. 'His doctor is with him.'

'Lord! He didn't say . . .'

I'm very sure he didn't say! He was dashing to get to Anne before anyone else. As her principal lady-in-waiting, I should be at her side, even if I have to interrupt my uncle, a duke.

I look around for her sister, Mary. 'Come with me?' I say.

'Not me,' she says rudely.

There is no one to help me. I go to the door of her privy chamber, tap on it gently, and go in.

Anne has half-fallen from a chair in a faint, Thomas Howard

holding her up by the shoulders. 'Here,' he says. 'Slap her, or something.'

Anne struggles in his grip. 'Jane! What's happening?'

'The king has fallen from his horse . . .'

She gets to her chair and rounds on her uncle. 'You said he was dead!'

'I said he looked as if he was dead,' he corrects her quickly. 'You have to understand that this is a moment of extreme importance. If he dies—'

'You said he was dead!'

'I did not. Listen, for God's sake! If he dies, we have to ensure that you are regent. If the child in your belly is a son, then you are queen regent for the next twenty-one years until he's grown. The sole ruler of England, good as a king.'

Anne looks wildly at me. 'Is the king dead? Is he dead?'

I shake my head and chafe her icy hands. 'No, no, the doctor is with him. He's not speaking; he's not conscious – but he's alive. Be calm, Anne.'

'Get George!' Her voice is a shriek. She jumps to her feet and sways with faintness.

I have to hold her from running out to find him. 'Anne, be still! He's with the king – all his closest men are with him. He's in his presence chamber; they brought him in. He fell, and his horse fell on him. But he was in full armour; he might just be faint . . .'

She pants and claps her hand to her belly. For a moment, nobody says anything. Then she breathes deeply; her colour comes back. She blinks; she recovers herself. I see her assembling her wits, straightening her back, calculating her advantage.

'There,' I say soothingly. 'There, there,' meaningless words while I watch the *hypothetical syllogism* work its magic on the two of them: *if, if, then* . . . *If* the king dies today, *if* Anne gives birth to a boy, *if* the Spanish party are weaker than the Howards, *then* there is a Howard regency for a Tudor-Howard baby king!

Anne turns to her uncle, who is standing beside the cold fireplace, looking down into the cold grate, waiting for her to become the skilled politician he knows that she is. She takes a shuddering breath. 'Regent,' she prompts him.

He nods. 'Understand this: the king's own sister Margaret was queen regent of Scotland when her husband died, leaving her with a young son. Queen regent until the boy was crowned. She's not the only one. Queen Margaret of Anjou was queen regent for her young son when her husband lost his wits. It's been done before. It's the right thing. You could do it. With my support, you could take the title. With my support, you could declare yourself regent and seize the power of a king. You would rule as a king with parliament and the privy council – we'd call it a regent council – until your son is twenty-one years old. Together, we could bring it off.' He looks at her, his dark eyes narrow with suspicion. 'Mind, neither of us could do it alone.'

'A Howard regency,' she says.

He nods. There is a long silence. 'We'd have to work together,' he specifies. 'No tricks.'

'We'd have to get rid of Lady Mary at once,' she says. 'Before anyone suggests her as the heir and queen . . .'

He nods. 'Marry her off. . . Or . . .'

'Send her to Spain?' I suggest quietly.

'No. I want rid of her forever,' she repeats. 'Permanently.'

He understands her before I do. He nods.

'I must go to him.' She takes two steps to the door, but she sways slightly, and I take her cold hand.

'Sit down, Anne. Let me see if—'

'No, let her go,' the duke orders me. 'She has to be seen, taking control, managing everything. I will take her.' He puts out his arm, and Anne understands exactly how they are to appear: the pregnant queen and her uncle, the duke, who will protect her and the unborn legitimate royal heir. Nobody can stand against the two of them. If the king is dead, her baby is his only legitimate heir, and Thomas Howard, with his own private army, will make her queen regent.

The baby in her belly is the next king, and Anne and her uncle will rule in his name until he takes the throne. This is the very script of Howard dreams.

Thomas Howard smiles one of his rare, sweet smiles at me. 'Quite so,' he says politely. He prompts Anne: 'Queenly. Undeniable.'

Anne puts her hand on his arm and stands tall as I go ahead of them and throw open the door to the presence chamber, where the ladies break off their panic-stricken gossip and sink into deep curtseys as the Boleyn queen and the Howard duke go by.

THE KING LIES like a dead man. They undress him and put him into his bed, and he makes no sound. He is alive, breathing and warm, but he hears nothing and sees nothing. There are a few who say this is the same curse that struck an earlier king Henry, who slept for more than a year and woke up to find his country at war and his throne lost.

'Not at all,' Thomas Howard says. 'The country is not divided. No one's claiming the throne. We are as one.'

Thomas Cromwell, waiting outside the king's presence chamber for news like the rest of us, exchanges one brief glance with me. Of course, there are other claimants; there are always other claimants. There is Lady Mary: now called a bastard but known as a royal princess and the true heir to all the Papists in the country and everyone abroad. There is the only legitimate child: the Princess Elizabeth, only two years old and a girl at that. If you count acknowledged bastards, there is Henry Fitzroy, betrothed to Mary Howard. Other claimants would be the endless royal cousins and nephews from the Plantagenets, the former royal family: the Courtenays, the Poles, the Lisles and their children.

'Do they think she will be regent?' Thomas Cromwell asks me, so quietly that I can hardly hear him as he steps up behind me.

'Yes,' I say shortly.

'Were they planning for his death?'

That would be treason. 'Of course, they're thinking what the king would want . . .'

Master Cromwell nods and works his way around the room to where Thomas Howard waits at the door to the privy chamber, Anne leaning on his arm. The two men confer rapidly and quietly; Anne listens in silence. Then the door to the king's presence chamber opens, and Anne goes in alone.

I see from the corner of my eye Henry Courtenay speaking quickly and quietly to one of his men, who bows and leaves the room. We are not the only ones thinking of Lady Mary as her father lies dying.

We all wait for an hour, incapable of going away, hardly daring to speak, though outside, the common people whisper and the tournament flags are stirring in the breeze off the river and the horses standing in their heavy saddles. Finally, Dr Butts comes out; the doors close behind him.

'I am pleased to tell you that His Majesty has recovered his senses,' he said. 'God has saved him; he is unhurt. God save the king!'

'God save the king!' we sigh – it is almost a groan – and then Anne comes out, white as a ghost and bares her teeth in a joyless smile.

'The king will rest in his bedchamber,' Dr Butts announces. 'I will stay with him.'

He turns back to the king's bedroom door, and the guards let him in.

Anne beckons me. 'Help me,' she says shortly.

She leans on me as we walk back to the queen's side, and I put her into her chair in her privy chamber. Her ladies straggle in behind us. No one wants to sew. Everyone wants to describe their own shock, what they saw, what they felt; but one look at Anne's pale face discourages them.

'You can all go and pray,' she rules. 'My sisters, Mary and Jane, will help me to bed. The rest of you change your gowns and go and pray for the king's health and thanksgiving for his recovery. Dine in my presence chamber, not in hall. No music. No dancing.'

W<small>E ALL DECLARE</small> that we have witnessed a miracle. A miracle! The king survived a fall that would have killed a normal man. But he jumped up unhurt. We tell ourselves this every day; we give thanks for his health in chapel four times a day. But though he is miraculously saved, he does not reappear. We hear that the old wound on his leg has opened up. He is in an agony of pain; he cannot get up for days. Anne, in her quiet rooms, is as pale as when she thought he would die. There are no more services of thanksgiving for the death of Katherine of Aragon, and the king does not send for Anne.

At last, he comes out of his private rooms, his shaven head printed with the bruise from his helmet, like a dark-blue mask that he can never lift off. He limps with the pain of his leg, which has worsened, and he looks oddly furtive – like a man hiding a terrible secret. He has learned his own mortality. Riding in the joust against young men to celebrate his first wife's death, he thought himself immortal. Now, he learns that he, too, can die, in a moment, alone as she was, cold as she was, with a great weight crushing the breath out of him.

'You have to be a very great scholar to be able to imagine death,' my father remarks, visiting me in my beautifully furnished Rochford rooms.

I am alone; George is keeping Anne company. These days, they sit for hours in silence, as if they, too, have suddenly thought that the king is mortal, and we have no future but the baby in Anne's belly.

'It's almost impossible for a man to imagine his death, except as a tragedy for others,' my father thinks aloud. 'How can a mind imagine its own absence? It's a paradox. And a king – who spends his life enforcing his will and embodying his desires – how can he imagine that will and those desires are no longer present? The absence of that will? How imagine a world without his orders?' Thoughtfully, my father opens his missal and scribbles a little note to himself on the fly leaf.

'He's always disliked the colour black,' I volunteer.

'He's always dreaded the thought of death,' my father agrees. 'But he will have to think of it now.'

'He has named it a treason to even speak of it.'

'We can be silent, but how can we not think of it? And Sir Thomas More was executed for unspoken thoughts.'

I frown. 'You didn't say. He was accused of thinking treason?'

'Yes, they argued that he would have spoken in good faith – silence meant treason.'

'Surely, that makes no sense?'

'It made sense to the Boleyns who ordered the trial,' my father says, smiling.

'It was terribly sad.'

'Any fool can feel sad – look at Master Somer the fool, who is grave now that the king has forgotten how to laugh. I must ask him if he can imagine not being? Perhaps a fool – who has so little will but so much imagination – can imagine his death.'

THE QUEEN IS buried with the scant honour of a dowager princess in faraway Peterborough Cathedral and not as a queen in Westminster Abbey. We pretend she was never married to King Henry, never a wife and queen of twenty-four years, never bore him child after child, never raised a beautiful princess. Her burial is done with respect and ceremony, but none of us attend. Nobody of any importance attends.

Even those who genuinely grieve for her as their dear friend are banned. Charles Brandon's new young wife, Catherine, and his daughter, Eleanor, are allowed to go as a favour to him. Spies go to watch, of course. My uncle Thomas Howard sends his daughter-in-law Frances, and Anne sends her friend Elizabeth Somerset to tell her who was there and to eavesdrop on the few mourners who dared to follow the coffin.

The death of the old queen should signal Anne's complete victory, but we cannot celebrate. Katherine's death makes Anne's great lie completely true: she said that the king's marriage was invalid and he had no wife but her – and now he does. She said there was only one queen – and now there is. She said the king had no legitimate child but Elizabeth – the other two are bastards – and now everyone in the country has sworn this is true. Anne's wildest claims become fact; reality itself surrenders to her. But though she is in the ascendant, Anne feels more uncertain than ever. She has the place of queen but not the favour of the king. He keeps to his rooms, his face still marked, the wound on his leg still open. Anne has won everything but it feels strangely like defeat.

SINCE WE ARE all agreed that the king was never Katherine of Aragon's husband, her few remaining treasures left behind at Baynard's Castle when she was exiled from court, are inherited by her daughter, Lady Mary. The king has no right to anything – except that he wants them, and claims them as her widower. Anne orders the old queen to be buried as a sister-in-law; but picks over her goods as her heiress.

Elizabeth Somerset, Jane Seymour, and I take the queen's barge with Anne upriver from Greenwich to Baynard's Castle like pretty buzzards circling a dead hare. Elizabeth Somerset is pregnant like Anne, and there is much talk of aches and pains and cravings for strange foods as we row inland on the flat tide. Jane, who is more insistently virginal every day, and I, a childless wife, sit stiffly in the prow and try not to hear these secrets.

They whisper that the midwife can bring on a slow birth by caressing the mother into pleasure until she dies away, and Elizabeth says: 'Not just a midwife – anyone could do it, I suppose? In case of need?' And Anne mouths: 'Mark Smeaton?' and Elizabeth says: 'How great is your need?' And they go off into gales of laughter.

Jane looks as if she is about to faint from excess of modesty, and I speak loudly to her about the likelihood of rain.

At the old castle, there is little value in the goods left behind by the old queen, but Anne picks out a horn cup with a cover, a chest covered in crimson velvet, a set of wooden trenchers, and an ivory chess set for the king. Jane finds a modest little box for her small pieces of jewellery, and Elizabeth chooses a table inlaid with dark wood for her rooms.

I take nothing. Our private rooms in the palaces are richly furnished; George and I pride ourselves on buying anything we want, and our home, the palace at Beaulieu, was furnished by the king himself before he gave it to us. I don't need the poor queen's little scraps of things: the king will give them at Christmas to people he dislikes.

Anne has a happy morning of triumph, disdainfully turning over tapestries, declaring them old-fashioned and hopelessly Spanish, opening chests and dropping the lids with a bang. But as she is bending over a box of books, she suddenly says: 'No, oh no.'

'What is it?' Jane Seymour asks eagerly, thinking there is an exciting find of a treasure; but when she sees Anne's snarl, she falls back, and I say: 'Is it the baby?'

Anne melts against me, like a woman of wax. 'Get me home,' she whispers. 'I have such a pain, such a pain!'

Thank God that the barge is waiting at the pier and the tide on the ebb. Elizabeth and I help her to it, ignoring the guard of honour of rowers, and order them to go as fast as they can to Greenwich Palace.

Even rowing hard with the tide, it feels like long hours on the water before we can sweep her through the chambers and straight into her bedroom. People fall back before our silent rush; it is like the king coming home on a table top, all over again. No one dares ask. Perhaps everything will be all right, as it was for the king. Perhaps Anne will rise up in triumph, like him.

In her rooms, we strip off her kirtle, her sleeves, her stomacher, her skirt. Our fingers tremble as we untie gold-tipped aglets on laces of silk. Off comes her outer linen, and then I see the spreading red stain on her underlinen. Jane Seymour flees the room; but has the sense to fetch Anne's sister Mary and their mother. Elizabeth Boleyn sends for the midwife, and we are as we were at that first time, gathered around the bed, doing nothing but telling each other lies: that this is not a miscarry, that it will all be all right, that it is a little bleed but only to be expected; and then finally – at the end of the long day, when the midwife has come and done her dirty work – that this is death, undeniable death.

We cannot bluster it out. Everyone saw us come home, everyone saw us dash into the queen's bedroom. Jane Seymour ran out and told them all that since she was a maid – such an innocent maid – she could not wait on the queen who was losing her baby. Everyone knows.

It takes a day and a night until it is all over, and when Anne is in a state of grim despair, they tell us that the king is coming to visit.

Elizabeth Somerset has the sense to make herself scarce. Mary Boleyn, a former fertile mistress, goes out of the room. Nobody wants to see a pregnant woman today; nobody wants to see a former mistress.

We sweep every disagreeable sight out of the room. No food, no drink, no linen, no water bowl for washing. We dress the room as if it were to be the background to a portrait, a masque version of a queen's bedroom. We make her bed into a bower, as if the king might be coming to make love. She is scented with oil of flowers and rosy-cheeked with rouge, her eyes darkly inviting with drops of belladonna, her hair a perfumed dark heap of curls on the top of her head, her nightgown demurely fastened to the neck, with ribbons that only need one touch to fall open.

They knock on the door and throw it open, and the moment he comes in, the moment I see how he is dragging his sore leg, his face crumpled, his mouth petulant, I know that Anne is lost. Henry has learned to imagine death – as my father thought he could not. Now, everyone else will have to think of it; Henry cannot keep a fear to himself. He is our head, and we are the *corps* – when he is in pain, we all hurt; when he is afraid, we are all sick with terror. Now he can imagine death, we will have to fear it all the time.

Anne's eyes fill with real tears – she holds out a trembling hand to him. 'My lord husband,' she says, and her voice quavers with genuine grief. 'An accident. We will have other children. For sure. For sure, we will. And the next will be better, stronger. Better made.'

His friends and companions do not come into the room but stand like a wall of hostile witnesses on the threshold. I see the hard faces of the old lords – among them, Queen Katherine's friends come to gloat at this new misfortune. Anne ignores them, whispering so that they cannot hear. But she should have said nothing, because the king has come with a speech prepared, and he is not a good company player who can say his lines off a wrong cue. He hates anyone else standing centre-stage. He draws himself up. I see him wince as he puts weight on his bad leg. He holds up his hand to silence her, so he can deliver his speech without interruption.

'I cannot understand such a thing,' he says. He knows he has struck the wrong tone, he sounds peevish rather than lordly. He clears his throat and starts again. 'I cannot understand such a thing. I am so healthy, so full of life. I cannot understand your difficulty.'

'It was my uncle the Duke of Norfolk,' Anne says quickly. 'He came to me in such a rush on the day of your accident! I thought you might have been dead! I feared you were dead!' Her voice quavers; but still his face does not soften.

Our uncle is among the king's companions listening in the doorway. He will step forward and contradict her if she tries to throw the blame on him again; but I cannot warn her of his darkening expression.

'And you've been attentive, to others . . .' Anne says reproachfully. She lowers her voice. 'You made me doubt your love . . .' She shoots a quick look at him under her lowered eyelashes. 'You have neglected me. You have hurt me. I have been bereft. You have pursued her and set her up as a rival to me – after all you promised . . .'

This would have worked when Anne was in her prime; but since the king has learned to fear death, he does not care for other people's fears, not even hers. Now, intent on his own speech, he does not even hear her. He has a question to test her: the worst question.

'It was a boy?'

It's too early to know; but it is more tragic for him if it was a boy. So he will think of it as a lost boy – another lost boy.

Anne hides her face in her scented hands like *Miseria* in a tapestry. The king will surely step forward and take her hands away and kiss her wet cheeks?

But no, this is his tragedy, exclusively his. He will not comfort her – everyone should be comforting him. He is the starring actor in the masque, not a supporting player.

'I see clearly that God does not wish to give me male children,' he says loudly.

There is a genuine gasp at these terrible words, and Jane Seymour lets out a little cry of sympathy. George shoots a startled glance at me: what is God telling the king now? That his marriage is barren? That Anne is no more wife than the previous one? That this miscarry proves the marriage is cursed? No better than the last one?

Henry stalks towards the door, and the old lords, Margaret Pole and her sons, Henry and Geoffrey, their cousins the Courtenays, their friends, our enemies, part before him and admit him to their ranks, enfold him with their sympathy, capture him.

Anne says: 'But, my lord—'

She cannot believe he is just walking out of the bedroom we prepared so carefully. She can see her ladies through the open door rippling down in a wave of curtseys; Jane Seymour's modest English hood on her fair hair is bowed low.

The king pauses halfway across her privy chamber, surrounded by our enemies, the Spanish party in triumph.

'I will come to you when you are recovered,' he says, as if she is unclean, and, limping to demonstrate his own pain, he is gone and they all go with him. The fool, Will Somer, hopping along behind in a wild parody of lameness – as if anyone would dare to laugh.

I close the doors on everyone and turn back to Anne.

'Get George back here,' she says through her teeth.

## GREENWICH PALACE, SPRING

# 1536

WE LEARN A hard lesson: Anne's power over parliament, church, and country, depends on her ruling the king. And she can only rule him if she captures him and holds his whimsical attention, and she has to do this all over again, after disappointing him, and disgusting him. All the Howards, all the Boleyns, all the placemen and women, all the supporters of reform, muster to return Anne to her throne as queen of the court of love, mistress of a hundred broken hearts, the most beautiful and desired woman, 'The Most Happy'. We have to persuade the king that she is the finest woman in the world, pre-eminent at his court; only then can she rule him, and the country. As soon as she can stand without bleeding, we have her on her feet. As soon as she can walk without fainting, we have her dancing.

The king goes away to Whitehall in London with a few friends – none of them our friends – but he will return, and we prepare dances and disguisings, jousts of poetry and masquing, tournaments of tennis, competitions of archery, balls, theatre, sports, games, every sort of distraction for when he comes.

Not one word does he send to Anne while he is gone; but a purse of gold coins is delivered to Jane Seymour – a prepayment for her maidenhead. She returns it without opening it. This could mean that when she weighed it in her hand, she felt it was too light for a prize so long preserved, or she may really not be for sale. At any rate, the king is making no progress with her, and we hope for a clear run to seduce him back into Anne's bed.

When the royal barge is sighted coming downriver, it is a confident Anne in a phalanx of Howards who goes down to greet it on the pier, in front of the beautiful palace, wrapped in her finest Russian furs, in a blaze of torches against the cold spring dusk.

George confers with our uncle the Duke of Norfolk, and we all agree that no one will ever mention the miscarry again: our uncle was not the cause of it, and it did not happen. It will be like the one before – quickly forgotten in the storm of amusements that only we can conjure. We unite against the Seymours, who move into Thomas Cromwell's old rooms adjoining the king's privy chamber. This is a great favour to the two Seymour brothers, and Anne says that it shows that Cromwell's influence is waning, if this mediocre family is given his rooms. I think, silently, that it could equally prove to be our influence that is the thinning moon – and Cromwell is obliging the Seymours now, just as he used to oblige the Boleyns.

But if the Seymours thought they had a hiding place for secret assignations with the king, we spoil sport. Anne takes Jane as her bedfellow on most nights, and the young woman remains the most virginal of maids-of-honour. There is no challenge and chase about Jane, no hide and seeking for the king. When he summons her to his side, she sits in dull silence beside him. When he says something witty and flirtatious, she is smilingly blank. The chattering court of gossip cannot see the attraction; but more than one girl tries on a new look of demure modesty, and the ugly English hood comes into fashion as a silent reproach to Anne's French style.

Thomas Cromwell takes over new rooms, further from the royal bedroom but grander, with a private stair to a room on the ground floor below, where he transacts his business. The ground-floor room has a grille on the window and a double door to prevent eavesdroppers. All of the letters for the king are delivered first to Master Cromwell's dark chamber for translating, decoding, and copying.

He comes to play cards with the king in Anne's rooms one evening and chooses me as his partner. When we put our heads together to count our winnings, he says quietly: 'I see you keep Mistress Seymour close.'

'Not as close as I would like,' I reply. 'She talks to Sir Nicholas Carew, and he is no friend to the queen.'

'Oh, does she?' is all he says.

'And Gertrude Courtenay,' I add.

'I knew you would find her of interest,' he says, as if pleased with his own foresight. 'Is she one of the Spanish party or just alongside them? D'you think she advises Gertrude Courtenay as to the mood of the king?'

I make a little face. 'What would Jane Seymour know of royal moods? The sun always shines on her.'

His dark eyes crinkle with amusement at my irritability. 'Indeed. D'you think she speaks to the king for Lady Mary?'

I think for a moment. 'I suppose she might. She's very tender-hearted.' By the tone in my voice, he may take that I don't think tender-heartedness a virtue in a courtier.

'Someone helpfully warned the Spanish party that Lady Mary must swear the oath or face a charge of treason.' He smiles at me. 'Lady Mary's friends are much dismayed. There's much fluttering in the hen coop, messengers going one to another. I believe they will try to get her out of the country?'

'How d'you know they are fluttering?' I ask.

'They write. They write constantly.'

'Your room receives all letters? Like the dark chambers of Venice?'

'I modelled my room on Venice. Information is the life blood of a powerful state. The Venetian Doge is a most successful tyrant.'

'Don't the Spanish party use code?'

He shrugs. 'I have the code. I have the names of the ship, the plan for escape, and the names of those who warned that she should run away.'

'You won't have my name,' I assert.

He nods. 'You can be sure, I don't. Lady Margaret Pole is a very discreet woman – unlike her son Sir Geoffrey: a blabbermouth. She never puts anything in writing. You did good work, Jane. They are desperate, and they will act desperately, and Lady Mary will be saved from sainthood despite herself, and they will talk themselves to the scaffold.'

## GREENWICH PALACE, SPRING

# 1536

ALL OUR FRIENDS and allies conspire to make Anne's rooms a whirlwind of play, sport, flirtation, music, and gambling. Mary Boleyn – 'Mistress Stafford now!' – goes back to rural obscurity – too slow for this whirling parade of provocation. We circle Anne as if she were the only woman left in all the world. Mary Shelton writes little riddles and poems for Anne to recite as her own; her sister, Margaret Shelton, releases her betrothed Henry Norris to kneel at Anne's feet. Every man who comes through the door of the queen's rooms is teased and badgered and courted, until he swears that Anne is the most beautiful woman in the world and the only woman he desires. Every dance presents her at her best; every disguising costume is cut to suit her; she wins every bout of archery, she wins at bowls, she wins at cards. She sings the king's love songs; she challenges the poets Thomas Wyatt and her brother George to admit that the king's rhymes are best; she partners the king in everything he does. She overwhelms him with the dazzle of her looks and charm. We create a frenzy of desire, and she is at the head of it, always directing it to him.

The usual subtlety of courtly love gets swept away as the court becomes more urgent, more bawdy. All the songs are love songs; all the love is heated. There are no steady friendships even between women. Everything is passionate; everything is quick and furtive. Hands roam freely. A woman's fingers touch her own lips, stroke along the line of the gown at her neck as if she has to be caressed, even by herself. Men adjust a woman's veil, touch her necklace, stray behind her ear. A kiss of courtesy on a cheek becomes lingering; a man feels a woman yield to his slightest touch. Courtships speed up – Anne Parr and William Herbert are openly besotted; Margaret Douglas and her young lover Lord Thom are always sneaking off together.

Even noble wives like me are fair game to the young men of court, who slide a hand up to touch the underside of my breast when they should be holding me by the waist to dance. I allow it. I am caught up in the frenzy of the court for love; we are all in season, we are all in heat.

Anne pushes her French hood further and further back on her head so her dark hair frames her face. When she gets up from her throne to dance, she whisks her skirts and shows the embroidered clocks on her stockings. When she leans forward to curtsey to the king, he can see the creamy curves of the top of her breasts. Everything which should be concealed can be glimpsed if you are quick enough – and everyone is quick to stare, and everyone is quick to show.

Only the king refuses to be swept along. He rollicks in the heated swirl of the queen's rooms, every evening, watches every woman with sideways secret glances; but he goes to his own rooms at night and sleeps alone. He has no desire for Anne though night succeeds night – and the wine flows into everyone's glass, and the music plays faster and faster, and we are like the girl in the story condemned to dance until death. We feel as if we are dancing for our lives in the scarlet shoes of whores. None of us are safe in our places, with our fortunes, until the king comes back to the queen's bed and gives her another boy. We have to whirl through this life of frantic extravagance and enjoyment until Anne is finally satisfied and the mother of a prince.

I brush her dark hair before the mirror, and I do not tell her that I can see a hair – just one – silver-white, in the sleek ebony mane.

'He's a man of contradictions,' she says, her eyes closed, nodding her head against the rhythmic sweep of the brush. 'A king who must have an heir but cannot bed his queen. His mother died after childbirth, as if to teach him that lust is fatal. He was raised by his grandmother, who declared herself celibate. Then he was married to a woman as cold as holy water, who gave him one girl and more than a dozen dead-borns. He thinks that lust for a wife leads only to death.'

'Conceiving a prince is an act blessed from God. It's not carnal lust; it doesn't lead to death . . .'

'But he's never managed it, has he? He lay in the old queen's bed, and he lay in my bed, and all he ever gets are girls and dead babies. It was me who told him that his marriage was sinful and that was why he had nothing but death from the old queen. The little coffins were the proof. Now someone – Charles Brandon or the Courtenays or the Poles or Nicholas Carew or some Papist – has told him that our marriage is sinful, too. You heard him! God told him that's why I lost the babies.'

'Just one,' I remind her. 'We only admit to one. But you're wrong. The Spanish party aren't plotting against you; they're in a panic about Lady Mary. Someone has told them she is in danger.'

'What if they think that the easiest way to save her, is to destroy me?'

I am horror-struck. I turn my face from her gaze in the mirror, until I can find a false smile. 'No, no – they wouldn't dare do that. They'll send for a Spanish ship and take her away. I am sure that's what they'll do. They don't have the power to attack you.'

'They'll send for Italian poison and do away with me.'

T HE KING GIVES George more lands and makes an inventory of everything that he has given us so far – as if to confirm our wealth before he adds more. I walk into Anne's bedroom, unannounced, to tell her the good news of George's new fortune, and she and Elizabeth Somerset spring apart as if I have caught them in a secret act. I am so accustomed to glimpsing couples hiding in shadows that for a moment my heart sinks, thinking that they are kissing or touching in some new love-play, and then Elizabeth tucks a purse into the top of her stomacher and flicks out of the room without another word.

'What was that?' I demand flatly.

Anne shakes her head as if to silence me. 'Nothing. She needed some money, and I lent it her.'

'How much?'

She laughs. 'Who are you? My treasurer?'

'She shouldn't be borrowing money from you. What's she done to earn it?'

Anne tosses her head. 'It's a loan only. I've lent her a hundred pounds.'

I gasp – this is the same as George's entire yearly wage as a senior courtier. This is a fortune and it will show up in the queen's accounts, and everyone will wonder what Elizabeth has done, or what Elizabeth knows.

'What d'you want me to do? Refuse a friend in need?'

'Yes,' I say flatly. 'Why can't she tell her husband?'

'It's a secret.'

'But she can tell you?'

Anne laughs harshly. 'She holds a secret of mine as security.'

'What does she know?' I demand, myself a trader and a broker of secrets.

Anne makes a little face. 'She caught me . . . talking to . . . someone.'

'Who?'

'Mark, beautiful Mark.' Anne gives a courtier laugh – empty of humour.

'The lute player?' I spell it out. 'The king's lute player?'

'There's only one beautiful Mark. And folly is cheap at a hundred pounds if it buys Elizabeth's silence. She'll be silent. She's no better than me. We are agreed: she's no worse than me and I no better than her, and all of us are going mad this season. I swear we have spring fever.'

I shake my head. 'Anne, you can't live like a lady-in-waiting – and a loose one at that. Elizabeth Somerset allows liberties that a queen cannot.'

Anne shrugs. 'Nobody knows anything about Elizabeth's liberties, and nobody knows anything about mine.'

I AM LONGING FOR summer even more than when I was in the cold and dark of the country. If we can get to May Day then we are in the happiest of all seasons at court. From midsummer the king and Anne will go on royal progress, hunting and travelling and living off other people's money in other people's houses. Away from court and from the frantic play of the queen's rooms, he will turn to her again. If we can get through to the summer, we will win him back, and she only has to have one lucky night. Once she is with child we are secure again – a royal family with a prince in the cradle. Then she can flirt with a lute player and nobody will care, and the Spanish party can steal Lady Mary away, and nobody will miss her.

The wound in the king's leg heals, and under our relentless joyfulness he becomes more cheerful. He comes to Anne's bed again, and we make jokes about his lustiness, about her fertility. Over and over again, we say how desirable she is, how every man is in love with her. Only a king could win her; only the most handsome prince in the world could hold her. The old Spanish ambassador, Eustace Chapuys, has no grudge against Anne now that the old Spanish-born queen is dead. He comes to court, and for the first time, they meet face to face, and he bows to her; she acknowledges him. It is a diplomatic triumph for us and a blow for the Spanish party, who see their own ambassador acknowledge Anne as queen.

George dines with Chapuys, sitting up over their wine late into the night, persuading him that the Boleyns are the ones who govern England. The ambassador's old allies, the Spanish party, who nag him for a ship for Lady Mary's escape, are yesterday's men. He need not trouble with them. We are the greatest advisors – and the ambassador will have to deal with us if he wants English soldiers for Spain's war against the infidel.

'And that's the turn of the tide!' George says with quiet satisfaction, coming into our rooms after showing Eustace Chapuys to his barge.

'If Anne can get a boy in her belly this summer, we are safe with no enemies,' I agree. He takes a chair beside me at the fireside. 'Lady Mary can run away to Spain, and the only legitimate heirs in England will be Boleyn Tudors.'

He puts a hand over mine. 'You've been invaluable,' he says. 'I couldn't have got Anne out of despair and back on show on my own.'

He has not always thought me invaluable. I don't melt at his touch. 'It's my duty to serve the queen,' I say steadily.

'For love?' he asks me.

I know he is amusing himself, speaking of love to me, who has never had his love, who will never have it. 'For love of my trade,' I say. 'I am a courtier. My father taught me to be a courtier, and your family taught me ambition.'

'I didn't marry a courtier, but a wife.'

'Yes, I know you did,' I say. 'And then you dropped me.'

He laughs out loud, it is nothing to him. 'Ah, Jane! Will you never forgive me for that? You know it was not my wish; you know I didn't mean to hurt you!'

'Would you do it again?'

'Only if I had to,' he says reasonably. 'And reluctantly, and with regret!'

'Then . . . reluctantly . . . and with regret . . . I will never forgive you.'

He smiles. 'We are to be fellow courtiers but not lovers?'

'We were never lovers,' I tell him. 'I don't think you know how to love any woman but Anne.'

THE SPRING FEVER of the queen's rooms continues through early summer, and, though the king is inspired by dancing and drink to go to Anne's bed most nights, he still moons around after Jane Seymour in the day, preferring her as his partner in every game of courtly love. The Seymour boys coach their sister in the lost art of simpering refusal, and people start to lay odds on how many days they will play this game, until they order her to yield to the king and get into his bed. The Seymours are not a wealthy family; they cannot afford to prolong a courtship where the drama is the refusal of rich gifts. It was a grave error for them to demonstrate her virtue by refusing money: she could have made a good profit from little liberties along the way; but they have staked everything on her maidenhead.

Most of the older men, the king's friends from his youth, hardly notice the new intense flirting and the playing of dangerous games in the queen's rooms. They were young men at the court of Katherine, they kept their lusts out of her rooms and safely in the alehouses and stews, where they were notoriously violent and vile. Half of them are too old to stay up late. Nor are they any threat to our reform of the Church and the diminishing of parliament. They don't understand the shift of power that we have made – they don't see the benefit to the courtier in making the court into a tyrant.

Some of the old lords see what we are doing and despise us for it. Francis Bryan turns his one eye on our games, and the scar beneath the patch on the other eye wrinkles up as if he is smiling behind his mask.

He greets me first as I am by the door, and beyond me, he sees Elizabeth Somerset playing cards with Jane Ashley for buttons rather than money, and beyond them, the king whispering to Jane Seymour, so close that his lips are against her little ear.

Francis rolls his one eye around the busy noisy rooms and misses nothing. 'In debt again?' he whispers, bowing over Elizabeth Somerset's hand. 'Who's going to pay for your new baby's cradle? The father? But who is he, exactly?'

'Not in debt at all,' she says in a peal of pretty laughter, and then – more quietly to him: 'Francis, be a true knight for me – don't mention I have no money to my husband?'

'I never thought he cared about your debts one way or another?' His mouth twists in a smile that matches his lopsided face. 'I thought it was your good brother Anthony, who kept you on such a tight rein that you have to play with buttons?'

She flutters her lashes. Even with a big belly, she manages to be inviting. 'Oh Lord!, I can't do a thing right!'

'You're fortunate,' he tells her. 'I never do a right thing, and nobody cares at all. But an attentive brother is in fashion at this court. Does your brother visit you in bed?'

She gives a little trill of laughter. 'Only to scold me!' she says and waves him towards Anne.

Sir Francis bows low, kisses Anne's hand, and presses it to his heart. With one eye on her smiling face, he slides her fingers down his chest, over his embroidered doublet towards his codpiece.

Anne snatches her hand from him. 'Sir Francis! You're very wild today. I don't know where you would take me.'

'Take you where?' Sir Francis asks, playing at stupidity.

'Why, where would you want to take me?' This is lacking in Anne's usual subtlety, but she has her eye on the king, who has now taken Jane Seymour's hand and seems to be imploring her for a favour.

'No, I don't like other men's leavings,' Francis whispers.

'The king has not left me!' She looks murderously across at Jane Seymour. 'You know very well that is courtly play.'

'Not him,' he says triumphantly. 'I didn't mean the king's

leavings. I meant Henry Percy's. Aren't you Henry Percy of Northumberland's leavings?'

For a moment, she is stunned into silence at this resurrection of old gossip. 'What are you saying? Why are you saying—?'

'Haven't you heard? Percy's wife has announced their marriage is invalid! Such a scandal! And worse, she is saying it's invalid because he was married: wedded, and bedded by you. She's left him. She says he's your husband and you can have him back?'

Thank God no one is close enough to hear him but me. Anne's dark eyes turn to points of black ice; but she never falters. She does not even shrink from him; her head is still cocked encouragingly towards him, her smile pinned in place. If the king were to look away from Jane, he would see Anne being courted by his old friend Sir Francis Bryan, in the very posture and place of courtly love.

'Years ago,' Anne says slowly in a low hiss, her smile never wavering. 'That was years ago, as you well know. And Henry Percy denied it on oath. Nobody even dared to ask me then. Nobody would have dreamed of asking me then. Not then, and not now. Then, it was a lie, a stupid lie. But now, it is treason, and whoever says it is a traitor. One more word, Sir Francis, and you're a dead man.'

'Poisoned soup?' he asks, smiling. 'Like you sent to Bishop Fisher? Or the headsman that you sent to Sir Thomas More?' He steps back before she can answer, bows as low as he should, hand on heart, and goes to the king, leans over his shoulder, whispers a bawdy joke, sets him in a roar, and melts into the crowd in the hot rooms.

Anne, left alone on her golden chair, throws back her head and laughs at nothing; only I see the shudder that runs down her spine. She looks blankly at me, as if she cannot believe what just happened. She beckons to Mark Smeaton. 'Play! Why aren't you playing?' she snaps.

'A song to stir the heart?' he asks, looking at her meaningfully, but she is looking past him, for George, who comes in, throwing a remark over his shoulder to someone else, as if he is casually passing through the room.

'Sir Francis has gone mad,' she whispers.

George does not hear her, he is hiding his own fury. 'I've not got the Order of the Garter!' he spits. 'Nicholas Carew has the place I was promised. I'm passed over again. They didn't vote for me. I'm not to be a Knight of the Garter this year. Again!'

'Carew? I won't have Carew preferred over you. This is to insult me and all of us. This is a vote for the Spanish party hidden under his name. I won't have it. I'll order him to step back – he's our kinsman. I'll tell our uncle the duke to make him step back.'

I am thinking furiously. 'Is this a move against us or just a jostling among the noblemen? Who voted for Carew and against George?'

'Hush,' George whispers to his sister. He takes my hand from his arm and raises it to his mouth in a pretty gesture of a kiss, but his lips don't touch my fingers: it's all show. 'Carew was nominated by King Francis of France, the man I thought was my friend. Someone must have told him I met with the Spanish ambassador.' He manages a wry smile to his sister. 'The Knights of the Garter choose their own; it's not in the gift of a woman. Not even you. I want to be known as a true knight, not as my sister's pet. I'll get it next year – I swear. I should've had it this year – but for sure I'll get it next.'

'The French king nominated Carew rather than you?' I go to the essential question. 'But why? He can't doubt that we're ruling the country? The monasteries are coming down, one by one; we're reforming the Church. Lady Mary will take the oath or go into exile. Why would France support Carew – of the Spanish party? Why now, when they are losing and we're winning?'

Both Boleyns look at me as if I am intruding on a private grief. 'I'll get it next year,' George repeats.

'That's not the point!' I say impatiently. 'Who is telling the French king that it is safe to overlook you this year? And why are they saying that? And how has Henry Percy's wife learned defiance? Why now?'

The double doors open, and Sir Nicholas Carew, the new Knight of the Garter, comes in, bows to the king, puts a hand over his heart in his bow to Anne, and nods at George. 'Better luck next time,' he says cheerfully.

'À Carew!' the king shouts, and everyone obediently choruses 'À Carew!'

'Congratulations on your well-deserved honour, Cousin!' Anne says pointedly, and she rises from her chair and goes to the king, her hands outstretched, ignoring Jane, who leaps out of her way like a startled deer. 'My lord husband, we must be merry and dance after dinner to celebrate my dear cousin's well-earned honour.'

Nicholas Carew's broad smile shows that he knows that Anne is choking on jealousy as bitter as poisoned soup. He bows as if grateful for her praise. 'I'm so proud,' he says to the king. 'I'm so honoured.'

'None more deserving,' says the king, though George is standing right beside his sister.

I am thinking furiously, while my hands are clasped in delight, and I am smiling at Nicholas Carew. Something's gone very wrong here: we've lost ground with our king, and even with the French king – what has he heard from his spies that I don't know? Poor miserable Mary Talbot left Henry Percy's house four years ago, why is she raking up his marriage to Anne now? Everything on the surface looks as if it is flowing our way, but something is wrong. Somehow the tide has turned, and it is against us.

I AM SURPRISED TO see my father enter with the other lords for dinner in the great hall. He is amiable with them, a lord among his equals, friendly with everyone – a true courtier. I wonder if he has found the time to ask Will Somer if his fool's mind can imagine death.

He comes over to me when they are clearing the tables away for dancing, and I kneel for his blessing.

'I didn't know you were coming to court again so soon,' I say as I rise, and he kisses me.

'Your mother needed some things from the London merchants. All well? In good spirits?'

He has never before come to court to enquire after me. 'Have you heard anything?'

'No, no, all's well,' he says. He tucks my hand in his arm and leads me away from a noisy dance. The music drowns out our conversation.

'Father, is everything all right?'

'Indeed, I hope so! You're obedient to the head of your house, the Duke of Norfolk?'

'I don't see him very often. He and the queen are barely speaking – since her illness.'

'Better not get involved in these family quarrels,' my father silences me, as if he does not want to know; but usually he is a man who wants to know everything.

'I'm not involved,' I say calmly. 'Father, have you heard anything? Is someone acting against us? Have you heard that the Boleyns are losing influence?'

'I've heard nothing. Are you losing influence?'

'George didn't get the Garter again, for the second year, though he was promised it for sure,' I admit. 'And Henry Percy's wife is making wild accusations . . .'

'Your patron, your advisor, is Thomas Cromwell?' he interrupts. 'You report to him? You confide in him?'

I nod cautiously.

'And he's still at one with the Boleyns? For the reform of the Church, for the destruction of the corrupt abbeys?'

'Yes – except Anne thinks the king should bring Master Cromwell under greater control – the abbeys should reform, not close; others should open as schools and centres for charity. She thinks that Master Cromwell is greedy and corrupt . . .'

'No – you be advised by him.' My father shakes his head. 'Nobody wants to give away Church wealth to the poor – certainly not the king. The wealth of the lords, of the king himself, is not to be decided by ladies.'

'But the reform of the Church came from the ladies!' I exclaim. 'All the new learning started in the queen's rooms . . .'

'Learning, yes, but now that great wealth is involved, it is of interest to the men. Faith can be the work of ladies, but wealth is the business of men. And nothing happens in this kingdom unless Thomas Cromwell agrees it. Even I am here on a commission from him.'

'What sort of commission?'

'As a judge on first evidence. A new inquiry.'

'Inquiry into what?'

My father glances around; but there is no one near in earshot. 'That's the thing. I've not been told. I've just been summoned to hear the first evidence, to see if there's a case to answer.'

I pause, thinking. 'Master Secretary is preparing another treason trial?'

He nods. 'For sure, but I don't know who is the accused.'

'Oh, Father, he's not going to act against Princess Mary, is he? Not now? Anne is demanding that she swear the oath. But they can't try a princess for treason?'

'Lady Mary,' he corrects me. 'No, the king would never use us lords against her; she's too well-loved. And Carew is one of her greatest advocates, and he just got the Garter. It has to be someone else. Someone whose star is falling.' He looks at me expectantly.

I shake my head. 'No one's really falling – Mary Shelton's been replaced as favourite by Jane Seymour, and the Seymours are in high favour – but that's just bedroom gossip. We're planning a May Day celebration, and George and Henry Norris are the lead jousters – so the king favours them. And then a progress to Dover and across the narrow seas to honour the Lisles at Calais, so the old royal family are in high regard. No one's out of favour?'

'Well, someone's going to face an inquiry by the lords,' my father warns me. 'So it must be either a courtier or a churchman. A commoner would go to the common courts. But Jane, if Master Cromwell asks you anything about anybody, make sure you tell him all you know – he's certain to know it already. Don't hold anything back. You don't want him to doubt you as well as . . . whoever he is doubting.'

'I do. I always tell him everything.'

We turn to watch the dancers. The king is seated on his throne, beating time with his hand. Anne is beside him; as we watch, she says something charming – I can tell it is charming by the turn of her head – and the king nods and smilingly replies, then looks across the room to where Jane Seymour is waiting, hesitantly, for her turn to step forward.

'Pity about the horse,' my father says.

'What horse?'

'Thunder, that big bay of the king's. The one that fell.'

'But I saw him get up? He was sound?'

'He was unhurt, but the king had him beheaded,' my father says. 'For treason, I suppose.' He has to hide a smile. 'Falling on the king is clearly the act of a traitor. The punishment for traitors is beheading. *Ergo*, the horse was beheaded. Rather like the beast trials of Prytaneum, Athens.'

I think of the beautiful animal, the bright-coloured coat and the big, dark intelligent eyes. 'Oh, poor horse, poor beautiful horse!' I exclaim. 'That's not justice!'

'He is Supreme Head of the Church,' he reminds me. 'And king of England. Justice is whatever he says it is.' He pauses. 'That's why I say to report everything to Cromwell.'

As if he knows my father has spoken to me, Master Cromwell summons me to his dark chamber next day. It is modestly furnished, as if the king's secretary needs nothing more than bare floorboards, a table, and a high-backed chair with a rush seat for him, and a second chair set on the other side. The writing chest that he takes everywhere is locked with the little brass key in the lock. There is a table and chair for a clerk, laid out with all the instruments for spying: knives for cutting letterlocks; a hair-thin wire for lifting a wax seal and replacing it unbroken; badger-hair brushes for dusting sand on invisible sticky letters; candles ready to make lemon-juice words appear on singed paper.

'What is this?' I ask, putting my hand on a series of copper wheels, one inside another, each wheel rim engraved with letters.

'An Italian device,' he says. He shows me how the inner wheel has a pointer to a letter of the alphabet, geared to the outer wheel so it can be set to show six letters forward or ten letters back, with another cog to alter the selection of letters between paragraphs. 'It translates in and out of code,' he says. 'You just agree with your correspondent what gearing to use and when to change it.'

'Clever,' I admire it. 'It must make a code very fast to write.'

'My clerks need to work fast. I've never known a busier time.'

'We are busy at court, too,' I agree, putting down the code wheel. 'The queen wants to make a special May Day for the king, as he cannot ride this year.'

'She has told her ladies that he cannot ride?'

'Everyone knows. Master Cromwell, why did you want to see me?'

'It's always a pleasure to see you. And does she speak of his poetry?'

'We all speak of poetry.'

'But the queen and her brother, your husband, and your cousin, Mary Shelton, and her friend, Thomas Wyatt – all noted poets, aren't you? Young Lord Thom Howard, too? You study metre and rhyme and all that sort of thing, criticise each other's work, write alternate witty lines – I wouldn't know; I'm not an educated man . . .'

'Of course, we discuss each other's poetry.'

'The king's poetry?'

'We all laugh at an awkward rhyme.'

'You laugh at the king's awkward rhymes?'

'Not especially. We all tease and torment each other.'

'Does the queen complain of his infidelity?'

'You know she does. The love that she feels for him cannot tolerate a rival . . .'

'And of his failure to love?'

'Well . . . she fears he prefers others . . .'

'But in bed? She says he fails her? She calls him incapable?'

'Of course, he was so badly injured just months ago!' I exclaim. 'And the wound on his leg won't heal . . .'

'She's told you this? She says that he is impotent?'

I feel cornered by my own patron. Everyone knows when the king beds his wife – he comes to her bedroom in a procession, accompanied by half of his friends. The nights when he lies stock-still as a statue are obvious to the lords who fetch him in the morning and find him as they left him, even the serving women changing unspotted sheets know that he has done nothing. No one says anything, it's treason to suggest the king is not in perfect health and vigour.

I lower my voice. 'Isn't every man—'

'And have you told many people?'

'No! I only told George. But that was an earlier conversation. Years ago.'

His broad brown face creases with sympathy. 'Years ago? How long has this been going on?'

'I don't remember . . . before I left court. After . . . About two years ago.'

'It must be a great concern for her? How are we to get a prince if the king is unmanned?'

'Yes,' I say. 'Exactly.'

'Does she do nothing to help him? To assist him?'

I think of George telling me that he got the king drunk, so Anne could mount him before he lost the will, that she must do anything: French practices, nakedness. 'She does everything a good wife should do.'

'Kissing, kissing with tongues, that sort of thing?'

I blush. 'Whatever is needed.'

'Sortilèges. French practices?'

'Nothing forbidden,' I tell him firmly.

'No potions or herbs? No spells?'

'She drinks a posset,' I say unwillingly. 'The midwife gave it her... After the last... the last time.'

'The last dead-birth?'

I nod.

'And that was the second?' he confirms, softly as a midwife himself, as gentle as the egg woman in the hen coop.

'We denied the first.'

'And the ladies all know the king is unmanned?'

'No, of course not – these are private matters between husband and wife... except that we all spend all our lives trying to encourage him,' I say in a little rush of resentment. 'It's hardly a secret. You know – you do it yourself?'

'I?' His blackcurrant eyes widen in astonishment that he might be thought part of the court's ceaseless encouragement of the king's potency.

'When we tell the king how much we admire him, how beautiful Anne is, how everyone is in love with her, how he is the only man who can hold her?' I challenge him. 'When everyone talks all the time about his strength and his manliness? His good looks?'

'You say this and don't mean it?' He looks astounded.

I ignore his false face. 'We all speak to encourage love.'

'She has created a court of constant love affairs to inspire him to love? To incite him? To arouse him? She creates sinful excitement with other men for this purpose? The masque is now *The Most Desiring*?'

'No! *The Most Desirable*...'

'But some of these love affairs are real,' he pursues.

'Of course they are. The game of courtly love often overflows into real love. Lord Thom and Margaret Douglas are courting, and Anne Parr and William Herbert, and Henry Norris and Margaret Shelton...'

'I'm just a simple man. I don't understand this game of courtly love.'

I smile at him, suddenly confident. 'Master Secretary, you

understand perfectly well. This has been the entertainment of every royal court since Eleanor of Aquitaine.'

'Eleanor of Aquitaine? The adulteress?'

'Well, yes. But that's not the point.'

'The point is that the court makes a game of adultery around the queen, to encourage the king in his love for her? Because everyone knows that he needs encouragement?' My friend Thomas Cromwell smiles kindly at me. 'Don't worry, Lady Rochford. All this, I know already. I use you as my touchstone for truth, not as a witness to be recorded.'

He rises to his feet, and I understand that our meeting is over.

'I thought you were preparing for a trial,' I remark.

He shakes his head and opens the inner door for me and bows as I pass into the gap between two doors, and open the outer door into the shadowy stone hall. The double doors mean that no one can eavesdrop.

'But what was that about Lady Margaret Douglas?' he asks me very quietly.

A man is waiting outside – Dr Richard Sampson: Anne's expert on church law. This is the advisor who produced all the church law to end the king's marriage to Queen Katherine. Master Cromwell does not acknowledge him; I assume he is to be invisible.

'She's courting Lord Thom, my uncle's young half-brother,' I say quietly, one eye on Dr Sampson, wondering what he is doing here. 'He gave her a cramp ring.'

'Does she suffer much from cramps?'

'Not now,' I say. 'Not now she's got a cramp ring.'

He gives a little chuckle at that. 'Anyway, nothing out of the ordinary for you ladies?' he confirms.

I shake my head. 'Just courtly love.'

'Tell me if it goes further,' he says casually. 'She's half-sister to the King of Scotland. He won't want her marrying a Howard. Whatever you Howards would like.'

He turns to Dr Sampson, who bows to me in silence, with a smile, and walks past me into Master Cromwell's private room to sit on the same chair where I was seated, and, no doubt, offer Master Cromwell information that he knows already.

W<small>E HAVE TO</small> plan a merry May Day for the king even though he cannot ride as his leg wound is still too bad. We declare loudly that Anne has begged him not to ride, she is so fearful for his safety – but the truth is far worse.

'He's afraid,' George says quietly, as if fear is a shameful thing, looking over the raked sand of the tiltyard. 'He dreams of being crushed under his horse, and he wakes up screaming. He keeps remembering it. It's as if he has realised, for the first time, that he is mortal. He's afraid that he's going to die.'

'We'll create a joust of poetry and music and let him win,' Anne says, gesturing at the space, as if she can fill it with dancers and musicians and drown out the terrible shriek of metal as the heavy horse went down on the steel-clad man. 'Something to make him feel young and strong again, the finest of everyone at court.'

'A joust without jousting?' he asks.

'Why not?' she says grimly. 'Isn't everything just for show now?'

We plan minutely, choreographing every move. There will be jousting at the centre of it all, but only the young men will ride. George and Henry Norris are principal challengers, and they will wear green for Tudor and green for spring, entering the arena one after another with their ladies' favours on their lances. Each jouster will recite a poem or sing a song on the theme of love on a May Day morning, and the king, seated in his viewing balcony with his lame leg hidden, propped on a stool, will reply with a poem of his own, as if he has composed it in that moment. Thomas Wyatt will be at hand to prompt him so that he looks as if he is composing poetry on the spot.

It will be a joust of wit and poetry – and the king's cleverness will defeat everyone else. The horse-riding will be the least important part, and when it is over, there will be a celebration dinner with more poetry and songs and dancing. But the dances will be for show, like the jousting; neither Anne nor the king will dance. There will be no tall king coming in disguise to surprise us this year; he cannot stand without pain, and his limping pace makes him furious, like a wounded bear at a baiting.

The maids are sewing ribbons on their headbands, with Anne irritably watching from her great chair at the centre of the queen's presence chamber, when George comes lounging into the room with Henry Norris. He bows generally to us all and then goes to Anne and kisses her hand. Anne waves Henry into a stool at her side and spreads embroidery threads on her knees so that he can sort them. He bends his dark handsome head into her lap, so close that he could be kissing her knees.

'Where's Mark?' George asks, looking round. 'I wanted him to play while I sing my song at the joust.'

'I'll play for you,' Mary Shelton offers at once.

'No, it's in the jousting area,' George says.

'Oh! Can't I go disguised as your squire?'

They both look at Anne, who must say at once that this is not allowed. A lady cannot cavort in squire's clothes in the tiltyard before anyone who has paid for a seat.

'I'll come, too!' Anne says immediately. 'What a picture we'll make! George, you shall dress me in your livery, and we can both be masked . . .'

I gently lean to whisper. 'Better not,' I say.

'Why not?' she demands. 'I'd look wonderful as a page boy.'

I shake my head. 'Too wonderful.'

She shrugs her arm from my hand. 'Oh, very well.' She thinks for a moment. 'But if I'm not going, then Mary's certainly not dressing up as a squire and showing off. You'll have to get one of the king's musicians or one of the choristers. There are enough wanton boys to choose from, God knows.'

George frowns at her bad temper and looks to me for help.

I shrug. Now the old queen is dead and the Spanish party silent, Anne has no enemies to plot against. Time hangs heavy in this fairytale life.

'I'll find one,' George says agreeably. 'D'you have a favourite? I know they are all in love with you.'

'There's a pretty lad called Peter Last,' Anne volunteers. 'He blushes like a rose when he sees me.'

'Then the Last shall be First,' George says pleasantly. 'I'll write a love song to you, and he can sing it.'

'Won't you write a song for me?' Elizabeth Somerset asks. George turns and whispers something in her ear and she giggles and draws him away.

As if she cannot bear a moment of George's attention on another woman, Anne rounds on Henry Norris: 'And what are you doing here, sitting mumchance?' she demands. 'You should be cooing like a dove to your betrothed, not getting my embroidery threads in a tangle? When are you going to marry poor Margaret?'

'I'll marry in my own good time.' Henry leans a little closer over the silk threads spread out on her knee, and touches one and then another, resting his finger on each one, so that she feels the warmth of his finger through her gown on her thigh. 'Besides, you have set me a quest to find the perfect rose – and I think it's here – not in the silks but in the blush in your lips.'

'I don't believe you have any honourable intention towards Margaret at all,' she scolds him, her mood sweetened by the flattery. 'Why d'you haunt my rooms all day? Like a lovesick ghost!'

'Because I am a ghost that has died of love!' he says extravagantly. He takes up a red thread and winds it around her finger above her wedding ring. 'It's only you, for me,' he says. 'No one else.'

Caught up in the flirtation, she slides her wedding ring off her finger, leaving the scarlet embroidery silk in its place and holds it out for him to admire. 'If anything were to happen to the king, I think you'd have me,' she whispers.

For a brief moment only, they are caught up in the game; then she realises what she has said. Awkwardly, she rips the thread from her finger and crams her wedding ring back on.

Henry Norris makes a muttered exclamation. 'I'd never lift my head so far . . . I'd rather it was off!'

Anne brushes the silks from her lap and jumps up. 'Good God! You would undo me . . . I'll see your head is off!'

George glances up from whispering with Elizabeth and sees my anguished glare at him. 'What's this?' he asks, coming closer, seeing the tangle of silks on the floor, Norris on his feet, Anne white.

'May Day madness,' I say, laughing my courtier laugh a tinkle as sweet as a warning bell.

Norris rounds on George; he is quite furious. 'I failed a riddle,' he said. 'I did not know the key to your sister's riddle. But it was not a riddle that Her Majesty should have told.'

'She's a very witty queen.' George struggles to understand the sudden switch from daring flirtation to what feels like panic. He offers Anne his hand as if to pull her out of danger, and she takes it and they walk away from the silks on the floor, their steps matching, moving as one being with two heads.

Henry Norris looks blankly at me, as if I can explain what just happened.

'Nothing,' I say again. 'That was nothing.'

'That was madness,' he says. 'Anyone could've heard her – she accused me!'

'Nobody heard,' I say. 'And it was nothing.'

'Half a dozen heard,' he said. 'And every man and woman at this court is a spy for someone. Someone's bound to tell the king. I'll go to the queen's almoner now and swear it was nothing.'

'It was nothing. And there are no spies here.'

I HURRY TO CATCH my spymaster on the stair on his way to the hall for dinner. We stand as close as lovers to whisper in the bay of the oriel window.

'Henry Norris misspoke,' I say. 'A joke about him loving the queen more than Margaret Shelton. But he went to swear to the queen's almoner that it meant nothing, so I thought I should tell you.'

'Yes. You're right.'

'Did you know already?' I ask curiously.

His smile is hard to read in the shadows of the stair well. 'Is Henry Norris the new favourite?' he asks.

'He's always been a good friend.'

'And Sir Francis is another?'

'Weston or Bryan?' I ask cautiously.

He smiles. 'Two Francises, a Thomas, and a Mark, and a Richard and a Henry. So many! William Brereton?'

I shake my head. It is a relief to say no. 'Elizabeth Somerset's brother-in-law? Never! He only visits us to scold Elizabeth . . .'

'And of course, George is constantly with his sister. In and out of her private rooms?'

'Oh yes,' I assure him. 'George is always at her side. George keeps her safe. He can vouch for her.'

I can hear a noise from the king's privy chamber above. I can hear Anne's voice, and then I hear the irritable whine of a spoilt child – she must have ordered them to bring Princess Elizabeth to the king.

'What's happening?' I ask Cromwell, looking up the stairs. 'Is that the princess?'

'The queen sent for her . . . after Norris misspoke, as you call it.'

'But why?' I ask. 'Why Elizabeth in the middle of all this?'

'It's always a masque, isn't it, with you people? It's always some sort of play. I think the title of this one is: *The Faithful Wife and the One True Heir.*'

I go to the top of the stairs, and I see Anne waving the little girl's nursemaids back to the nursery, putting her hand on the king's arm and looking into his face, as if to persuade him of something. She is smiling her confident smile, baring her teeth, but he is oddly impassive, standing stiffly on his painful leg.

'All's well,' Cromwell says reassuringly, coming up behind me.

It does not look as if all is well.

'Is the king in pain?' I ask. 'Has his wound opened up? Will he be able to take part in May Day and go on progress to Calais?'

'Oh, that's been cancelled,' he says casually. 'No Calais.'

'Cancelled? Why?'

He gives a little shrug, as if he does not know. 'Perhaps Sir Nicholas Carew advised against it.'

'Since when does Nicholas Carew say where we go on progress?'

'Because he's a friend of Spain, and now Spain is our friend.' Cromwell smiles, as if it is a neat riddle that I might enjoy. 'The Spanish party is our friend and so are the Lisles who keep Calais for us, trusted friends and kinsmen, just like the Poles and Courtenays.'

'The Spanish party are our friends now?'

'Dear friends,' he agrees.

'Even Sir Geoffrey, the blabbermouth?' I query.

He smiles. 'Sir Geoffrey is the most friendly of all, he keeps nothing to himself.'

Thomas Cromwell has been a trader in wool and secrets for so long that no one can tell whether he is showing the front or the back side of the weave.

'You are joking with me,' I say uncertainly.

He shakes his head. 'I am very serious.'

Above, the music starts playing for the ladies to dance; the tune filters down the stone stairwell like an invitation to light-hearted play to those with happy feet. It is a summons to courtiers to take their place.

'Are you coming, Master Cromwell?'

He shakes his head. 'I must catch the tide back to Stepney. Tonight, I have work to do at my home. Tell me, what d'you think of Mark Smeaton?'

'The lute player? The singer?'

His smile is inscrutable. 'D'you think he will sing for me?'

'If you ask him. But he's very attached to the queen.'

'So I hear,' he says.

## PHILIPPA GREGORY

## GREENWICH PALACE, MAY DAY

# 1536

May Day morning is magical as always. The choristers get up in the middle of the night to sing at sunrise under Anne's window. We wake to the soaring sound of a May Day carol mingling with birdsong and swing open the shutters to hear them. There are gifts at the maids' doors from their lovers, little things like crowns woven of white-flowering hawthorn and buttery primroses: real things as if it were real love.

We walk to the jousting arena carrying wands of willow like country girls, and the maids wear their hair down over their shoulders, plaited with white and coloured ribbons. Everyone is carefree but Anne, who is wound as tight as a silk bobbin, desperate that the king shall enjoy the day and not be reminded of the last joust when he thought he would die. We all pretend that he is young enough to joust, and strong enough to joust, but that he has decided – quite freely – not to ride today. His fear of falling, his terror of injury or death, is an open secret that no one mentions.

Never before has he sat in the royal viewing balcony in the octagonal tower for a whole May Day. He built the towers for an admiring crowd to watch him; not to be a spectator, seated in the king's tower, surrounded by the Spanish party: Henry Courtenay of the old royal family on one side, Nicholas Carew the friend of Spain on the other. The Seymour boys pour wine and joke with him. In the opposite tower, the queen's tower, Anne compresses her lips in a hard smile and puts Jane Seymour in the front row of the ladies, in the hopes that the sight of her will tempt the king over.

The jousters ride around the arena, their lances raised in salute to the king and the queen, and they halt between the two towers to read the poems they have composed. The king leans forward and makes his reply, reciting Thomas Wyatt's poetry as if it were his own, with little pauses as if he is waiting for inspiration. Everyone cheers his extraordinary talent and he signals that the jousting can begin.

The challengers bow their bare heads, canter around the arena and go out to arm themselves. The servers pour wine and pass sweetmeats, and Anne in her balcony watches and applauds each passage, showing every sign of pleasure at the day, with one eye always on the octagonal tower opposite, where the king is drinking heavily and dining well and laughing with his men friends: the ringing bark of men without real amusement.

The last joust of the day is George and Henry Norris, evenly matched; but Norris' horse won't go forward, almost as if it knows that the joust is unreal and the joy manufactured. Norris spurs it on, and his squire runs up with a long whip to crack behind the big animal; but still George waits at his end, his horse sidling and ready to go, as Norris' horse steps backwards and sideways, and tosses its head and shows the whites of its eyes and rears and turns and will not go on.

Some stupid girl – of course it's Jane Seymour – says, 'The horse! The horse knows something's wrong!'

Margaret Shelton gasps to see her future husband fighting to control his horse and says, 'He should get off. He should withdraw. Remember how the king—'

Anne throws back her head and laughs – a shriek of defiance. 'It's just a badly trained horse!' she says rudely, and she calls out to Norris: 'You can't carry my favour, if you can only go backwards!'

We can't see his face behind his visor, but he will be grinding his teeth in rage.

The king hauls himself to his feet and leans over the balcony of his viewing box. 'Borrow my horse!' he yells. 'Yours is afeared. You'll not get a good charge out of it.'

Henry Norris, rescued from public shame, pulls up his sweating horse and thankfully salutes the king. As soon as he turns his horse's head away from the tilt rail, it becomes docile and walks easily from the arena to the saddling area behind the public stands.

We wait for a few moments as they hastily change the barding from Norris' horse onto the king's new charger and heave Henry Norris, stiff in his heavy armour, into the saddle. He rides up to the king's viewing balcony, bows low, and thanks him for his generosity. The king is all smiles, showing his royal favour, as the crowd cheers him.

The big horse lifts its head, as if it knows the job it has to do, and Norris raises his lance first in thanks to the king, then in salute to Anne, and finally to George, who has waited all this time, walking his horse around the arena to keep it warm and ready. Norris canters around the arena. People cheer him: he is a popular challenger on the king's own horse.

The two horses wheel and canter to opposite ends of the list. The riders tighten their reins to make their horses wait, while they press their spurs against their sides to urge them to be ready – to go from standstill to gallop at the signal. Anne rises to her feet, waits for all eyes to be on her, raises her handkerchief, and lets it fall. Simultaneously, they dig in their spurs and loosen the reins, and the animals leap forward into a flat-out charge, straight towards each other, a thundercloud of dust rising from their hooves. There is a tremendous smack as George's lance catches Norris square on his armoured belly and splinters with a crack. Norris keeps his seat on the king's horse, though the blow must have knocked the breath out of him.

They pull up at the far end and wheel around, cantering the circle of the arena, to settle the horses to their work, and to catch their breath behind their helmets. They ready themselves at the foot of the rail, turn their metal faces to watch Anne, who drops her handkerchief, and they spur forward again, and George has the best hit for the second time. They are usually evenly matched, but this May Day, Henry Norris is riding a strange horse and is angry with himself. Only at the last charge does he break his lance on George, redeeming himself before the crowd, who roar for him, and the tournament is over, and George – my George – is the victor.

The riders canter around the arena, steeled fist raised to acknowledge the applause; the musicians play, the ladies throw flowers, and I beam across the arena to Nicholas Carew in the king's box – so who is the greatest knight today? Who should have been the new Knight of the Garter? But Nicholas Carew is alone in the king's tower: the seat before him is empty; the king has gone – gone without awarding the prize, gone without accepting the cheers, gone without a wave at the crowd who have come all the way from London to see him.

His throne is empty; there is no one left in the viewing tower but Seymours and Henry Courtenay and Nicholas Carew – all men of the Spanish party and the old religion. Have they offended him? Can we be so lucky that they have offended him, and he walked out on them without a word? Have we won some extraordinary victory against them without doing anything? I don't even know if the king saw the last tilt – did he see nothing but George's triumphs? Or has he been taken ill and gone back to his rooms?

'The king's gone,' I say quietly to Anne as I hold the box with chains of gold for her to award the winners.

'Where?' she asks, without turning her head.

'I don't know. He must have just left.'

Anne leans over the edge of the balcony to give the prizes; but only George rides up before her for the gold chain.

'Where's Norris?' I ask him, leaning over the side of the balcony as Anne drapes the chain over his bare head onto his metalled shoulders.

'Was he in a temper?' Margaret Shelton asks from the other side.

'No,' he tells her. 'The king came behind the stands and said they must go at once – back to Whitehall.'

'By barge?'

'The king said he would ride and Norris ride with him.'

'He can't ride,' I say. 'His leg . . .'

'He's gone on his horse,' George answers.

The applause trails off, and people start to rise to their feet and climb down from the stands and leave. George's horse sidles as he holds him close to the balcony to whisper with Anne.

'Why? Why has he gone?' she demands. 'Without a word to anyone? We have the masque and the dancing to come? And the dinner? He's learned a poem to recite at the dinner?' She straightens up and smiles broadly for the people still watching, and claps her hands to praise her brother.

'It must've been planned,' George says quietly. 'His groom had a fresh horse saddled and waiting. His outriders were waiting for him. Norris didn't know. He stripped off his armour and left just as he was.'

Her smile never wavers. 'Oh God, he's impossible,' she says through her teeth. She waves at the crowd of Londoners who raise a cheer. 'I wish to God he had—'

'—stayed,' George finishes the sentence quickly.

Anne leans over the balcony as if she is kissing the winner's brow. 'Go after them,' she whispers, so softly that only I, standing beside her, can hear. 'Go after them and make sure that he's happy and that Norris says nothing stupid about me. Especially after yesterday. Make sure Norris says nothing about anything.'

He reins his horse back and salutes her; then he turns and canters around the arena, raising his lance in recognition of the straggled cheers, and rides out. We get up, gather up our flowers and our favours, and walk back to the palace. I am thinking that we have special gowns and costumes for the May Day masque; but it's hardly worth the effort if the king has chosen to leave his favourite palace on the best night of the year, to dine alone in London with Henry Norris, and George chasing after the two of them as they left him behind.

A ND THEN, BEFORE dinner, as the choristers come in to sing the May Day carol, Mark Smeaton the lute player is nowhere to be found

'Where is he?' the master of the revels hisses at the master of music, who shrugs. They both look at me, since Mark is the king's servant, attached to the queen's household, and my responsibility.

'Perhaps he's died of love,' Mary Shelton says. She turns her laughing face at the queen. 'It's all been too much for poor Mark, and now he's died of love for you.'

Anne laughs as if she is amused. 'We'll sing without him, and it shall be his lament,' she says. 'Poor Mark, to die of love!'

Jane Seymour and Margaret Shelton, missing their partners George and Norris, have to find other partners for the dance – the fool Will Somer jumps up and does some clowning steps with Margaret. In a parody of courtly love, he kisses her hand and pretends to lift the hem of her gown to kiss her feet. He claps his hand to his heart and then – shockingly – to his groin. We laugh; anything is allowed. It is May Day – the usual rules are broken. Jane Seymour turns her blushing face away.

The king was never going to dance or act; but all this was planned to amuse him, the choreography designed for his gaze; the masque is a celebration of a scholar king – King Arthur the lawgiver. But all the compliments are aimed at a vacant throne, and the golden stool where he rests his foot stands empty. What's the point of us pretending to be merry when he does not see our pretend joy? We dance and drink and sing until midnight, but we are discordant and out of time without our audience of one.

As soon as the great clock strikes twelve, and May Day is over, Anne gets to her feet, unable to conceal her boredom, and everyone bows, and all of us ladies withdraw with the queen. Three of us help her undress and get ready for bed, prepare her hot posset and turn down the covers of the great bed, although we know that the king is far away tonight, and will not bed her and make a baby on this most special night of magic and love. Instead, he has chosen to be a good ten miles from his wife – and no way of getting back by barge, as the tide is against us. A big milk moon has drawn a high tide westward up the river, and it feels as if all the waters of England, river and sea, sweet and salt, are in full flood against us.

Anne orders me to be her bedfellow, and she says her prayers and gets into bed. I lie awake beside her, thinking of Henry Norris' horse and how its big hooves tore up the ground as it refused to go forward but reared and clawed back. How the king disappeared without a word, as if he had been only waiting for it all to be over. And why ride to Westminster on the best night of the year? Why take Henry Norris? Why him and no other favourites? Has he gone to meet Master Cromwell, engaged on private business at his house at Stepney? And where is Mark Smeaton tonight? Is he singing for Thomas Cromwell?

IN THE MORNING, Anne leads the ladies to the chapel as usual, though the king is missing from his place and the royal balcony empty. We trail back to the queen's rooms with nothing to do. Of course, we have had a court of ladies before – the king has been absent on business – but never before like this: without preparation or announcement.

We talk over the joust and the evening dancing as if it was a pleasure to watch, as if anyone enjoyed it. Nobody mentions the sudden disappearance of the king and his absence this morning. There is no word from George, and Margaret has not heard from Henry Norris. Mark Smeaton does not reappear with a new song and an apology. Anne sets everyone to sewing shirts for the poor and makes Jane Seymour read aloud from an improving book in English – the country girl has no Latin.

We are sitting in busy boredom when there is a rap at the door of the queen's presence chamber, and then the yeomen of the guard swing open the double doors, and Anne's chamberlain announces:

'The king's council to meet with the queen.'

Anne gasps and rises slowly to her feet, her cheeks flushed, one hand on the back of her chair to keep her steady. She stands tall, her head raised for a crown.

I know at once what she is thinking: perhaps it has come, perhaps it is now: her great moment, the greatest moment of her life. Perhaps the king dropped dead on his ride to London, and the council has come to tell her that she is the mother of the first queen of England and will be queen regent for eighteen years until Elizabeth comes of age. Queen regent, and our time has come at last.

But her uncle the Duke of Norfolk is looking dark-faced and grim, not folding his thin lips over his excitement, as he did before when he thought the king was lying dead and his niece was carrying the next heir to the throne. Then, he was at her side for every step; now, he looks across a wide expanse of wooden floor, and says coldly: 'We would speak with you, alone, Your Grace.'

Anne's eyes narrow, trying to read his impassive face; but she makes a little gesture with her hand, and all of us ladies, even me, have to sweep from her presence chamber into the gallery outside, and there, stationed at the door, to make sure we don't listen, are two yeomen of the guards, who close the double doors and stand before them, their pikes crossed.

We have to wait, standing about, one or two with sewing still in their hands. Jane Seymour takes a seat by the window. She closes the book as if she knows she will not read any more today and folds her hands, her head bent as if she is praying. Something about her snags my attention; she is oddly serene, when the rest of us are flustered.

We wait. Nobody even wonders aloud what is happening inside Anne's presence chamber. Nobody even whispers, we are all straining to hear through the thick doors. There is the rumble of angry male voices, again and again, as if they are asking questions, and we can't hear more than her short retort. It sounds like an argument – but the council cannot argue with a crowned queen. One thing is for sure: they are not begging her to accept a regency.

Then there is a quick tap on the door, and the yeomen fling the doors open, and Anne is standing before them, her face quite blank, her eyes quite black, the lords half a pace behind her.

'Her Grace's cloak,' my uncle the Duke of Norfolk snaps at me, and I run through the presence chamber to her bedroom to fetch it, as if I were a chamberer.

By the time I am back with it, they are gone: my uncle Thomas Howard; John de Vere; William Sandys, lord chamberlain of the household; and Anne, my sister – gone with three men who hate her. But where have they gone?

'To the barge,' Margery Horsman says to me.

I turn from her and run down the little stone stair to the garden and the pier, and she trots beside me, as if she is helping; but really to see what is going to happen next.

By the time we arrive at the pier, they have handed Anne into the royal barge; she is sitting in state, on the throne at the back, her uncle beside her, and the other two men are ashore, waiting for the cloak. They take it from me on the riverbank; I make a little gesture to the frozen figure on the chair.

'Don't I go with her?' I ask John de Vere. 'What about her ladies?'

'You don't want to go with her!' he says, laughing as if this is a great joke. He takes the cloak from me, strides up the gangplank, and they run it on board and cast off.

Margery and I stand on the pier and watch the oarsmen take up the rhythm of the drumbeats and row to the middle of the river, where the flow of the stream catches it, and the barge picks up speed and goes rapidly upstream on the incoming tide. Anne hasn't moved an inch; and though they have her cape, she has not put it on.

I am the chief lady-in-waiting; but I have no idea what I should do. George is at Whitehall Palace with the king; Anne has gone upriver – I assume she is summoned to join them; but nobody knows. I look at Margery Horsman and see a blank fear in her face that I must wipe from my own as we go back inside to the queen's rooms.

'Well, you can get on with the shirts for the poor, at any rate,' I say in a weak attempt at discipline, and I wave the ladies and the maids back into the presence chamber, but one by one, they put down their work and slip away, and I know they are going to tell their patron or their mother or their spymaster that the lord chamberlain has taken the queen upriver to London, without a companion and with nothing but her cloak. Jane Seymour did not even wait for me to come back from the riverbank – she was gone from her seat in the window when I returned from the pier.

I leave the younger maids sewing with Margery Horsman, and I go through the bedroom door to the king's side to see if George has returned. Our room is empty; the bed has not been slept in. It doesn't even look like our room, where we have lived, husband and wife, for eleven years. It looks like a stranger's room, readied for strangers, with a chill tidiness about it, as if the room itself is waiting for someone who will not come, someone who will never come again.

I go down the gallery to the Howard rooms and tap on the door. The usual manservant answers, and he knows perfectly well who I am; but today he pretends not to know me and does not admit me.

'When is His Grace returning?' I ask at the threshold, peering over his shoulder into the hall.

He bows. 'His Grace did not say.'

I turn from him as if it does not matter at all. 'Where did he go?'

'He did not tell me, your ladyship.'

I walk down the king's gallery and down the little stairs past Cromwell's dark chamber to the stable-yard. At least here, everything is normal. The grooms are filling their buckets at the well, someone is whistling while mucking-out, and three horses are saddled and waiting for their riders. George's horses are in their usual stall, and the groom is brushing one of them down.

'Get ready to go to Whitehall Palace,' I say. 'I'll give you a note for your master. You can take a wherry.'

He nods, and I step into the office of the master groom, where there is a desk with pen and paper for sending orders to the corn merchants and hay farmers. I take up a blunt pen and dip it in the sticky ink and write:

*Our sister has gone by barge upstream with our uncle and others of the council. Please write what I should do. J*

If it falls into the wrong hands, it is not incriminating in any way – nor does it even identify us Boleyns. I cannot think why I am worrying about this simple note. I add another line.

*Don't fail to reply.*

And then I give it to the groom and send him on his way with a sixpence.

It is the strangest evening. We dine in the queen's presence chamber; nobody talks above a whisper at dinner, and though the tables are laid with cards after we have eaten, and the servants are pouring wine, no one plays or laughs. The musicians thump out dances by rote, with their eyes on us; but nobody stands up. The men dine on the king's side and visit us, after they have eaten, aimlessly, as if they have nothing else to do. When they see Anne's empty chair, they go quietly away again. Everyone looks at me, as if I must know what is happening, and I turn up my mouth in a false smile and look around as if I am ready to be amused; but I know nothing, and George has not replied to my message.

I even get hold of Jane Seymour, who reappears, blank as vellum, and I ask her where has she been all day, and if she knows when the king is coming back? She shakes her fair head and looks at me with her grey-blue eyes and says that her brothers needed her for family business and that she knows nothing.

I sleep in my own quiet room, in my marriage bed, restless, hoping that George will return in the night, having sailed home to me on the ebb tide. But he does not come.

When I wake early in the warm sunshine of a May morning, I throw a robe over my shift and go through the little door to Anne's bedroom. It is empty; she is not back either. I cannot think where she might be, nor what she can be doing without me, without her ladies.

As I am standing helplessly before her chest of gowns, wondering what she has at Whitehall and what she will need, there is a knock on the door of the privy chamber outside. I leave her bedroom and cross the privy chamber.

'Yes?' I snap.

'The Boleyn groom for Lady Rochford,' the guard says outside the door.

I open the door, and there is my groom, and in his hand is my letter to George.

'Why didn't you give it to him?'

'He wasn't there.' His face is set in the same expressionless mask that we are all wearing. 'I went to his rooms at Whitehall Palace, and he was already gone. His horse was in the stables where he left it – he went by barge.'

'But our barge is here? Whose barge did he take? And where's he gone now?'

'It was an unmarked barge,' he says very quietly. 'An unmarked barge with no standards. It took him to the Tower. Him, and Henry Norris with him.'

This means nothing; I need fear nothing. The Tower is a royal palace; we have our own rooms there.

'Henry Norris went, too? With my husband in the barge? As good company?'

He spreads his hands as if to tell me it was not a pleasure trip, but he does not contradict me.

'Good company. Very well,' I say as calmly as I can; my voice trembles, and I clear my throat. 'Don't gossip of this in the stables. It's probably just a game of the king's. You know how he loves disguising and surprises. It'll be a masque – a May Day masque.'

He nods uncertainly.

I tuck my note to George in my pocket to burn later, and I go back to my own rooms to dress. Foolishly, I hesitate over the chest of clothes, and when my maid comes in, I don't know what I should wear. I don't know what I am doing today. I don't know if I should dress prettily, for a May dinner in the greening woods, or warmly, for the barge to the Tower. My head hammers as if I have a fever. I cannot decide on my gown; everything whirls past my eyes. I keep seeing Henry Norris' horse backing and nobody able to make it go forward.

When I am dressed and walk stiffly into the queen's presence chamber, there are just a few of the ladies – and half of them disloyal – stitching shirts for the poor. As if they care about the poor! I look around at the missing places.

'Where's Jane?' I demand. 'Where's Jane Seymour?'

Margery Horsman looks up. 'She's gone. She's gone with Sir Nicholas Carew to Beddington.'

Everyone looks blank, as if a maid-of-honour is allowed to leave her post, go off with a courtier, without a word to the mistress of the maids or the chief lady-in-waiting. As if Nicholas Carew can command a maid in the queen's service. As if he is a courtier of any importance. Carew Manor at Beddington is his family house. He has taken Jane Seymour from her hard-won place in the queen's rooms; he has taken her out of court without permission and without notice. And Jane is not the only one missing.

'And where are the others?' I look round. 'Who isn't here? Elizabeth Somerset, Lady Worcester? Anne Braye, Lady Cobham?'

'The privy council sent for them,' Margery Horsman tells me. Everyone has their heads bowed low over their sewing, as if they are afraid that if they look up from their work, they, too, will be summonsed.

'What for?' I ask.

'They said there is an inquiry.'

'Oh, that inquiry,' I say confidently. 'Yes, I know all about the inquiry.'

I walk confidently towards the door, and the yeomen of the guard swings it open for me without hesitation. I go down the stair to Thomas Cromwell's dark chamber, and I tap on the first and then the second of the double doors. He is not there; but his clerk is carefully sorting papers, deeds of lands into separate piles. When he sees me, he turns the deeds face down, as if to hide the names of the owners, and bows.

'Lady Rochford.'

'Where's Master Cromwell?'

'I don't know, your ladyship.'

'He told me that he was going home to Stepney for May Day?'

'He was leaving home as I came here.'

'By horse? Going to join the king at Whitehall Palace? By barge? Has he gone to the Tower?'

'I don't know, your ladyship. I don't know where he is.'

I come a little closer. 'I have to tell him something important.'

'Would you write it for him? I am going home to Stepney shortly; I can carry a message.'

This is no help to me, for I have nothing to tell him – unless he does not know that Anne has gone from court and that George has gone to the Tower, Jane Seymour to Beddington, and Lady Worcester and Lady Cobham to the inquiry. But surely, he must know this? The council could not act without his knowledge.

'I'll write to him,' I decide.

He gives me a sheet of paper and a needle and thread, a knife, a pen and sealing wax, but I have no time to make a letterlock. I write what anyone can read:

*Sir,*
*As you may know, the council has taken Anne in a barge to*
*London? I believe that my husband has been taken to the Tower.*

*Please tell me if I should join them, and how long a stay they will make so that I can send their clothes? Should I attend the queen?*
  *Yours aye,*
  *JB*

'Don't give it to anyone else but your master,' I tell him. He bows. He is of the Cromwell household; he would never give anything to anyone but Cromwell.

I cannot go back to the queen's rooms and the frightened women sewing shirts. Instead, I go to the king's side and knock on the door of the Boleyn rooms. I stare at the bright newly painted heraldic shield, the three black bulls and the red inverted chevron, before the door opens and the groom of the household bows to me.

'Is Lord Wiltshire here?' I ask.

'No, your ladyship. He is at Westminster.'

'Do you expect him home tonight?'

'No, your ladyship; he is lodging with the other lords at Westminster Palace.'

I nod as if this is what I expected and go down the gallery to my own rooms, the Rochford rooms. I don't know what else I can do. If Anne's father is at Westminster, sitting with the other lords on the inquiry, then he will be guarding the family interest: his son George and his daughter Anne. I have nothing to worry about, since all four of our allies: my mentor Cromwell, my father, George's father, and even our uncle Thomas Howard, are judges on the inquiry. It is packed in our favour, and I don't even know the subject. I have nothing to fear.

It's not yet noon, and I am as tired as if I have been up all night watching for an enemy from the tower of a besieged castle. But I don't know who the enemy is, and I don't know who is in the castle and who is without.

I GO ON KNOWING nothing all day and all night until the next day, when Thomas Cromwell comes back to Greenwich alone, without the king, or George, or my father, or the other lords. But my heart leaps to see the familiar big cob horse in his stall, and at the end of the day, I wait for my spymaster at the door to the stable.

'You startled me,' he says as I step out of the early evening dusk.

I know I did not. 'I wrote to you yesterday. I asked you what I should do.'

'I could not then tell you. I was as much in the dark as you are.'

'Not in the dark now,' I observe.

He nods. 'But there is great darkness,' he says piously.

I feel a wave of impatience, like a disregarded daughter. 'Master Cromwell, if I am to work for you then I have to know what is happening, to avoid accidental error.'

He smiles. 'I am sure you would make no error, Lady Rochford. You have already been very helpful. Matters moved rather swiftly and unexpectedly; but I can tell you everything now.'

I know he will never tell me everything. 'Where is my husband?'

'At the Tower. He is under arrest.'

I gasp and put my hands behind my back, my palms flat against the roughness of the bricks, as if I need the walls themselves to support me. 'And Anne?'

'The same.'

'What for? What for?'

He clears his throat. 'As I say, it has become rather complicated. I was instructed by the king to set up an inquiry into the validity of the royal marriage. Obeying his command, I summoned reputable lords – your father one of them – to rule that the king is in forbidden intimacy with the sister of his former lover. As everyone knows, he married Queen Anne though he was her sister Mary Boleyn's lover, and so he has offended God.'

'They got a dispensation from the pope,' I point out.

'Yes. But – remember? – the pope has no authority to give a

dispensation in England. And two dead-borns are proof to the king that the marriage is an offence to God.'

'One,' I maintain stubbornly. 'Only one.'

'Two,' he says gently. 'One was wrongly denied.'

I am silent; he meets my eyes as guileless as a child.

'This is *superstitio* – a belief standing over a fact,' I tell him.

'But it is the king's *superstitio*. And the king's belief comes from God Himself.'

'Like Moses?'

Thomas Cromwell hides his smile in a nod. 'God speaks to the king and that overrules everything, even the facts as we – er, lesser men – might think them.'

For a moment, I could almost laugh. Here are Thomas Cromwell and Lord Morley's scholarly daughter agreeing that Henry Tudor's fears are more true than reality. This is to take courtier work to an extreme. But these are extreme times.

'Oh, that's why they were singing the old song of Henry Percy's betrothal to Anne!' I exclaim, as this part of the puzzle falls into place. 'To discredit her marriage to the king.' Suddenly, it is all clear to me. 'Master Cromwell – this is the work of the Spanish party! Francis Bryan insulted Anne to her face – called her Henry Percy's leavings. It was the very day they got the Garter for Nicholas Carew! They have been stirring up the king to think his marriage invalid – they must be telling him there was no dispensation for his affair with Mary Boleyn and that Anne was married to Henry Percy.'

From his silence, I know I am right.

'And that's why you were meeting Dr Sampson: to prove invalidity!' I say triumphantly. 'I saw him outside your door that day. Dr Sampson advised the first marriage, Katherine of Aragon's marriage was invalid. Now you've brought him back to deny this one.'

He nods, saying nothing.

'The Spanish party has persuaded the king that his marriage is invalid,' I say slowly. 'And you have set up an inquiry into it.' I enjoy the step by step of the discovery; but I know that this is a path that winds to the end of the Boleyns. 'Master Cromwell – I cannot believe you are siding with the Spanish—'

'Obeying the king,' he interjects.

'—siding with the Spanish to say that Anne is not a valid wife and so she is not queen?'

'Alas, since the king knows it from God, there can be no denying.'

'But what about the oaths? All of England swore that she was the one and only wife and queen. You swore it! I did! Why did Sir Thomas More die if Anne is not the only wife and queen?'

'He died for denying that the king is supreme. Nobody can deny that.'

I open my mouth to say that if the king is supreme, then he can give himself a dispensation and continue married to Anne. I close it again.

'Quite,' says Thomas Cromwell. 'The Supreme Head of the Church has received a new vision. Anne is not in it.'

It takes me a moment to realise that this is the end of Anne as queen. She will have to withdraw to the country, perhaps even go abroad. George and I will have to keep out of the way until this scandal is succeeded by another and all forgotten, or until the king's new vision requires our services. This is going to be a difficult time. We cannot repay all our loans and return our gifts; our court debts alone are far beyond our income. And if we're not at court, we'll get none of the riches from the abbey fines, or any fees or bribes. God knows how we will manage; God knows what we will do. We've lived all our lives at court, George as a diplomat and me as a spy. We have lost our fortune, our life and our work.

But this is a blindingly brilliant victory for the Spanish party, who have rid themselves of an enemy queen and all her supporters. When Anne is gone, they can return Lady Mary to favour; they will make her an heir to the throne; she will supersede our Princess Elizabeth. The king will be free to marry again, and, of course, he has already chosen his bride, who is completely under their control and living at Sir Nicholas Carew's house.

The king can marry Jane Seymour tomorrow; he can marry her in a Roman Catholic church if he wants; the damned pope can marry him in the damned Sistine Chapel if he likes, and Lady Mary will carry her new stepmother's wedding train with a happy heart. This is her triumph over Anne and the final revenge of her dead mother. They have won, and we have lost, and it was all over in four days in May.

'What a turn against us,' I say, thinking of the debts and packing our goods and vacating our rooms. 'What a change of season. And are they coming back here?' I ask. 'Anne and George? Or do we have to leave court at once?'

'I had planned they would come back here, sign all the contracts and then retire,' Master Cromwell takes his time, speaking lawyer-like, slow, so that I understand. 'That is what I thought would be the conclusion of the inquiry. But then there was a development – not of my making. My inquiry was complete. And successful. But then – to my surprise – new evidence was volunteered.'

'What new evidence?' I am barely interested. George's falcons alone cost us more than we earn in rents.

'Evidence of adultery, of infidelity.'

Now he has my full attention. 'Whose adultery?'

'Adultery by the queen,' Cromwell repeats. 'Out of thin air, they produced evidence of adultery by the queen.'

I scrape my knuckles against the bricks behind my back, as if to wake myself up from a nightmare. 'That is *antinomic*.' I grasp at scholarship. 'If they proved her marriage was invalid, then she is a single woman. Any love affair of hers is no adultery. She is free to be promiscuous, as free as any single lady-in-waiting.'

'I agree with you. And that is why they are not stopping at adultery; they accuse of worse. They say there was perversity, even magical entrapment . . .'

'But this is ridiculous!' I catch a breath. 'Master Cromwell, I know you would never bring a case to court with faulty accusation and hearsay evidence. My father says you're the greatest lawyer in England. You'd never allow such gross gossip as evidence.'

He smiles. 'Your father is generous.'

'But you never would.'

'Indeed. I would prefer not. But my opinion is now irrelevant. They have taken my little inquiry and whipped it into a panic.'

'Panic?' My voice is too sharp, as if I am infected with groundless fear. I take a breath before I speak again. 'Adultery is no cause for panic?'

'But treason is,' he says. 'A huge treason plot in the heart of court. Sexual perversion, a ring of corruption and witchcraft.'

I burst out laughing at the story as wild as the oldest Romance. 'No, no, this can't happen!' I exclaim. 'Anne wrote the laws of treason! She can't be prosecuted by the laws she invented. Master Cromwell! You cannot allow the Spanish party to whip up a story like a spinning top. They can't invent accusations and take it into a trial! Where will it stop?'

'That's the very point,' he says, as if glad that someone agrees with him. 'They won't stop – and I will let them go to the utter extent of folly. They will overreach and destroy themselves. They are planning on naming dozens of men, citing incidents that could never have happened – accusing her of meeting a man when she was miles away that night and in bed with the king. Accusing her of grossness, of perversions, even witchcraft. Their accusations against the queen are so wildly exaggerated, it will become obvious to everyone that they are lies. I am giving them the rope to hang themselves. They think they are trapping her; but they are trapping themselves.'

'So, what happens when the trial collapses, for going *ad absurdum longitudines*?'

'Then the king will round on them for failing to give him what he wants, and he will destroy them.'

'And you rescue the whole thing! Anne retires, and the king can marry Jane Seymour.'

'It's not going to be easy,' he concedes. 'But think of it! The Spanish party ruined forever and exposed as madmen and -women, Anne's marriage annulled as the king wishes, but nothing against her as a woman or queen, the Boleyns without shame, and you and George can keep your places at court. You can keep Beaulieu Palace and your fortune. Anne can even visit you if she wishes.'

The fear leaves me in a gust of giggles. 'I don't think anyone would want that! She'll be safe, but she won't thank you!'

His laughs with me. 'No, you're probably right.'

Another night alone in my bed as Henry Norris' big horse backs through my dreams, forever refusing to go forward. When I wake, I am so haunted by the memory of the charger's hooves tearing up the tiltyard that I go down to the stables to see his big head nodding over the door. I thought for a moment that the king might have had him beheaded for disobedience, just as he executed his own horse for falling. I reach out a hand, and he sniffs at me with his sweet oaty breath; then he backs off again, away from the door, as if he can smell bad luck on my fingers.

A messenger in the livery of the Archbishop of Canterbury, our old friend Thomas Cranmer, rides into the yard. I open the door of the stable and slip inside with the restless horse to hear Cranmer's man say to the groom: 'Give him hay and water. I have a message for the Master Secretary, and I'll wait for a reply.'

'Don't tell me the archbishop is locked up in the Tower as well!' is the lame attempt at a joke.

'No – His Grace is safe in Lambeth Palace. But anxious. Praying. Weeping. He says over and over: "How can it be? How can such a woman be?"'

'He's the only one'll weep for her,' the groom replies truculently. 'She were a false wife to the king and no good queen to us. Not like good Queen Katherine.'

'False?' the messenger asks.

'A dozen times over with a dozen men,' the groom says with certainty. 'In two places at once, on a witch-wind, to have her will.'

They go their separate ways – the messenger to the Cromwell's rooms; the groom leads the horse to an empty stall, and I creep out. I wish I had not listened. I wish I had not heard that. It is a sample of what we are going to have to endure as we let the Spanish party exaggerate and overreach themselves.

In the afternoon, I sit in the queen's half-empty privy chamber with a handful of ladies: all Boleyns. Everyone else has melted away. Someone says that Francis Weston, the king's favourite, was missing from his place at dinner and that the king, who was drunk, told someone – who immediately repeats it to everyone – that Anne bedded up to a hundred men. I think: this is good news, this is *ad absurdio* – a claim so extreme that it makes the point ridiculous. Our enemies are overreaching themselves as Master Cromwell said they would, and we are entrapping them. All we have to do is wait.

THE NEXT DAY Thomas Cromwell's clerks come to the queen's rooms and take every book from her shelves and every piece of paper, even scraps of poems and riddles and letters. I watch them pack every note from her writing table into the green sacks that lawyers use – as if any of this will be used as evidence in court! The books are dangerously Lutheran; but Anne has read every single one of them to the king himself, and Thomas Cromwell has his own copies of most of them. The safest man to hold them is Thomas Cromwell, who will defend her and George against a charge of heresy, which the Spanish party are certain to bring along with other mad exaggerations.

After the clerks, come the grooms of the royal wardrobe, who take all her clothes: gowns, capes and hoods and sleeves. The grooms of the treasury collect the jewels, even the pieces that are her own; they don't listen to me when I say that I know that this bracelet or these pearls are Boleyn family treasures. It's all to be stored for safekeeping in the treasure house at the Tower and I make sure everything is properly labelled. When this is over, she will want her personal treasures back.

I finish tidying and clearing the queen's rooms and then, while I am waiting for a groom of the household to lock the great double doors behind me, Elizabeth Somerset comes past with a wooden ribbon box in her hand. 'It's my own things!' she says quickly. 'Things that I lent her.'

I take her word for it, though I think her a thief.

She drops her voice to a whisper. 'What did you say to the inquiry?'

'They haven't called me yet.'

'I said nothing about my brother-in-law William Brereton.' She is anguished. 'William would never do anything. Why would they arrest him? And I said nothing about Anne but what is common knowledge . . .'

'What did you say?' I demand.

'Nothing to the inquiry, just – earlier – to my brother Anthony. He was shouting at me – you know how strict he is. He was reviling me – you know how we quarrel! I said I had done nothing worse than the queen herself. And he took me up on it – you know how he is – and next thing I know he and Thomas Wriothesley – as if he has any right to question me! – are asking me what I mean! And saying that they will have to take it further.' She breaks off as she sees my face. 'I said nothing. I meant nothing. I told him it was nothing. It's all just courtly love.' She gestures at her growing belly. 'What more can I do than talk? All Anne and I ever did was talk!'

I try to smile and agree with her, but my whole face feels quite frozen. 'If she gave you that hundred pounds for you to keep silent, then she got a bad deal,' I say nastily.

She turns without a word and hurries away, down the gallery, away from the locked doors of the queen's rooms where nothing happened.

The court is buzzing with gossip like a troubled beehive, a low angry murmur that falls silent when I walk past. There's no doubt that my family and I are the centre of the scandal. But I know courtiers, and I know that when Anne is cleared, they will all be my greatest friends again. The Spanish party will overreach themselves, and the inquiry will be led into ridiculous claims. But then I think: my father will never be led into ridicule. I should warn him that this is a conspiracy by the Spanish party and that they should be encouraged to hang themselves. I send an urgent message to him for permission to visit him at Westminster – I have something that I want to tell him.

He replies at once:

*Daughter,*
*Information from ladies has already been submitted in writing, and nothing more is needed. Since you know nothing, you need not visit. Say nothing to anyone – especially not to the king, who is rightly much offended. The inquiry has arrested Thom Wyatt and Richard Page and summoned Sir Francis Bryan.*
  *Morley*

My father never signs his letters to me with his title, and from this I know that he is writing a letter to be read by any spy. Even so, he manages to give me much information. That I am to say nothing, and especially that I know nothing. That Sir Thomas Wyatt is arrested, who has loved Anne since she was a girl and is certain to defend her. Richard Page has no enemies and must be here as a strolling player to swell the scene. Sir Francis Bryan is Jane Seymour's host and sponsor, a blatant friend to the Spanish and enemy to us: his spite against Anne will tempt him into telling a cartload of lies, winking at them behind his eye patch. He will betray their conspiracy – just as Master Cromwell promised. A conspiracy against the queen is treason, punishable by death. They will regret starting this hare which will circle as hares always do.

I go quite cheerfully to dinner in the great hall; the royal table is weighted with silverware and the servers will bring twenty courses out of respect to the absent king, who is still at Whitehall but said to be dining out in London in the happiest of moods. We all enter in order of precedence and bow to the throne. Half a dozen ladies sit with me at the ladies' table, and we eat in silence. There is no music, and nobody wants to dance when half the court has a kinsman in the Tower tonight.

After dinner, some of the gentlemen sit over their wine, but the ladies disappear to their own rooms. I am at the doorway to the Boleyn rooms when Thomas Howard appears. He steps inside with me, without asking permission, and waves away the servant.

'Has Cromwell promised you safety?' he asks without preamble. 'You and George? I know you've not been called to give evidence – and he's going to get Thom Wyatt off – has he promised to release George too?'

'He's made me no promise,' I say, which is true: he has not. 'I need none. No inquiry can find anything against me or George. It is a plot by the Spanish party against Anne, with imaginary accusations. It will blow up in their faces.'

His sharp face is more hawklike than ever. 'Of course it's a plot,' he says grimly. 'But it's a good one. They'll prove their accusations. They'll drag her down. Question is: will they take you and George, too?'

'If the marriage was invalid, then she is no wife,' I explain patiently. The duke is deadly at the head of his men, but not the sharpest blade when faced with ideas. 'If she is no wife, there is no adultery. As her uncle, as the head of our house, your task is to wait for them to make fools of themselves, and then take Anne away.'

His laugh is like the sharp bark of a dog. 'You're behind the times, Jane – it's gone far beyond validity; it's gone far beyond adultery! If she's not his wife, then adultery doesn't matter – suppose Anne kissed Henry Norris? Even if she swived him? The archbishop will rule that she's adulterous and send her to a nunnery. A modern Guinevere. That's not enough for them – now they want her dead!

Some fool told them that Anne said it was her or Lady Mary. So they're all out for the death sentence on Anne. They're throwing every filth they can. They say she was plotting with her own brother for the king's death, in an enseamed bed? They'll both have to die for it.'

'Treason? With George? It's ridiculous!'

'Worse! They say they bedded. Brother-and-sister lovers! Incestuous lovers!'

He has knocked the breath out of me.

'You think you're so clever,' he says, with lightning malice. 'The three of you. So clever and young and sinful. Were you in the bed, too?'

'Nobody can say it! Nobody will have witnessed it! There's no evidence for it!'

'Everyone's given evidence of it,' he jeers. 'Everyone witnessed it.'

'Lies! And such a thing to say? Such a wicked . . .' I break off. Actually, it's clever; everyone knows their intimacy. I, myself, said to Cromwell that George is always with his sister. Impossible to deny what happens behind a closed door. But it is the worst of accusations, made by the worst of imaginations. And why attack George? And why add incest to the accusations of adultery?

I can feel my uncle's hard scrutiny of my white face, and I look up, hoping for help. 'But – why?' I ask simply. 'If this is an attack on Anne by her enemies – the Poles, and the Seymours and the rest of the Spanish party, all working together – why so gross an accusation? Why incest as well as witchcraft?'

'Something so ungodly that it drives the king mad,' he tells me. 'Nobody's going to ask "but was she married before?" when they hear about this. Nobody will care. It's such a vile sin that everyone will call for her death. The king loudest of all. They'll frighten him half to death about the lust he felt for her. By the time they've finished, he'll think of her as a witch who tempted him and destroyed his life, made him impotent, dropped a horse on him, killed his first wife and sickened his daughter. Nothing will satisfy him but her death.'

'Wait!' I say. 'I can vouch for George. At least I can save him. There was no treason. There was no incest. There was no plotting the death of the king. I was there at every meeting.'

He grips me by the arm and draws me close. 'If you were at every meeting, then you are a traitor and part of the queen's adulterous murderous witchcraft,' he growls in my ear. 'If you were there at every meeting, then you were in bed with the two of them, hanging on each other, kissing with tongues, hiding dead babies, cursing the king into impotence, taking potions. You choose! Go to your spymaster Cromwell: his book is open at the page for confessions.'

His grip is tight, but I hardly feel it; I sway with sickness. He pauses and looks into my ashen face. 'D'you want to die? D'you want to die as an incestuous witch-traitor with George and Anne?'

'They're not going to die.'

'D'you want to die with them?'

I know that I don't. 'No.'

'Then do as I do: condemn them.'

'You can't condemn them – your own niece and nephew. You can't send them to their deaths without a word?'

He grins, showing his yellow teeth. 'Oh, I'm going to speak a word,' he says mirthlessly. 'I'll speak a word all right. I'm going to say: "Guilty".'

N O ONE TELLS the ladies to leave; but there is nothing for us to do here without a queen. Those of us who have families in rooms at court can go to them, and the others – like Anne Basset whose mother is in Calais – stays with friends in London. Sir Nicholas Carew does not open his grand house at Croydon for any other maid-of-honour but Jane Seymour, who does not reappear to help as we pack up our things.

'Where will you go?' I ask Margery Horsman.

'Home,' she says shortly. 'I've told them everything they asked. I don't have to stay.'

'What d'you mean, everything they asked? Who asked you?'

'Master Cromwell asked me; his clerk wrote down my answers. "Who spoke to who? Who danced with the queen? Who did she favour?" I told them that I saw what everyone saw – the king himself saw everything. Master Holbein could've painted it! There's no news to be made from it. Masquing, dancing, plays, courtly love, everything as normal. Will you go to Beaulieu?'

I shake my head. 'I'll wait for George in our rooms. He'll come back here as soon as he's given his evidence.'

She lowers her voice. 'Did you hear? They've arrested Thomas Wyatt?'

I think of Cromwell saying: *Two Francises, a Thomas, and a Mark, and a Richard and a Henry. So many! William Brereton?*

I shake my head. 'I've heard nothing,' I lie. 'I've seen nobody all day. But it can't be an arrest: Wyatt is a great favourite of the king, as is Henry Norris. They'll have called him in to give evidence, like George and Francis. Nobody would believe anything against Francis.'

I go to our rooms, and I write a letter to George.

*Dearest Husband,*
*I send you these clothes and some writing paper and new pens and ink. I will see the king and speak for you, if I can.*
   *Your faithful wife,*
   *Jane*

I take the letter to the stables and find our groom. I offer him another sixpence, but he hesitates.

'Beg pardon, Lady Rochford, but I can't go for less than a shilling. By the time I go there and back, I'm likely to be turned off.'

'You work for me,' I tell him. 'No one can turn you off.'

He twists his cap in his big hands. 'They say there'll be no Boleyn money to pay my wages, and already, there's no place for me at the royal groom's dinner table. I used to get my keep – I used to eat in. Now there's nowhere for me to sit and no dinner for me.'

I am not going to protest our family's innocence to my husband's groom. I give him a shilling. 'Take the message and bring me back an answer,' is all I say.

I could have saved my money. George's answer is so short and formal that he must know his letters are being read and trusts me to do whatever I can. But I am glad of a letter that says nothing – it means he is thinking of his safety, not raging in defence of Anne. The accusation of adultery and treason will fall of its own overweight – it will crash down on those who raised it. The worse they try to paint us, the worse will be their defeat. All we have to do is say nothing.

The Spanish party's accusation of the four commoners accused of adultery with Anne opens – in all its ridiculous illogicality – at Westminster Hall in front of a thrilled audience of Londoners. Ridiculous – because everyone knows that the charges are false. Illogical – because if the four men are found guilty of adultery with Anne, she will come to trial with a verdict already cast against her. Is the Queen of England to be condemned for adultery because a lute player admitted under torture that he swived her? With no witnesses? With no evidence? It's so far-fetched that I am reassured that no one can take it seriously. It's only at the end of the day, when I meet that fool Elizabeth Somerset, that I realise that the collapse of the Spanish party plot is coming dangerously late.

Broad-bellied, she is climbing awkwardly into a litter in the stable-yard, and tries to make a grimace at me, as if to laugh at her predicament. Her face is gaunt and strained. The pretty flush of pregnancy is a livid stamp on her pale nose and cheeks.

'I'm going home for my confinement,' she calls out as I come through the archway. 'My husband ordered me home the minute they went to trial! So sad! Who'd have thought anyone would have taken it all so seriously!'

'What?' I ask tightly. 'Taken what so seriously?'

'Haven't you heard?'

'No.'

'Oh! I don't like to be the one to tell you!' she pauses.

I come close to the litter. 'Tell me, Elizabeth. I've heard nothing, and nobody talks to me but you.'

'Well, they wouldn't,' she exclaims. 'Oh! My dear! So sorry! So awful! Well! Anyway . . . poor Smeaton confessed, though he looked awful – terribly bruised around the head. The noblemen denied everything, of course. But the lords found against their own! Think of that? Guilty.' She looks ready to cry. 'Of course there'll be a pardon. But it's such a scandal, and it looks badly on all of us. My own reputation . . .'

'Guilty?' I repeat.

'Yes! All our darling friends. Thank God, George wasn't there. He and Anne will be tried by the lords, not in a common court. And darling Norris and Francis Weston will be pardoned for sure. And nobody could think anything against William, though he is so disagreeable. Smeaton confessed; but of course, nobody believes him. But even so, my husband says I have to go straight home!' She leans towards me to whisper. 'He's trying to deny the baby is his! Says we're all as bad as each other. Which is what I said in the very beginning! Meaning innocent, of course!'

I recoil from her, but she goes on.

'Think of me! The only good thing about it is that I won't see my husband for nearly two months . . .' Her voice dies away as she realises that I have not seen my husband since May Day. She beckons me closer to whisper: 'Did you hear about Jane Seymour?'

I shake my head.

'Moved from Nicholas Carew's house. Too far from Whitehall for convenience! She's at Sir Francis Bryan's house on the Strand. So Francis Bryan is released to play host – he was just called in for questioning, nothing against him – though he's the worst man at court. Now the king dines there nightly! Not bad for a half-wit from Wiltshire.'

'Sir Francis' house?' I repeat.

'The king dines there every night. Goes by royal barge with the musicians playing.'

'Does he?'

'Yes. You can hear them from the pier.'

The muleteers, tired of waiting, turn and look at her.

'Oh! I suppose I have to go. Well, goodbye,' she says simply.

'Good luck,' I say, and I see the quick movement of her fingers, the thumb going between the index and the third finger, the old sign to ward off witchcraft – as if I am so unlucky, as if we Boleyns are so unlucky, that my blessing on her is a curse.

# THE TOWER OF LONDON, MAY

## 1536

IT TAKES THEM three days to make the scenery for the masque at the Tower of London which is to be Anne's trial. They build a stand for spectators and bring in great tables and heavy chairs to make the court look more important than a bear-baiting, certain to end in death. There is no doubt about the outcome: just as one dog is thrown in after another until the bear goes down, they have added and added to the charges until a saint would break under the weight of them. It is not only my uncle the Duke of Norfolk who comes to say 'guilty': no one can claim Anne is innocent when the lower court has already found against her lovers. The judges go through the motions like old partners rehearsing a familiar dance;

but the verdict is obvious. She cannot be innocent if four men have already been found guilty of adultery with her.

I don't attend her trial; my fury at the Spanish party is greater than my scholar's desire to know everything. I know that she is innocent of the charges, but I know she is guilty of worse. She did not plot the king's death, but she did cause the deaths of Bishop Fisher and Thomas More, and the law she wrote would have killed the old queen and Lady Mary. Our enemies were driven to destroy Anne from the moment that they realised it was her or Lady Mary.

I fuelled their fears, so I am guilty, too. The Spanish party learned of Lady Mary's danger from me. I asked my father to warn her. I told Lady Margaret Pole that she should escape. I was advised by Thomas Cromwell; I thought I was doing the right thing, but I did not foresee this *hamartia*, this tragedy blooming from one mistake. I never dreamed that a courtier's word, which is always half-lie and half-truth, would bring us Boleyns to death.

They tell me that Anne is unyielding as they find her guilty. I can imagine her, listening to the verdict from the men who rode on the hem of her skirts to power and favour, her own father, her uncle, even the man who married her in secret, Henry Percy, who denies her now. I can imagine her dark gaze going from one face to another, her head tilted, listening to one Judas word after another, and her quick-witted nod when it is all over and they tell her she is to be beheaded or burned, at the king's discretion. Even the judges murmur at the terrible sentence. A little murmur, painfully quiet.

GEORGE'S TRIAL COMES after his sister's condemnation, and the court is betting on his acquittal – they want a more cheerful afternoon after the monstrous tragedy played in the morning. The love of gambling is as strong as ever among courtiers, and there are no other entertainments for us but the trials. Facing his judges, his father and father-in-law among them, his uncle as the lead judge, he becomes again the George that everyone has always adored: witty and cool under attack, charming in agreement, fiercely clever – no one doubts that he will argue himself out of the stand and get himself off. The odds rise to 10:1 in his favour, and someone offers me a share of a bet. I don't take it. I tell them that I will not attend his trial, but I wear a thick veil to hide my lying eyes and my false face, and I slip into the back of the court.

The judges sit at a long table, facing George, who stands before them like a sword fighter, lightly on his feet, one hand resting on his belt where his sword should be. He looks at each one of them – every one a kinsman who has known him from childhood, or a friend at court. He responds confidently to every charge, proving easily that he was not where they say he was, that he was not even at court that night or this, that no one ever saw him in Anne's bedroom, that no one has any evidence but hearsay, and no one is called to speak against him. He is the king's favourite, a trusted diplomat, the king's brother-in-law. He is certain to be proved innocent.

I nod at every well-made point, and I force myself to sit still, but the whole of the gallery is on his side. I am not the only woman leaning forward, watching through a veil, following every neat step he takes on the rising stair to his acquittal.

But then he is handed a note and warned that it is a report of his own speech. The chief presiding judge, the Duke of Norfolk – our uncle Thomas Howard – asks George if he said the words written on the piece of paper. They are such dangerous words, such treasonous words, that he warns George not to read them aloud.

George opens the paper, studies the words in silence, and raises his dark head. He looks scornfully around the court, his dark eyes bright with contempt, and he reads aloud, in his ringing, defiant voice: 'This says: "The king is unmanned and cannot get a woman with child".' He crumples the paper in his hand, like a player enacting contempt. He tosses it to the floor.

'There is no need for this to passed around like a disgraceful riddle,' he says. 'It is a lie and should not be elevated to evidence. I did not say it. I would not say it. I know it to be untrue. The allegation of impotence throws doubt over the fathering of all the king's children, and – even worse – over any royal heirs that may bless the king in future – as we all loyally pray. This should never have been written down, never have been submitted in evidence. These are not my words, and I deny them.'

There is a horrified gasp. Of course, everyone knows that the king is now and then impotent – actually, those of us who serve in the queen's bedroom know that he is impotent often. But such an allegation recorded in the court reports puts a question over our Boleyn heir – over Elizabeth's fathering. Four men were found guilty of adultery with Anne – any one of them could be named as Elizabeth's father if the piece of paper is entered as evidence. Even if George had only looked at it and denied it – it would have gone into the court records. By throwing it to the ground, he has discredited it.

He knows this. He read the words aloud and denied them for the sake of his sister Anne and her daughter, Elizabeth. If he had remained silent, they would have let him off. But his defiance of the court – his contempt for their plan – is enough to condemn him. He lies on his oath, to say the king is not impotent, has never been impotent, to insist that Elizabeth is the king's own daughter. He has put his own head on the block to leave no question over his little niece's fathering.

I should remember him as a hero for this. But I am so furious that his last act is to save the rights of his sister's daughter that I am numb with rage. I cannot feel anything. He has defied the court – and for what? For love of Anne and her little daughter, Elizabeth. Now, I cannot save him; no one can save him. He has condemned himself. He has chosen to die so that his niece may keep the title of princess. The Boleyn ambition and his love of Anne means more to him than life.

I push my way past the people straining to see his smiling face, the defiant cock of his head as he steps into a guilty verdict and strolls towards his own death. I get out into the cold east wind and the glaring sunlight blinds me. I will never forgive him for this. It is the final betrayal of me. It is his final act of love towards his sister and her daughter. I stalk across Tower Green to the dark gateway and think I will never come here again. I will never see George again.

I am completely ruined. The queen I served will die named as a witch, a creature of perverse lusts, an adulterous wife, a treasonous queen. My husband is named for terrible crimes with her and has chosen to die with her rather than live with me. At his death, I will lose my fortune and my home. At her death, I will lose my place at court and royal favour. I will be poor; I will be homeless; I will be out of favour. I don't know what will become of me. As a Boleyn, I will be reviled as the wife of an adulterous, incestuous brother, and the sister-in-law of a lust-crazed witch. History will name me as a bawd, a procuress, lust-mad myself.

GEORGE DIES ON Tower Hill; Henry Norris and his friend Francis Weston and William Brereton follow him to the scaffold keeping the order of courtly precedence, even when going to their deaths. The commoner, Mark Smeaton, is last on the scaffold drenched in other men's blood, and he makes a poor end.

This is all incredible to me. I cannot understand it. I cannot even think it. I feel like it is a concept too difficult for study, even for a scholar. I live in a state of burning fury with Anne, with George, and with all Boleyns: my mother- and father-in-law, who have made no effort for their own son and daughter, with all the Howards, who have distanced themselves from their kinsmen so far that they have been practically Seymours this season. Mary Boleyn is nowhere to be seen, shunning, disaster as she shunned success.

Anne has to wait, hoping for a pardon, in pleasant rooms overlooking Tower Green for a swordsman to come from France for her death. She is to be beheaded with a sword, not burned. And so her final scene is delayed, waiting for a unique prop for this special masque. The court does not know the etiquette for beheading a queen. There is no agreed ritual in the king's grandmother's book of the court. No one has ever killed a queen on a scaffold in England. Actually, I don't believe anyone has ever executed a queen anywhere. There is *Clytemnestra* and *Penthesilea* in the Greek legends, but neither of them were legally beheaded before a select crowd of a thousand family and friends on Tower Green – the grass scythed especially short for the occasion. I cannot understand this either. I could almost laugh at the thought of Anne, who always preferred French fashions, getting a swordsman from France.

People don't know whether to wear mourning or not. They decide on best clothes in bright colours for a queen's beheading. I don't pick out a gown. I won't attend. I can't bear to see it. But I know when it is done because, as I am sitting in the empty bleakness of Greenwich Palace hall, the cannon of the Tower shoots off a roar, as for a great celebration. The king has ordered a full cannon salute loud enough for him to hear upriver at Chelsea, where he has timed the dance so that he should lead out his new bride at the very moment that the great love of his life was beheaded.

The next day, his betrothal is announced. He is going to marry Jane Seymour.

## GREENWICH PALACE, SUMMER

### 1536

I HIDE IN THE Boleyn family rooms instead of my own, avoiding any snares on my usual pathways like a hare with a chewed-off foot. George's mother and father left for Hever straight after the sentencing, before the deaths. Their horses were standing by, waiting for Anne's father to give his verdict with his fellow-judges. He said 'guilty' of his own son. He said 'guilty' of his own daughter, and he and his wife left for Kent as soon as his wife's brother, our uncle, put on the black hat, turned the blade of the axe outwards, and declared the sentence of death.

Their servants were dismissed but for one groom of the chamber to hand over the keys to the new tenants of their rooms at Greenwich Palace. They did not forbid me to hide in these empty rooms, my last home at court. But nor did they offer me refuge. They did not speak to me at all.

In their absence, in the absence of incomers, the servant and I camp out like beggars in a barn. He sleeps on the floor in the men servants' room; I have a truckle bed, little and low amid the dust of old strewing herbs in the grand Boleyn bedroom, and a blanket that they left behind in a forgotten box. I am not cold. I have a stool at the fireside and a few boxes of my own things, saved from George's debtors: some clothes, a pair of shoes, my books – I saved my books, although I can't be bothered to read any of them.

I dine in the great hall with the few remaining courtiers, though I am never hungry. Every day, I walk to the ladies' table half-expecting a groom of the household to turn me away, but no one objects when I take a lowly place with the other single and widowed ladies of court. They too, have nowhere else to go and are neither dismissed from court nor invited elsewhere. No one speaks to me; this is not hurtful as I have nothing to say to anyone.

We bow our heads in silence for Grace, and we eat in an unbroken silence, like Benedictine nuns. After dinner, I walk down to the river to watch the water flowing out to sea, as if it, too, is leaving without a word. I walk back through the weary gardens, the leaves crumpled by the summer heat. The sun beats down on the winding paths of the privy gardens, the white stone paths too bright to bear; but I am not hot.

The king stays away from court, the remaining noblemen go to their estates in the country, and the servants clean their rooms. I have to pick my way over wet floors in the galleries, and there are buckets and brooms in the open doorways to the great rooms.

## BOLEYN TRAITOR

The weather turns suddenly cold and rainy, and the Boleyn groom and I draw coals and candles from the royal household stores and light the fire in the Boleyn hall in the evenings. I am not cold.

I am neither cold nor hot. I think of God saying: *For thou art lukewarm, and neither cold, neither hot, I shall begin to cast thee out of my mouth. Thou knowest not, that thou art a wretch, and wretchful.*

I think *Revelation 3*; but I don't pray. I think if I am a wretch and wretchful, then I have nothing to pray for. The souls of George and Anne, and the souls of our friends, beheaded with them, will go to hell, I suppose, for their terrible sins. Unless they were all innocent and go, headless, to purgatory. It will depend on whether *particular* judgement is under the control of the Spanish party or of the Boleyns? Whether the old faith is right and they are waiting in purgatory for masses to be sung to release them to heaven; or they have gone at once to bliss or hell as we reformers believe.

I suppose I shall have to go to the living purgatory of my home at Morley Hallingbury. I have nowhere else to go. There is no place for me at the palaces and castles of my bridal days and I cannot afford to run Beaulieu Palace, or pay the servants. I have been dropped again; but this time, no one will summon me back to court, and my father will never forgive my disgrace. I suppose I shall live and die there and be buried in the parish church under a modest stone, fitting for a widowed daughter of no importance.

I cannot bring myself to write to my father to ask him to send his grooms to fetch me home. My paper and my pens are in one of the boxes with my books. I cannot be troubled to look for them. For the first time in my life, I have no interest in study.

Days pass. A week passes. Then I come back to the rooms after dinner, and the groom of the chamber is waiting for me. 'You've got a letter,' he says. 'Special seal.'

I take it without interest, and I stare blankly at him until he ducks his head in a bow and leaves. I take my seat on the stool by the mean fire and look at the letter – the first I have had, since George's final note.

I feel a stir of interest like the rising of temptation. This is no ordinary letter – it is letterlocked: the tongue of the page intersects itself and is pasted down. Who would writing something to me, which is to be read only by me?

I look at the wax seal. It is Thomas Cromwell's crest.

*I have obtained for you the place of chief lady-in-waiting to Queen Jane. You can draw gowns, etc., from the royal wardrobe, and your fee from the treasury. Other ladies will come to Greenwich Palace shortly. Please ensure they are housed in the queen's rooms, as they should be, and that the rooms are ready for Her Grace, who will come within the week.*

I look at the stroke of the *T* and the half-moon of the *C*, and I think: good God, I am not going to die wretchful; I am not a wretch and wretchful. I am going to survive this. Good God, my life is going to begin again.

Thomas Cromwell has not packed his bags and gone to his country house while the king dallies with a new bride, like the old lords. Thomas Cromwell does not hide from failure like the Howards and the Boleyns. Thomas Cromwell continues, as always. Probably, he never stopped, not even for the trials. The dark chamber is still taking in the king's letters – probably everyone's letters – reading them, resealing them, and sending them out again, apparently untouched. The Cromwell men are still in post: sheriffs, mayor, justices of the peace, middling men, and wealthy merchants. The Cromwell machine of government rumbles on, unstoppable. The Cromwell Court of Augmentations takes in and redistributes the wealth of the monasteries; the Cromwell inspectors travel the land to find corruption in the rich monasteries. Amazingly, in all this work, Cromwell still thinks of me.

He is not thinking of me – I, myself, Jane Boleyn, pauper widow. He is thinking of how he can use me. He needs a spy in the court of the new queen; he needs someone to watch the Seymours, someone to watch the Spanish party, someone to predict the king's next idea, someone to create the king's new idea and slide it into his wishes. I will be more use than ever before, now that the Spanish party think I am their friend; warning them of the danger to Lady Mary. They think I gave evidence against Anne and brought her and George to their deaths. Thomas Cromwell has written a part for me in this masque, as the traitor-sister to a queen, whose star was falling, and as a friend to the rising star, the new queen, and the Spanish party that has put her in place.

Jane Seymour will be so glad to have a lady-in-waiting familiar with the private rituals of the queen that she will overlook the *froideur* natural between a man's new wife and his former sister-in-law. Her brothers will disregard me, thinking all women as dull as their sister. The king himself sees me more as palace furniture than Boleyn – I have been here for nearly twenty years, single and married and widowed.

I shout for the groom. He is so startled by my raised voice after days of silence in the empty rooms that I hear him scramble up and fling open his door. He comes at the run.

'What is it? What did the letter say?'

'You can move my boxes,' I tell him.

'Where to?' His eyes are wide and frightened. 'The Tower? You too?'

'To the queen's rooms,' I say triumphantly. 'To the rooms for the chief lady-in-waiting.'

IT TAKES ONLY a few days and everything is restored. Everything is as it was for the last queen – and for the one before that. The maids-of-honour return; I greet the familiar ladies-in-waiting. Even the king's friends, coming and going with compliments and invitations, are the same. Why should there be any difference? It's only been two short weeks between the death of one queen and the arrival of another.

Jane Seymour sails downriver from Chelsea in Anne's barge, wearing Anne's clothes, and sleeps in Anne's bed, in Anne's sheets. The monograms on the sheets and towels and linen are picked out, and the *A* under the coronet is replaced with a newly embroidered *J*. In the evenings, we light the candles that Anne ordered; they have not even burned down. Everything is the same; only the queen is different, and the newly joyous mood of the court.

We are merrier than in April, happier than we were at May Day, at the May Day joust that nobody ever mentions. The king is in a most boisterous mood: pleased with everything. The same entertainments and games planned by the same master of revels now bring him delight, as if before he was pretending happiness – as false as any courtier. He comes into the queen's rooms with his face wreathed in smiles, his limp hardly noticeable. His fool, Will Somer, gambols like a lamb at the heels of a well-fed lion, as if none of us need fear anything.

There are a few faces missing: the lute music is bright, but it is not the ripple that only Mark Smeaton could play. The king's friends still come running with messages that the king is on his way and we had better be looking our best, but we miss Francis Weston's boyish laughter. There is no Henry Norris, lounging through the door, flirting with Margaret Shelton and winking at me; no William Brereton frowning at Elizabeth Somerset, and she is still away from court in the confinement that she and Anne thought they would share. Now, Anne's baby is long gone and forgotten, and Anne is dead, too.

And – of course – there is no George. My husband's body is buried with his decapitated head in the chapel in the Tower. His sister Anne lies beside him, in an old arrow box, her head pushed under her feet – they forgot to order a coffin for her. They are as inseparable in death as they were in life – and I am very far from them both.

I cannot make myself understand that everything is the same – except that six of us are missing. I cannot make myself understand that I am in my accustomed place, on the right hand of the queen's chair, ready with a smile or a prompt to cover an awkward silence – but those six are absent. I cannot believe that when I glance to my left, there is the queen on her heavy carved chair – but it is not Anne; it is not even Katherine of Aragon. They are both dead. It is little Jane Seymour, with her ugly English hood crammed down over her pale hair and her white face shining with astonishment at finding herself in Anne's chair, with Anne's friends, at the summit of Anne's court.

There are new ladies, of course; the Spanish party has won and are taking the prizes. They appoint Poles, Courtenays, Greys, Darcys, and Husseys, and of course Seymours. Almost none of the new ladies have been chosen by the new queen – Mary Brandon, the daughter of Charles Brandon's first marriage, has been foisted on her, and she cannot possibly have wanted Margaret Douglas, whose heated flirtation with Lord Thom – the boyish half-brother of our uncle Thomas Howard – is going to blow up like a purse of serpentine now that we have a queen who notices nothing and commands no one. Eleanor Manners, Mary Zouch, and Anne Parr have returned, even though Anne Parr is red-hot for the reform of the Church and sits uneasily in this court which is going to bring back the old religion as soon as it can.

How can any of us treat Jane Seymour with respect, when she was our despised junior and we laughed when Anne slapped her face for perching her arse on the king's one good knee? The newly made queen appoints ladies who are not worthy of their place: Margaret Dymoke, who was a hard-hearted spy on Anne in the Tower, and some vulgar Seymour countrywomen: Anne Seymour is the worst of them, now that her sister-in-law is queen.

They look at me with disdain and suspicion, wondering how I have clung to my place, despite all that has happened, and I smile my courtier's smile. I may no longer be kinswoman to the queen – as they now are. I may not be of the royal family – as they now are. I may not be rising upwards on the skirts of my sister-in-law as once I did – as Anne Seymour does now – but I have survived, though my fortune, my friends, my husband, and my queen have been taken, in a great *auto-da-fé* by the Spanish party, who are now triumphant.

And here – as if to prove their ascendancy – comes Lady Margaret Pole, visiting the new queen to arrange for the return of Lady Mary to her proper place at court. Her ladyship strolls into the royal rooms as if she owns them once again. Two sons and her cousins are in the king's favour; she and her kinswoman, Gertrude Courtenay, are welcomed in the queen's rooms and honoured at every great occasion. Her cousin, Arthur Plantagenet, Lord Lisle, commands the key fort of Calais; her scholar son, Reginald, is high in the favour of the pope at Rome, and now his great book is going to offer a brilliant compromise between reform and the old church: a way for our king to return to Rome. This is the end of Anne's reform, the triumph of the Spanish party and the restoration of Rome.

They have thought of everything – except they forgot, or perhaps they never knew, the quiet power of Thomas Cromwell. The only thing that gives me any pleasure this summer is watching their realisation dawn, like a pearly summer morning when the birds are loud at four o'clock and the sun is hot by eight, that Thomas Cromwell is a great power, and – now that Anne is gone – there is no power to rival him.

The Spanish party are welcome at court and showered with honours, but they do not take control of government. They pray fervently with the king in the chapel night and morning, but he still signs his name during mass to the orders of examination of one religious house after another and levies great fines on the church. Thomas Cromwell puts the papers before him, and takes them away to execute. The Spanish party speak fondly of Lady Mary and the king smiles and nods, but she will not be excused the oath: she has to swear that she is a bastard if she wants to come to court.

The reform queen is dead; but reform still goes on. How can this be? Thomas Cromwell is a greater threat to them and to their faith than Anne ever was. Thomas Cromwell, the quiet commoner, is more than a mere clerk doing the king's will. Slowly, they understand that they have done Cromwell a great favour by destroying his only rival. Now, there is no advisor to the king but him. He keeps his place at the king's ear; his wooden chest holds the royal orders that he translates into laws. It is his administration that enforces them.

The Seymour brothers can bob about, babbling suggestions, but they don't have royal business at their fingertips like Cromwell. The Pole family are of the old royal house, and Sir Geoffrey Pole can tell everyone that he knows great secrets; but they have no network of foreign agents and spies.

The king comes to Jane Seymour's bed every night and passes me in the queen's bedroom with a warm smile and familiar greeting for a beloved friend, his eyes on the big golden bed and the fair head in the prim white nightcap where Anne used to be lazily smiling. Being shamed as a cuckold has cheered him; being publicly named as impotent has stimulated his ardour. A new wife with absolutely no allure has achieved what the most desirable woman in England could not do: incite his lust. Jane's pallid lack of enthusiasm reassures him that bedding her is holy work without sin – clearly without pleasure for her. The mockery of his poetry inspires him to write – he has completed a three-act tragedy based on the events of his life, and he reads it to anyone who he thinks learned enough to understand it. To me: he reads it to me.

I freeze my face into an expression of polite interest as he goes on and on, through three acts of clanking pentameters about his seduction with French practices and sortilèges, his betrayal by a witch-wife with hundreds of men, and the final act of his righteous wrath when he strikes her head from her body as you would behead a serpent. Surely, the king must be mad to read a play about a man's incest with his sister and their bloody execution to the man's widow?

'You are the only one who understands what I have been through, Jane,' he says to me, his voice choked with tears.

'I share your grief,' I say.

He takes my hand and kisses it.

The king is the only one to speak of Anne and George; but he makes up for everyone else's silence, for he speaks of them all the time, as terrible events in his distant past, a time near the creation of the world – the Fall, and Anne and George as a mythological monster like a double-headed serpent. No one else speaks of the absent six at all.

We call Jane 'Queen' from the day she is proclaimed, a little more than two weeks after the swordsman took off Anne's head. Nobody remarks that Anne's beautiful gowns must be cut down to fit Jane's bony frame. Nobody says that Jane's English hood is like a nun's wimple; she looks like the king's grandmother. Nobody asks why the queen's ladies are now famous for modesty when – only two weeks ago – we were famous for wit? Nobody remembers that last summer, the royal progress went to Jane's home, the Seymour home, Wulfhall, and it was a little house, badly placed, not big enough to house the court. The drains overflowed, and her family were an embarrassment – how can a young woman from there now sit on the throne of England?

I remember us Boleyns as a unified three: a *troika*, going like the wind, inseparable all day, and every night I slept with either one or the other of them. Now, I am a third of the being that I once was. Now I am alone, the only point left from an erased triangle.

I cannot see how to be myself, for I don't know what I am, now that I am not beside George or one step behind Anne.

The lords of the inquiry hold a great dinner at Greenwich to celebrate their work, before they disperse to their country houses. I find my father in a guest room, ready to leave. 'I can't live without them,' I say simply. 'I can't live here without them.'

'You've no choice in the matter,' he says irritably. 'If you leave now, we'll never get you back to court again. And, without your salary as a lady-in-waiting, you'll have no money. George has left a heap of debts; the king has confiscated all his goods as a traitor, and the Boleyns aren't going to be generous with your jointure – not to a childless widow to a traitor son. You have no expectations, Jane. You'd have to marry again, and who would have you, looking at what you did to your last husband?'

'I didn't give evidence against him,' I say wearily. 'You were judge on the inquiry; you, of all people, know that.'

'Well, you didn't try to save him, as Francis Weston's wife tried to save him.'

'You told me not to!'

'Yes,' he says. 'That's true. But anyway, you can't come home; you'll have to stay at court.'

'I don't mean that I can't live at court without them. I mean that I can't live without them at all! I mean that I cannot be myself without them! I am a third of a person without them. I am two-thirds dead!'

For a moment, he looks interested. 'Are you really? Do you imagine yourself two-thirds gone? How do you imagine your absence?'

I think for a moment. 'No,' I say. 'You're right. I can't imagine my absence, but I do feel a void. But, Father, I didn't mean philosophy. I just mean I am in despair. Such despair.'

'Despair at court is an appropriate emotion,' he tells me. 'The courtier's disease is despair.'

'I want to go to Beaulieu! I want to live as a widow.'

'It's been returned to the king.'

I look at him blankly. 'But it is ours for life.'

'George's life is over.'

'Mine isn't!'

'I thought you said it was? So, we make progress. Your husband is dead, your sister-in-law is dead, but your life continues, *ergo* you will live, *ergo* you have to live somewhere, *ergo* you will stay at court. Agreed?'

'Father, this is logic – but it brings me no comfort.'

'Logic should always comfort a scholar. Now, I have asked Master Cromwell – y'know he's to be Lord Cromwell? His reward for this solution to the paradox of how a man divorces a woman who is not his wife – anyway, I have asked him to consider your widow's pension from the Boleyns, and he has promised they will make a fair settlement on you. You are fortunate in your patron. No man but Cromwell could have survived the dislike of the queen, the rivalry of the Howards, and the enmity of the old royals and the Spanish party. But he turned them on each other. And now, they will destroy themselves.'

This is more comfort than logic. 'How will they destroy themselves?'

'You know that Lady Margaret Pole's son Reginald has been working for years on his book of theology, commissioned by the king? To bring together the reformers and the traditionalists in the Church? Well, he's finished it. And it's not at all what the king commissioned. By all accounts, it denies the king's divorce of the first queen, his reform of the Church, it says he has no right to the Church lands in England. It destroys the king's case from the bedroom to the treasure house. Reginald Pole has shown it to the pope. The pope has adopted it as his own creed and will issue a bull of excommunication against the king.'

I look at my father in complete horror. A man excommunicated from the Church cannot take mass, cannot enter a church. Every good Christian is obliged to disobey him or arrest him, and if he is an excommunicate king, it is a holy duty for all the faithful to make holy war on his country. The French and Spanish kings will be ordered on a new crusade, against a new infidel – against England. It is a declaration of war from Christendom on Henry's England.

I am stunned. 'My God! How could he? Has he got his mother away to Rome? He cannot have done this with his mother at court! Has Lady Margaret Pole gone, and all her family with her?'

My father looks as if he could laugh. 'He lives for the truth, not for courtier truth. He's not published. He's sent a private copy to the king; he's asked that someone read it to him. He wants to discuss it.'

I could laugh at this unworldly scholarship if I did not know how dangerous it is to try to teach the king anything. 'Not you?' I demand. 'You won't be the reader!'

'Not I! I saw only one chapter, and that was incendiary. I wouldn't read it to the king for a fortune. I've no interest in arousing royal rage on my own account, and none on turning it on the Courtenays and the Poles, the kinsmen of Reginald Pole.'

'Thomas Cromwell will not be so considerate. He'll use it to destroy them.'

He nods. 'I expect so. You'll see Anne and George avenged. The Courtenays and the Poles will be suspected traitors, constantly watched, and poor Lady Mary will be left without friends, without a party to support her.'

My father pauses for a moment. 'It's ironic that it will be the flower of the family, the king's scholar, Reginald Pole, a royal heir, a Plantagenet prince and scholar, who brings them down. How true it is, as Machiavelli would say: a friend is more dangerous than an enemy!'

## ON PROGRESS, SUMMER

### 1536

IT IS CLEAR to the Spanish party that they have not yet won Lady Mary's return as princess, and when Henry Fitzroy, the king's bastard son, the Duke of Richmond, opens the parliament at Westminster, they realise they have not even put her into first place in her father's erratic affections. Fitzroy is proud as a prince. The whole ceremony is designed to honour him. He walks before his royal father, seventeen years old, carrying the cap of estate. Parliament, instructed by my spymaster, invites the king to nominate his own heir – an extraordinary idea, nodded through lords and commons as if it were not the destruction of the rights of Englishmen.

In this one move, the monarchy of England, always hereditary and always confirmed by parliament, has become a Caesarship, the property of Henry Tudor, to be left by him like his goods, like a tapestry, like a barge, to his chosen heir. The long public discussion between God and Henry Tudor, if his marriage (first or second or third) is to be blessed with an heir, has been abruptly resolved by Henry simply taking it out of God's hands. God is to have no say in it. Henry Tudor will decide if he is blessed with an heir, and who it shall be. He can nominate a true-born princess, Lady Mary, or he can nominate the girl he has named as his bastard, our Lady Elizabeth. Or he can nominate a true-born bastard: Henry Fitzroy. Neither their mothers, nor God, have anything to do with their claim to the throne. Our king has become a Fallen Angel; he sets up his will against God.

I meet with Cromwell – now Lord Cromwell – in the rose garden at Greenwich, and I say: 'I think I am going mad, Master Cromwell. I think I am going mad.'

And he says, very soothingly: 'Lord Cromwell. It is Lord Cromwell now. It is a new reign, and I have a new title.'

'It's not a new reign,' I protest. 'It is the same king but now immeasurably greater, a king so mighty that he needs a succession of queens. I am serving a third queen – the third in four years! And everyone acts as if it were normal. And now he does not need to conceive a son with her anyway! He can just name one! So what's it all for? I think I am going mad!'

'There's no need for you to go mad,' he says soothingly. 'You are accused of nothing.'

'What?'

'A madman cannot be executed,' he says, smiling. 'Nor can a madwoman. But since you are accused of nothing, there's no need for you to be mad, my dear Lady Rochford. You don't need that refuge.'

'I'm not pretending!' I exclaim. 'I feel mad! – or as if I am the only sane person in a mad world?'

He nods sympathetically. 'Oh yes,' he says. 'Now I know what you mean. Yes, I feel that, too.'

For a moment, our eyes meet: his, blackcurrant and implacable; mine, grey and blinded with tears.

'You're alive, aren't you?' he asks gently. 'Alive when they're not? You're still in play, aren't you? In the game that they lost? You see and speak, though they are still and cold and see nothing and hear nothing?'

'Not even buried with honour!' I gasp. 'Not even in the family vault. I won't lie with my husband in death!'

'Unless you're executed for treason and buried in the Tower chapel!' he says with a weak attempt at humour. 'Then you could end up side by side. It could be easily arranged?'

'I miss them. I miss them, Lord Cromwell.'

'Ah – I miss them, too,' he says, surprising me with the emotion in his voice. 'And that brave old fool Bishop Fisher, and Sir Thomas More – God knows what we lost when we silenced him – and the monasteries, and the nunneries, and the houses and the art and the beauty and the choirs. I miss them all. I remember Queen Katherine when I first saw her; I was a rough young fool, and she was a beautiful princess, and everyone thought that it was a new reign and a new king and new queen and a new dawn for England.

'It's not without cost for me – don't think that it doesn't cost me, too. I can see where it's going; but I can't see where it'll end. One decision leads to another and then another, and then a host of them have to run after. I believe I'm serving God, and I know I'm serving my king, and I know I'm surviving – but for sure it's not without cost.'

'You make it sound like a *via ad insanium*,' I say bleakly. For a moment, we look at each other like people in the middle of a wasteland that we have made ourselves: as if we inherited a rich green forest and burned it to blackened stumps and twigs of smutty charcoal.

Cromwell lifts my hand comfortably into the crook of his elbow and leads me towards the courtyard. 'Assure me that you're not out of your wits,' he says gently. 'Because I want you to think about Mary Howard.'

His question, as much as the warmth of his touch, restores me to my courtier-self. 'Thomas Howard's daughter? My cousin? Why?'

'If the king names his own heir, he seems certain to choose Henry Fitzroy? His beloved bastard son? And Fitzroy is wedded for three long years; but has still not bedded Mary Howard. Her father must be at the end of his tether? Mary Howard married to the lad who'll be the next king of England, and yet the marriage not confirmed by bedding?'

I smile at my patron's obvious pleasure. 'My uncle has said nothing to me – does he press the king?'

'Doesn't dare. Would he put them to bed and risk it?'

'Never.' I shake my head. 'She wouldn't do it. She wouldn't trust her father; none of his family will ever trust the duke again . . .' I break off. '. . . after all . . . after that.'

Cromwell makes a little side-to-side nod as clothiers make, haggling over the value of a kersey. 'All that. Well, I'm not going to bless the wedding bed. Henry Fitzroy ought to marry a foreign princess. Where's the gain in ridding the king of Anne, to put another Howard girl on the throne?'

'Actually, Mary Howard would make a good queen,' I point out. 'And she's in favour of reform.'

'But her father . . .' is all my lord says, with a shrug. 'I'd rather have a well-trained German princess, even a Lutheran, than another Howard girl. No offence.'

'None taken.'

'If you hear any Howard plans, let me know,' he says, so casually that I know it is important. 'If her father commands her home, if he throws her together with Fitzroy – anything like that. I count on you, my dear Lady Rochford. And I will reward you. I am aware – well aware – that the Boleyns will never pay your jointure, they will never take care of your debts. I am working on that, you can trust me.'

He shakes his head to forestall my questions. 'And now,' he says politely, 'are you ready for progress? The queen knows that we don't sail to Calais? We're just going to Dover?'

It is part of the everyday madness that the May Day progress delayed to entrap and kill the queen, will now take place with her replacement – just as it was before: the same route and stops along the way to Dover, the same horses and clothes and attendants.

'I am ready . . .' I say – but I am not ready. I think I will never be ready to take my place behind Anne's red embroidered gown and lift Anne's heavy red embroidered train and walk behind Jane Seymour, who minces, hesitantly where Anne strode.

Lord Cromwell bows to me and goes back to the house, and I go to the courtyard, where the ladies-in-waiting are mounting their horses and fussing about whether it will rain. Jane will not ride, not even her steady horse – God forbid that she should fall! She sits in Anne's litter, drawn by the white mules that George brought back from France. She looks very small and pale among the rich cushions, and I tuck Anne's sables around her; she feels the cold as much as Queen Katherine. Now both Katherine and Anne are forever cold, and Jane is in their sables. This is the new play and the new actors. I mount my own horse, my Norfolk roan, well accustomed to riding beside Anne's litter, but he sidles sideways and turns his head to look at the billowing curtains, as if he knows that the wrong woman is inside.

The king heaves himself into his saddle and gives the signal; the noblemen follow him through the great stone gateway. Sir Geoffrey Pole rides in the front, the young man's face bright with self-importance.

I am about to move off, when I notice that Lady Margaret Douglas, the king's niece, is not where she should be, immediately behind the queen's litter. Her expensive high-bred horse is still waiting by the mounting block – there is no sign of her. Even the daughter of the Queen of Scotland, half-sister to the King of Scotland

and niece to our king, should not delay Jane, who, though only a Seymour, is queen.

Irritably, I throw the reins to my groom, dismount and make my way up the stone steps to the door to the queen's rooms, when my uncle the Duke of Norfolk strolls out. 'What's the delay?'

'Lady Margaret Douglas,'

'Not coming.' He bares his yellowing teeth in a joyless smile. 'You can set off without her. No need to make a fuss.'

'Not coming?' I ask. 'Is she ill?'

'No . . . no . . .' he starts. He glances around furtively. 'She's being questioned. No need to tell the queen and the other ladies. It'll all blow over – it's courtly love. Nothing but courtly love. No need to cause a scandal for nothing.'

'I've caused no scandal,' I say instantly, to the man who sent his niece to the scaffold for scandal. I drop my voice. 'But why is she being questioned?'

'Hush, hush,' he says. 'No need to bring it to the attention of the queen. Will she notice that Margaret is missing?'

Jane Seymour is so new to her part as queen that she has no idea who should be waiting on her and who is absent.

'One of the ladies will tell her. I can divert her if I know what Lady Margaret has done?'

He makes a grimace as if he is chewing on a lemon. 'Margaret's done nothing – it's another attack on me, on our house. The Spanish party accuse my half-brother Thom of flirting with Lady Margaret.'

'Have they told the king?'

'It'll blow over,' he says certainly. 'Lady Margaret'll be in disgrace for a few days. I'll take young Thom home. Keep it quiet.'

I turn back to the stable-yard and smile at the queen and say: 'No need to wait for Lady Margaret. My uncle says she's delayed on the king's business.'

Jane peeps up from the sables in the litter and asks stupidly: 'But what business can have delayed her? What business does she do?'

Jane is easy to silence. I lean down and I whisper against her jewel-encrusted hood: 'She's in trouble for loving young Lord Thom Howard. Didn't you know?'

Jane goes as white as the curtains of the litter. 'I don't know anything!' she peeps.

I nod. 'That's what we'll all say. We'll say that we didn't know anything, and nothing happened anyway.'

She looks sick with fear. 'My brother . . .' she says, looking round for help.

'Let's keep this to ourselves, to us ladies,' I advise. 'Let's say that you know nothing. Everyone will believe that, after all!'

'But, Lady Rochford, I really do know nothing!'

'I know,' I say reassuringly. I prompt her to raise her hand, and the muleteers start, and the rest of us follow her litter on horseback, and we leave the Duke of Norfolk on the steps, waving us out of sight as if he hadn't a care in the world.

The first night of the progress we stop at Cobham Hall – showing royal favour to Anne, Lady Cobham. Nobody asks what she did in May that is rewarded by this royal visit in July. She is at the door of the great hall with her husband to welcome the king and Jane. I wonder if Jane remembers that Lady Cobham curtseyed as low to Queen Anne, and kissed her with just as much affection, and if Jane knows that she offered evidence that took Anne to the scaffold? I doubt Jane minds either way. Since she was dancing with Anne's widower at the very moment that Anne died – why should she balk at her betrayer?

Jane waits politely to hear the speech of welcome from the Cobham herald, but the king hurries into the house, with Lord Cobham scuttling after him to show him his bedroom. His leg will be aching from a long day in the saddle, and he will need to piss and eat sweetmeats.

The next day, the court is ready to go hunting, but the king says his horse is overtired and blames his groom for not keeping it in good heart. The groom bows a contrite head and begs pardon.

Will Somer the fool says that he is too tired to go another step and demands that the groom to carry him to his bed and mount him for a gallop in the morning, and the king roars with laughter, his good mood restored. I see Jane look inquiringly from her husband to the fool – either she does not understand the pun of 'mounting', or else she has decided – with the *non exemplar* of Anne before her – to hang on to her virgin innocence.

We take a rest day, and the day after, the king complains that now his horse is too fresh and ill mannered. We all know from this that he is still tired and probably in pain; but he cheers up as his horse goes steadily down Watling Street, the broad pilgrim road from London to the shrine of Thomas Becket at Canterbury. The king waves to groups of pilgrims lining either side of the road as the heralds blast on their trumpets and shout: 'Make way for the king!'

But something has soured in England this summer, like cream left out in sunshine. People still push back their hoods or pull off their caps as the court passes by; but there are no smiling faces turned towards us. Everyone making a pilgrimage from one religious house to another knows that the convents and monasteries are being inspected. Everyone knows that they are mostly well-run, and devout; but wrongly accused of being corrupt or wasteful or ill disciplined. They are harshly fined for imaginary misdeeds and sometimes even closed down, their treasures taken away, and their great lands given to court favourites.

And then what will happen to the hospital? To the library? To the school? To the church where people have prayed for hundreds of years? Will Saint Thomas Becket's own shrine be one day taken by the king and its rich treasures sucked into his treasury? Will his sacred body be kidnapped and slung into a storeroom with all the other relics, even though everyone has seen and heard of miracles they have done? An assault on Thomas Becket's body would be a second martyrdom by a second King Henry – and everyone fears that this Henry may have even worse advisors than the other, for these have killed not one turbulent priest but a bishop of Rochester,

Sir Thomas More, another priest, four monks, a queen and even the whore who took her place and half a dozen men accused with her.

The king sets his shoulders square, and his little mouth pouts beneath his moustache. He orders the heralds to push people back – right off the highway, into the ditches and hedges. By the time we get to the Lyon Inn at Sittingbourne, we are all as quiet as Jane, who sits like a little doll behind her curtains of white silk and leans forward to draw them tightly closed when she hears someone shout defiantly: 'God bless Bishop Fisher!'

We are dismounting in the inn yard, and the gates are closing on the staring crowd outside, when there is a shout from the high road and a band of exhausted riders wearing the livery of Henry Fitzroy rattles in.

Thomas Cromwell, who rides ahead of the court to ensure the king's reception, is out of the inn to meet them before the lead rider has even dismounted, and he rushes Fitzroy's herald into the great hall to speak to the king in private.

Jane, climbing slowly from her litter, asks me: 'Who was that? They were in such a hurry?' and when I tell her, she says: 'Oh, what should I do?'

I gesture that she should go forward to stand beside the king, to receive whatever news Fitzroy has sent with such urgency, and I take her gloves and follow behind, feeling that I am pushing an unwilling broodmare into a pen. But she is so slow that Cromwell has already closed the door on the king's private room.

Jane looks from the panels of the closed door to me, and I whisper: 'Better wait.'

We stand awkwardly before the door, everyone watching us, and then I hear a great bellow from inside, as if the king has been gored by a bull or stabbed to the heart. I nearly run in I am so sure he has been attacked, and I hear him shout: 'No! No! No!'

Thomas Seymour barrels his way through the shocked courtiers to get to his sister. 'You've got to go in,' he says urgently. 'I think Henry Fitzroy is dead. I think they've just told him.'

'Oh no!' she says. 'Oh why? Poor boy! But – oh no, Thomas, I can't go in there . . .'

Even in my shock, I could laugh at this new brother pushing this queen towards the door, and this one – so unlike her predecessor – refusing to seize her chance.

The door is suddenly thrown open before us, and the messenger and Thomas Cromwell stride out. For a moment, before the door is slammed shut and the guard takes up arms before it, I can see inside: the king on his hands and knees on the rush-strewn floor, bellowing like a stag brought down by a spear. He looks wounded beyond recovery, his big mouth gaping wide with screams of pain. It is like a death, a moment of shocking intimacy.

Jane clings to me. 'I'm not going in there,' she tells her brother.

Only one person, Lady Margaret Pole, born royal, the king's cousin, has the courage to intervene. She says a quick word to her sons, Henry and Geoffrey, and takes Jane by the hand. 'We'll both go in to him,' she says firmly.

The guard lifts his halberd for her as for a royal princess, and she leads Jane inwards. The door closes behind them, and Thomas Cromwell is at my side. 'Send the ladies to their rooms, dinner will be served late,' he tells me. 'Henry Fitzroy is dead – a short illness. The king will dine alone in his privy chamber.'

From behind the door, we hear agonised sobbing. 'Fitzroy! My heir! How could God do this to me? How can God turn against me? Why would God punish me? This must be women's sin? Women's sin! Cursed be the woman that did this!'

We stay at the Lyon for three days; the king keeps to his private rooms. We don't see him. We don't even hear him after that first night of screaming. Jane, legless with fear, comes out of the room clinging to Margaret Pole and the king locks the door behind them. He only admits servants with trays heaped with food: unbelievable amounts of food, enough for half a dozen men, as if he is choking down sobs with manchet bread and butter.

Everything is ended: his secret triumph that he had a strong son, ready and waiting to be named as heir. His pushing the new law through an obedient parliament. Even the Howard plan to put Mary Howard into the royal line is valueless: her husband, Henry Fitzroy, is dead; and all the plans are for nothing. The king has no heir but girls: Lady Mary a named bastard, Lady Elizabeth another one, and Lady Margaret Douglas, a legitimate half-Tudor niece, has disappeared and nobody even knows where she is.

'In the Tower,' Thomas Cromwell tells me by the way, as if it is of little interest. 'Arrested for marrying young Lord Thom Howard without permission.'

I have to school myself to keep my face perfectly still. 'I thought my kinsman, Lord Thom, was going home to Kenninghall?'

'I'd drop the connection if I were you,' Lord Cromwell advises me. 'He's in the Tower, for seducing an heir to the throne. His baby face won't save him. Courtly love has become treason.'

I find my hands are trembling, and I put them behind my back. 'A secret marriage is not treason . . .'

'It's against the law.'

'No, it isn't . . .' I know it is not.

'A new law, not yet passed. A new law that will say that the royal family can only marry with the king's permission. If Lord Thom and Lady Margaret married in secret then they have broken that law.'

'But it was not written when they married . . .'

Blandly, he nods.

'This is not justice,' I say, thinking of the last time that I said that something was unjust. Then it was the king's warhorse, beheaded for treason. Since then, he has beheaded his wife and my husband. Will he behead his niece as well? Will I say nothing for a niece – just as I said nothing for his wife or his warhorse? Just as I said nothing for my husband?

'The king is the law,' Cromwell reminds me. 'He cannot be unjust.'

'*Rex non potest peccare?*' I quote. 'The king cannot be wrong?'

Cromwell smiles. 'Quite so.'

Sir William Paulet, the comptroller of the new queen's household, comes up to his patron, Lord Cromwell, to ask him for orders.

'Are we staying here another day, my lord?'

Cromwell nods. 'Another day, I think.'

'I'll have to order mourning clothes for the queen and her ladies from the royal wardrobe in London,' I say to Sir William.

Lord Cromwell shakes his head. 'No mourning.'

'When we get back to Greenwich? For the funeral?'

'No funeral.'

'No funeral for the king's own son?' I ask disbelievingly.

'Dead,' Cromwell mutters in my ear. 'So nothing to do with the king after all.'

'The king has ordered the Duke of Norfolk to organise the burial of the body in his family chapel at Thetford Priory,' Sir William says, as if this is completely normal.

'Thomas Howard is to bury the king's son?' I ask incredulously.

'He is his father-in-law,' Sir William reminds me pompously. 'Henry Fitzroy will be buried by his father-in-law, in his family vault.'

Thomas Cromwell and I silently enjoy the irony that my uncle, who so longed for Henry Fitzroy in his short life, now has him in death. The dead youth is all Howard and no Tudor. The king has sworn he will have no more dead sons, so his beloved boy has not died but vanished, like a seraph in a miracle play. It is as if he never was, and the court has another ghost that we will never mention.

THE KING EMERGES from his rooms without a word about his vigil of gorging, and we resume our journey to Dover, as if nothing has happened at all. Jane hardly dares to look at him; she was so frightened by the roaring and then the solitary feasting. When she has to stand at the king's side, for the presentations at Dover, I have to prop her up from behind; she floats away from him unless she is anchored.

Lord Lisle and his wife Honor have sailed across the Narrow Seas from their fortress at Calais to greet the king and his new queen and hide their delight that his heir is dead. Not even the king's sullen greeting overshadows the splendour of their rising sun. They are of the Plantagenet family, old royal blood and the traditional religion, they loved the old queen and pray for her daughter Lady Mary. After the banquet – where the king crams food into his mouth as if gorging on despair – they slip away to the Pole rooms to celebrate the triumph of their family over the Boleyns. Everything is going their way: Anne Boleyn the reform queen disgraced and dead, Henry Fitzroy the Protestant heir, dead, too, Elizabeth is declared bastard, so their darling, Lady Mary, is the only possible royal heir and who could be a better husband for her, and king consort for England, than the favoured son of the old royal family: Reginald Pole himself? The red rose of Tudor Lancaster and the white rose of Plantagenet York will unite to bring lasting peace, and the young royal couple will return England to the Church of Rome. Sir Geoffrey Pole – hopelessly indiscreet – is radiantly happy and all the way home from Dover to London, the Poles and the Courtenays ride with shining faces, as if they have been called to greatness.

Lord Cromwell drops back from the king's side to bring his big cob beside my pretty roan.

'Looks as if they didn't overreach after all – they have greatness in their grasp,' I remark to him.

'They've been lucky,' he says grudgingly. 'They killed Anne the Protestant queen, but God Himself took Fitzroy, the Protestant heir. Now, they think they've won – they've got the only heir left standing.'

'It is an *annuntiatio*,' I say sourly. 'And Sir Geoffrey Pole as the Virgin Mary.'

I smile at his snort of laughter.

## WESTMINSTER PALACE, SUMMER

## 1536

But the king surprises us. As soon as we arrive at Westminster he forces Lady Mary to take the oath, and the young woman, very far from triumph, has to deny her mother's marriage and declare herself illegitimate. The king's wound has opened up on his leg again, he can barely walk, and there is no heir to the throne. Lady Mary declares herself illegitimate; Lady Elizabeth is illegitimate and too young; Lady Margaret Douglas his niece is still in disgrace in the Tower.

'Whatever has she done?' Jane whispers, beckoning me closer.

'She married young Thom Howard, half-brother to the Duke of Norfolk. Thom is arrested and is being questioned, too.'

She goes even paler. 'We know nothing,' she whispers her lesson.

'Quite right. And anyway, this all happened . . .' I trail off. Anne and her reign, and even Queen Katherine and her reign, are never mentioned in Jane's court, which has no knowledge of anything, especially history.

'But they'll blame me,' Jane predicts dolefully. 'My brother Edward and his wife Anne will blame me. They'll all blame me, though I know nothing.'

She is right. The Seymours blame her for Margaret Douglas' deception, but it is worse for the Howards: the king accuses them of creeping into the line of succession for the third time. First, there was Anne Boleyn with sortilèges then there was Mary Howard with a marriage contract, now there is Lord Thom Howard with a secret marriage. What is this, if not a conspiracy of Howards?

To cheer the king, Thomas Cromwell suggests a legal device, to speed up executions – a 'writ of attainder'. Now the king can demand an execution without trial, and no one can appeal against sentence of death. Thom Howard is not accused nor tried nor defended; the king declares him guilty, and parliament slavishly agrees that he must die.

I pass Lord Cromwell on the winding stair. 'Are we madder than ever?' I ask.

'Lady Margaret Douglas had better be mad, for nothing else will save her,' is all he says, and he goes on down the winding steps to the dark river below.

## WESTMINSTER PALACE, AUTUMN

### 1536

THE SOUR MOOD of the pilgrims on the road to Canterbury rumbles through the country like a late summer storm. All the lords report that the workers on their lands and the tenants on their farms are surly, saying that the church, their own parish church, their mother church is under attack. They have given their halfpennies and farthings to the church for feast days and candles for centuries and won't allow their treasures to be stolen and their windows smashed out. Each village demands that its own abbey or monastery or convent is spared, whatever happens a country mile away.

Even the poorest people hear of the king's excommunication and there are terrifying rumours that the pope is going to move against the king in a crusade, and Reginald Pole will lead a holy army to invade and restore England to the true faith. At court the Poles, especially Lady Margaret's youngest son Sir Geoffrey, are ostentatiously loyal. They are never seen together, never even speaking to each other, so I am certain they are organising and the tenants on their vast lands – almost the whole of the west of England – are ready to rise in rebellion the moment that their favoured son, Reginald, lands at the head of a crusade. Lord Cromwell brings the two princesses, Mary and Elizabeth, to join us behind the walls of Westminster Palace and musters men and goods and weapons ready for a siege of London.

Lady Mary stalks into the queen's rooms, wearing royal purple, and curtseys to Jane Seymour. The angle of her head under the jewelled hood is exactly right for a blood-royal princess to a queen by marriage. Jane, who wisely persists in knowing nothing, jumps up from her throne and kisses her stepdaughter, and Lady Margaret Pole, who escorted her *protégé* back to her place at court, steps back and smiles at me. The victory of getting Lady Mary to an honoured place at court has been accomplished almost unnoticed – the luck is running with the Spanish party again.

I go to the royal nursery to greet my niece Lady Elizabeth and find an imperious little girl who hides her fear at the strange surroundings by demanding one thing after another from her harassed governess. She is instantly recognisable as Anne's daughter, though she has the king's colouring. The look she throws me under sandy eyelashes is as swift and calculating as Anne. Already, aged only three, she knows to hide her emotion; the chubby cheeks of babyhood are her mask.

I take her hand. 'I think you're going to be the greatest courtier of all.'

'I'm not,' she disagrees instantly. 'I was Princess Elizabeth, but now it is Lady Elizabeth.' She has the slightest infant lisp, but there is nothing childish in her dignity.

'I am Lady Rochford,' I tell her. 'I am your aunt.'

'Tudor?' she asks keenly.

'Boleyn,' I say.

She turns away – the tilt of her little copper head is in an exact copy of Anne's disdain.

'Good day, Lady Elizabeth,' I say.

THE KING'S DAUGHTERS take refuge behind the great walls of Westminster Palace, safe inside the walled City of London, because the men and women of Lincoln and then Yorkshire and then, one after another, all the great counties of the north, declare they will not have their faith destroyed and their beautiful churches emptied of treasure. Every day, news comes in – from one lord or another – of rebels who call themselves pilgrims, marching under banners that show the five wounds of Christ. It is the old crusader banner: a call to all faithful; no Christian will raise a sword against them.

Of course, my uncle the Duke of Norfolk is immediately forgiven any offence. Nothing matters when the king needs a reliable killer. He is ordered to raise his army and go to Yorkshire. He rides out, ready to kill a couple of hundred peasants armed with staves; but finds himself surrounded by fifty thousand men, led by mounted armed gentry, determined that the houses of religion founded by their forefathers and serving their people, shall not be slandered by Cromwell's inspectors and swallowed by the king's treasury.

My uncle, outnumbered five to one, takes in his desperate situation and pledges his empty honour to be their friend. He swears to the rebels that the king only needs to know their grievances to set everything right. All these changes – heretical changes – are the fault of the king's wicked advisor, Lord Cromwell.

Thomas Howard kills two birds with one stone: buying time against the rebels and turning them against his greatest rival – Cromwell. He guarantees that the king will reopen closed monasteries, repay all the stolen treasure, and reunite with the pope. He offers a free and complete pardon to every man, praises them for doing God's work in protecting the Church against the infidel Cromwell. My uncle is St Paul – he has seen the light. I imagine him gritting his teeth as he smiles at them and sends panic-stricken messages demanding help to the frightened court at Westminster.

'Pardon them!' Jane drops to her knees in a flurry of pale silk and lifts her earnest face, framed in the ugly square hood. 'Mercy!'

There is a stunned silence in the privy chamber. It could not be more awkward. Lord Cromwell pauses in the middle of reading aloud a grovelling letter from the Duke of Norfolk listing the endless reforms he has had to promise in order to save the king's army from being butchered.

Nobody is talking about a real pardon. Nobody would ever talk about a real pardon, only Jane would think that it could be a real pardon.

I glance around for help in getting Jane out of the way of the royal temper. Nobody responds. Lady Mary, the pilgrims' princess, is too wise to make any move forward or back. She folds her hands in her sleeves like a nun and looks down at Jane, kneeling at the king's feet.

'Pardon them? Pardon them?' The king repeats Jane's words in a mocking falsetto voice. 'Madam, you would do better to get an heir to the throne than advise me to throw it down.'

It is a shocking insult to a new wife in honeymoon days. I glance over at Cromwell and see that he will make no move to rescue Jane, who is now frozen on her knees, condemned as a fool before the entire court, and a barren fool at that. Jane's brothers coached her to do this queenly ritual; but they could not have been more mistaken. This is not Katherine of Aragon asking pardon for a dozen rowdy apprentices, condemned to death and snivelling. These are powerful rebels with the Spanish party, the Church, the old royal family and most of the lords of the north on their side. They speak with one coherent voice – the king does not want to hear them. They are calling for the death of Cromwell – he's not going to offer a pardon.

The two men let Jane kneel; it is the fool who saves her.

'Pardon them!' Will squeaks, throwing himself to his knees and putting his hands together in mimicry of the queen. 'Pardon them! And get their leaders to London and execute them when you've got them here! That's what I meant to say. Not pardon them and forgive them and put the abbeys up again. And certainly don't give the lands back. And don't repay the money! Quite the opposite! Take more!'

Jane, completely baffled, turns her head to stare at Will, kneeling beside her, and then the king roars with laughter, and everyone throws back their heads and laughs, too.

I shake my head at the fool's cynicism, and laughing loudly, I step forward and haul Jane to her feet, my hand under her elbow. She is white-faced and near to tears. I give her a little pinch on her inner arm.

'What?' she gasps.

'Laugh,' I order, and she manages a little squawk.

'I'm damned if I don't!' the king bellows. He turns on Cromwell. 'This fool is a better advisor than you! And a better soldier than Thomas Howard!'

'Almost everyone is a better soldier than Thomas Howard,' Cromwell agrees, smiling. 'And if the fool's strategy captures Robert Aske, the rebel leader, then the royal fool will meet the pilgrim's fool!'

The king narrows his eyes into little blue slits. 'Will they trust my word? Will they come to London for talks if I offer them safe passage? Will they halt the rebellion?'

'They're on a pilgrimage,' Lord Cromwell observes. 'They believe in miracles.'

## GREENWICH PALACE, CHRISTMAS

## 1536

WE HOLD CHRISTMAS at Greenwich, and it is the falsest feast I have ever known in many years of fakery. More self-serving than the loveless gift-giving, more calculating than when courtiers had to choose between Queen Katherine's Christmas court and Anne's rival one in Whitehall. Lord Cromwell disappears in apparent disgrace, and the rebel Robert Aske is favoured guest, high in the love of the king. Dazzled with honours and drenched in affection, he swears he will send the rebels – half of England – back to their homes as the king declares a new Jerusalem of holiness.

Robert Aske is a handsome, courteous provincial man – a lawyer and a gentleman. I don't think the court has met such an honest man before. He describes the love that the poorest people have for their religious houses and their determination that the bells for Matins should always ring over the green fields of England. He tells the king that their children are taught at the monastery schools, their sick nursed in the Church hospitals, that pilgrims travel from one religious house to another trusting in the hospitality of the Church to always have a free bed for the night, that the prayers of the chantries save the souls of their mothers and fathers from the pains of hell. He asks the king to be a good father to his people, to consult with parliament – not command them, to be advised by the pope – not defy him.

We are so enchanted by this vision of an England at peace with a beloved king and respected Church that we all fall in love with Robert Aske. Indeed, the only ones who avoid him are those who most agree with him: the old royals, the Spanish party: Poles, Courtenays, the Spanish ambassador. They are never seen talking with their hero, but smile distantly at his friendship with the king. Sir Geoffrey Pole, Lady Margaret's spoiled youngest son, leaves court and spends the season in their great London house rather than say a Latin grace at dinner with Robert Aske the pilgrim.

The king calls Robert Aske his good angel and his saviour – the man who has rescued England from error. Robert Aske does not queue for the begrudging trading of gifts. The king takes a golden chain from his own neck and his own scarlet jacket of velvet from his shoulders and puts them on this new dearest friend. Jane clasps Aske's hands in thanks for his gift of an ancient missal in Latin.

He seeks me out, as the queen's trusted friend, and asks me the names of the people who come and go; he asks me to point out the great landowners. In return, I ask him about the pardon he has won for all the pilgrims. 'Should the Courtenays ask for a pardon, too?'

'Why would they?'

'Didn't Reginald Pole, Margaret Pole's son, promise to lead the pilgrims?'

He shakes his head. 'I know nothing about it,' he assures me. 'I was just in Lincoln and Yorkshire with the humble people who love their religion when they called on me to speak for them. I never knew any of these grand people until I came to court.'

I nod, and smile, and make a note.

ROBERT ASKE TAKES the place of Lord Cromwell as the king's new advisor. He recommends that a special council meets at York, to hear all the grievances of the pilgrims. The king says that the whole court will travel north and Jane will be crowned in the city as a sign of forgiveness and unity. Robert Aske says the church bells will ring out over moorland and river valleys. Monasteries and nunneries will be restored; the king will restore the Roman Catholic Church to England. Lord Cromwell will be exiled as a bad advisor, Reginald Pole will come home to his loving family.

All of this is proclaimed with such certainty by the king and greeted with such joy by court and country that even I start to believe that we are dancing a new masque – *The Renaissance* – and that good times are truly coming. This is the end of Anne's reform, the end of my spymaster, and the end of my spying. I will become a courtier at this new court, of one true faith and one true word. I will be friend to this new advisor, Robert Aske. I will be re-born.

HE IS A man for the season, the highlight of the Christmas feast, like a roasted suckling pig paraded on a trencher of gold with an apple in its dead mouth. The new year sees the handsome young man leave, loaded with gifts and blessings, riding north to take the good news to the pilgrims that they have won, the Church will be restored to them.

But, as he rides out of the Hall Gate to the north, Lord Cromwell rides in at Sovereign's Gate at the south, imperturbable in his dark-black suit, sitting deep in the saddle of his big cob horse, greeting old friends with a smile.

'You just missed Robert Aske,' I tell him.

'I think I will meet him in future,' he says.

He invites me and my father to a new year ritual of gift-giving in his old rooms at court – reclaimed from the Seymours – and now enlarged and redecorated. My father has a treasure for him.

'My translation of Machiavelli's *The Prince*,' he says to Cromwell, who reaches eagerly for the handwritten manuscript, beautifully bound by my father's bookbinder – once a highly regarded crafts-woman in charge of a bindery in her nunnery, now travelling from door to door and working for food.

'I'm very glad of a copy in English,' Cromwell exclaims. 'I shall be glad to see what you've made of it. Does "duplicity" translate, or is it only an Italian concept, d'you think?'

'It is *duplicità*, so an easy translation; but an un-English concept.' My father smiles.

'No duplicity in England?'

'The tool of a courtier,' my father says. 'But a man such as Robert Aske would be a stranger to it.'

'I think he'll learn what it means,' Cromwell remarks.

*The Prince* is a book that advises all rulers on how to gain the power they need to rule. It is far – very far – from the belief of first among equals that was the code of the Plantagenet kings who came before the Tudors. The kings of Margaret Pole's family believed that they ruled with the support of the lords, who ruled in their turn with the consent of the people: power sitting on a sturdy base of love and loyalty, and the founds going deep. But the advice from the Italian philosopher Niccolò Machiavelli is that nothing is given for love: everything is traded for power, and a ruler who wants to command must promise anything and give away the least he can.

'D'you think the scholar is right – that a perfect king is a tyrant?' Cromwell asks my father.

'A perfect king must enjoy perfect power – so, logically, he must be a tyrant,' my father replies.

Cromwell laughs shortly. 'It's better to tyrannise people than have their love?'

'I don't know about love,' my father says. 'It's not easily measured.'

The two men smile in accord. 'And does your pretty daughter put the pursuit of power over the pursuit of love?' Cromwell asks, turning their attention to me.

'I hope no daughter of mine would pursue love,' my father says disdainfully.

Cromwell smiles at me. 'Ah, Jane,' is all he says.

## GREENWICH PALACE, SPRING

# 1537

'IS THE QUEEN merry?' Lord Cromwell asks me, watching her and the king play a quiet game of cards with her brothers. There is not one word of witty talk and no laughter at the table. The king seems discontent as they all frantically discard good cards in order to lose to him. The pile of coins at his elbow grows higher, but since it is money from lands and places that he gave them in the first place, he takes little pleasure in winning it.

'She never complains. She shows us what it is to be a truly womanly queen.'

He raises dark eyebrows. 'You admire her?'

'She seeks no manly power,' I say, as mincingly as a Seymour.

'No studies strain her mind. She takes no interest in theology nor reform, so the king can say anything and she never disagrees. She doesn't advise like a counsellor; she doesn't plot like a courtier. She's all wife: what your friend William Tyndale called an empty vessel.'

Cromwell grunts with laughter behind his black leather gloves. 'That vessel had better fill,' he warns me.

I shrug. 'She does her duty. But you can rest assured there are no sortilèges.'

Jane Seymour has neither power nor influence, nor does she want any. Her few pleas for mercy for individual religious houses are completely ignored by the men who advise the king and make their livings from ransacking the old Church. She is kind to her stepdaughters and keeps Lady Mary at court, but there is little joy in it.

Queen Jane has the royal wardrobe and treasury at her command, but she orders no masques and dances where she could wear rich jewels and fantastic clothes. The king has given up dancing, and no queen of England should ever go hand to hand down a chain of smiling handsome men again. The only time I see her animated is when she plans her coronation at York. For a few brief weeks in January she was elated, and the centre of her brothers' attention – but it turns out to be yet another empty promise. The king used Jane's name to pacify the rebels; now they are quiet and waiting for us to arrive at York, he need do nothing more.

'No sign of a baby?' Thomas Cromwell asks.

'No sign,' I reply.

'Has anyone else taken his eye?' he asks me.

I glance over at the king, who is looking idly round the room. His gaze rests on Margaret Shelton, on Anne Basset – bright girls, witty girls, pert girls. 'Not yet.'

'And what d'you think happens then?'

'Most girls would rather be a mistress than a queen,' I suggest. 'Ambition is out of fashion since Anne Boleyn.'

It is the saving of Jane Seymour that she missed her course in January, and, on my advice, told the king that she was with child when she missed another in late February. I swear, if she had left it until March, he would have declared war on Spain or France, or reformed the Church to Jewry, or married someone else – he was so unspeakably bored.

Under cover of feeding a pregnant queen, none of us fast for Lent. We eat like princes and pile food into her thin frame as if she were laying eggs in a hive of bees. Lady Lisle sends quails from her aviary at Calais; the Poles send salmon from the River Test. Nothing is too good for the wife whose family is famously fertile, whose line runs to men – she has six brothers – three living – who has conceived in her first year of marriage. We carry her around as if we were parading a Madonna statue, and she gets fatter and fatter, with thick ankles; even her toes are swollen.

I believe this baby is truly the miracle that we call him. The king eyes every lady in the room, and his hands wander over their necks, but he beds no one, not even when Easter ends his Lenten piety. I suspect, that though his eyes still twinkle and his fingers paddle, his other parts are sleeping, and this baby is a triumph of will by his father, hand-pumped into a silently humiliated mother. Such a baby, conceived without lust, will be a godly baby in the opinion of his father: he should be born alive, he should survive.

Though unborn, this baby is serving his father already. He is the king's excuse to stay in safe lands all the summer. The king does not want to meet the people of the north as they learn of the depth and breadth of their betrayal. He hides behind Jane and sends my uncle northwards.

That man of faith, Robert Aske, has disbanded the huge rebel army on the word of the king, and then he finds that the Christmas promises were empty air. Thomas Howard the Duke of Norfolk and an army of thousands follow him up the north road handing out meaningless general pardons for everyone, followed by orders of execution.

Robert Aske, who was so happy and handsome at court in the king's red silk jacket, is arrested at York and begs – as a gentleman's privilege – not to be disembowelled before his hanging. My uncle – with the charm for which he is rightly famous – promises that Robert Aske will be spared the insult of hanging. Instead, he bolts him into an iron cage and suspends it from Clifford's Tower, until the handsome young man dies of starvation, dangling over the city that called him a hero, and the crows and buzzards pick his flesh.

Queen Jane's brothers promptly change their tune, and she never says one other word in Robert Aske's defence, nor breathes one whisper for pardon for the thousands of others that Thomas Howard rounds up for the king and hangs at the crossroads of their villages.

The king will not set a foot on northern soil until every rebel is dead. There is no chance of a York coronation for Jane. He does not want to see thin starved faces and hear resentful muttering when he rides by on a horse better-fed and better-housed than his people. He is sure he has conceived a son; and this proves he is blessed by God. They are dying in their hundreds, which proves that they are not. He wants to forget his fear of them, and my uncle reports there is nothing to fear, there is no one left. Satisfied his country is at peace, the king takes short hunting trips, never going far from the bloated queen and her big belly.

Her blessed condition does not make her any more interesting to him, and court is dull, as her ladies are devoted to keeping her quiet, not whipping up excitement around him. He visits us briefly and goes off with his men friends, roaring at their release, while she endures the months of aches and pains and the loneliness very sweetly, with no complaint.

## GREENWICH PALACE, SUMMER

## 1537

I WATCH HER AS I watched the other two queens, waiting for her to double up in pain, clutch at her belly and rush to her bedroom to start the long vigil of bleeding and weeping. But Jane – calm, stoical, and uncomplaining – seems to have a womb that her betters did not. Her baby sits still and calmly in her belly, just as she sits still and calmly wherever we set her down, and her brothers visit with sweetmeats and pastries as if they were stuffing a white goose for pâté.

While she eats and sleeps and smiles – acknowledging our concern, always replying that she feels well but just a little tired – the business of the queen's rooms goes on, and I become more and more important to the smooth running of a court, like a worker bee with a completely idle queen. I order her summer clothes from the wardrobe, and I audit her jewels with Anne Parr. I decide on the payments to charities, and I hear petitions from the poor women who come to the palace seeking justice and favour. I check with her treasurer that we are receiving the correct rents from her royal lands at Midsummer Day, and I make sure that the Court of Augmentations does not forget us when they disburse the profits from the savage fines on monasteries. When they close a rich monastery and give us gold crucifixes and jewel-encrusted church-ware, I send for goldsmiths and get them remade into jewellery. I check that new laws for the parliament do not damage the interests of the queen's lands and rights. I agree with the Archbishop of Canterbury who shall have the queen's patronage in the Church, and I sell her priestly livings to the highest bidder.

On the rare occasions when she makes a public appearance, I am at her side, prompting the part she must play, knowing her lines better than she does. She depends on me as a friend, and I sit with her ladies in her privy chamber or alone with her in the bedroom. God knows, she is not a demanding companion. I study as she dozes; she does not interrupt my thoughts. She rarely sews and never reads; she is content to the idle, saying nothing, with her white hands nesting on her curved belly.

Sometimes, I ask her what she is thinking, and she opens her eyes wide at such a question and says: 'Nothing. I'm thinking of nothing.' She is silent for a moment, and then she says, a little anxiously: 'What should I be thinking of? Is there something I have to do?'

I have to suppress a laugh. 'No, I have taken care of everything.'

Now that I no longer have a husband in the king's service, I have no rooms on the king's side. The Parr family shield is hammered onto the door of my old rooms, and William Parr lives there alone, his wife never comes to court. His mother and his younger sister, Kateryn Parr, stay with him when they visit. Instead, I have a suite of rooms on the queen's side: a bedroom, a tiny chapel for my private prayers, and a small stool room. My maidservant sleeps with the other maids, and the royal servants clean my rooms and make up my fire. The royal grooms care for my horse in the stables. I have sold all George's falcons; they fly to another man's whistle. All our wealth is gone; it is as if we were never man and wife. I thought I would feel ashamed to lose my great house and servants, our new furniture and our treasures; but instead, I feel strangely free. All I have to guard now are my own interests and myself.

Without plotting, without effort, I rise in importance at court as I do the work that others skimp, the work that the queen avoids. I am a woman in my prime; my girlish prettiness has refined into confident beauty. My ambition is satisfied. I am a widow without grief. Nobody ever mentions George or Anne, and they would not recognise what remains of their court. I don't think they would recognise me either. I am not the girl that George married; I am not the wife that he dropped. I have become a great courtier in my own right, the greatest courtier in the queen's rooms.

## HAMPTON COURT, AUTUMN

## 1537

In the autumn, we all go to Hampton Court for Jane to give birth in the newly renovated queen's rooms – beautifully designed by Anne, who made the rooms into a glamorous shell to house a dazzling queen. Jane is overawed by the gold leaf on the wooden carvings, the heraldic beasts, the massive wood shutters, the heavy wood furniture. She looks like a country cousin on a visit and perches uncomfortably on the edge of her throne.

It is a small court – only a few ladies are admitted. There is plague in London, and the king, always terrified of illness, insists that Jane is locked into the empty palace, as he hides from illness at Esher. He does not even say a proper goodbye in his haste to get away.

I have seen two queens miscarry. All through the birth, which lasts a day and a night, I expect something to go wrong; but Jane labours with the trappings of her old-fashioned faith all around her: the unrolled manuscript which she calls the girdle of the Virgin around her straining belly, the communion wafer in a huge crystal monstrance in her sight, holy water on one side of the cradle, blessed wine on the other, holy oil in a jar, a piece of the true cross on her table, some saints' bones enclosed in a crystal, half a dozen things – mostly fakes – and the prayers of a hooded priest muttering through the grille of a closed door. In the early hours of the second morning, she gives birth to a boy.

The messengers in the presence chamber, who kept their horses saddled and ready all night, race to be first with the news to the king, to the lords, to London. I don't need to tell my spymaster; his pigeon master frees his fastest bird from one of the towers at Hampton Court. He will have the news before anyone.

There is a huge service of thanksgiving in St Paul's and in every church in the country, and at once, the machinery of the court grinds into motion. The builders make the last touches to the royal chapel, and the palace fills up with nobles for the christening. The king greets the guests but will not attend the royal christening. He prefers to conform to tradition and stay away than risk being upstaged by a baby.

My father is honoured to walk four-year-old Lady Elizabeth up the aisle of the royal chapel, carrying the vial of oil for anointing her baby half-brother, Edward Seymour, on her other side. Known Papists, and Anne's enemies are honoured with prominent roles. Gertrude Courtenay of the Spanish party carries the precious baby, her husband beside her, Lady Mary is godmother. The final insult to Anne is that the wife of her jailor at the Tower, Lady Kingston, carries Lady Mary's train. The men who gave fatal evidence against Anne – Sir Francis Bryan, Sir Nicholas Carew, and Sir Anthony Browne – are the guardians of the font. Anne's judges: my uncle Thomas Howard, and Charles Brandon, and her confessor Archbishop Cranmer, are godfathers.

The king does not see Jane alone, he will not meet her privately, until she has been churched and emerged from her confinement rooms. Loving husbands break these rules, but the king, equally horrified by illness and female mysteries, keeps his distance. So he does not see Jane's quiet pride when we bring the baby back to her room and tell her that he has been christened Prince Edward for the saint's day of his birth, like a good Roman Catholic baby.

Indeed, the king never sees Jane again, as she dies of a fever a little more than a week later. He is not missed – Jane would have been horrified by a deathbed visit, and how could we have welcomed and flirted with him, when we were distracted by her dying? Without him, she makes a good death – better than her two predecessors: in comfort, fully shriven, drenched in the oil of extreme unction, revelling in the only moment of triumph of her entire selfless life.

## BOLEYN TRAITOR

## GREENWICH PALACE, WINTER

### 1537

THE KING DECLARES that he will never marry again, that he has lost the love of his life. The part of heartbroken widower is new to him, though this is his third dead wife, and he takes to it as his greatest role. He orders her buried at Windsor and swears that he will lie beside her; they must enter heaven together. He likes her far better dead than he ever did alive. Her final service, is to restore his sense of eternal youth. She was a young woman, and yet she died before him: in his mind, that makes him her junior. He is elated to be alive though she is dead, to be healthy and strong, while she is in her grave, to have his whole life before him, while her life is over. And now he has his own baby, a son and heir, and no woman can claim the credit of having birthed him; he feels divine: like *Zeus* he can produce a child from his forehead.

Once again, a queen is dead, and once again, the queen's ladies are not dismissed. The queen's chambers are closed, but the king cannot live without women admirers. We have to stay at court. Married ladies live with their husbands, young women return to their fathers. My uncle invites me to an elegant suite of rooms in the Howard chambers. This is not for love nor family loyalty; my uncle knows that my patron is on the rise: Lord Cromwell has taken the post of lord privy seal from Thomas Boleyn and has been awarded the Order of the Garter that George wanted so much.

The king's daughter, Lady Mary, has outlived two stepmothers and is now the first lady of the court. Lord Cromwell is negotiating foreign marriages; but with a boy in the royal cradle, the king can spare no thought for either of his daughters and cannot be brought to say whether Lady Mary is a legitimate princess or a bastard by-blow. Not even the Howards dare to ask about Lady

Elizabeth, whose servants are transferred to serve a true, legitimate baby prince.

Margaret Douglas, also displaced by this baby boy, is released from the Tower, desperately ill, and sent to Syon Abbey to recover. Her husband, poor Lord Thom, has died of fever, so she is a widow who was, so briefly, a secret wife. If she recovers from gaol fever and heartbreak, she will return to court to join this strange half-life that we all now live: ladies-in-waiting with no one to wait on, princesses without titles, heiresses with no inheritance, the queen's ladies without queen's rooms to attend or a queen to serve.

It is a sign of how little the king truly values the ladies that he keeps us on with nothing to do, except for the evenings when he wants company, or dancing or singing. The grooms would not leave his horses standing idle; the huntsmen would not leave his hounds cooped up; but the ladies of his court are picked up and dropped.

'He has no special favourite?' Lord Cromwell asks me again, as the tables are put away after dinner in the king's presence chamber and the musicians tune up for the ladies to dance. We go through our paces like mares in a market as the king watches and taps his one sound leg. 'I don't want to arrange a marriage for him with a foreign princess if another Jane is going to pop up from the countryside and overturn everything.'

'He's attentive to Anne Basset,' I warn, looking towards the dancers where the king is taking his place in a circle dance which will take him around every lady. 'Daughter of Lady Lisle of Calais, the Spanish party put her forward. And Mary Shelton as well as her sister. But he likes an audience more than a partner. He likes us in a flock.'

'Bedding any?' he asks me.

It is treason to say that the king is impotent. 'Not that I've noticed,' I say discreetly. 'Not noticeably at all.' I am rewarded with his little grunt of amusement.

'I understand you. Tell me if there is a rising star. Or if anything is rising at all . . .' He lets the sentence trail away, and I incline my head with a hidden smile. I know what he means, but Jane taught her ladies to ignore bawdy jokes.

'Won't your cousin Mary Howard have a try at the king?' he suggests. 'She's pretty enough, and clever enough? I can't believe her father hasn't suggested it? He's always pushing a Howard into a royal bed. He wouldn't wink at her marrying her father-in-law.'

I shake my head. 'She's a young woman of principle; she's adopted the reformed religion, and she's sincere about it.'

He crinkles his dark eyes in a smile. 'And what about you, my dear Lady Rochford? You don't deploy your charms – you don't try sortilèges?'

'No,' I say. 'I am no longer mad, Lord Cromwell. I am sane and cold and dry. I live my own life, and I want neither court nor love nor courtly love.'

He gives me a sympathetic, crooked smile. 'I am a widower myself,' he says. 'There is a lot to be said for sane and cold and dry.'

## GREENWICH PALACE, SPRING

# 1538

THIS YEAR, MY father's new year gift to Lady Mary is a translation of *Psalm 36*. It is a hint for her to keep her friends – the Poles, the Courtenays, the Spanish ambassador and his spies – at a safe distance. The Spanish party are at the peak of their power. I cannot think they will ever overreach; nothing seems to be beyond their grasp. It feels part of their triumph that my mother-in-law, Elizabeth Boleyn, dies without returning to court, and my father-in-law faces the rest of his life alone, one daughter estranged, his two favourite children and his wife dead.

My father is right to warn Lady Mary: *Let not the foot of pride come against me.*

May Day is a muted celebration, appropriate for a king who swears he will never be happy again. Lord Cromwell talks to all the ladies and praises the king, whose leg is healed so well that he can take part in a circle dance and works his way around the ladies to arrive at me. I curtsey low to him as my new partner and observe the barrel circumference of his chest, the broadening of his belt, and the exaggerated embroidered codpiece thrusting between the thickly jewelled skirts of his jacket.

'Pretty Jane,' he says to me, and then his big round face flushes, and tears come into his eyes. 'That's what I called her.'

I take his hand. 'I know,' I say. 'And she was very pretty.'

'She adored me.'

'She did,' I agree. 'All the ladies do, Sire. But the greatest honour for her was that you loved her. You were her knight errant.'

The musicians pause the music. Everyone is standing still, waiting for the king to start the dancing, noting the warmth of his gaze on my face, his head close to mine.

'You understand me.' He smiles through his tears. 'Like she did.'

'I have been at your court so long . . .'

It is a mistake. I bite back my words. He does not want to think of my long service to three queens at an ageing court. He must be seen as a young widower, grieving for his one and only wife. He flushes with annoyance and drops my hand and repeats reproachfully: 'You call it so long?'

'Long enough to know and love you,' I say quickly. 'Not long enough at all! And you never seem a day older!'

He smiles again; he kisses my hand. The musicians strike up and we dance together, and then he goes on to the next partner, Anne Basset, who sinks into a curtsey so deep that her smiling mouth is level with his codpiece.

The dance finishes, the dancers disperse, and I find myself beside Lord Cromwell. The choristers begin the May Day carol of spring and youthful hope, promises, and love that will never die. I don't smile at the words. My May Day is an anniversary of terror and loss.

'You offended him?' Cromwell asks me.

'Who does not? It was a little slip of the tongue. But I recovered. I'm glad to see you, Lord Cromwell.'

He tucks my hand in his arm, and he walks me away from the dancers towards the card tables. He presses me gently into a seat and takes a deck of cards and starts to shuffle. The pictures, each with a secret meaning, like a pack of codes, flicker through his strong hands.

'You have news for me?'

'I do. You remember that Lady Margaret Pole has an abbey, her family foundation, at her palace at Bisham?' I ask him.

'It was closed by my inspectors for corruption and harbouring a runaway heretical priest.'

'The king has reopened it. He has promised it will never be closed again.'

There is no check to his smooth shuffling. 'I didn't know this.'

'It is to be a chantry for Queen Jane's immortal soul. The king's paying for a permanent foundation with nuns singing daily masses for Jane. The holy women will be housed at Bisham Abbey, under the protection of Lady Margaret Pole.'

We reformers don't believe in the existence of purgatory, nor that masses will release a sinner early from torment. It's so obviously a ruse to fleece grieving families of their money. Once, the king agreed with us, but His Majesty's grasp of theology is rarely as strong as his whims.

Cromwell turns over cards at random. 'Not quite the glorious Pilgrimage of Grace that Lady Margaret's son Reginald promised to lead, is it?' he says, unimpressed. 'One abbey, reopened – just one – and that at the Poles' own expense? But no doubt it will be a great joy for Lady Margaret to reopen her family abbey in defiance of my closure. This must give her hope.' He pauses. 'And if you see any other signs of hope: reading books against reform or letters from Reginald or Rome, or any sort of thing, you will let me know, dear Lady Rochford.'

'I will,' I say. 'But she didn't get to sixty-four years old, through four reigns, by leaving signs of hope lying around for a casual passerby.'

'No,' he says with a smile. 'But she's not surrounded by casual passersby but by a large family, indiscreet and all needing money. One of them is sure to betray her.' His eyes rest on the youngest brother, Sir Geoffrey, the least handsome and least likeable of a handsome, likeable family. 'Would you like to take a wager on which one?'

## WESTMISTER PALACE, SUMMER

# 1538

I AM TOO WISE to risk good money gambling on the unreliability of Lady Margaret's youngest son. Sir Geoffrey is taken to the Tower for questioning in the dog days of August, while his powerful kinsmen are at their country homes, the king on progress, and all the court dispersed. No one notices that the young man has disappeared into the unbearably hot rooms, under the leads of the roof of the Tower, and Sir Geoffrey, simmering with resentment against his older brothers, heated by Lord Cromwell's questions, melts into spiteful gossip.

When the court returns to Westminster Palace in autumn and finds Sir Geoffrey under arrest, everyone assumes that he must have been taking bribes from the Spanish ambassador or even from the French, and is to be taught a lesson by a brief imprisonment. The Pole family are glacially disapproving of one of their kinsmen falling below their high standards, but we are all sure that his name and his debts will be cleared by the matriarch of the family: Lady Margaret Pole.

There are other portents. The eternal chantry for Queen Jane, the Pole family's abbey at Bisham, is closed again, only months after its brief reopening. The king has changed his mind. Now, he thinks it is ridiculous to believe that souls wait patiently in purgatory to be bought into heaven by thousands of sung masses. And if there is no purgatory, then there is no need for an expensive chantry, and the Pole family's abbey can be closed again without regret – for anyone but the Poles: they are anguished, of course.

This is not the only straw in the changing wind. The tomb of Thomas Becket, a sacred destination for the hundreds of pilgrim ways that cross and recross all Europe, is closed, too; the jewels gifted over centuries disappear into Thomas Cromwell's Court of Augmentations, and the priceless bones of the saint are robbed from his tomb and promptly lost. The great ruby of Thomas Becket – the greatest treasure of the shrine – vanishes with the bones of saint but reappears – a *resurrectionem* – on the king's fat thumb.

The heartbreak in Canterbury is completely silent. I think of the priest in my father's village church cutting all references to the pope from his missal; now he will have to cut out St Thomas Becket as well. He might as well throw away his Latin Bible. Every church is to have a new one in English; God will no longer be addressed in Latin. The king knows that God speaks English. It is an English God for an English pope and king.

These are heavy reverses for the Papist Spanish party, but not their downfall. They believe that they are safe – their weakest link, Sir Geoffrey, has fallen silent in the Tower. They admit to nothing more than his minor indiscretion, and no one can be executed for an indiscretion.

'I have good news for you,' my spymaster tells me, finding me idle on the pier at the river, watching the fish rise in the still water.

'Always welcome,' I say.

'I promised you a reward for keeping faith with me.'

I wait.

'Your father-in-law sees reason at last. He's wanting to settle his accounts and – as luck would have it – your widow's jointure gives you a life interest in the lands that he wants to leave to his only surviving child.'

'He's never paid me a penny of the rents,' I say resentfully. 'And Mary was not so dear to him when his other daughter was queen.'

Cromwell smiles at my resentment. 'I know. But I have put together an agreement that gives you good lands in Cambridge, in return for your jointure in Buckinghamshire. And –' he pauses smiling – 'you will be a tenant for life at Blickling Hall.'

'Blickling?' It was the Boleyn family home, before they had Hever.

He nods. 'I could not get it for you outright, but it is yours for life, and I will have it confirmed by Act of Parliament. The king himself will agree to it.'

This man, this blacksmith's son, has done for me what a duke of England, my uncle, would not do for me. He has turned around my fortunes, I am a woman of property once again. I can pay off my debts and my bills at court. I can buy gowns and horses and jewels that match my station in life. I can hold up my head. I am Lady Rochford with a grand house and lands to match my title. I am Jane Boleyn and I have the Boleyn family house as my home. I choose to live at court, it is a free choice, I am nobody's dependent. I have a place of my own again.

'I don't know how to thank you,' I am quite breathless with joy.

'You don't have to thank me,' he says. 'You've earned it. I promised that if you told me what I needed to know, you would be rewarded. And you told me – and it cost you your house and your husband. It's only right that I give you the house back.'

'Wait,' I say. 'I said nothing that led to George's death. I gave no evidence, I signed nothing.'

He bows. 'Then the house is payment for nothing.'

## HAMPTON COURT, WINTER

## 1538

As if to defy the shadow over the old royal family, Lady Lisle braves the stormy Narrow Seas in November and visits us from the English fortress of Calais, to see her daughter Anne Basset, who is slowly inching her way forward to be the king's new favourite. We hold a banquet to celebrate Lady Lisle's arrival. She is a big-boned, handsome woman, and Thomas Culpeper, the king's new favourite groom of the chamber, has obviously been primed to show her all sorts of little attentions. Anne Basset – who had her eye on Thomas Culpeper herself – is hugely offended by this flirtation and is heard to say that if Master Thomas Culpeper wants a hawk from Calais, he can no doubt pay for it like anyone else, and there is no need for him to make sheep eyes at a woman old enough to be his mother.

Lady Lisle stays at court for several days, hunting and hawking, walking in the gardens – friendly with everyone and wheedlingly flirtatious with the king. I never see her alone with her many kinsmen – the Poles, the Courtenays, and the Roman Catholic lords – she only meets them casually in public. She is in a position of high trust: her husband, Arthur, Lord Lisle, is of the old royal family the Plantagenets and holds the English fort of Calais for England, and the English Church in the sea of envious papistry that is Europe. He could not be in a more tactically important position; he could not be more trusted. Lady Lisle, walking into a banquet in her honour, on the king's arm, reminds everyone that the former royal family, the Spanish party, are still riding high, and she and her husband are trusted with the keys to the gateway of the kingdom.

But after she has said her farewells and set sail for Calais, as the court prepares for Christmas, we hear extraordinary news from the Tower. Sir Geoffrey Pole has confessed to a plot against the king and against the Church of England. He says his family supported the rebellion of the pilgrims and planned an invasion of England to be led by their exiled son, Reginald Pole, who was going to throw down king and Church, marry Lady Mary and take the throne.

No sooner has he signed his name to this death warrant for his family than he lapses into remorseful panic and stabs himself in the heart with his butter knife, after enjoying the good dinner that was his reward for betrayal. If he had used a proper knife and succeeded in killing himself, his family would have declared him insane and his words valueless: the ravings of a madman. But he did not hurt himself enough to save them. His blunt knife, his weeping survival, only proves his sanity and their guilt. An avalanche of arrests follows.

His brother, Henry Pole Lord Montague, is taken to the Tower with Sir Edward Neville. Henry Courtenay the Marquess of Exeter and his wife Gertrude are arrested for treason as well. Even the children of the family are taken with their parents: Edward Courtenay and young Henry Pole disappear into the darkness under the portcullis.

Sir Geoffrey names others: a canon from Chichester cathedral, a priest from the newly closed Bisham Abbey, a merchant who carried secret letters to the traitor Reginald Pole. Even Sir Nicholas Carew – who got George's Order of the Garter – is arrested. One of the old lords, poor Lord De La Warr, says no more than that he cannot bear another trial of old and loyal friends, and is arrested for that – and held in the Tower along with them.

None of them confess anything. Gertrude Courtenay declares that everyone is innocent of everything, and she herself is a fool whose word cannot be trusted, and the many things she said in defence of Lady Mary, her insistence on calling her 'Princess', were nothing but feminine folly.

The old lady, Margaret Pole – too tough for feminine folly – is questioned, her home Bisham Palace is searched, and she is taken to Cowdray Castle in Sussex and interrogated for hours, day after day, by William Fitzwilliam, the newly appointed Earl of Southampton. The old lady is too wise and too brave to be caught by Fitzwilliam's bullying. She does not break or even bend while her beloved son Geoffrey and his brother, his cousin Henry Courtenay, and his kinsman Sir Edward Neville, and their priests and messenger are tried for treason as the court has a merry Christmas. We do not even pause the music when we hear that Henry and Edward have been beheaded.

I MEET LORD CROMWELL at the king's gift-giving, and companionably, we watch the courtiers coming forward as if to pour sacrifices of blood on a reeking altar.

'You are keeping Lady Margaret Pole and Gertrude Courtenay in the Tower with the little boys?' I confirm. 'But they will be released?'

'Of course – nobody would execute such great ladies, and the boys are just children. But I've no doubt they will return to plotting as soon as they are free. I'm surrounded by rivals who take the king's fancy and drag him their way. There's always some bright lad coming up through the ranks; there's always a pretty Howard girl in the nursery.'

I laugh at the truth of this. 'My uncle was speaking to me of a cousin – Katheryn Howard, his niece – who should come to court. And the king's rooms eat up young men like a *manticore* – he needs a constant supply of companions. But you are secure?'

'While the king wants a well-run country, a fortune without the trouble of earning it, and everything done his way before he's thought of it – I am secure.' He looks at the king, receiving gifts that cost a fortune and handing out baubles. 'But serving a man of power is to feed a furnace. The more that he has, the more he wants.'

'Wealth?' I ask.

'Wealth I can easily get,' says the destroyer of the Church. 'It is power that is harder. The greatest want for a rich man is power over others.'

## WHITEHALL PALACE, SPRING

## 1539

Nicholas Carew is tried and beheaded in the spring for the crime of questioning the arrest of the Pole family. Since he dies for asking a question, no one dares to inquire about him. I think someone should speak out for him; but he was no friend of mine nor friend to my husband, so I don't speak.

In May, Lord Cromwell brings the case of his old enemy Lady Margaret Pole before parliament, as if it were another May Day joust. He shows the House a silk tunic found in the bottom of an old trunk at her home, embroidered with the five wounds of Christ – the old crusader badge that the pilgrim rebels wore when the north rose up. There is nothing to connect the banner with the rebellion; there is nothing to prove that the old lady even sewed it, that it was not laid away by an old crusader's wife, years before. But a single silk banner is enough for this cowed parliament to condemn her to death without trial.

Nobody dares to defend a disgraced princess – we have three of them already, silent at court. Nobody is going to speak up for the mother of a cardinal. The old lady waits for her death in the Tower of London, where her son Henry and his kinsman were killed. Her twelve-year-old grandson Harry, Gertrude Courtenay, and her son Edward visit her in her cell.

'But she won't be executed?' I ask Lord Cromwell. 'You said she would not be executed?'

'No,' he reassures me. 'In time, she'll be released, but she'll never again have the power to raise the north or kill a queen, your sister, or your husband. It is the end of the Poles and the Spanish party, as I promised.'

We exchange a smile. This is our revenge.

## BOLEYN TRAITOR

## WESTMINSTER PALACE, SUMMER

### 1539

THE COURT'S MOOD swings against old families and the old faith. At midsummer, we have merry joust of barges on the river. On one side is a barge dressed in imperial purple, crewed by a gross figure, fattened on indulgences, waving a papal crook, and a whole college of fat lazy cardinals splashing about with oars. On the other side of the river on their barge are Tudor green rowers and black-and-white soldiers of reform. Fireworks explode around them, mock cannon fire roars, and jets of water spurt, as battle is joined, and the royal barge, with the king and the ladies of the court, rows close enough to see the action and be thoroughly splashed. We scream with delight and encouragement as the reform barge throws grappling irons and boards the papal barge. There is rough and dirty fighting until the righteous reformers triumph and tip the pope and his men overboard into the river, where they bob about, pleading for rescue.

The king orders them fished out of the water with boat hooks before they drown in their great robes and applauds both sides for the spectacle. The court and the people watching from the riverbank loudly cheer and read this entertainment for the lesson that it is: the old faith, the old Roman Catholic families, the Spanish party have overreached themselves and are defeated as surely as if they were tipped in the river and left to drown.

## WINDSOR CASTLE, WINTER

## 1539

The king, who will never marry again, sends the court painter Hans Holbein all around Europe to take the portraits of young women. There is Mary of Guise, the favourite, who chooses to marry the King of Scotland, which gives much offence; but she has two sisters, Louise and Renée. There are two daughters of the Duke of Cleves; there is Christina Duchess of Milan, or Anna of Lorraine, and the French king's sister, Marguerite.

Thomas Cromwell does not want England allied by marriage to either France or Spain, but to be an independent power, playing one side off against the other, so he chooses a bride free from the power of the pope: Anne of Cleves, a princess raised as a Lutheran – the most anti-papal of all the religions. Her dowry – her only dowry – is an alliance with the Lutheran princes of Germany.

The king announces that he has made his choice and orders her bridal journey by sea in winter so that she can admire the power and strength of the king's naval escort. Thomas Cromwell takes pity on her and sends her the safer and easier route overland.

In early December, Arthur, Lord Lisle, rides out from his fortress town of Calais and brings the new queen into his domain. He has survived the scourging of his family and remains our trusted commander of Calais. William Fitzwilliam the Earl of Southampton, high in favour after bullying Lady Margaret Pole, escorts the new queen into her fortress, and finally, after a noisy merry Christmas – with much flirtatious teasing of the most handsome bridegroom in Christendom – the returning ladies of the queen's rooms go to meet their new mistress at Rochester and welcome her to her new country, where we tell her that we hope she will be happy and never admit that it is almost certain that she will not.

## ST ANDREW'S ABBEY, ROCHESTER, KENT, JANUARY

## 1540

She is a pretty young woman in her early twenties – slim and white-skinned, though her gown is padded to make her as big as a horse, and the hood on her head is like the roof of a house. I am to be chief lady-in-waiting again. Who knows better than I how to run the queen's rooms for my fourth queen?

I curtsey to her and suggest that she change into the gowns we have brought from the royal wardrobe before she continues her journey to London.

She widens her brown eyes at me, and she smiles: '*Was?*' she says encouragingly. '*Was?*'

'God save me, does she not speak English?' I exclaim to the Duchess of Suffolk, who greeted her at Dover.

Catherine Brandon is twenty years old now, and she's been married to old Charles Brandon since she was fourteen – she should know better than to giggle.

'You're the first person to wait for an answer,' she explains. 'Everyone else reads aloud the ceremonial welcome in Latin, and she nods and smiles and doesn't speak. My lord husband bellows at her like she was his cavalry. He hasn't noticed she never answers. I don't blame her – never answer him myself if I can help it.'

I glare at Susannah Hornebolt, the artist. 'You were supposed to teach her English!'

She spreads her hands in apology; I can see a stain of paint on her forefinger.

'You've spent all your time painting,' I accuse her.

'No – I am teaching Her Grace English – she is making good progress.'

I turn to the silent queen-to-be. '*Français? Parlez-vous français?*' I ask her.

The pretty smile widens, but she shakes her head.

'Latin?'

She laughs. '*Kannst du Deutsch?*'

'Yes,' I reply in German. 'A very little. But we'll have to teach you English at once.'

She claps her hands at my reply and says in German: 'Of course I must speak English. I have started to learn, but everyone speaks so quickly!'

'I will speak slow,' I say in measured tones, and Katheryn Howard, a new maid-of-honour, niece to the duke, giggles like a naughty schoolgirl, nudges Catherine Brandon, and whispers: 'I vill speak slow.'

I go with the queen to her bedroom to look at the gowns in her heavy travelling chests. She refuses to wear English dress but insists that she will make her grand entry to London in her best cloth of gold gown that her mother told her to wear, with a hood that looks like an anvil stuck on her head. There is no point arguing with a queen in a language that only she speaks fluently, so I leave her ladies to dress her in her ugly heavy gowns. I am going to my own rooms, when a manservant asks me to come to the hall.

I see at once why I have been summonsed. Half a dozen gentlemen are in the hall, boisterously swinging marbled masquing cloaks around their shoulders, throwing off large glasses of wine, musicians with them, dancers trying out steps around them. In the middle is the noisiest of them all, an instantly recognisable figure: broad as a beam, swathed in a cloak swirling with colours, a hat pushed back from his wide face, a brightly coloured mask stretched from forehead to smiling mouth.

I drop into a curtsey, my hand to my heart as if I am breathless with surprise.

'You guessed!' he says. 'You guessed at once! I had a bet that you would! Didn't I say that Jane Boleyn would know me anywhere? In any disguise?'

The others whoop and laugh and clash their gold cups together in a toast to me.

'Now, Jane, you're going to have to join our band and be sworn to keep our secret.'

I come up, smiling. 'Your Majesty, it could be no one else but you! So tall and so handsome and so gaily dressed! And what lord but you would ride all this way to surprise his bride?'

'I am a fairytale prince out of the old Romances!' He roars at the thought. 'I did as my brother did all those years ago – he rode halfway to greet his bride on the road to London. Everyone said he was a true knight errant, and now I have outdone him.'

'You have far outdone him.' I pick up my cue, and one of the men behind him, richly dressed and masked, shouts: 'Hurrah!'

'I will keep your secret,' I promise. 'But I must go and get your bride ready for her surprise.'

I am absolutely determined that she won't wear her ugly hood when she meets the king, and I turn to go back up the stairs to her rooms.

'Not so! Not so!' The king grabs me by my sleeve and then draws me down the stairs with an arm around my waist. His breath is a hot gale of stale wine in my face. 'I'm not having you spoiling our surprise, Jane. I mean it. You shall stay with us and have a cape and a mask of your own, and you shall join my band. We'll come in with music while she's watching the bull baiting – we have it all planned. We'll dance with her and her ladies, and you shan't betray us.'

'I won't tell, I swear.' I am desperate to get her out of that ridiculous hood and into a low-cut gown. 'But she'll want to look her best. You must surprise her at her best.'

'Is she not pretty as she is?' he asks, instantly suspicious, his eyes sharp through his mask. 'Pretty as my Jane?'

'Very pretty,' I say at once. 'Who is a better judge than you? Who catches a likeness better than Master Holbein? You couldn't be mistaken in your choice. I just want to—'

'No, no,' he says. He hands me to Sir Anthony Browne, whose

evidence brought my sister-in-law to the French swordsman and my husband to the block. We greet each other with clasped hands and warm kisses. 'Sir Anthony! Give my sweetheart Jane a cape and a mask and a hood!' the king exclaims. 'She is my man for the night!'

I laugh with everyone, as if this is the best joke in the world, and Sir Anthony takes me to the back of the hall and gives me a little silvered looking-glass to hold, as he swirls a marbled cape around my shoulders and turns up the collar.

'I have to go to her . . .' I say urgently.

'First swop your hood for a bonnet,' he says, and with a strangely intimate gesture, he unpins my hood and replaces it with a man's hat, pulled down over my eyes like his own. He ties the brightly coloured mask on my face and pulls up the hood of the cape so that my face is in shadow.

I look at myself in the mirror and see that my anxiety does not show behind a smiling face, which is hidden by the mask, and concealed by a hood.

'I wouldn't know myself,' I say.

'We all have many faces,' he replies. 'Come on – we're going in.'

'Wait,' I say. 'I have to—'

But he takes me by the hand and makes me follow the others up the broad stone stairs.

'Where's Lord Cromwell?' I demand desperately as the noise from the courtyard below swells to tumult and I guess the bull has been loosed and they are throwing dogs into the yard for him to gore.

Sir Anthony laughs recklessly. 'Left behind in London! This is courtier work! Not for an old counting-house clerk!' He pulls me by my hand up the staircase. 'Tonight's our night! The king and his comrades! King goes in first, we come behind, musicians follow us! King greets her, gives her a gift, steals a kiss, musicians strike up, we all dance. Usual. Dance is a gavotte.'

'But she won't know him,' I say urgently. 'Sir Anthony, let me go and tell her. She won't know that she's supposed to recognise him only after he unmasks. She doesn't know to pretend not to know him before unmasking. She doesn't know how it's done . . .'

He laughs. I think he's too drunk to understand that this is going to go terribly wrong; but in any case, it's too late. The door before us opens, and we pour into the queen's great chamber.

She's at the window, looking down at the bull baiting below. She looks up when we come in, and her smile of welcome dies as she sees the troop of drunk men, strangely masked, with musicians coming in behind them. For a moment, she looks at bay, like the bull in the courtyard below, facing the dogs running in to torment her.

Sir Anthony has tight hold of my hand and is readying me for the dance.

'Let me go!' I wrench my hand from his. 'I have to warn her—'

The king lurches at the still figure at the window, and, horrifyingly, he pulls her into his arms and plants a hearty kiss on her lips. She recoils immediately, jumping back, shoving him away from her, looking around for her guards. She shouts something at him in German. She wipes her mouth on her sleeve, and terribly, she spits on the floor. She whirls around to turn her back to him, snapping an order at her servants that they throw him and all the half-drunken minions out of her rooms.

The musicians shudder to silence; everyone is frozen with horror. The king stands alone, his mask pulled half-off; he looks completely stricken. He has kissed his bride, and she spat his kiss out of her mouth. He looks nothing like the most handsome prince in Europe – he looks like an overweight man of nearly fifty who has been knocked back hard. He looks around, as if for help. He looks around for someone to laugh it off. He looks around as if his legs are weak and he wants to sit down, to sit on a throne, so everyone knows he is king.

Nobody moves. Nobody says a word.

And then little Katheryn Howard, the newest arrival, the most junior of all the maids, trips forward. 'The king!' she coos. 'So handsome! I would know him anywhere. See, my lady! It is our handsome king!'

She breaks the spell that holds us frozen. Catherine Brandon darts forward and tells the queen that this is King Henry and not – as she thought – a drunk fool with a band of mummers. Anne turns back to him, sinks into a curtsey, scarlet with mortification, and Henry laughs it off with a harsh, ragged laugh.

Everyone laughs with him, wide-mouthed, as if they were shouting. The musicians bravely strike up the gavotte again but straggle off into silence when nobody takes a partner, nobody moves. Nobody wants to dance a gavotte with its climax of a kiss, seeing how the last kiss was received.

I look at Sir Anthony. 'You should've let me prepare her.'

He is beaming. 'Better that the king sees Lord Cromwell's choice as she truly is.'

Something is happening here that I don't understand. 'She was the king's choice—'

'From a short list of two Lutheran duchesses.' He takes my hand and kisses it. 'She's Cromwell's choice. His lordship picked her for his own good reasons. Now he'll have to answer for them. And if the king doesn't like her – Lord Cromwell will have to answer for that, too.'

I realise that this is not a masque that has gone wrong; this has all gone exactly right. The king's first meeting with Cromwell's bride is a disaster; but the Howard girl saves the day. I have just witnessed the first move in the Howards' brilliant bid for the throne, and another Howard girl is in play.

I send a letterlocked note that night by one of Lord Cromwell's messengers. I mark it *haste*, and know that the man will ride all night.

## GREENWICH PALACE, JANUARY

## 1540

Lord Cromwell's response is a magnificent reception for the queen at Blackheath, with all the theatrical extravagance that the king loves. The king, escorted by hundreds of noble courtiers, wearing imperial purple velvet, with a cloth of gold jacket, rides on a great horse as Anne of Cleves emerges from a tented pavilion like a princess in a tapestry, mounts a white horse, and rides forward to greet him.

Three thousand Londoners cheer their king as he welcomes his queen to her home at Greenwich, and Anne smiles and waves and then rides hand in hand with her husband up the new road that Cromwell has bored through the woods towards the riverside palace.

Lord Cromwell greets all of the queen's ladies at the doorway as they dismount, and as he takes my hand, I pinch his fingers. I need do no more; he leaves the dinner table as they are putting out the voider course of fruit and sweetmeats, and I slip away from the ladies' table and find him waiting for me in the gallery.

The happy buzz of the court talking, laughing, flirting in the great hall echoes through the stone arches to where we stand like lovers, half-hidden in a doorway.

'What did she do?' he demands tightly. He has already faced the rage of his royal master: horribly betrayed into a marriage he never wanted, with a woman too ugly for him to bear.

'She offended him, but it was planned. I swear it,' I say in a rush. 'As I wrote you. Nobody prepared her, and the king strode in, greeting her like a knight errant in a masque. Unannounced – you know – unknown revellers – he could have been in Russian furs or Turkish turbans. They came in shouting; they frightened her, and he grabbed her. She pushed him off and spat out his kiss. She swore at him as if he were a common drunk. It was a disaster. The new Howard girl, Katheryn, saved the day. But it wasn't her doing, I swear. Not her words. She's too young and untrained to be that quick on her feet. But she jumped forward and flattered the king and smoothed it all over. She was brilliant – she was well-prepared.'

'Howards?' he muses. 'A new Howard play?'

'They wrote the script, I'd swear it. But the attack on the Cleves princess is an attack on you – the Spanish party's revenge. I bet you that Honor Lisle wrote to her friends, the old lords, the moment that Anne of Cleves rode into Calais. I bet she told them: the duchess can't speak English; she's not pretty and witty and clever; she can be made to look a fool. The old lords and what's left of the Spanish party don't want a Lutheran queen supporting reform in the king's ear. They don't want an alliance with Germany against the Spanish. And they don't want you as a successful royal marriage broker.'

He nods. 'They want revenge on me for the deaths of the Poles.'

'They couldn't predict exactly, but they knew that if he burst in on her, disguised and drunk, she wouldn't know what to do. They got hold of me so I couldn't warn her, and now the king's horribly shamed and he blames it all on her. The Howards knew there'd be a set-back and readied their girl to be his salvation – they're playing their own game. The Howards and all the old lords jump forward, and the reformers of the Church – and you especially – are pushed back.'

His face, shadowed by his simple hat, is grim. His clothes, still clerkly black, are now made from silk and embroidered velvet. 'Only a small step, I hope. If he likes her better now, after this grand reception with everyone cheering, he'll overlook the first meeting. He'll forget it – it'll never have happened. If she gives him a son, all this will be forgotten. And whatever the old lords think, there is no future for England but an alliance with other Protestant countries. Charles of Spain is meeting Francis of France right now and swearing alliance against us.'

'He'll never desire her,' I warn urgently. 'Believe me, my lord. She cut him to the bone.'

He grimaces. 'And she? Does she still find him disagreeable, now that she knows he's king?'

I shrug. 'She doesn't confide in me, not even in her German ladies in her own language.'

'You listen?'

'Of course. She says nothing. Not even in her prayers.'

'She's discreet,' he approves. 'If I can get the two of them wedded and bedded, I'll trust to that sturdy German nature to do the rest.'

'She's a duchess, not a Groningen cow,' I say acidly.

He smiles again. 'Don't mince words like a Seymour. All we need from her is that she gets into calf.'

'You won't get him into the field – you won't get him through the gate,' I say, and he laughs at my bawdiness, kisses my hand, and goes back to the great hall, where the king sits scowling beside his blandly smiling bride.

Four days later, I am standing behind the bride in the queen's rooms at Greenwich Palace, straightening the train of her gown. I keep my expression as pleasant and smiling as those of the other ladies, who tighten the gold chains at her slim waist and comb her hair over her shoulders. Her round face is pretty and flushed; she wears a jewelled coronet on her beautiful golden-brown hair. Her wedding gown is made from cloth of gold encrusted with flowers made from huge pearls, as if she were turning to stone before our eyes. She carries a little posy of rosemary for love and fertility, and I see it tremble until she grips both hands before her and sets her jaw square. She is determined to show no weakness to this court of unfriendly strangers.

She knows – we all know – that the king has demanded the wedding is delayed until her earlier contract of marriage is shown to be properly cancelled. As a little girl of eleven years old, she was promised in marriage to a neighbouring duke. The contract was revoked, the duke married someone else, and the cancelled contract was tossed into some vault at Cleves – who cares?

But now the King of England cares, and he is saying that his marriage cannot go ahead until the cancelled contract is in his hand. She knows he is hoping to get out of marrying her on this slender excuse. Of course, this is nonsense. Not even Henry can bring a royal duchess across Europe in the worst weather for a midwinter wedding and then cancel the ceremony for a piece of paper that he never wanted before.

Meanwhile, France and Spain have sworn to a ten-year alliance not to make war without the other's agreement – so our enemies are united against us; we must find new friends. If Paris or Toledo want war, our only safety is the German bride: she is our defence, as essential as the castles that the king is building at all the southern ports. The wedding has to go ahead for the safety of England.

It must take every ounce of courage for her to hold up her head, to smooth back the fall of beautiful hair over her shoulders and greet Henry Bourchier Earl of Essex, late as usual, who leads her down the long gallery to the king. His Majesty is magnificently dressed in a crimson satin coat with diamond buttons and a gown of cloth of gold. He manages a sulky little bow in reply to her three deep curtseys. She looks magnificent, gowned and crowned, gleaming with pearls matching her pearly skin. Beside her, the king looks old and sulky, his dazzling clothes contrasting with his pouting mouth and his strawberry moon face.

Count Overstein from Cleves steps forward and takes the duchess by the hand to lead her into the queen's close for a private ceremony with our old friend, Archbishop Thomas Cranmer, officiating, his smiling round face showing no glimmer of self-doubt.

As we wait outside in a reverent silence, one maid is not standing still, eyes downcast as she should be. Katheryn Howard, new maid-of-honour and evening star of the dreadful night in Rochester, is lifting the hem of her sage-green gown to examine the rosettes on her satin shoes. She is expensively dressed for a poor relation: someone is betting good money that Kitty will take the eye. She looks like a little doll beside the older women; she is so small and dainty. Her hair is a wonderful bronze, her eyes hazel, as green as her gown in the candlelight. Trained by the Dowager Duchess of Norfolk, she is as graceful as a dancer; she walks as if to music. Her manners are beautiful, her education completely neglected. She senses me watching her, and when I frown at her to stand still, she gives me an apologetic smile and continues to fidget.

Once again, I put a queen to bed and wait at her side as the great double doors are thrown open and her husband the king and his drunken friends enter. Once again, Henry passes me in the royal bedchamber, his gaze on the bed. This time, he doesn't smile at me, nor at anyone. He limps towards the bed like an unwilling old man on his way to an arduous chore.

She looks up at him as he stands by her bed. She says carefully: 'Goot evening!' Her smile does not waver at his dark scowl; her expression of courteous welcome does not alter, not even when he sits down heavily on the side of the bed and his grooms of the chamber heave his bandaged leg up and bodily push him in beside her.

The queen's ladies trail out of the wedding chamber and take a glass of wedding ale in the presence chamber with a pretence of goodwill, before I send them to their beds. Kitty Howard, her face bright with mischief, says: 'Goot evening!' as she leaves, and the younger maids snigger.

The noblemen leave in a hurry to drink in their own rooms, as if there is nothing here to celebrate. My uncle gives me a satisfied nod; he knows the king's vanity will never allow him to forgive his bride her first, fatal misstep. 'Going well,' he remarks to me with a sly smile.

'Very well,' I reply instantly and curtsey as he leaves.

Lord Cromwell says goodnight to the ladies and pauses, bowing over my hand. 'She looked pretty enough,' he says. 'You turned her out well. A pretty face.'

'She has a pretty face,' I say simply. 'But it's not a false face. And he's seen nothing but false faces and painted smiles for all his life. D'you think he wants an honest woman now? Does any man want an honest woman as his wife? Don't you all prefer liars?'

She is no fool. She doesn't understand half that we say, but she doesn't need to be told that he doesn't desire her. The king leaves her bed after a few hours the first night, and there is not a mark on the sheets and her hair is still in the fat blonde plait, tidy under her nightcap in the morning.

Kitty Howard, a noble-born maid who should have no knowledge of such signs, gives me a knowing look as the queen sits before her mirror and we unpin her nightcap and brush her hair.

Anne, the new queen, sees the exchanged glances and says nothing.

'Early days,' Thomas Cromwell says to me stoutly, as the king and queen process to mass and breakfast and sit side by side, smiling, like gold icons of marital bliss.

'Not through the gate, not into the field,' I say crudely.

'You're sure?'

'I'm sure.'

He scowls. 'He told me that he knew by certain signs that she is no maid.'

I fold my lips over a sharp retort. There's no point arguing with the king's certainties.

'But you would say she's a maid?' Cromwell asks me carefully.

'A beautiful and clever maid. Fully fitting to be a young queen.'

'That's what I think,' my spymaster says firmly. 'It's early days.'

I get hold of the serving girls and tell them that if anyone breathes a word about clean sheets and a tidy bed, I will see them hung up by their thumbs amid the hams in the meat larder. The gossips learn nothing from the queen's attendants – though I don't doubt Kitty Howard reports to our uncle the duke, Thomas Howard; Catherine Carey to her mother, my sister-in-law, Mary Boleyn, and from her to the supporters of reform; Anne Basset reports to her mother Lady Lisle and she to the old lords. The Spanish spies – whoever they are – report to Don Chapuys and to Lady Mary; the French spy earns his pension with information to the French ambassador. But the king and queen go through the celebrations of January in perfect public accord, and the wider court does not know that at night they sleep side by side, like statues on a tomb, never touching.

Every day, the Howards send Kitty Howard out in a prettier gown and a smaller hood, and their spies and placemen remark in the king's hearing that it is a pity that the new queen is taking so long to learn to dance or sing or play an instrument or write a poem – and how strictly raised these Lutheran duchesses must be, that they take it as a holy duty not to delight the eye or entertain the mind! Every day, the Seymours loudly remark how charming the new queen is and what a worthy heir to their girl. The Seymours don't care if the marriage is a *mariage blanc* – one for public show. They prefer it. The last thing they want is a little half-brother to their prince; they want all the attention on him and on them.

Every day, Lord Cromwell looks across at me at prayers in the morning and just raises an eyebrow as if to say: *and has the bull got through the gate into the field?* Every day I minutely shake my head. The king spends most nights in her bed, but I think he has lost the power to do it.

'She's got to please him,' Cromwell says bluntly, catching me as I am waiting for the grooms to bring my horse for me to ride out with the queen. She looks wonderful on horseback, when she's not afraid of saying or doing the wrong thing. She's at ease with her big Holsteiner horse, and she rides as fast as any of the young men. They whoop and holloa as she keeps up with them, and scramble to help her down from the saddle when we come home.

'She has to invite him,' Cromwell urges me. 'She has to incite him to happiness. She has to encourage him. She has to inspire desire. Do I have to tell her chamberlain to tell her? Or will you speak to her?'

'Sortilèges?' I ask, blank-faced. 'You want sortilèges now?'

He narrows his eyes. 'Don't,' he says shortly. 'Don't be amusing with me. It's no joking matter. She has to do something. Anything. Anything to attract him. If he's not encouraged, he won't get a boy. If he doesn't get a boy, he'll say it proves the marriage isn't blessed by God. And if God is against the marriage, he'll want to get out of it – and I tell you, Jane, neither God nor I can get him out of it. Not without upsetting all the German princes and leaving us open to attack from Spain and France. Not without setting back the cause of reform. Not without the king needing another bride so his pride isn't humbled – and where do I find her? Who would be a fifth wife?'

'She can do no more than she does,' I say flatly. 'She greets him with pleasure every time she sees him; she's learning English as fast as she can; she's learning the dances; she's learning our entertainments. If he comes again in disguise, she knows to act falling in love with him. She's changed her clothes to French fashions. She rides like a *centaur*, and she has the patience of a saint. What more d'you want of her?'

'I want her to be like Kitty Howard!' he exclaims as if it is forced out of him. He immediately drops to a whisper. 'I want her to flirt.'

'Kitty Howard was born a flirt and raised a flirt. If the king had married her, you'd have an inquiry into her lovers in the first year.'

'She has lovers?' he demands, alert to any Howard weakness.

'God only knows what her step-grandmother the dowager duchess allowed in Norfolk House,' I say. 'She's already in love with three different courtiers. Currently, it's Thomas Culpeper – the king's new favourite.'

Cromwell grins with genuine amusement. 'How will she take the king's eye if she's courting with the groom of the bedchamber?'

'She's a Howard girl,' I say shrewdly. 'She can do both.'

## WHITEHALL PALACE, FEBRUARY

# 1540

In February, I find boxes in the Howard hall and my uncle's travelling cape thrown over them.

'You're going away, my lord?' I ask, curtseying to him.

'To France,' he says. 'To persuade Francis of France that whoever our king marries, even if his bride is a Lutheran, we are still their friend – and a better friend than they'll find in Spain.'

'God speed,' I say piously.

The duke takes my elbow in a hard grip. 'You can tell your patron, Thomas Cromwell, that if I can turn the King of France back to our side, then we won't need friendship with Cleves, nor with any paltry German princes, nor with any whining Lutherans. And if we're not bound to them, we can be rid of the heretic queen and – more – we can say a fond farewell to the fool who made the marriage!'

I stand stock-still, and he releases me.

'Not if she conceives a child,' I say, to test his knowledge.

The scowl from under his craggy eyebrows tells me that he doesn't know the king's failure. Kitty Howard has not reported to our uncle; the queen's secret is still safe. I rather like Kitty for this unexpected loyalty to her queen.

'When pigs fly with their tails forward,' he says; but he is bluffing.

'He comes to her bed every night.'

'He complains she's not inviting,' he says uncertainly.

'A king doesn't need invitation. No man in England is more potent than him.'

My husband died at the hands of this man, for questioning the king's potency. 'Of course,' he replies. 'We all know that.'

Kitty Howard and I are supposed to be laying out the queen's evening gown; but she is prancing about with a cape over her shoulders instead of spreading it out on the chest.

'I'm glad you don't tell your uncle all the secrets of the queen's bedchamber,' I remark. 'Take that off, child.'

'How d'you know that?' she asks wonderingly. 'Do you know everything that happens everywhere, your ladyship?'

'Yes,' I say, laughing. 'I am the she-pope, all-seeing and all-knowing.'

'But you are terribly clever, aren't you?' she asks engagingly. 'I mean, you read all the time, and you can understand Latin and everything.'

'You could understand Latin,' I say. 'I could teach you?'

She makes a pretty little pout. 'I don't need to know Latin,' she says. 'I have enough trouble reading and writing.' She looks shyly at me. 'But could you advise me about my money?'

None of the maids can resist buying ribbons and jewels with their salaries; they are always in debt. 'I can try,' I say.

'I have a hundred pounds in coin, and I don't know where to keep it safely,' she says. 'It's not mine, or I'd just spend it. I've promised to keep it: but where?'

'A hundred pounds? That's a fortune. Where did you get it from?'

She looks both embarrassed and defiant. 'My young man – a young man of my acquaintance – left England and gave it to me for safekeeping until he returns.'

'Is it stolen?'

'Oh no! Well, at least not a robbery?'

'He's cheated someone out of it?' I hesitate. 'It's not counterfeit money, is it?'

'No . . .' She wriggles like a child at the question. 'I don't know for sure. I didn't ask. I didn't think. I think it may be . . . I think it is profit from his work.'

'That's very profitable work,' I comment acidly. 'And a lot of money for a young man to trust to a friend. Are you betrothed, that he should give you his life savings?'

'Oh no!' She laughs, blushes, and then catches at my hands. 'Oh, don't ask me! You know what it's like, when you're first in love – you make all sorts of promises, and you do all sorts of things! But now I'm come to court, I see that it was nothing serious. He means nothing to me now that I've met young noblemen. Fancy giving me money but not for spending! Saying he may never come back!'

'You'd better give it to me, and I will keep it in my treasure chest in my room. It'll be safe there. If he comes back, you can tell me, and I'll return it to him myself. That way, you're not obliged to him, nor him to you. And if he doesn't come back, then I'll return it to you and we'll say no more about it. As long as you're sure it's not stolen, Kitty? What work did he do to earn such a fortune?'

'He was a purveyor for my grandmother's household at Lambeth,' she says airily. 'So you can see, I would never have been betrothed to a young man like that.'

'Indeed not,' I say. 'He's far beneath you, and our family would never have consented. But at any rate, we can see how he made his profit: he stole from the dowager duchess.'

She looks stricken. 'I suppose he must have done,' she says. 'I thought he was wonderful when I lived there. But now I have come to court and seen gentlemen like Master Culp—' She breaks off.

'There are many handsome gentlemen and noblemen at court,' I say severely. 'Far better suited for you than your grandmother's purveyor. But there are rogues and tricksters at court, as at Norfolk House. You must take care, Katheryn. You'll have to marry where you're ordered, not where you like. You're the daughter of a great house. Our good name is your name. You must carry it with pride.'

'Oh, I do!' She widens her hazel eyes; she is completely unconvincing. 'I really do.'

'Did the duchess or your uncle promise you a great marriage?' I ask curiously. 'Did they tell you what to say when the king came in disguised at Rochester?'

She gives a little giggle. 'Over and over again! They tried it out a dozen different ways. They rehearsed it like a masque until I knew exactly what to do. But it was easy – the king is such a sweet old man, and old men always like me.'

'You can't allow any favours,' I warn her. 'Not to old lords any more than young ones.'

'Oh no!' she says. 'My grandmother is very strict. She says I may be surprised at my good fortune if I can stop myself behaving like a slut.'

'Good advice,' I say. 'Though rather blunt. But you do that.'

## WESTMINSTER PALACE, SPRING

# 1540

LORD CROMWELL SUMMONS me to his grand rooms in a tower of the Palace of Westminster. The secret of the queen's cold bed has got out but not from us. The king has betrayed his own secrets. He has chosen to tell his friends that he is impotent with her – the most extraordinary self-shaming. No man at this court of boisterous cavaliers and seducers would ever admit to such a weakness. But the king has done so. He is so desperate to tell the world that he doesn't like her, that he is ready to call himself unmanned, to say himself what it is illegal for us to say: that he is impotent.

I find my spymaster gazing down from his window at the little garden below his tower. Daffodils dance at the foot of a tree of springing green; a blackbird is singing in a ripple of notes. I don't think I have ever seen him idle before. I close the heavy wooden door and take a seat.

His counting-house books are one end of the table: he uses the Italian double-entry system, counting what goes out of his purse as well as what comes in and calculates his wealth by comparing the two of them. The old lords, my uncle among them, only count income: rents, fees, gifts, bribes, and pensions and hope they are spending no more than last year. If their steward tells them that the stocks are running low in their treasure room, they increase the rents or sell land or get a loan. I never knew until I worked for Lord Cromwell that it was possible to know to a penny what I was worth. From him, I have learned to calculate my treasure chest, the rents from my new lands, and the cost of running my house at Blickling. And – more importantly – I account for my own life: ambition against defeat, advancement against being dropped. I double-entry my power and influence and watch my value rise.

'The king says her body is slack with use.' Lord Cromwell turns from the view to scowl at me. 'He says her belly is fat, like a woman who has given birth, her breasts hanging down like a woman who has given suck.'

My courtier mask falls from my face in my amazement. 'She's a virgin of twenty-four years old! Her breasts are plump and high; her belly is round and firm. Susannah Hornebolt could paint her as *Beauty*.'

He snorts. 'Holbein painted her as a beauty; that's why she's here.'

'Does the king complain to Master Holbein?'

He shrugs away the question. 'He says she stinks.'

Lord Cromwell knows as well as I do that the king suffers from constipation and purging that brings on stinking farts, and the sore on his leg oozes a noisome pus. The grooms of his chamber and Dr Butts change the bandages three times a day, but still the reek goes with him everywhere. We all carry pomanders for when he is close, and we launder the queen's sheets every day to be rid of the familiar stench of king.

'D'you deny it?' he demands.

I give him a long level look. 'Obviously, she doesn't smell.'

'Then he must be suffering from a delusion,' Cromwell says, pleased, as if this is a good answer. 'He must have been bewitched. Someone has put a spell on the king to make him find his Lutheran wife displeasing. Who would do such a wicked thing as that?'

'Bewitched?' I repeat slowly, as I take in a new move.

My spymaster tuts at my slowness. 'Jane, please. Let's assume, for the sake of argument, that the king has been bewitched so badly that he is unmanned.'

'We can say unmanned?'

'For the sake of argument.'

'*Petitio principii*? We agree a false supposition and then we try to prove it?'

'As scholars,' he says. 'Let's proceed by logic and never mind about truth for a moment. Say someone is discouraging him from bedding the queen – who would do such a thing?'

I restore my courtier face and join the masque of false accusation. 'All the Papists, the Spanish party, the French party?'

'She, herself?'

'Why would the queen cast a spell to make him impotent?'

'Out of disgust, to avoid him. Or to speed his death so she can be dowager queen? She has ambitions. She wants to be a regent queen?'

I don't answer; it is too ridiculous. I shake my head.

'Well, put that to one side for now. Someone else? Any family putting a pretty girl forward to take her place? Who's new to court?'

'Catherine Carey – Mary Boleyn's daughter – as pretty as her mother; but she's the king's niece, perhaps even his daughter. He likes Kateryn Parr, visiting her sister Anne; but she's married to Lord Latimer. Or Mary Norris – the daughter of – er – Henry . . .' I break off. 'But his favourite by a country mile is Katheryn Howard?'

'No, I can't name a Howard girl for witchcraft,' he says briskly. 'Thomas Howard's star is rising since he killed so many rebels at such speed. If he comes back from France with an alliance, he'll be unassailable.'

'No, my lord,' I say primly. 'You can't name a Howard girl, nor any innocent girl for witchcraft, because it would be her death – and none of the maids-of-honour or ladies-in-waiting are guilty of being anything but silly and flirtatious. No one is casting spells.'

'Agreed, but – just for the exercise, remember! – let us assume that someone *is* casting spells. Never mind who.' He slaps his hand on the table and startles me. I've never known him less than courteous. 'For the sake of an argument, Jane.'

'As you wish – as a "useful fallacy".' I pause to consider the holes in this confection. 'But my lord – who is left? Gertrude Courtenay and Geoffrey Pole are released and terrified into obedience? And if Lady Margaret Pole can summon a witch from the Tower, then the keeper of the Tower is dangerously at fault.' I pause. 'And that's you, my lord.'

He gives his familiar little snort of laughter. 'All right. Not her. What about Lady Mary?'

'Nobody would ever believe that Lady Mary would instruct a witch,' I say flatly.

'Then it's got to be the Lisles. Lady Lisle with her pretty daughter Anne Basset at court, working her wiles on the king to replace the Lutheran queen. Anne Basset as their favourite horse in the race, Arthur, Lord Lisle, betraying Calais to the Papists – that might even be true. And the Lisle family are of the old royal family, Plantagenets, founder and key members of the Spanish party . . . and kin to Lord Hungerford!' he finishes with a flourish.

'What's Lord Hungerford to do with it?'

'His wife has evidence that he's a traitor and a Papist! And he hired a witch – name of Mother Roache – to predict the end of the Tudors. There's your witch: Mother Roache. There's your motive: a Papist plot. There's your guilty party: the Spanish party, old royals, Plantagenets and Hungerford. There's their candidate for queen: Anne Basset – and therefore your conspiracy!'

'It hangs together as an argument; but it'd never stand up in a trial. Nobody would believe that Lord Lisle and his lady are anything but loyal, and she's far too grand to have anything to do with a drunk like Hungerford and some grubby hedge-witch. Even if anyone can be brought to believe that Lord Hungerford hired a witch in the first place.'

'Oh, that bit's true,' Cromwell assures me. 'I've got sworn evidence from Eliza Hungerford. She wants a divorce, and she'll say anything to be rid of him. But you're right: it won't go to trial – I'd do it with a writ of attainder. I'd just tell the Houses of Parliament that he's guilty and get a death warrant. Trials are uncontrollable; defendants say too much. I won't use a trial again.'

I pause at that. 'You do remember that a fair trial is the right of all Englishmen – won by the barons in the Magna Carta? What will we become, without justice in England?'

He touches my hand, gently, almost apologetically. 'We'll become a good tyranny, run by godly men. It's the best way to rule; it's the most efficient.'

We are silent for a moment; his fingers are warm on the back of my hand.

'And anyway,' he says softly, 'what else but witchcraft could cause His Majesty to fall impotent?'

He dares me to say that the king's grossness, his drunkenness, and his superstitious fear of sin stands between him and normal, healthy lust. I don't even think of love. He has no ability to love. I think he lost it when he exiled Katherine of Aragon, the love of his life.

'Well then,' Lord Cromwell says, taking silence for agreement – as tyrants do. 'So you see. I solve the mystery of the king's impotence. He's been bewitched by Lord Hungerford in conspiracy with the Plantagenets, to turn him against the Lutheran queen and replace her with one of their own. Conveniently, in one stroke, I am rid of Lord Hungerford, his wife Elizabeth is rid of Lord Hungerford, and we reformers are rid of the Lisles and the last redoubt of the Spanish party. It's neat, isn't it, Jane?'

'It's neat,' I say. 'But what if you kill everyone and the king is not restored to vigour? What if you execute Lord Hungerford and the poor old witch, Lord Lisle and his affinity – and the king still doesn't bed his wife? Still doesn't want her as his wife?'

He nods gravely. 'Yes, that's true, Jane. You're right. The work is half-done. The king can't have a wife who does not incite him. We'll have to get rid of her. Behind the plot, there is the queen – unmanning him.'

I am horrified. This is worse than accusing innocent ladies-in-waiting. 'No, no, my lord. You really can't say that. You can't accuse her of witchcraft. Even a whisper of it would be her ruin.'

He shrugs. 'What can I do? If the king does not want the marriage, it has to be dissolved, one way or another.'

'Yes! I understand!' I am desperate that she is not smeared with a witchcraft accusation. 'But he can annul it? He's Head of the Church?'

He smiles at me. 'Wouldn't that be tyranny?' He stops teasing when he sees the fear in my face. 'Oh, very well, it can be done! If you insist on it – for argument's sake. We can say that her childhood betrothal still stands, that God spoke to the king at the altar, so he did not consent in his heart and did not consummate his marriage. And as it is not consummated, it's easily annulled. How's that?' He looks at me with an air of triumph.

'Prior contract again?' I ask incredulously. 'Is Queen Anne to be the third royal bride that was married before? Isn't that rather a lot?'

'Would you prefer that we go down the Papist and witchcraft route so that Lord Lisle dies, Lord Hungerford dies, his priest and his physician and Mother Roche die on the common scaffold, and even poor old Lady Margaret Pole? And all their evidence leads to the queen as master-planner and witch?'

'Nobody would believe the queen is a witch.'

He shakes his head. 'People believe anything if it is said often enough, loudly enough. You of all people know that, who lost your family to noise.'

'There's been enough deaths,' I say quietly; my lips are so cold that I can hardly speak. 'Someone should speak up against the deaths.'

'You speak up!' he says encouragingly. 'You save them! Help me save them all! If the queen will agree that her marriage was no true wedding, that she was married before, then the king's not impotent but guided by God to holy celibacy. There's no fat ugly woman, no smells, no bewitching, and no witch – even the Lisles are safe! She can stay in England for the rest of her life. I will see she's paid a pension: 8,000 nobles a year – a fortune – and she shall have Richmond Palace as her home.'

It is a fortune; but it is a poor exchange for the throne of England.

'It's not in exchange for the throne of England,' Lord Cromwell says, reading my thoughts. 'It's instead of a scandalous accusation of witchcraft that would be the deaths of a dozen people and blacken her name forever as a fat, stinking woman that a king could not bear to bed.'

'There must be another way!'

'Not that I can imagine.'

My head is whirling. I can't imagine another way out either. 'Then – yes,' I say simply. 'I'll advise her to lie. I'll tell her to say that she was precontracted and take an annulment . . . if you swear she has no other choice.'

He bows his head. 'I always prefer to leave people without a choice,' he says. 'It makes deciding so much quicker.'

## HAMPTON COURT, SPRING

# 1540

THE SEASON OF Lent is observed only lightly this year. We eat no beef, but the new Church of England confirms chicken and game and eggs as 'fish' for the forty days of fasting. Lady Lisle sends quail from her aviaries and dotterel for the queen's table, and her daughter Anne Basset gives the king marmalade to her mother's recipe. But neither quails nor marmalade take the king's gaze from Kitty Howard, who encourages him like a demure granddaughter hoping to be given a pony. Her inviting smiles disappear the moment that our uncle, wearing a new French cape, strides into the queen's rooms with the other lords before dinner.

'You won't tell him about Thomas Culpeper, will you, Lady Rochford?' she whispers urgently to me. 'It was a kiss on Shrove Tuesday; he said he would give me up for Lent. I'd never do it again; it was only because it was Shrove Tuesday – like a pancake, you know. So sorry.'

'I won't mention it,' I say, and she fades away among the other girls and keeps a good distance from her overpowerful uncle, who comes to me and kisses my cheek.

'All well?' he asks.

'All well,' I say. 'Did you have a successful embassy to France, sir?'

One glance at his hawk-faced gleam tells me that he has won a treaty with our nearest neighbour and separated them from the alliance with Spain.

'I did. But I came back to news that I should've heard first from you. Remember you're a Howard, whoever your paymaster is. I expect you to keep me abreast of things in the queen's rooms.'

'I've withheld nothing,' I reply, wondering what he can have learned on the road from Harwich. 'I have no paymaster. I couldn't have written secrets to you, anyway.'

'The king told his council that he can't consummate his marriage. You didn't tell me.'

'He said that?' I show him a shocked face. 'But he comes to the queen's bed every few nights? And she's said nothing to anyone.'

I see he is uncertain. He was sure that I had played him false; but now he is wondering if his informant is lying. 'She's said nothing?'

'No, my lord. I would have told you.'

'You must know! Don't you listen at the door? You must have heard . . .'

I shake my head. 'Sometimes His Majesty stays all night, and sometimes he calls for his page and goes to his own bed around midnight. He's never said anything to us ladies. Nor has she. We've been hoping for a prince, as you know.'

'Forlorn hope! The king says that nothing's happened and it never will.'

'Oh!'

'He says God has saved him from the sin of bigamy.'

'Oh.'

My uncle narrows his eyes to glare at me. 'So, the council must decide if the queen is a bigamist. What d'you say about that? Going to say "oh" again?'

'No, my lord. I'd heard there was a childhood betrothal; but the new Cleves ambassador is coming to Hampton Court for Lent. Won't he bring the papers to show the childhood betrothal was ended?'

'Better for us, if he doesn't,' my uncle whispers. 'If the king's marriage was annulled, he'd be free to marry. And he's seen the bride he wants, hasn't he? He's all over Kitty?'

'He's given her several gifts.'

'And she's behaving herself?'

I nod without committing myself to words.

'Very well. If the queen asks you for advice, you know what your answer should be: that the king can't and won't consummate, and she should admit a prior contract and let the marriage be annulled, and the king can be free to marry our girl, and Cromwell's girl can go back to Cleves. We own the queen, and he looks like a fool.'

THE KING REVELS in the Easter rituals of the old church, creeping to the cross, blessing cramp rings, washing the feet of the poor men, and the queen obeys him in this, as everything else, though the traditions must seem completely pagan to her. They take Easter mass dressed in cloth of gold, side by side before an altar smoking with incense and drenched in holy water.

After the long church service, there is a dinner with roast beef, veal, lamb, porpoise, and puddings to celebrate the end of Lent. Then there is masquing and dancing by the younger noblemen and the queen's ladies. The king's older friends stand beside him, drink and watch the girls dance with a new generation of handsome sons of the great houses: Lord Lisle's stepson, John Dudley; Anthony Kingston, son of my husband's gaoler; Richard Cromwell, my spymaster's nephew, and Gregory Cromwell, his son. George Carew, Sir Nicholas' kinsman, is home on leave from Rysbank Fort, Calais, and there are several handsome young Howard men newly come to court, including Charles, my cousin. Margaret Douglas, back at court having learned nothing from disgrace and widowhood, dances twice with Charles Howard; but I tell the queen to nod her to a new partner for the third dance.

My spymaster, Lord Cromwell, is smilingly watching the dancing, chatting from time to time with the other lords and the king. My uncle's belief he would fall is proved wrong by the king, who rewards him with a great honour: the title of Earl of Essex. Lord Cromwell takes the news with quiet pride; the king gives a dinner for him in the council chamber. Cromwell himself heads the table; and the court is treated to a new masque which could be called *The Rise of the Common Man*, as the new earl is seated on one side of the king, and Thomas Howard the Duke of Norfolk, stiff with offended pride, on the other.

## WESTMINSTER PALACE, MAY

# 1540

THE MAY DAY joust is held at the beautiful tiltyard in Westminster Palace, and Thomas Seymour is the king's challenger. He defeats all comers. Queen Anne, with the restored

*H* and *A* curtains billowing in the warm breeze, awards him the trophy with a smile. Lord Lisle's stepson John Dudley rides well, as does George Carew, who hopes to take the king's eye for promotion before he returns to service at Calais. Gregory Cromwell, as brave as any nobleman's son, breaks a spear on my young cousin Henry Howard Earl of Surrey, and Thomas Culpeper carries Bess Harvey's favour.

'Not yours?' I ask Kitty.

She is red-eyed and defiant. 'No!' she says sharply. 'He seems to prefer Mistress Harvey to me.' Her lower lip trembles. 'I don't care, I am sure, Lady Rochford. If you see him, you can tell him that I don't care at all.'

'He probably decided to avoid you when he saw that the king favoured you,' I comfort her. 'The king makes much of you, doesn't he?'

'Yes,' she sniffs. 'He gave me a gold chain, which is nice, but he's older than my uncle!'

I laugh. 'Not at all! His Majesty is in the prime of his life!'

She gives me her courtier smile. 'I just forgot for a moment,' she apologises.

On the day after May Day, Richard Cromwell, my spymaster's nephew, is knighted and is now Sir Richard, and Lord Lisle, visiting from Calais, hosts a great banquet at Dereham House. The queen looks beautiful in the French hood which I have persuaded her to wear, and the king beside her is noisy and cheerful, praising the jousters and the dinner. The wealth of the monasteries and the abbey lands pouring into the royal treasury makes the king as generous as *Plutus*. He gives every one of the champions a purse of a gold and a house of their own. Lord Lisle beams at the honour shown to his stepson and applauds the wildly extravagant gift to the jousters. Lord Cromwell, dressed plainly as usual in his black suit, claps his boy Richard on the back when no one is looking.

Lord Lisle is a tall, handsome man, good-looking and charming as all the royal Plantagenet family – all of them more kingly than any Tudor. He is high in royal favour; he, too, is to get an earldom for his loyal service in holding and managing Calais – a difficult posting, so close to France and so far from London, an exchequer for all spies and heretics going between France and Spain, Scotland and England. He has no idea that Thomas Cromwell and I imagined his downfall, and I am glad that the plot stayed as a speculation.

The deaths of my husband and sister-in-law have been fully avenged by the fall of the Courtenays. I don't need more. I hope that Lord Lisle will use his time basking in the king's favour to speak for his kinswoman, Lady Margaret Pole, who should be released from the Tower to finish her long life in the comfort of her own home. I will believe that a good tyranny is in power when I see her return to Bisham Abbey.

Lord Lisle attends a meeting of the privy council, confidently expecting his earldom to be announced by his beloved cousin the king, and I have the ladies ready in our best clothes for a late dinner to celebrate his new honour, though the queen is looking strained and Kitty Howard dazzling. I expect the king and his friends to come late after drinking the health of the new earl, and I take a moment to look out of the window of the queen's chamber, over the river to the gardens and fields on the south bank, and upstream where the sun is setting over Lambeth Palace.

Below me, threading through the little boats on the Thames, is a dark barge silently rowing upriver, turning on the flat water and mooring, in complete silence, at the pier. As I watch, Sir William Kingston – the constable of the Tower – and his friend Lord Lisle come out of a little garden door below my window and walk through the golden light of the garden, down the stairs to the quay.

Lord Lisle is wearing his cloak, though the evening is mild. Sir William Kingston keeps pace beside him with his head bowed. They're not arm in arm chatting, as if they were leaving a joyful party; they are both silent as they walk along the pier, past other gaily-painted barges with standards flying, up the gangplank of the black unmarked barge. They cast off and row away without a word, without anyone on the bank saying farewell. There is no escort to honour the new-made earl; there are no trumpeters. There is no sound but the crying of seagulls, no cheers from the rowers, no word from the bargemaster. It is all silent, like a bad dream. It can be nothing but an arrest; it has to be an arrest, though they are old friends and their sons were jousting together as comrades on May Day only yesterday.

I stare out of the window without moving, without a word. For once in my life, I don't think: what does this mean, and how should I use this information? For once in my life, I think nothing, and I do nothing. I don't even tap on the window so that his lordship knows someone has seen his departure and will write to his wife Lady Lisle in Calais and warn his stepdaughter Anne Basset, who is practising dance steps in the room behind me, with no idea that her stepfather has just stepped into the Tower barge and gone swiftly and silently downstream, like a dark cormorant speeding east, low over shining water.

Only at dinner, when everyone notices that Lord Lisle is missing from his place and his chamberlain says he has been summoned to London, do I allow myself to think: can this be the false supposition, the *petitio principii* that Thomas Cromwell and I played when we said: suppose that the king is unmanned by witchcraft? Suppose that Papists have hired a witch? Did I help my spymaster imagine a supposition which was not an intellectual game but a new masque of entrapment?

L ORD LISLE'S SILENT disappearance launches a wave of arrests, as a stone thrown into a millpond sends ripples spreading in dark water. Dr Richard Sampson, the king's reliable advisor on divorce, is arrested, too – no reason is given out, but perhaps he thought – as I did – that three prior contracts for three successive wives was straining belief.

George Carew, young kinsman of the executed Sir Nicholas Carew, follows his commander, Lord Lisle, into the Tower, both of them accused of giving the keys of England's last foothold in France to our enemies.

Anne Basset cries all day in her room for her mother Lady Lisle, who sends an anguished note to say that she has been turned out of her home in Calais, and her household goods and her wardrobes of beautiful clothes have been taken from her. Even her famous aviary of quails has been seized by Robert Radcliffe the Earl of Sussex – one of the king's brutish old lords who wins not only the quails but the captaincy of Calais, too.

'Poor little birds!' Kitty Howard says, holding Anne Basset in her arms. 'He'll never look after them properly.'

THE EARL OF Sussex dives into the riches of Calais and all the spy records. It's a town riven with gossip, heresy, disloyalty, and treason. Thomas Cromwell has friends throughout the Staple where the merchants gather, half of them Lutherans, some even worse. Reginald Pole is said to have the keys to the castle; the King of France is said to be a friend of the Lisles. Robert Radcliffe finds a document which shows that Lord Lisle once sold a horse to the emperor of Spain: a dishonest broker can make much of this – and he does. And if Arthur, Lord Lisle is accused of treason, will the imaginary plot run on? Will Lord Hungerford be accused of witchcraft next? And then, will anyone mention the queen?

Every day, we hear of another arrest and not all of them are Papists; many are Lutherans, the queen's religion. Suspicion spreads like a plague mist as I walk around the Palace of Westminster, wrapped against the cold like a masquer, with a cloak hiding my gown and a hood hiding my face. It is so like the May of only four years ago, when nobody knew what was happening and who had offended, that I feel as if I am reliving the days when I wrote to George and wrote to my father and met with Master Cromwell and the duke, and asked everyone: what is happening? What is happening?

This time, I don't need to ask. I can imagine it all; because I was in the room where the unthinkable was first thought, built like a dark downward stair: one step after another – and the lowest point was naming the queen as a witch.

I think: I must speak to her. I must warn her against any questions about witchcraft. I must make sure that she knows the words: witchcraft, enchantment, sortilège, dark arts, curse, impotence, and death, to deny them if they are ever put to her in questioning. I must warn her to tell someone that she fears that her marriage to the king is not valid. She should do this today, before the music changes again and someone – like the Earl of Sussex, who is dancing through Calais, or William Fitzwilliam, who was such a strong partner to Margaret Pole – gets hold of her and swirls her around in a new dance called the *Liar's Volta*.

Only Thomas Cromwell can reassure me that the queen is safe, and I lie in wait for him as he arrives early one morning, with a servant carrying his great wooden box full of warrants for the king to sign as he prays at Prime.

'Lord Cromwell?' I curtsey. 'My lord?'

He beams at me. 'Lord Essex it is now, Lady Rochford!'

'Lord Essex, I will not delay you. I know you're going to mass.'

'I have a moment for you, Lady Rochford. The bell is not yet tolling.'

'The ladies in the queen's rooms are much concerned about the arrests, Lord Essex.'

'Are they?' he asks me, smiling. 'I would be surprised if they thought about anything but their own ambition. Or is it just you? Just you who is concerned? Since I have a moment. But only a moment?'

I step closer. 'You're not pursuing the *petitio principii*?' I whisper. 'Not the witchcraft accusation?'

'I am,' he says frankly. 'But not up to the queen's door. She can be kept out of it as long as she agrees to an annulment. The matter can begin and end with the unfortunate Lord Hungerford and his friends on one scaffold and the unfortunate Lord Lisle on another, and no connection from them to the queen at all.'

'But there *is* no connection,' I point out. 'No connection to the queen at all!'

Lord Cromwell smiles. 'None at all, none will be made – if she agrees to an annulment.'

'But if she does not, then you have this . . . this possible third act?'

'This inducement,' he says gently. 'She can make a false admission of invalidity or face a false accusation of witchcraft – it can be her choice. I have no preference. They both achieve the same end – I want a final blow to the Spanish party and to set the king free of a marriage that he doesn't want.'

He is so smilingly cheerful that I feel foolish when I take hold of his hands and say, breathlessly: 'But, Lord Essex, one way gives an innocent woman 8,000 nobles a year and the Palace of Richmond and the other names her as a witch. And the punishment for witchcraft is death.'

He bows over my hands and lets me go. 'That's why I know that you will advise her to make the right choice. Will you bring ladies to the Tower to give evidence, Lady Rochford? I will send a barge for you. I should like one – no, I should like two other ladies to sign evidence. You choose whomever you think would be the most convincing.'

I put a hand on his arm. 'I know you wouldn't hurt her,' I say earnestly. 'She's very young. Her father is dead; her brother doesn't protect her. She's not even fluent in our language. She could be easily entrapped by a bad advisor. But it was you who brought her to England, Lord Essex, and she has done nothing wrong. You would not hurt her.'

He puts his hand over mine. His hands are still callused from hard work, though he has sat among the nobility for years. 'I won't hurt her,' he promises. 'But she has to help me to set her free. You have to help me free her from this marriage.'

It is like the other May Day. I have the same swirling sense of darkness behind my eyes, and I seem to be running wherever I go, though I don't really know where to go, and certainly I should not be seen running and breathless.

I skid to a halt before the double doors of the queen's rooms as they are opened, and I curtsey as the queen and her ladies come out for mass, their heads veiled, holding their prayer books. I snatch up a scarf to veil my head and step into the procession behind the queen.

In the royal chapel, everything is comfortingly unchanged: the king in his balcony, his foot propped on a stool, half-listening to the priest, who is saying the prayers in Latin although today the Bible readings are in English. The king holds a pen as Cromwell, steady as a turning water wheel, bends forward, slides a paper before him, whispers in his ear, and the king signs without reading. Behind Cromwell, his clerk scatters the new signatures with sand to dry the ink, before putting them in the great wooden box. Kneeling in prayer on one side of the king is his new favourite, Thomas Culpeper; on the other side is his brother-in-law, Thomas Seymour, and standing at the back of the balcony, Sir Anthony Browne.

Everything is as it always is, as it always will be. Except that I know that this time next year, there will be a new queen beside me, looking over at the king and bowing with respect, sliding to her knees and praying earnestly that God will give her a son, as the king cannot. Today, the fate of this queen lies in my hands, and Thomas Cromwell has shown me a way to bring her out of the valley of the shadow of death into safety and freedom.

I kneel beside her, and I proffer my missal for her to share. I have knelt close before, to prompt her in the ritual which is strange to her, but this time I whisper: 'I have to advise you, Your Grace.'

I speak in German, so none of the English ladies will understand if they overhear us.

She is no fool. Not a flicker of an expression crosses her face. She keeps her eyes on the words of the service, her lips moving in prayer; she does not even steal a glance at me.

'The king's minister is going to end your marriage,' I say. I don't know the word for annulment in German, and this would sound more tactful in French; but we are safer in her language. 'Please stay still and quiet.'

She keeps her eyes on the altar. She says: 'Amen,' to the end of a collect, and I take it as agreement.

'There are two ways this can be done. One is very bad for you. Very bad.' I wait until I see her half nod. She knows what 'very bad' means for a queen in England. 'The other way gives you a pension, two beautiful houses. You would be a single woman, an Englishwoman, as free and as wealthy as a rich widow. You would be respected.'

She has gone very white; I am afraid that she is going to faint. Under the shelter of the velvet shelf where our prayer books are resting, I clasp her hand. She does not take her eyes from the officiating priest but she minutely nods. '*Sprechen*,' she whispers. 'Speak.'

'They will ask if you were betrothed to the Duke of Lorraine.'

'They asked me already. I told them no.'

'I know. But they will ask again, and this time you must answer differently. Don't deny it this time. Just say that you don't know. You were only a little girl – you don't know what your father agreed. And now your father is dead, you can't ask him. How would you know?'

'Because I have seen the contract of release,' she says simply. 'I swore on my honour I was free to marry the king, my husband.'

'You have to say that you may be mistaken,' I tell her. 'On your life – for your life – you have to do this.'

'But it is a lie,' she observes quietly, her gaze on the crucifix on the altar.

'I know. But you must say it, and then the churchmen will inquire, and they will decide that you were married before and your marriage to the king is invalid.'

'So, I am married to the Duke of Lorraine?' she confirms quietly. 'And I have been married to him since I was eleven years old?'

'It doesn't matter that this makes no sense. It is a pretence, like a masque. But it's going to save your life.'

Again, she goes a terrible waxy white.

I pinch her soft palm. The priest has started the bidding to mass. I don't have long to make her understand. 'You have to say that the marriage to the king has not been consummated,' I whisper. I have no idea of the word 'consummated' in German. 'You have to say he hasn't swived you. No bed. No bed. No fuck. No baby. You understand?'

'Because he is old?' she whispers. 'He cannot?'

'No, no! Never, never say he cannot. If you say it, they will say there is a witch – an overlooking – evil magic. You say that you don't know what should be done in bed. You are a maid. You know nothing about it. He kisses you goodnight and good morning, and you thought that was all that was needed to make a baby.'

'He knows better . . .' she observes.

'Yes, but he says that he does not do it, he chooses not to do it, because he knew as soon as he met you that you are the wife of the Duke of Lorraine.'

Even in this terrible danger, she has a sense of the ridiculous. She lowers her eyelids to hide the gleam of amusement in her dark-brown eyes. 'How does he know this?' she whispers in English.

'God told him,' I say without a smile.

She hides her face in her hands as if praying.

'Whatever you think, whatever the truth, it has to be done this way,' I say sternly.

The priest has started the confessional; the ladies behind me follow the strange English words in a whispered chorus.

I hold up the prayer book to hide the queen's face from the officiating priest. 'You have to agree that the king has not bedded you; then the marriage can be annulled, and you can get your pension and your lands, and you will be safe. You have to agree that you were precontracted; you have to say that you're still a virgin; you have to agree that the king has slept by your side but never touched you. You didn't know there was more. You kiss goodnight and good morning, and that is all.'

'It's not true,' she says flatly. 'Everyone will know it is not true.'

'If you don't say this lie, then the king will say he is impotent, and others will say it was caused by witchcraft.' I press my words into the side of her hood with my lips, as if I would force them into her head. 'They will say someone put a spell on him, to make sure that he never had a baby with you. They may even say that you knew, that you wanted the king unmanned. They may even say it is you who is the witch.'

I thought she might be frightened, but under her heavy gown, I see her shoulders make a tiny shrug. 'Is as stupid as the other,' she says in English, and if we were not in chapel with the king opposite and Cromwell putting down death warrants before him, she would have shocked me into laughter.

T HE WEATHER IMPROVES, and May is a merry month of arrests. Lord Hungerford is taken into the Tower for questioning. It is announced that he foretold the king's death with a witch, and they produce the poor old woman and his priest and his doctor, too. They are all accused of plotting with the dead rebel pilgrims for the return of the old royal family – Reginald Pole and Arthur, Lord Lisle. Such wickedness earns them all the death sentence. Justice must be swift, and there is no need for a trial; they will be executed by a writ of attainder, nodded through by an appalled House of Parliament.

The queen's lord chamberlain Thomas Manners Earl of Rutland comes to me in the middle of June and says that the king's council advise that there is illness in London.

'Not plague?' I ask.

'Alas, yes,' he says, glassy-eyed. 'The council thinks it would be best if Her Grace moved to Richmond Palace.'

We both know that if there were plague in London, the king would be in Windsor by now. But we have our parts to play. 'Richmond Palace? Will the king join us there?'

'In a few days,' he lies, so smoothly that only I – another smooth liar – would detect it. 'Please do explain to Her Grace that the palace is known for its healthy air.'

'I will,' I say.

I have not spoken to her since the morning in the chapel. I hope she understands the arrest of Lord Hungerford and his witch is part of the plot that could bring her down, but I don't know what she is thinking, nor if she has plans of her own. She cannot get a secret message to her brother in Cleves; any letter would immediately be delivered to Thomas Cromwell's dark chamber for opening, translating, and reading, and only sent on if it suits his plans. The queen's ambassador, newly arrived from Cleves, has no money and speaks no English. He can be no help. The people of London liked her on sight, but they can do nothing, and she knows nobody in England but her ladies. Her most trusted friend is me – and I am plotting for the annulment of her marriage and her shame.

I curtsey to the lord chamberlain and go slowly into the queen's rooms.

Queen Anne is playing cards with Catherine Carey and red-eyed Anne Basset. I am hoping that Anne's tearful face will remind the queen of her danger. If a royal cousin like Lord Lisle can be arrested, a friendless young foreign duchess can disappear overnight. A lie to save yourself is allowed by God, Jews call it the *pikuach nefesh*. The most faithful Roman Catholic Christian in England, Lady Mary, swore that she was a bastard. If Lady Mary can lie, this Lutheran surely can.

The girls at the card table try to smile when I come in.

'Ach, Lady Rochford,' the queen says. 'These girls are robbing me.'

'They are terrible thieves!' I say, laughing, and Anne Basset flushes red. I rush on: 'I have just spoken to your lord chamberlain, Your Grace, and we are to move to Richmond Palace tomorrow. I think you will like the palace; it is one of the most beautiful new buildings on the river and more healthy than London at this time of year.'

Not by one flicker of expression does she betray that she knows Richmond Palace is to be part of her settlement. 'Does His Majesty come with us?' she asks.

'He will follow,' I say. 'When he has completed his business in London.'

At the mention of the king's business in London – the execution of her stepfather, Lord Lisle – Anne Basset excuses herself and dashes out of the room.

I sit in her place and pick up her cards, and the queen nods as if she is pleased and picks up her cards again, as cool as if I had told her nothing but a detail of housekeeping.

'It is your deal, I think, Mistress Carey,' she says.

## WESTMINSTER PALACE, JUNE

### 1540

I GO TO SEE if my spymaster is at work in his dark chamber after morning prayers. There is a yeoman of the guard barring the way before the locked door, and I walk briskly past, as if his room was never my destination. The warm air drifts through the open door to the gardens and invites me to stroll through the courtyards and the jumble of pathways of the old palace.

I find myself at the royal stables. Thomas Cromwell's big cob horse is in his usual stall; his groom is polishing the big leather saddle on a bench outside.

'Where's your master?'

He jumps to his feet, pulls his cap from his head and bows. 'I don't know, your ladyship,' he says. None of Cromwell's men ever tell anyone anything.

'When he comes for his horse, please tell him that Lady Rochford would like to see him,' I say, and as I am turning to go back to the queen's rooms, my uncle Thomas Howard Duke of Norfolk rides in and jumps down from his horse like a man half his age.

'Ah, there you are, Jane,' he says cheerfully. 'And here am I, early for a meeting of the privy council. We have much to do today.' He laughs. 'Much to do.'

I fall into step beside him up the stone stairs into the open doorway. 'Really?' I say. 'About the arrests?' I lower my voice. 'My lord, anything about the queen?'

'Arrests!' he exclaims. 'They're shipping them over from Calais as if they were quails! A baker's dozen, all heretics.'

I have to steady my voice before I can ask him again: 'My lord uncle, anything about the queen?'

'It's not the queen you need to worry about!' He laughs at me, showing his yellow teeth. 'Not her! But one of your other fine friends. You'll know it all in good time,' he declares. 'But I'll see you at my door, claiming kinship and wanting friendship. I will see you, all pretty smiles, at my door, Jane.'

'I'm always proud to be of the House of Howard,' I say cautiously. 'I am always glad of your friendship, Uncle.'

'Never more than today!' he taunts me and heads up the stone stairs to the privy council chamber.

THOMAS CROMWELL MUST be at the privy council meeting with my uncle and the other lords, and I expect he will find me when the meeting is over. The meetings usually take all morning, especially in these troubled times when the king's wishes are uncertain and changeable, and one group rises and the other falls, and only Thomas Cromwell – Lord Essex as he is now known – rides the crest of every tide.

In the queen's rooms, the girls are sewing, and Kitty Howard is showing the queen the steps of a new dance. I walk past them to the tall Venetian glass windows and look down to the quayside and the river beyond.

The barge from the Tower is moored by the pier again – I rub my eyes as if I cannot believe that I see it again, as if it is a ghost, a harbinger. A black-painted barge without a flag or standard, rocking lightly on the ebbing tide, the oarsmen in their places, as if ready to go in a moment, the gangplank against the pier, the stanchions in place, the bargemaster waiting at the pier as if he has to stand to attention because his passengers will be here at any moment.

And then I see the prisoner: bare-headed, slightly stooped, stumbling as he comes down the stone stairs, along the paved quay, one hand clasping the front of his beautiful black jacket where it has been ripped in a struggle. Someone hurls his cap after him, and as it flies through the air, I recognise it. It is the neat black velvet embroidered cap that Thomas Cromwell always wears – little different from the cap that he wore when he was a wool merchant. The man walking behind him catches it and hands it to him with an odd little bow, as if he does not wish to be impolite to this man who is limping as if fatally hurt, to this man who says nothing as he stumbles along, to this man who ruled all of England this morning and is being hurried into the Tower barge to catch the ebbing tide, to take him to the Tower this afternoon.

It is Thomas Cromwell under arrest. It is Thomas Cromwell, bare-headed, with his cap in his hand, his jacket torn where someone has ripped off his insignia, his breeches tattered where someone tore off his precious Order of the Garter. This is a disaster for me, for the queen, and for Thomas Cromwell himself.

I glance back to the room, at the ladies so pretty and comfortable and busy in their little occupations, and I think: nobody will ever know the terror that is gripping me in this pretty room, as I turn from the window and smile and say that we must start getting ready, for the king and the noblemen will come soon, and it will be dinnertime.

I supervise the dressing of the queen; I am most particular in the placing of her jewels and the positioning of her hood on her fair hair. I meet her questioning brown eyes in the mirror, as if she is asking me why any of this would matter, if she is to go to Richmond Palace tomorrow? If she is to declare herself a duchess of Cleves and not a queen of England? Why dress like a bride to agree to the annulment of her marriage?

I don't tell her that this poor outcome is now our most ambitious hope – that the man who planned to end her marriage and save her neck is going swiftly downstream in an unmarked barge to the Tower of London, and I don't know what will greet him when he gets there. I cannot tell her that there was another plan, all in place and ready to hand, a plan where she dies on the scaffold, just as my sister-in-law died.

I don't know who will become head of the dark chamber if Thomas Cromwell is beheaded, who will open the box of secret letters, who will choose what plan grinds into place. Both plans for the removal of the queen are equally ready, but one gives her Richmond Palace and 8,000 nobles a year, and the other deals her disgrace or even death. I don't know what will happen to her, without Cromwell shuffling the pack of picture cards; I don't know what will happen to me without his protection.

I smile confidently and say to her: 'Will Your Grace dance tonight?'

'Oh, do let's,' says Katheryn Howard.

The queen laughs at Kitty Howard's unending desire for dances and young partners, and says: 'Yes, why not?'

As my uncle the Duke of Norfolk predicted, I am at his door the very next morning, although the queen's barge is at the pier, waiting for the flowing tide to Richmond Palace. I ask his servant if His Grace is at home and if I may speak with him, and the duke himself comes to the door smiling.

'Ah, Jane. I was expecting you,' he says. 'Do come in, dear niece.'

He leads me to his inner chamber. The empty grate is filled with herbs, and the room smells of lemon balm and hyssop. 'You'll be anxious about your spymaster.'

I nod. There is no point in denying it.

He gleams in his triumph like a well-fed falcon. 'Lord Essex – now once again Master Thomas Cromwell – is being questioned in the Tower for heresy and treason. He'll be executed within the month.'

I feel cold. 'You seem very sure, my lord?'

'They're dancing in the streets for joy.'

'Might there be a pardon? Or some mistake?'

'The king's archers have collected sacks of gold plate from Austin Friars, chests of money, and Cromwell's debt book. D'you think he's going to give it back?'

'His lordship is to face a trial?' I ask.

He shakes his head. 'As he says himself, trials take too long, with too many opinions. Quicker and easier for us all if I put the evidence before the Houses of Parliament and they issue a writ of attainder, and he is executed.'

'That's not justice,' I say simply. 'Nobody can think he has been treasonous to the king.'

'As I say, I don't need opinions. Clearly, he forced the king into a marriage which was against the king's best interests. Clearly, she's a Lutheran bride and he's a Lutheran spy. The marriage will be annulled, and the man who treasonously forced this marriage on the king will die for it. The king's true friends, the old lords of the realm, the true nobility will be restored as his only advisors. We've all had enough of new men. We won't be ruled by merchants and mayors. The king will be free to marry whoever he chooses. As it happens, he will choose my niece.'

'Kitty?'

'Mistress Katheryn Howard. So she's not going with you to Richmond. You can make up some excuse to tell the duchess.'

'The duchess?'

'The Duchess of Cleves.' He sees my face. 'Oh, all right: the queen. But anyway, Kitty Howard won't serve her any more. She's going home to her grandmother. The king can court her there without scandal.'

I am completely silent. Of course, the king, nearly fifty, in the first months of his fourth marriage, cannot court a girl of sixteen, his wife's maid-of-honour, without scandal – not at Lambeth nor anywhere else.

But my first thought is for my own safety: 'Thomas Cromwell's servants will be fearful – many people inform for him: the investigators of the monasteries, the network of mayors and sheriffs and merchants . . .'

'You mean you, I suppose? For Christ's sake, Jane, don't waste my time pretending you care about Cromwell's slaveys. Your name needn't come into it – if you're prepared to be helpful now.'

'What can I do to help you, Uncle?'

'Did Cromwell have a plan to release the king from this false marriage? He says that he did? He says that he can set it in motion in return for his freedom. D'you know what it is?'

I don't hesitate. 'Yes, I do.'

'What is it?'

'He can tell you it himself? In return for his freedom?'

My uncle looks at me, hawklike. 'Or you can tell me now?'

I have no choice. 'The queen is to have Richmond Palace and 8,000 nobles a year,' I tell him. 'In return, she has to agree to an annulment – that she was precontracted.'

'Precontract again?' he says incredulously, just as I did.

'Yes,' I say firmly. 'He thought it the only solution.'

Thomas Howard takes my chin in his hand and turns my face towards the light. I don't waver under his eagle-eyed inspection. 'Not the only solution, I think. Wasn't there some discussion of a witch overlooking the king's marriage bed? Some enchantment cast on the king's potency? D'you know why Lord Hungerford is in the Tower?'

Something about the way his thumbnail digs into my chin reminds me that he is strong and I am only a woman, but I know that my woman's frailty has taught me to be quicker-witted, more cunning. I can fool him. I can fool him now.

I gasp and cross myself. 'God save us all. I know nothing about Lord Hungerford but what everyone knows: that he was cruel to his wife and perverse.'

'So – no queen witch this time around?' he asks. 'Not like t'other one.'

'There's no need for accusations of witchcraft, it's all done by agreement,' I urge him.

'Then why is Lord Hungerford condemned to die?' he asks.

I turn a blank face to him; he will believe I know nothing. 'For rebellion, isn't it? And predicting the king's death?' I give a little start. 'Oh yes, they say he used a witch, didn't he? In Wiltshire, though? An old woman? Nothing to do with the queen?'

'Quite separate?'

'Oh yes.'

'Very well.' He is satisfied. 'And have you brokered this agreement with the queen? Is she ready to declare herself as good a maid as when she came into this country and that the king was inspired by God to leave her as that?'

'She'll consent,' I assure him.

'And you've got ladies lined up to give evidence that the king was in her bed, night after night, and chose not to consummate the wedding, for his conscience's sake? Nothing about impotence?'

'Nothing about impotence,' I repeat, as if learning from him.

'Very well,' he says, with quiet satisfaction. 'Cromwell is a master at this stuff; I give him that. You take the queen to Richmond Palace on the tide and bring your ladies back to swear their evidence when I tell you. And prepare the duchess to swear an oath as well.'

'And if this is all done as Thomas Cromwell planned, does it earn him a pardon?'

'Why should you care?' my uncle demands. 'Unless you share his faith, his treasonous faith? Unless you have worked with him as his spy and his crony in treasonous plots? Unless you're a traitor like him? Are you a traitor? Another Boleyn traitor?'

I am silent. My spymaster, with his dark-eyed smile and reluctant snort of a laugh, will have to fall without a word from me. He has hundreds of friends, thousands of dependents. Someone should speak for him; I cannot. 'No, of course not. I'll do what I ought to do, in obedience to you, Uncle.'

'Good,' he says shortly. 'And if this is successful, with the queen and ladies-in-waiting, with sworn evidence and legal annulment, then we'll never say it was Cromwell's plan, Jane. I will take the credit and earn the favour of the king.'

'Very well.' I think: yes, you braggart. You take the credit, and you'll never know that it was my plan. I am too clever to take the credit. I will see this through from the shadows, and only I will know that you are all dancing to my tune.

'You'll never mention Thomas Cromwell again,' he tells me.

I know that this is the death of Thomas Cromwell, who was a friend to me when I had no friends and made me feel loved when nobody loved me. He was my tutor, my spymaster – he taught me all about treachery; it will come as no surprise to him when he learns that I have let him go to the scaffold without a word in his defence.

'Very well.'

## RICHMOND PALACE, SUMMER

# 1540

WE TELL THE queen that we have come to Richmond to avoid the plague and the heat of the summer city and that the king will join us shortly. We embroider this lie by assuring her that the king always leaves London in summer on a progress to beautiful country houses and that she will enjoy this.

Katheryn Howard is missing: the Norfolk barge took her on the high tide to her family house at Lambeth before we embarked. She did not say goodbye to the queen, nor to any of the ladies but only to her bedfellow and cousin, Catherine Carey, who says that she cried a great deal and said that she would never be happy again. For once, I think that the foolish child is right. She has the most glorious prospect of any girl in England – but I doubt that she will find happiness.

We tell the queen that Kitty Howard's step-grandmother, Agnes Howard the Dowager Duchess of Norfolk has been taken ill and that Kitty has gone back to Lambeth. The queen glances at me, as if to ask me if this is another lie, like all the others we are telling her now, but she can read nothing from my expressionless face. 'But she will come back?'

'I don't know when.'

Nobody tells the queen that parliament is in daily session, but in early July, we hear that they have passed a new law to say that a second marriage, undertaken after one that was not consummated, is legal and not bigamous. The queen does not ask me what this law means, and I don't volunteer that the king can marry a new wife at once; he need not wait for any annulment, all he has to do is prove his marriage to her was not consummated.

Three days later the king's new advisors – old noblemen and favourites, not one scholar or lawyer among them – are rowed upriver in two barges, with her new ambassador Herr Harst. I stand beside the queen as her lord chamberlain tells her that the privy council has implored the king to hold an inquiry into their marriage. Her ambassador is silently furious; her receiver general is embarrassed. I am as empty of emotion as a mask laid aside.

They give long speeches in English that are translated laboriously into bad German by that established liar Richard Rich. Queen Anne gives no answer, not in English nor German. In the afternoon, they come again to explain what was completely clear to her from the day I told her in chapel: that she must pretend to believe a string of lies. They tell her that she was precontracted to the Duke of Lorraine when she married the king, that God warned the king of this on their wedding night, and that their marriage was never consummated on all the nights after.

'You'll have to see them again,' I tell her. 'You'll have to reply that it shall be as the king wishes.'

She looks at me. 'Whatever he wishes? Whatever it might be?'

'It's not the king you need fear,' I tell her. 'The king has new advisors, and I don't know what they will do. They have all the power, and you have none. Your brother will not defend you; he's in France. He's given up on you and on England. You've got no choice but to accept.' I hesitate. 'I beg you to accept . . .'

'It is not the king who does this?' she asks me.

I shake my head. 'He doesn't do anything – they do everything for him, before he even says what he wants. Now, he wants a new wife.'

The king's men come in: Charles Brandon, the king's brother-in-law, and Thomas Audley, sailing before a new wind. William Fitzwilliam comes in with Bishop Stephen Gardiner. Sir William Kingston the constable of the Tower, who escorted my husband George to the scaffold and Anne to the block, follows them. My heart misses a beat. Has he come to arrest his queen? Like he arrested his friends, Lord Lisle and Thomas Cromwell?

She tries to stand to greet them, but when the five of them march in – so hard-faced and old, so unflinching before her young prettiness – her legs fail her, and she falls back into her chair. Charles Brandon – the most senior and the stupidest – hardly waits for her to recover before he says that they have documents to prove that she was precontracted to the Duke of Lorraine.

Ambassador Harst blusters in German and demands to see the documents; nobody pays any attention to him. It is a masque not a real consultation. They don't even have the documents to hand, they mime, gesturing with empty hands. The king's men are blockheads; I have seen them in a dozen masques, as Russians, as Turks: now they enter as hangmen. Queen Anne, silent on her throne, is like a woman playing *Mischance* seated on a painted wood wheel of fortune. Impossible to take this theatrical confrontation seriously – except that it could not be more grave. If we do not play our parts in this masque which is called *Surrender*, there can be no doubt that we will be dance in another called: *Witch-hunt*.

I lean forward and whisper to her. My part is *Kind Counsellor*, and I play it as well as ever. Obedient to my advice, speaking my script, the young queen raises her head and tells them that she is always content with His Majesty the king, and that of course, he must be right in whatever he says. If he says that there was a precontract and the marriage should be annulled, he cannot be mistaken.

The Lords Audley, Suffolk, and Southampton bow low and manage to restrain themselves from slapping each other on the back.

They stay overnight at Richmond Palace, and they eat well and drink deep in the great hall, while the queen and us ladies dine in her rooms. They come in after dinner to say goodnight, and William Fitzwilliam beckons me to see him out.

'Tomorrow morning, before breakfast, please bring two ladies with you to swear that the marriage was not consummated,' he says. 'I take it there will be no difficulty?'

'None.'

'Who will you bring?'

'I thought Katherine Edgcumbe?' She was in service with me to Katherine of Aragon, and dropped her without remorse. 'And

Eleanor Manners the Countess of Rutland?' I suggest. Eleanor was Anne's lady-in-waiting and gave evidence against her and my husband. Swearing on oath that a marriage was not consummated is nothing compared to what she will have said then.

'And they know what they have to do?'

I could almost laugh at him telling me of my own plan. 'Yes, my lord. We all know very well what we have to do.'

We prepare our statement like three Judases on the first Spy Wednesday, sitting in the back of the barge, wrapped up warmly in our capes, hoods together like three witches, rewriting the past so the future will read as we want. We devise an unlikely account of a conversation, ignoring that Katherine and Eleanor have no German and the queen knows no English words for intimacy. Never mind that the queen would never have spoken to anyone about her marriage bed and her husband. Never mind that nobody could seriously believe one word of the conversation that I scribble in the back of the barge, that springs forward so powerfully as the rowers pull and reset, that we look as if we are in a masque, miming the rocking of a pretend boat on the painted waves of a silk sea.

'We could say that we asked her if she thought she might be with child?' I start, as the oars creak and the barge heaves.

'She'd never have discussed that with us,' Eleanor objects, letting likelihood get in the way of a good story.

'Doesn't matter. She's not going to deny it,' I remind her. 'She wants this over as much as the king does. She knows we have to say this. We all know this is not truth but an escape for them both.' I look from the cold determined face of one career courtier to another and I think: Christ! Do I look like this?

'All right,' Eleanor says. 'I'll say I asked her what he does when he comes to bed.'

'And she can answer that he kisses her and takes her by the hand and lies down and sleeps the night beside her,' Katherine agrees. The two of them snigger like whoremongers.

'We have to say that she knows nothing,' I remind them. 'We have to say that she is innocent.'

'Oh, we can say I asked her what he says in the morning, and that she told me he says: "Farewell, darling, until mass!"'

The two of them collapse at this high wit. Really, I should have hired Will the fool to write a merry masque.

'D'you think it likely that one of us would have asked her for more details?' I enquire, writing to their gleeful dictation.

'I shall say that I said: "Madam, there must be more than this, or it will be long ere we have a Duke of York, which all this realm most desireth",' Eleanor says grandly. 'I don't mind swearing to that.'

I make a note of the superbly unlikely dialogue. 'And we stick to this,' I urge them. 'We're swearing on oath. We can never betray our word; we can never betray each other, nor the queen.'

'The king wants this?' Katherine asks, as if it is the only question. 'He wants rid of Anne and to marry Kitty?'

'This is what he wants,' I say. 'And this is the only way to get the duchess out of this snare that the men have put her in.'

'Oh! The men!' Eleanor says, throwing her hands up as if she has one scrap of fellow feeling for another woman. 'Yes, yes, Jane. We have our script, we know our parts, we'll never let you down. And there will be a reward?'

'There will be a reward,' I confirm.

I am satisfied with the words I have noted. There's nothing about witch-given impotence blighting the royal bed. There is nothing to suggest the king is impotent now or was earlier – essential if everyone is to believe Prince Edward is his son, essential if he is to be credited with fathering any future son. The king and his line must be free of any suspicion of lack of vigour. He will tell everyone that God warned him not to bed his bride; all we have to do is to confirm that he did not. The completely ridiculous dialogue, all in English, invading royal privacy, makes it clear that Anne of Cleves is a maid – even more virginal than her predecessor Anne Boleyn, who once told me that she was as virginal as the Virgin Mary.

The barge slows, and the oarsmen spin it round so that it will face upriver, ready to take us home on the flowing tide when our work is done. Charles Brandon steps on board to help us down the gangplank and along the quay. The other two lords fall in behind him. It is a guard of honour, although it feels for a moment unpleasantly like arrest. I suddenly think: is this a double-cross, and am I leading the way to my confession, and am I not the spider here but a stupidly buzzing fly?

Brandon leads the way through the maze of courts and gardens to the heart of the palace, to the room I know well: my spymaster's room. It is clean and bare – just as he always has it – his big chair one side of the table and two smaller ones set opposite, convenient for conversation or confession. I can't think how many times I have sat here and seen his slowly dawning smile or heard the quiet click of a letter falling through the slit behind me and known that the sluice gate of the Cromwell information mill is open, and it is grinding grist. But today it is my dark chamber; I am the spymaster.

It takes us about an hour to finish, and the clocks are striking the half hour when Charles Brandon's young wife Catherine knocks on the door and enters the room, followed by a clerk carrying a great wooden box.

'My lord requires me to invite you ladies to breakfast,' she says with studied indifference. I know she is sulky at having to obey him and meet with us. She is a reformer, a secret supporter of Lord Cromwell; she welcomed the Lutheran queen. 'And here is my lord's steward.'

Silently, the man opens the wooden box like a gaping jaw for me to drop our signed pages inside. There are papers at the bottom of the box already. I recognise the regular clerkish hand of Thomas Cromwell, the half-moon loop of the *C* of his signature like a smile. He has signed his statement, and here it is in the box, sitting neat and orderly below mine. I cannot see what he has written, but I trust him, as I always did. I know it will be an accurate account of the coming of the queen to England and the king's immediate rejection of her – inspired by God – and how her precontract means the marriage must be annulled with no blame to her but a handsome pension.

Beneath his statement are more papers – every courtier will have wanted to demonstrate his support for the king's case. They will repeat the cruel and disgusting lies the king told about her – that she is fat, that she smells, that her breasts are slack, that she is no maid. Dr Butts will witness that the king is as lusty as a bull in the meadow, but God spoke to him and warned him the queen is the wife of another man.

I remember saying to Cromwell: *You won't get him through the gate*, and for a moment, I could almost laugh at this box of scripts, this enormous theatrical production, this great masque – one of the greatest that the court has ever produced – and all to slide the king from the bed of one beautiful young woman worthy to be queen and into the bed of her maid. This is the third time we have rid the king of a good woman for a lesser one. But I am the first advisor to achieve this without bloodshed, and I give myself credit for that.

We eat a good breakfast with the sulky young duchess, and then take the barge on the flowing river back to Richmond. As soon as we enter the queen's pretty rooms, she asks us where we have been all morning? The other two ladies leave it to me to curtsey while they whisk away to change their gowns. I tell her we were called in by the convocation to say that we believe her marriage was not consummated.

She gives me one dark look, as if I have betrayed her to her enemies, and I lean close to her and whisper in her ear: 'You know I had to do this. You know this is the only way, the best way, that you set him free so he does not fight for his freedom. I did it for your good.'

She says: 'Yes, I know. I am not his wife but his subject, in his country. He has all the power.'

'But think of this lovely palace being your own, and 8,000 nobles a year!'

She looks at me gravely and turns away and goes into her private closet.

Next day, she keeps to her chamber; she wants no company. When I tap on the door and go in, she says she is reading; but she's staring out of the window with a closed book in her lap, and her cheeks are wet.

The day drags by with no amusement, and nobody visits. The weather is sunny, and the birds are singing and singing, but she does not want to walk in the garden, nor take a boat out on the river. We are waiting for something to happen, but nobody comes to Richmond Palace all day.

We undress her and put her to bed like a lonely child, and we have all gone to our own beds when there is a hammering on the door, and it is Ambassador Harst, who has rushed to us with the decision from the convocation.

We tumble out to wake her, but she is wide awake already, with her beautifully embroidered night robe over her gown, a white-worked nightcap on her fair head.

He tells her in German that the convocation has agreed unanimously that the marriage was illegal and shall be annulled. While he is speaking, messengers from the convocation are announced, with papers to be signed. They must have jumped in a barge and rowed as fast as the bargemen could go, to catch up with Herr Harst; they are only minutes behind him.

It is not enough for them to tell her the decision all over again, they want her to acknowledge that she will abide by it. She has to sign a letter of acceptance. As they watch eagerly, she signs herself the king's sister and servant and five of the ladies-in-waiting sign as witnesses after me. We all want our names on this document that will give the king so much pleasure. He will see my name is first. The brief marriage and short reign of Queen Anne is over.

At once, Richmond is no longer a royal palace – now, it is the private home of Anne of Cleves, a German duchess – no longer the Queen of England. She is to be known as the king's sister – and take precedence over all the ladies but the next queen – though with ponderous tact, they don't say who this might be. She has a handsome income, of course, but not enough for her current household of one-hundred-and-thirty servants. As a private single lady, she will need a lady companion or two – not dozens of us.

The master of the royal wardrobe comes to collect furs and gowns; the master of the jewel house boxes up precious diamonds and rubies and the pearls that suited her so well. I sit with her in her closet and listen to the men and the ladies outside in her bedroom, packing up the queen's treasures so neatly and prettily that they will be a pleasure for the new queen to open. Her other ladies are packing their own things and preparing to leave on the barges that are taking tapestries and carpets from the palace.

'You stay with me?' Anne of Cleves asks me in English, so calmly that it does not sound like a plea.

Of course, I could live with her as a private lady, withdraw from royal service and become a nobody. But I couldn't do it – not now, while I have achieved something no one has done before – ended a royal marriage without a death. Nobody, not Wolsey, not Cromwell – no one has been able to do this before. If I were a man, I would be lord chancellor for this. I have invented a new sort of woman: neither wife nor maid nor widow, I am a *femme sole* of court life. I am only thirty-five years old, I would be mad to retire with a discarded wife to a quiet house on the riverbank when my cousin is to be next Queen of England and only I have the skills to make her marriage possible.

'I am commanded to return to Westminster with your jewels, Your Grace. I'm in the king's service; I'm not free to choose where I live.'

'You go now?' She is startled. 'No one stays with me?'

'Your German ladies will stay with you,' I say gently. 'And your lord chamberlain will find new English ladies to keep you company. Many of your servants will stay.' I smile. 'You must keep your cook, now that you have taught him to make *birnentorte*: pear tart! And you will keep your horses and your own barge. You've got a country house, too – Bletchingley Place. I believe it is very beautiful – quite near here, in Surrey.'

Bletchingley was Nicholas Carew's house – seized by the crown after his execution for treason, now given to Anne of Cleves.

'And they're offering you Hever Castle as well! That was my family home in Kent – a proper little castle, very pretty. The king is generous to you. People will visit you, and you will visit court. The king has promised to be your friend and to treat you as his sister. You will be happy.'

'I shall be an English lady,' she says uncertainly.

'An English noblewoman,' I correct her. 'A rich English noblewoman!'

'You go back to the court at London?' She twists the ring off her finger. 'Take this,' she says. 'My wedding ring. It should go with all the other things.' She drops it into my hand: a gold ring engraved with the motto: *God send me well to keep*. She is quite expressionless; her enemies would say she is too stupid to feel grief at being abandoned and despised. But then she says: 'Tell the king that I said he might break it up and melt it down for the value of the gold. Tell him it has no other value, God knows.'

## OATLANDS PALACE, SURREY, SUMMER

# 1540

'My darling, darling Jane!' Kitty Howard flies down the long sunny presence chamber of Oatlands Palace, hands outstretched, her bronze hair streaming out from under a tiny cap. 'At last you've come! I thought you'd never come! My uncle said that you shall be my chief lady-in-waiting and I said: of course! She knows everything!'

There is no time for me to curtsey; Kitty flings herself into my arms in a swirl of silks and a mist of expensive Turkish perfume: oil of roses. 'Jane – I have the whole royal wardrobe to choose from. And you won't believe the jewels! Oh, of course you will! You know them all! Well, anyway, they're all mine now! And Jane, I have houses of my own. He has given me two dead men's houses! I shall have rents! I will be wealthy! Just think what I will buy!'

I detach myself from her clinging hug and sink into a curtsey.

'You don't have to curtsey to me!'

'Yes I do,' I tell her. 'All your ladies have to curtsey to you. You cannot be Kitty Howard any more. You're going to be the Queen of England.'

She pouts. 'But what's the point of that, if I can't do what I want?'

I see that a stay with her step-grandmother, Agnes Howard, the dowager duchess, has done nothing to prepare little Kitty Howard to be Queen Katheryn. The old lady is notoriously careless and trains all her daughters and nieces to be exquisitely mannered and completely thoughtless.

'Your Grace, you can't do just what you want. You know as well as I, that a queen is not free. You get all the jewels and all the clothes and all the money; but you have to play your part.'

'He says I'm perfect as I am,' she says, showing me a sulky face. 'He says I'm never to change, not by a single inch.'

'Please God, he always thinks so,' I say carefully. 'But you wouldn't want to disappoint him? And you certainly wouldn't want your uncle to think you're not fitted for this great place to which God has called you?'

She turns away, and I think: this is not going to be an easy queen to serve – maybe the hardest of them all. She is still only sixteen years old; but she's going to have to grow up fast. I can teach her cunning, but nothing will teach her wisdom.

'Don't be angry with me because I teach you queenly ways, Kitty. I am your friend as much as I was when I tried to teach you to be a good maid-of-honour.'

Instantly she turns, all smiles. 'No, I know you are my friend! But don't be dull and cross when it's my first day in my first palace, and I'm to be married to the King of England tomorrow! Tonight, we can drink wine and dance and misbehave, can't we?'

'Not really,' I say.

Despite my caution, it is a merry dinner in the great hall of Oatlands Palace, and I am not surprised that when the dancing starts our uncle Thomas Howard, flushed with drink and triumph, beckons me to his side.

'You're going to have to keep her on a tight rein,' he says shortly.

'I am?'

'She can do no wrong now. He adores her. But we're not safe until she's in pup.'

'You always seem safe, my lord. Whatever happens. You always return; you always rise.'

He narrows his eyes to look at me. 'I could say the same of you,' he says pointedly. 'But you know as well as I, this isn't the first time a Howard has made it to the throne of England. She has to give us a royal heir. Your fortune depends on this one.'

I glance over at the dancers. Kitty is whirling around with other girls, as wild and as flushed as *maenads* in a *bacchanal*. The king smiles dotingly on his young bride; his poisoned leg, swollen and bulky with bandages, rests on a stool before him. He leans back in his throne so his belly rests across his big body like an incubus wreathed in cloth of gold.

'There's no reason to think that she is not fertile,' I say carefully. 'There's no reason that she should not have a child.'

'The king's own doctor says he has his full powers,' my uncle points out. 'Now that he's married to the right woman – a Howard, not a Cromwell choice. You'll observe the wedding night closely, Jane. She's got to please him. She's got to entice him. He has to conceive a child for the good of the kingdom, not only for us.'

I see that I have become a full Howard; I will do nothing now but sniff shifts. There will be no discussions of philosophy or theology and the shifting ground of politics. There will be no wider horizon of Europe, of Christendom; there will be no *petitio principii* – false arguments for the sake of logic. As a lady in the House of Howard, I am good for nothing but sex, birth, and death.

The duke puts his stale mouth near to my ear. 'She's sixteen years old to his fifty,' he says. 'This is not just a Howard queen; this will be a Howard queen regent. You keep control of her, and we'll rule England through her.'

It is a quiet wedding – a secret wedding – at Oatlands Palace, in a summer heat so stifling that more than one lady-in-waiting faints and has to be taken out. Bishop Bonner officiates; there is none of the glory that Kitty was hoping for – not Westminster Cathedral, not even Greenwich Chapel, no cheering crowds, no admiring ambassadors. Truth be told: there would be no cheering crowds even if wine was flowing in the fountains of London. The city is weary of Tudor wives; the city is sweating, as hot as Venice, and racked with plague. While we are at the wedding breakfast, a messenger comes to the king and is beckoned to the high table to whisper in his ear.

I have a moment of complete dread: that Anne of Cleves, left alone at Richmond Palace, has taken some fatal step: thrown herself in the river and drowned on this summer morning. But the king's smiling nod tells me that no disaster has overshadowed his wedding day: it is good news, his beam tells me it is very good news.

Not until the tables have been cleared and Kitty is dancing again do I learn that it is a death. A death that leaves the king smiling and beating his hand in time to the tune. The musicians do not miss a beat for this death. The choir does not catch a breath. It is the death of my friend. It is the death of a man I loved, who was neither lover nor husband nor father but something dearer to me than all of these.

'Thomas Cromwell has been executed,' Catherine Brandon tells me, her voice carefully modulated, expressing no emotion. 'The old lords have won against the upstart, the old ways of religion against reform, and we are all to be Papists again.'

My sense of loss comes in a sudden sweep, like a flock of crying gulls along an empty shore. I think: Thomas Cromwell? Thomas Cromwell? I didn't say goodbye to you; I didn't ever tell you . . . I feel I should go to the City and wash his head on the spike of London Bridge, just as Thomas More's daughter washed her father's serene face. I should go to George and Anne's tomb in the chapel at the Tower with flowers for this new grave; they will have dropped his body in the vault beside them.

I wish now I had told him how glad I was of his protection; I wish I had told him how much he taught me. I wish that I had told him that – in a way I don't try to define – I loved him. He was my *magister* – my master, my tutor, the mirror of the world to me. I listened so carefully, so often, to what he said that I can hear his voice now, although his neck is hacked through. I can see his smile and the knowing cleverness in his eyes, although they are closed in death. I can hear his voice. I think I will always hear it.

'God save the king!' I say stoutly, looking at Catherine Brandon's young pale face.

'And God save the queen,' she says, not at all like a shouted hurrah – but as if she thinks that being married without consent, to a man nearly old enough to be your grandfather, is not the greatest chance for every girl. She should know – her guardian, Charles Brandon, took her and her fortune in one smooth gulp.

Queen Katheryn's motto – chosen by the king in doting confidence – is: 'no other will but his'. He has no idea how ironic this is – of all the king's wives, this is the most wilful and the most selfish. She is the last person in the world to put anyone else's wishes before her own.

But Kitty, a girl barely out of the schoolroom, knows better than any of them how to enact obedience, and Henry pours wealth on her: the royal treasury is mined to bring up jewels for her hair, for her hat, for her fingers, for the hem of her gowns. The royal wardrobe is harrowed for cloth of silver for new gowns. Seamstresses throughout London embroider pearls onto stomachers and rubies into sleeves, while Katheryn and her husband ride out every day into Hampton Court Park, along the riverside and deep into the country. The king is back in the saddle; he rides a great horse beside his bride for hours every day. Even the wound on his leg seems to be healing. The bandages get lighter and thinner, his limp less noticeable; the smell fades away. His colour improves; he loses weight; his doctors speak of the miracle power of true love.

'Is he swiving her?' my uncle asks, bringing his horse up beside mine as we watch Katheryn take the hand of her master of horse, John Dudley, to step onto the mounting block in the courtyard under the great clock tower.

'My lord?' I say irritably, pretending I can't hear him above the yell of the Irish wolfhounds giving tongue and the shouts of the whippers-in.

'You heard me.'

'I can guess. For you never ask me anything else.'

'Is he?'

'Yes. He is.'

'Fully? Completely?'

'So she says.'

'And she'd know?'

I say nothing. All royal brides know. It is their one and only task. The suggestion that Anne of Cleves was ignorant about her one duty as queen was ridiculous.

'So, we can expect a baby?' he pursues, as keen as the wolfhounds who are baying with impatience.

'We can hope for a baby,' I correct him.

'I'm not a man for hope. You tell me when she's expecting. I don't care about your hopes.'

'I'll tell you. But remember: even if she does conceive, even if it's a boy, he won't be the next king; he'll only be a second son.'

'Prince Edward's sickly,' he says cheerfully. 'Plenty of second sons take the throne. The king himself was a second son.'

I bow my head. I wonder who would be interested in the information that the Duke of Norfolk is hoping for the death of the Seymour boy? Everyone would be interested; but I have no one that I want to tell. No one will turn a dark, smiling gaze on me and say: *You have news for me?* No one will make me laugh when he says: *The one thing I like about your uncle is that he is always so predictable.* I think: no one enjoys the endless theatre of court ambition as Thomas Cromwell did – and without him, it's not as good.

They bring up Katheryn's well-trained palfrey, and she is helped into the saddle. They check her girth, her bridle, that she is holding the reins correctly, that she is not nervous, and she brings her horse alongside the king. The huntsmen know not to let the hounds go too fast. The king swears he feels like a twenty-year-old; but he is not the rider he was, and Katheryn is not a horsewoman like my sister-in-law Anne, though she wears her red velvet riding jacket.

The hunt moves off; the hounds and the whippers-in first, the king's master of horse next, John Dudley beside him, and then the king and queen, side by side, like a doting old man and his favourite granddaughter. The rest of us follow behind them, chattering and looking forward to the day, as if we have not ridden out like this, hundreds of times before, following four previous queens.

## ON PROGRESS, SUMMER
### 1540

In August, we move from hunting lodge to hunting lodge, which pleases the king as a prolonged honeymoon, but disappoints Katheryn, who wants to be queen of a palace. The heat of the summer goes on; some days, it is too hot to ride out at all, and Katheryn stands beside the king and watches him fish in the moat or practise archery at the butts. Every catch, every bullseye, he turns to her, as proud as a spoiled boy, and she smiles with delight and sometimes prettily claps her hands. Of course, she is getting more and more bored by this old man in the first flush of his happiness.

I make her rest alone in her bedroom in the afternoon, so that she can have time away from blushing and smiling. I bribe her to good behaviour with sweetmeats and sugarplums. The king has bought himself a little pet like Anne's lapdog Purkoy, and it is my task to train her to do pretty tricks to please him. She dances like an angel; she walks as if she was dancing. Purkoy used to beg, sitting up on his hind legs, most prettily. I teach her to beg.

She is rescued from boredom by the appointment of her ladies-in-waiting. Many transfer so fast from Queen Anne of Cleves to Queen Katheryn that they just come back to their old places. Katheryn has to employ ladies of her own family: her sister Isabel Baynton, whose husband Sir Edward Baynton is vice chamberlain; Catherine Tilney, her kinswoman and childhood friend from Norfolk House. Even the queen's step-grandmother, the dowager duchess, has a place as chief lady if she comes to court. Katherine Edgcumbe and Eleanor Manners the Countess of Rutland are rewarded for their outstanding skills as the writers of an impossible conversation with Anne of Cleves about virginity. Mistress Stonor, who spied on my sister-in-law Anne in her final days in the Tower of London, gets a place. Anne Parr – now Mistress Herbert – takes charge of the royal jewels, having served every one of the four previous queens with me. Back in harness like the white mules of the queen's litter, we are accustomed to the pace of royal service. The burden is a different woman, but it makes no difference to us.

Katheryn has scores of men servants – her master of horse is John Dudley. Thomas Manners the Earl of Rutland will manage her lands – she is given everything that Jane Seymour had – though she had to earn it with a fatal pregnancy. An entire council of treasury and land agents and managers meets weekly to manage her vast estates. She does not attend; she says it is too boring, and I must go in her place. She has a stable full of grooms and two muleteers to drive the French litter.

The entire household was barely appointed to their roles, hardly started work, when we go on progress with a small riding court for the summer. It is rushed – almost a flight – as if the king is avoiding a state entry to London with yet another queen, as if he doesn't want the people to see that he is getting older and the wives are getting younger and younger. The progress feels like a rout, without a plan.

For the last ten years, everything was meticulously organised by my spymaster. All the departments of government that he created grind on: reporting, inspecting, and taxing; but they are the turning sails of a windmill catching a passing wind. There is no miller watching the clouds, steering the sails; the cogs and gears are not engaged. The old lords have no skill in business, church reform, taxation, running the counties or controlling the towns. They cannot manage the Houses of Parliament. They have influence only in their own areas; they have no nationwide view. They have no idea of foreign alliances and overseas trade. They have no unified policy; they rule for themselves, only themselves.

No one can plan a route as Cromwell did: threatening restless towns with our armed retinue, rewarding supporters with a smiling visit, weaving a path between threat and bribery. The old lords don't even know the country outside of their own borders; they have no maps of any lands but their own.

SEVERAL LADIES COME on progress only long enough to secure their places, before they announce that they are pregnant and retire to their homes for the summer, perhaps for the rest of this reign. Anne Parr now Mistress Herbert gives the keys to the jewel house to Elizabeth Tyrwhitt and tells me that she is going to leave when we reach Ampthill. It's a bad evening on another disorganised day: the queen's own brother-in-law and fifteen men of her household got drunk and fought with the porters the night before.

'You can't leave us!' I exclaim. 'Not until I've got some proper order in the queen's rooms!'

'I can't stay,' she says. She gestures to her belly, which is flat as a board. 'You can see that I have to leave.'

'I see nothing, Anne Herbert!' I say crossly. 'And I can't be everywhere. The queen likes the place in chaos; she likes everyone running around screaming. And if her own vice chamberlain is going to brawl . . .'

Anne Herbert leans towards me to whisper. 'You'll have seen her brother, Charles Howard, is courting Lady Margaret Douglas?'

'Jesu save us!'

'Another coup for the Howards,' she observes neutrally.

'It didn't work out so well the last time.'

'No – but this time, with a Howard queen on the throne . . .'

'I doubt that even Kitty Howard can persuade the king that his royal niece should marry her brother Charles. Remember what he said last time about entrapment! Lady Margaret's only just got out of Syon Abbey, you'd have thought she'd have learned her lesson.'

'It's not as bad as last time. Not a betrothal – only poetry-promises. But I wouldn't leave court without warning you.'

'You shouldn't leave court at all,' I say crossly. 'All the queen's friends are young and foolish, and the king is not a young and foolish husband.'

'She can enchant him, and you can manage her,' she reassures me.

'Oh, he dotes on her; but a young court reminds him that he is old enough to be their grandfather. Her youth is a *memento mori* for him.'

'A courtier's work is to build up the king,' Anne Herbert warns. 'Not diminish him.'

'She's just seventeen!' I say despairingly. 'How can she not make him feel old and tired by comparison?'

## WINDSOR CASTLE, AUTUMN

# 1540

WE ARE BARELY returned to Windsor Castle when Lady Agnes the old Dowager Duchess of Norfolk announces that she is coming to visit her beloved step-granddaughter.

At once, the vain young queen becomes a frightened schoolgirl again. 'Don't leave us alone,' she begs me. 'You don't know what she's like when she's angry. And I always make her angry, whatever I do!'

'She can't be angry with the Queen of England,' I point out. 'Threaten her with a writ of attainder for treason and throw her in the Tower.'

'Oh!' She gasps on a little laugh. 'Oh! If only I could! But you can't put old ladies in the Tower.'

I don't disagree, though Lady Margaret Pole is still waiting for her pardon in the Tower. 'Well, at any rate, she can't scold you,' I assure her. 'You only owe obedience to your husband the king, and to the head of your house. And the duke isn't coming with her, is he?'

'Oh God no!' she says, more afraid than ever. 'Is he? I can't face the two of them together. I'll say I'm ill.'

'No, you can't,' I tell her. 'But I'll stay with you. She can't scold you in front of me. It's part of my duties to make sure that you are happy.'

'Really?' She is diverted at once. 'Is it your duty to make me happy?'

'Lawful joys,' I say dampeningly. 'Only lawful joys.'

THE DOWAGER DUCHESS is not overawed by the greatness of the motherless girl that she raised – nourishing her with neglect – in her country house at Horsham and in the shabby grandeur of Norfolk House, Lambeth. The old lady, lean as a well-bred old hound, is accompanied by her daughter the Countess of Bridgewater, a woman so honed by disaster that nothing can hurt or frighten her. Together, they walk into Windsor Castle, like a pair of raiders, scanning for loot in the echoing great state rooms, as if they see nothing to admire: not rich tapestries on the walls, nor gilding on the dark-blue beams, nor the view of the Thames winding through the woodlands of the valley below.

They both curtsey as low as they should to a queen.

'Lady Grandmother. Dear Cousin,' the queen says feebly. 'So welcome.'

Behind them comes the queen's uncle Lord William Howard and his wife Lady Margaret, behind them, her brothers Charles and George. That is when I know that they have come in force, to make Katheryn do something for them.

'I'll trouble you for a chair, Your Grace. I'm not any younger than when I took you in, a nobody without a penny to your name, no mother and a worthless father,' the dowager duchess begins.

'Very grateful,' Katheryn whispers, sinking into her throne and waving that everyone can sit. I stand behind her.

'We'll speak with you alone,' the old lady announces, glaring at me.

I swore to the little queen that I would not abandon her to this family visit even before I knew the old dowager duchess was so terrifying, and her daughter, flinty-faced.

'Stay,' Katheryn squeaks.

'The queen requests my presence,' I say grandly.

'Then you'll keep this between ourselves,' the dowager duchess commands, turning sharp blue eyes on me. 'You're a Howard by marriage, if not by birth.'

I curtsey. 'Like yourself. For you were a Tilney before you were a second wife.'

Grandly, she ignores the impertinence. 'It's that fool Francis Dereham,' she says abruptly. 'My purveyor. Went to Ireland to make his fortune and came home without it. Now he wants a place at court. In your service.'

'He can't,' Katheryn says instantly.

'Better that you give him a place and a small fee to make him happy than he chatters away in the London alehouses,' Lord William Howard points out. 'All you young people were as wild as each other, though I know you were warned more than once . . .'

'We did nothing.'

'Nothing that matters,' the dowager duchess corrects her. 'I've taken a handful of letters and poems and nonsense from half a dozen girls off him. I've not looked at them, but I take it you were as bad as the rest?'

Kitty gives a little moan. 'Nothing.'

'Well, anyway, I've got them locked up safe, so he has no evidence. But he's running around saying that you two were beloved and betrothed and God knows what else. He says he gave you a hundred pounds before he went away, and that now you're queen, there must be some good to come to him.'

'I'll give him his money back; I haven't even spent it,' Katheryn says crossly. She looks at me. 'It's that purse you have, Jane.'

The dowager duchess turns a sharp gaze on me. 'You have it, do you? You're in her confidence?'

'I know nothing about it,' I say quickly. 'I just held the purse. I will return it to you today to give to him. I thought it better that Her Grace did not hold money that belonged to a young man, even before she was queen.'

'Excellent.' Lord William Howard clasps his fat hands together, and his wife Margaret repeats his gesture, as if she is following him in a dance, copying the steps, one beat behind. 'Then all that's needed is to find a place for him in your household.'

'We don't need a purveyor,' I remark quietly.

'He can be her secretary!' the old lady tells me. 'He can write.'

'It's not enough to write,' I point out quietly. 'The queen's secretary is a post for a man with money to pay the entry fee, a family to ask for it, an education to match it. And faultlessly discreet.'

'Dereham is distantly related to us Howards,' the dowager duchess says, as if that is a connection good enough for any post. 'And who cares about his education?'

'The queen's vice chamberlain would care.'

'My step-grandson-in-law! He'll do what I say!'

'No!' Katheryn interrupts. 'Not secretary. Couldn't he do something else?'

'I'm sure we can find some kind of post,' I offer glacially. 'If you insist, Your Grace?'

'Why can't you keep him at yours?' Katheryn asks plaintively. 'He was always your favourite?'

There's a brief, awkward silence. Only the Countess of Bridgewater, who has seen worse and survived far worse, breaks it. 'He's a little shit,' she says crudely. 'Better for you, Your Grace, if he is shitting in your stool house than shitting over us all with the enemies of our family and a bunch of reformer preachers. If he says anything at court that you don't like, then you'll be first to hear it, and you can have him beaten at the first word and arrested at the second.'

'It's treason to speak against me,' Katheryn whispers, so pale that I can see blue veins at her temples that match the looped chains of sapphires on her neck.

'Then hang him,' the countess says simply. 'But don't leave him gabbling and scrabbling around St Paul's and telling dirty Lutherans that the queen – a Howard queen – is a whore as bad as her cousin Anne.'

Katheryn gives a little scream and jumps up. 'How dare you!'

Everyone has to rise as she is standing; but her grandmother takes her time getting to her feet.

'My Lady Bridgewater . . .' I say furiously to the countess. 'You forget the respect that you owe . . .'

She shoots a hard look at me. 'Oh, aye – I forgot you were her sister-in-law. But am I right? Or not?'

'You're right,' I say unwillingly. 'We don't want gossip in London.'

'Lord William'll bring him to court and introduce him. He can be a groom of your chamber,' the dowager duchess rules.

'Not I!' Lord William says hastily. 'Can't stand the man. My wife can do it. She's your lady-in-waiting; it'd come natural to her.'

Lady Margaret turns a horrified gaze on him.

'Very well,' the countess says agreeably. 'Lady Margaret can do it.'

'There you are!' Agnes, the dowager duchess, says. 'I knew it'd come out all right.' She turns for the door. 'I won't stay to dine. I'll tell Dereham to start at the autumn quarter. Hallow's Eve. Lady Margaret will present him.'

Lady Margaret murmurs something which might be a refusal; but all the Howards ignore her.

'Does my lord uncle the duke know of this?' I ask the flint-faced countess as she follows her mother.

'No,' she says shortly. 'Best not trouble him?'

'Yes,' I say. 'Best not.'

THOMAS HOWARD THE Duke of Norfolk, with a hunter's instinct for hidden prey, comes to his niece's rooms before the rest of the lords and the king before dinner. He bows low to the queen and steps aside to me. 'I hear that my lady stepmother visited you today?'

'She wanted a favour – to put her old purveyor into the queen's household.'

'Very well. Anything else?'

'Nothing,' I say.

He turns to the queen. 'Your Grace, you are to be congratulated. You are to receive some more lands. Gifts from the king, your generous husband.'

Kitty Howard, who has no more idea of landowning than of coal mining, beams at her uncle. 'He's so kind to me!'

The double doors open, and she dances off her throne towards the king as he comes in, leaning slightly on Edward Seymour's arm.

'Thank you, my lord husband! My uncle just told me you're giving me more lands!'

'Thomas Cromwell's fortune,' he tells her, taking her hand and kissing it. She does not flinch, though his kiss shines on her knuckles like slime. 'You're sharing it with young Thomas Culpeper here.'

She turns and smiles radiantly, as though she has quite forgotten that he preferred Bess Harvey to her. 'Oh, congratulations to you, Master Culpeper!'

'Great work to take them from a rogue and give them to two people that I can trust,' the king says. 'But land is wasted on you, pretty one. I know you only like jewels.'

'Oh no, Your Majesty. I like jewels as well!' she says, so earnestly that everyone laughs at her childish greed.

'If you dance very prettily for me after dinner, I shall give you a ruby ring,' he promises her. 'Who shall you have as your partner?'

She turns to consider her ladies: Mary Howard is the best dancer, but Kitty prefers a dark-haired partner as a contrast.

'Take Thomas,' the king says. 'You're well-matched.'

Their eyes meet; Culpeper's smile is warm, amused. He knows full well that she is still offended with him. But she cannot refuse a partner proposed by the king. And Culpeper knows – as a handsome man always knows – that she still likes him.

'Would you honour me, Your Grace?' He bows.

'As His Majesty wishes,' she says coolly, and she takes her husband's arm, and they lead us into dinner.

THE COURT IS to celebrate the feast of All Hallows' with all the Papist rituals unchanged, despite the disappearance of shrines and the end of chantries. The king will spend the day in prayer, and despite Kitty's protest, she has to attend two-hour-long masses three times in the day, wearing sombre clothes, and ostentatiously pray for the soul of Queen Jane. She endures this very well, though I know she is almost crying with boredom and she aches from forcing herself not to fidget.

When she is in her rooms, waiting for the king and a reduced court to arrive for a quiet dinner, Lady Margaret Howard, wife to Katheryn's uncle William, presents herself, as ordered, with a handsome, dark-haired young man following her at a respectful three paces. Charles Howard, Katheryn's brother, comes in as well, as if to keep Margaret to her script in the masque.

Margaret curtseys to her niece, whispers a few words so inarticulate that no one hears the introduction she is supposed to make. Charles Howard has to say loudly: 'Why, Francis Dereham! I've not seen you for months!'

I dislike him on sight. He looks like a handsome rogue, a man you would trust with neither a secret nor money. Katheryn is superb; she gives him her fingertips with the slightest smile and an inclination of her head. She acts as if she dimly remembers him from her childhood, welcomes him to Windsor Castle, says that her step-grandmother has asked for a place for him in the Autumn, and hands him over, before he can say a single word in reply, to her vice chamberlain brother-in-law Sir Edward Baynton, who discreetly sweeps him away back to Norfolk House.

No one seeing Dereham's modest bow and cheerful acceptance of the queen's dismissal can imagine there was anything between them. I dare to hope that the young man has reached the top of his ambition and that he will serve the queen's household for a season, skim what profits he can, get bored and run away again, and we can all forget about him.

## WOKING PALACE, AUTUMN

# 1540

WE SPEND LONG days at Windsor, make another dull visit to Oatlands Palace, and arrive at Woking Palace as the drought breaks and it starts to rain. Kitty's days become even more empty. The court cannot go hawking, the birds will not fly in the rain, and we have to stay indoors, as rain streams down the windows all day. The king and his young men friends stay in their own rooms, gambling and drinking. Kitty walks around her quiet rooms, restless and bored, repeatedly asking if I know when we are going to London, when her wedding will be announced, when she will be proclaimed queen, when she will be crowned?

'She'll get no coronation until she's with child,' my uncle Thomas Howard predicts. 'The king'll never crown a barren queen. Never again! Does she know that?'

'She knows it,' I say. 'But she's determined to be proclaimed as his wife and queen even if the actual coronation comes later. And really, she's got to be proclaimed. Half the country doesn't even know he has married her.'

'Oh, he'll announce her. He'll do it at Hampton Court before the Christmas feast,' he promises. 'I've made the arrangements. Unending detail, thousands of invitations. Christ knows how Cromwell ever did everything. My daughter will carry her train.' He suddenly remembers his widowed daughter. 'Mary's got to be seen. You make sure she's front and centre of any masques or dancing.'

'She wants to marry again?' I ask, knowing that she does not.

'Thomas Seymour,' he says very quietly. 'The heir's uncle. It's the very best I can get. We have to be allied with them when . . .' He trails off.

He does not need to say more. When the king dies, the Seymours will be the closest kin to Prince Edward. If there is a regency council, the two Seymour brothers, Edward and Thomas, will lead it. Mary Howard would be wife of the lord protector. If the widowed Queen Katheryn was named queen regent, Thomas Howard would have his only daughter and a niece at the very centre of power.

I think of the darkly handsome Thomas Seymour and Mary Howard's glacial beauty. 'I can't see it,' I say.

'You will,' my uncle replies. 'If bribery and force can make it happen.'

'Who are you going to bribe?' I ask curiously.

'Thomas Seymour.'

'And who are you going to force?'

'My daughter.'

## HAMPTON COURT, WINTER

## 1540

ALL THE NOBILITY are summoned to greet the new queen in December at Hampton Court; the marriage is formally announced, and Queen Katheryn finally gets the reception she wants, dining under the cloth of estate, with the duke's daughter, the young widow Mary Howard, holding the golden bowl for her to dip her fingers, and the Duchess of Suffolk, Catherine Brandon, holding a towel for her to dry her hands. Neither of them betrays the smallest flicker of disdain for the girl that they first met as a junior maid-of-honour, one of the silliest of the new cohort. This is not hard for Mary Howard, who learned to hide her true feelings in the cradle, and Catherine Brandon knows better than most that queens come and go.

The Christmas feast is the merriest that the court has held in years – the king adores his young wife; we are at peace with the other countries of Christendom, and the king's interest in reform has declined so much that only a few heretics are burned this holy season.

He drowns his little queen in new year gifts, table diamonds, ropes of pearls, a muffler of black velvet edged with sable fur, spattered with rubies and hundreds of pearls. She claws the jewels towards herself like a gambler raking winnings from the table, and the constant stream of gifts keeps her temper sweet, even when she is tested by long days of bad weather when the king stays indoors and plays cards and riddles with her.

Lady Mary, the king's eldest daughter, visits us from her own household at Hunsdon, and the entire court is agog to see how the daughter of a princess of Spain, herself a full royal, seven years older than her dainty stepmother and a cruel lifetime wiser, greets this former maid-of-honour sitting on her mother's throne, flaunting her mother's jewels.

'I'm going to get her married off to one of the French princes,' my uncle remarks in my ear as the first of Lady Mary's outriders clatters through the clock gateway.

She is on a magnificent Spanish horse, a deep chested bright chestnut Andalusian, and wearing a purple riding jacket – a colour for royals and emperors, with a purple velvet bonnet. A purple feather pinned with a magnificent amethyst sweeps around to frame her intense, pale face. It is an entrance shadowed by storm clouds, as theatrical as the masque before a joust, when the challengers parade their standards and people pick their favourites.

'Why would you make a good marriage for her?' I wonder, as the cavalcade pulls up the princess looks towards us, and we bow in welcome. 'What's the benefit?'

'I don't care for her,' my uncle says, out of the corner of his mouth. 'But if she's married out of the kingdom, then the oldest royal child left in England is our Tudor-Howard girl. Elizabeth will be more noticed.'

The princess dismounts and comes up the steps, where Sir Edward Baynton waits to escort her to the queen's rooms, her mother's rooms. She knows the way better than he does.

'You once told her you would bang her head against the wall until it was as soft as a baked apple,' I observe quietly.

'Love talk,' the duke replies with one of his hawkish smiles. 'Fatherly love.'

LADY MARY'S PALLOR is the only sign of her distress at seeing a second Howard girl throwing down another better-born queen. Her curtsey in the doorway of the queen's presence chamber, before she approaches the throne, is to the exact depth required – she has been curtseying to inferiors raised to be her stepmothers for all her life.

'Was that a proper curtsey?' Kitty demands of me, in a hissed whisper behind her hand.

'Perfectly proper,' I say, admiring the hollow show of deference.

I lead Lady Mary to the queen. They exchange kisses, both of them kissing the air on either side of the other's cheek, both cheeks barely touching, cold as eels.

Katheryn rushes to sit before Lady Mary sinks into the window seat, hurrying to claim precedence, and then she has nothing to say.

'You are welcome to court, Lady Mary.' I fill the awkward silence. 'My father sends you his best wishes. I know he has sent you his translation of Cardinal Torquemada's psalms this year.'

Lady Mary turns her head from the rigid little queen. 'Please send him my thanks. I am always so interested in his work.'

Still the queen says nothing. She sighs as if exhausted by boredom and looks out of the window to the garden. It is sleeting down on the formal garden; the different coloured squares of gravel divided by little hedges of herbs are all slowly going grey and white. The gaily painted wooden statues of heraldic beasts are growing crowns of melting snow; the river beyond gleams silver in the cold air. Kitty gazes out of the window, as blank as snow clouds.

In the queen's silence, Lady Mary and I go from a comment on the weather to the many words in English for rain.

'The dialect of Venice has a word for the reflection of light from water on the ceiling of a room,' I tell her. '*Gibigiana*. Reflected light.'

'What are you talking about?' Katheryn demands abruptly. 'I don't know what you're talking about! What are you going on about?'

I could blush for her rudeness. Everyone in the room stops their low-voiced conversations and looks from the queen to Lady Mary.

'We were speaking of an Italian word, Your Grace,' Lady Mary explains politely. 'A word that means both reflection of light and – interestingly – a gaudy or glittery woman.'

I keep my face perfectly still at this unexpected, unwanted demonstration of Lady Mary's scholarship.

Katheryn, dazzling as a magpie in Lady Mary's mother's jewels, goes white but for two spots of red, as if someone has slapped both cheeks. 'Lady Rochford,' she squeaks. 'A word, if you please?'

I rise at once and go behind the queen's chair to lean over her shoulder so she can hiss a hysterical complaint.

'She insulted me!'

'She meant nothing.'

'She should be talking to me, not you!'

'You've said nothing to her.'

'She didn't call me "Majesty".'

'She called you "Your Grace" which is quite adequate since you're not crowned yet.'

'I won't have her at court.'

I steal a quick glance at the princess. Now, she is talking easily, in a ripple of low-voiced Spanish, to Catherine Brandon, the half-Spanish daughter of Katherine of Aragon's most beloved lady-in-waiting. This visit is getting worse and worse.

'You've got to welcome her for the season,' I say flatly. 'The king has ordered it; you're her stepmother.'

'You tell her: I want respect. She was respectful to Jane Seymour, wasn't she? And to Anne of Cleves?'

'My dear, she was as respectful to them as she is to you. Believe me, there is nothing to make a quarrel about. And you'll make yourself look foolish.'

'I'm not foolish!' She gives a little scream.

'You'll look foolish if you quarrel with the king's daughter over nothing.' I gamble on Kitty's love of appearance.

Her restless glance goes past me to Lady Mary's entourage. 'And how many ladies-in-waiting has she brought with her? She's only allowed two. I know it. She's only allowed two.'

I follow her gaze. Four ladies are talking pleasantly to old friends.

'It's hardly worth making a fuss . . .'

'You tell her. I'll cut down her household. She will lose two attendants.'

The door is flung open; the king, on this boring afternoon, is playing the part of a delighted husband and father visiting his wife and his daughter. He is wreathed in smiles. The noblemen come in behind him, all delighted to see us ladies in such picturesque harmony.

Kitty jumps to her feet with delight and takes Lady Mary's hand to lead her forward.

'I'll tell her later,' I say.

To my surprise, my father is in the king's entourage. I curtsey to him, and he rests his hand in blessing on my hood and kisses my brow. When the queen plays cards with the king and Lady Mary, we sit together in the window seat.

'Why are you at court, my lord Father?' I ask nervously. 'Not an inquiry or anything?'

The king is talking pleasantly to Lady Mary. Katheryn is pulling at his sleeve.

'You make me sound like a *Cassandra*, constantly bringing bad news,' he smilingly complains. 'Of course there's no inquiry! Who could organise one, now that Lord Cromwell is gone? I only came to present my compliments to the king and my translation of the *Commentaries of the Turk* for his new year's gift. I'm not a born courtier like you, Jane. I don't enjoy the life as you do. I don't have the patience for it.'

'I don't enjoy it as I used to,' I tell him. 'I know too much. It's as if I've gone behind the scenes of a masque and seen the machinery that makes the thunder and the wheels that turn to make the waves of the sea. I don't delight in the spectacle now that I have to put my weight on the wheels. I'm part of the machine, not the audience.'

He is more interested in the metaphor than in me. 'Make great waves then,' he recommends, glancing at the king. 'Make sure you're the one working the machinery.'

## HAMPTON COURT, JANUARY

# 1541

In the end, we all have to set our hands to the wheel to make the magic of a royal court for the new year celebrations. A visit of Anne of Cleves throws the machinery into its highest gear. She curtseys as low to Kitty as if her former maid is an empress, and she sits with the duchesses, halfway down the table that she once supervised as queen. After dinner, there is dancing, and the king watches his two wives take hands as partners, and he beats his hand in time to the tune.

Everyone seems to have forgotten that Anne is so ugly that no man could desire her. Nobody thinks that her breasts are slack and that she smells. She is beautifully dressed – she must be spending a fortune on new clothes, all cut revealingly in the French style to suit her curves. She has brought lavish gifts for the king – two horses barded in imperial purple velvet – and he repays her generously. Even Katheryn shares some of her spoils, passing on the king's gifts that she doesn't want: two puppies that Anne snatches up and kisses, and a gold ring that Kitty puts on Anne's finger.

After her short stay, when it's time for her to go, Anne bids a cheerful farewell to all her old false friends, and I walk with her to the clock tower yard, where her horse and guards are waiting.

'You are happy?' I ask.

'Happier than you, I think,' she says. 'For I am as you said I should be: free of the show and free of the fear. I live without a master. Just think: I'm going to ride six miles through the frosty park and get home before dusk in time for my dinner. I shall eat what I like; I shall sleep alone in my big bed. I shall wake tomorrow, and then – I shall do whatever I want to do!'

'I'm glad for you.'

'But what will happen when he dies?' she asks in German, so that no eavesdropper could understand us.

Even so, I glance around. 'It's against the law to speak . . .' I start to caution her.

'I know. But it can't be long. Look at him.'

'Your place is secure,' I say. 'He made it the law that you should be paid your pensions and recognised as his sister.'

'And you?' She looks at me. 'Katheryn Howard's young; she'll outlive him by decades, just as I thought that I would. I thought that I would be a regent queen, ruling over England until my stepson was of age and then he would honour me as a good stepmother. But it will be Kitty, not me. The king will name her as regent in his will, and then you and the Howard family will be the power behind the throne of a queen regent ruling England.' She looks at me, speculatively. 'You know how to do it. Actually, you'd be good at it!'

I lower my eyes so that she does not see the flare of my ambition. 'I've thought of it,' I admit.

She laughs in genuine amusement. 'It would be funny, after his hunger for a son, if his kingdom was ruled by a woman! It would be so funny if the woman was a Boleyn.'

I REMEMBER MY FATHER'S gloomy prediction that no one could pack a jury like Thomas Cromwell when Sir Thomas Wyatt, our old friend, the poet, is arrested suddenly without warning and taken to the Tower. He is wearily familiar with the prison rooms; he was released last time only because Cromwell had enough evidence against Anne without having to throw Thomas Wyatt into the scales against her. But this time, Wyatt's only friend is Sir John Wallop, ambassador to France, and he is suddenly recalled from Paris, and they are imprisoned together.

And that is where it rests, in an eerie silence and stillness. Their houses are searched and their servants questioned; but nothing is found against them. The two men are housed in the Tower but not charged. It is as if someone knows there is a crime, but he lacks the skills to make a water-tight case against them. No one seems to know how to write a writ of attainder to have them killed. All the old lords are on edge, waiting for news, terrified that something will point to one of them: an embroidered banner in the bottom of an old chest, a receipt for a horse. But whoever has ordered this inquiry does not know their business. They have started with accusation and now look for evidence. But a clever advisor sends *bread on waters passing forth*. My spymaster spread lies to breed lies long before he made an accusation, knowing very well, *thou knowest not what evil shall come on the earth*.

I loiter in the gallery outside the privy council room when the old lords are coming out and talking indiscreetly to their friends; but since they know nothing, I learn nothing. If there was a circle of hidden plotters, they have been well-warned by the arrests. It is true – as my father said – that nobody can run an inquiry now Cromwell is gone.

'Is Thomas Wyatt actually guilty of anything?' I ask my uncle.

'He's too clever by half,' my uncle says crossly.

'It's not an offence to be too clever, is it?'

'It's an offence to flaunt your learning, to say that none of us old lords can muster more than one wit between all of us, to suggest that England cannot be ruled without a Wolsey or a Cromwell and that the king's poems don't scan or rhyme or have enough words to a line or whatever,' he says irritably.

I scrutinise him; I don't fear his ill temper now that my future is secure. I am a wealthy woman in my own right, I am indispensable to a favoured queen, and if she becomes a regent queen, I shall be her chief advisor. Her inexperience and ignorance are my advantage. No queen before her had so poor an education; no queen before her had nothing to fill the empty days. English-born, she cannot serve as an ambassador like Katherine of Aragon. She has no interest in

Catholicism like the first devout queen, nor reform like the second. She has not a thought in her head about the running of the country, no interest in the poor, nor in rescuing those who have nowhere to go now that the monasteries are closed. She has no clever brothers like the Seymours to support her authority. She was raised as a pillion wife, who sits sideways behind her husband on a special saddle and cannot even see where she is going. If the king makes her queen regent at his death, I will rule England through her.

## HAMPTON COURT, FEBRUARY

### 1541

In February, the king, tiring of a lack of evidence, goes to London with his advisors to speed the execution of his friends Thomas Wyatt and John Wallop. My father meets them there; but does not come upriver to Hampton Court to visit me. From this, I understand that he is content with my progress from queen to queen. The Duke of Norfolk goes north, alert to the threat of the Scots on the borders. The court, suddenly free of old lords and the old king, makes every day a May Day at Hampton Court. The weather turns icy, and Katheryn, a snow princess from a fairytale, in bright blue with swansdown at her wrists and neck, leads her ladies at a scampering run through the formal gardens, jumping over the herb hedges and scuffing the coloured gravels in a wild battle of snowball fights. The king's young men – unemployed and unsupervised while the king persecutes old friends in London – see us from the windows and come whooping and hollering out of doors, throwing handfuls of fresh snow.

We run away laughing and order pages and chamberers to roll up a store of snowballs, and we set up an ambush beside one of the yew-tree allées. As they dash down the tunnel, with brown needles underfoot, we storm snowballs down on them and jump out of the yew trees to surround them. Trapped under the green boughs on dry ground, they have no snow to make more ammunition: it is our victory. They surrender, holding up their hands and demanding a parlay.

Thomas Culpeper steps out of the laughing crowd of young men and faces Katheryn, her hair tumbling down, her cheeks rosy as a child.

'Mercy,' he pleads, kneeling at her feet, but his brown eyes looking up into her face say: *kiss me!*

'Are you very, very sorry?' she asks him. She is panting from the running and the play-battle, but I think she is breathless with desire.

He pulls off his red cap from his thick brown hair. 'I lie beneath your feet,' he says. 'You can do what you want with me.'

'You are beneath my feet,' she agrees. 'I shall hold you to that.'

They don't move, and all of us are frozen, captured by this tableau of sudden desire, under the dark-green shadow of the trees, surrounded by the bright whiteness of the sunshine outside. We are hidden with them in a private world, in the secrecy of the greenwood tree, breathing the peppery scent of the fallen fronds crushed under Culpeper's knees as he sits back on his heels, as if he would stay all day looking up at her, as if time has frozen like the dripping icicles, as if she is a snow princess who will melt into his mouth.

Slowly, as if she is skating on thin ice, Katheryn glides forward and extends her hand to him. The white swansdown on her sleeve flutters under his warm breath as he takes her fingers and drops his curly dark head over her hand. In one fluid movement, he rises to his feet, lifts her hand to his mouth, turns it over, and puts a kiss on the inner softness of her wrist, where the blue veins run direct to her heart.

Everyone sees this gesture of courtly love; it means nothing to them – but it means something to me. For a moment, I see the two of them, illuminated in the darkness by a bright shaft of winter-white sunshine; I think I see a heart in a heartless world: love among the loveless. Nobody watching Thomas' lips on her wrist and the colour rising from her swansdown collar can blame the pretty queen for giving her fingertips to him. No young man would blame him for taking the soft palm on his cheek. All of us are spellbound in the moment, as if there is such a thing as true love. As if, in this grinding exchequer that is the court, there can be desire: freely offered and lovingly taken.

For once, there is no one to remind us that nothing is free: everything is bought and paid for. Thomas Howard Duke of Norfolk is far away, guarding the north gate of the kingdom like a bad-tempered old dog. The other older lords are in London with the king, sifting evidence against one of their own. The queen's older sister Isabel Baynton is warm indoors; her husband Sir Edward with her. The queen's uncle, Lord William Howard, is packing his bags to go to Paris as the ambassador, newly promoted into dead man's shoes. The whole young court is like a pleasure garden where the hard lord and schoolmaster have gone away. They have not conspired to be free, suddenly they are.

We go hunting with the king's hounds, but nobody cares about the kill; we are riding for the joy and excitement, recklessly following the hounds wherever they lead, half-hoping to be lost in snowy woods, finding our way to the warm dining tents for dinner, drinking too much hot wine, and riding home singing love songs. Mary Norris rides hand in hand with her new husband George Carew, Catherine Carey is inseparable from her husband Francis Knollys, Charles Howard and Margaret Douglas are always together, and the queen herself and Thomas Culpeper are like the point and the pencil of a drawing compass: wherever she sits, he seems to circle her, always staying out of reach but never too far. Wherever he is, she looks up as if to measure the distance from him. They are never again as close as they were at the snowball fight, and strangely, this careful distancing is more hauntingly erotic than any embrace.

They are like two beautiful wild creatures circling each other, alert only to each other and blind to anyone else.

When we dance in a circle, and she can see his place, two girls away from her, and then one and then the next step will bring him to her – she steps back and excuses herself from the dance and waves a maid-of-honour forward, so that she does not go handfast with him or step into his arms. I would praise her for her discretion, but then I see the triumphant smile she throws at him as she avoids him, and I realise that she is only playing at retreat to bring him on, closer and closer. He watches her go, turns the bright heat of his charm on the girl she has put in her place, and waits, without looking, until she comes back to him.

I speak to her; a queen of England, especially the fourth wife, should be beyond suspicion. 'Like Caesar's wife,' I tell her.

'Who's Caesar's wife?' she asks.

'I'm saying that no one can speak slander against you.'

'They can't,' she says simply. 'Thomas Culpeper has never done more than kiss my hand once, and we were in front of all the court. You saw it yourself. Only once.'

'I saw it,' I say – and I think: it is my fault not theirs that I keep seeing it in my mind, that I keep seeing her hand against his face, his mouth on her wrist as a moment of quite extraordinary beauty.

ONE FROSTY DAY at noon before dinner, Kitty takes a fancy to dance on the frozen grass of the archery lawns, and we summon musicians and choristers to play and sing country dances and gallops, changing partners at every chorus. As we fall on cushions and carpets, hot and laughing after romping through a circle dance, we hear a drumbeat, ominous as a roll of distant thunder on the bright day. They are the drums of the king's barges coming steadily upriver, insistent as drums of war. Then we hear the sharp blare of trumpets as the king's barge draws up at the pier.

At once, we grab the capes and hats and muffs that we had thrown down while dancing and hurry down to the pier. Nobody needs to be told to tie their capes and straighten their hats: none of us want to look tousled by play. The older people come more slowly out of the palace, eyeing us with quick suspicious glances to see that we don't betray their lack of supervision.

We knew the king would arrive today or tomorrow, but we still feel caught out. The king's companions dash ahead to line up in the correct order of precedence, stiffly waiting to greet the king, as if we had not been rioting as dancing shepherds and milkmaids just moments ago.

I look from the flushed young faces turned to the cold river, to the heavy barges of the old men waiting to land, a sluggish armada of wealth and age, and I think: if the king ever comes to know himself as one of the old, bad-tempered men, cold and distant, and his court as young and playful and hot-blooded; then he will hate us. Katheryn and her maids-of-honour look like runaway schoolgirls recalled by a strict teacher. They press their cold hands to their rosy cheeks and try to pretend they are not heated by dancing and flirtation. Kitty looks as guilty as a child with a smear of jam on her smock.

'Smile, Your Grace,' I whisper urgently. 'The king will want to see a pretty face to welcome him.'

'But he's been in London executing people!'

'No need for you to look as if you should be in the Tower.'

She turns her lips up in a smile; but as soon as I see the king rise heavily from his throne at the stern of the barge, I know that we are all in grave trouble. I can read his resentment in the set of his padded shoulders, the way he scowls at the heavy snow clouds overhead.

The barge spins expertly, the rowers leaning on their oars, to bring it parallel to the pier. The king is unsteady on the rocking deck; his hand tightens on the bargemaster's shoulder, his fat face is furrowed with lines of pain. His eyes are squinting against the bright winter light, dazzling on the sparkling river.

He cannot get down the gangplank without leaning on the

bargemaster, and at the foot, he snaps his fingers for Thomas Culpeper, who pulls off his cap and springs forward to kneel.

'Get up, fool – I need your arm,' the king says, pulling him close and putting all his weight on the young man.

Culpeper staggers for a moment and then bears up. They start to walk, the king as unsteady as a drunken man. Culpeper hesitates as they go past the queen. Katheryn sinks into a deep curtsey, exquisitely graceful, and comes up with a radiant smile.

The king makes a noise as if he is hawking up phlegm and says: 'Keep going, you damn fool. Every moment on my leg is like a year of pain.'

Culpeper can do nothing but heave the king past Katheryn as if she were not there.

John Dudley ducks around the two of them to arrive on the other side. 'Would Your Majesty take my arm as well?' he offers.

'You think I can't walk?' the king demands, shuddering to a standstill. 'You think I can't walk through my own garden into my own palace? From my own damned barge?'

'A wound that would have killed another man,' John Dudley exclaims.

'It's killing me,' the king says dourly. 'Give me your arm and take me to my rooms.'

The younger men of the court trail behind the king, watching for their chance to help, wondering how they are going to get him up the huge flight of stairs. We ladies are left completely rejected on the riverbank. The playful spring day has come to a sudden wintry dusk.

The noblemen's barges, following the king, line up to dock like heavy-laden trows, one after another, and the old lords stamp down the gangplanks and into the palace without a courteous word to anyone, except a token bow to the queen and a nod to summon their young kinsmen or their spies.

'Shall we go in, Your Grace?' I prompt Katheryn.

She is staring after the king with John Dudley holding up one side and Thomas Culpeper bearing up the other. She looks quite appalled, as if she had never before realised that the king is a bad-tempered old invalid, thirty-two years her senior, who can only get older and sicker; and that all her youth and joy and prettiness are wasted on him.

Her lower lip trembles. 'What's the matter with him?' she demands. 'Did he not see me? Did he not see me curtsey?'

Ever since that day at Rochester, when she stole his gaze from his rightful bride, he has not been able to look away from her.

'What's wrong with him? He's so old – all of a sudden! Has he gone blind?'

'Shut up,' I spit. 'Shut your mouth.'

She gasps at my rudeness; she is stunned into silence, long enough for me to bundle her indoors, out of earshot of anyone, into her bedroom.

'How ... how dare you?' she whimpers, as soon as the door is closed behind us.

'You could die for those words,' I rejoin. 'Don't ever say them.'

She sinks onto a chair and blindly feels for her hand mirror as if she has to see herself, as if she has to make sure that she is as beautiful as ever. 'But what's the matter with him?' she demands, never taking her gaze from the portrait of young sorrow reflected back at her.

'He's an old man with a terrible old wound from jousting,' I tell her bleakly. 'He's nearly fifty. Most men die before his age. And he's been working hard in London while we've been merrymaking here. He's been hearing evidence against a boyhood friend – a man he's known all his life, a man he pardoned once before. You can't imagine what it's like to be surrounded by friends that you can't trust – but the king has lived like that ever since ... ever since ...' I think: it was before the death of Thomas Cromwell, before Anne, before even Thomas More – even before Cardinal Wolsey who guided him so faithfully, even before Queen Katherine. He has been untrusting and untrustworthy from the moment he secretly exulted at his brother's death and jumped into his shoes.

'He's terribly alone,' I say. 'Grief and anger keep him from sleep, so he's always tired, and he's always in pain – he's terrified of loss, and yet he executes his friends. He wants to be loved, and yet he has no heart. I've seen him like this before . . .' But never so bad, I think to myself. 'The important thing, the thing you must remember, is that you can never, never say one word, not a single word, that suggests he is old or ill or . . .' I break off; I don't think I can say the word 'impotent' to this child, watching herself in her mirror as a single tear rolls down her face.

'You can't say anything but praise. It's against the law to say that he is old or unwell. It is illegal to say he might die. It's against the law, Katheryn.'

'But that's a stupid law,' she observes. 'Everyone dies.'

'Still the law,' I tell her. 'You can be tried for treason and beheaded for saying – as you did at the pier – that the king is looking old or sick. You must never say it.'

'He walked right past me as if he didn't see me.'

'He didn't see you; he didn't see any of us, because he's in so much pain and he's so—'

'But it wasn't just the king! Everyone walked straight past me!'

I think: oh, this is Culpeper. But she has to learn that the king comes first. To a courtier, the king must always come first.

'Nobody matters more than the king,' I tell her firmly. 'We all put him first. Thomas Culpeper has to put him first. You too.'

'Why, what can I do?' she demands, opening her hazel eyes wide at her own reflection.

'You have to smile as much as you did as when you were happy with his gifts. You have to be pretty even when no one is watching. Even if he – or anyone else – fails in their manners, you never fail in yours. You are always as beautiful and as beautifully behaved as when you first popped up before him.'

This, she understands. She was raised to be a Howard girl: the most charming, the most beautiful, the most desirable. This court – an illusion – has a fitting queen at last: one who only cares how things look, not how they are.

'I'll wear my dark-green gown and my emeralds to dinner,' she says as a solution to unhappiness.

'Yes. I'll send them in to get you dressed, and I'll find out if the king wants to dine in his presence chamber or wants to come here.'

'And order the musicians to come—'

'There won't be dancing,' I warn her. 'He won't want dancing when his leg hurts.'

'I'm not going to dance! But I want to refuse to dance with—'

'There won't be dancing.'

THE KING IS in too much pain to dine with the court; he does not even want to dine privately with his bride. He only wants the company of a couple of his most favoured friends: Thomas Culpeper must stay at his side, sitting with him all day and sleeping in his bedchamber at night. No visitors are allowed: hundreds of plaintiffs come to court, and there is no one to hear their requests. Noblemen and their ladies – elegant beggars themselves – get no closer to the king than the presence chamber, and he never comes out there. Only the doctor is admitted to his privy chamber by the guards on the door, and Dr Butts comes out grim-faced, saying – as he is legally bound to say – that the king is healthy and strong.

A week goes by; the court freezes into stillness and quietness in the dark days of February. It snows silently, most days, thick heavy flakes, and the river starts to freeze, crackling among the reeds, and it is dark by early afternoon. No one dares to raise their voice or run with their heels tapping on the wooden floorboards, for fear of disturbing the king's sleep. The doors of the king's room are barred, and blank-faced guards stand before them, pikes crossed, to block anyone from even approaching. Nobody can linger outside to see the doctor enter and leave.

One afternoon, the snowflakes are a soft pattering swirl of grey against the windows, the sky so dark that we have candles lit at midday, and everyone is bored of card games and riddles by mid-afternoon. The queen looks longingly at the white gardens where we played at snowball fighting, where we danced on the archery lawns; but she knows better than to run out in the snow while the king keeps to his shuttered rooms like a sleeping beast, like a mole deep underground in darkness. She is imprisoned in the blizzard, and there will be no tracks of her little boots in the drifts, running away.

'But what's wrong with him?' she whispers to me.

'His doctor says he's very well.'

People start to whisper that the huge trays of food are a deception, and he is not in there at all. I wonder if there is another greater deception: if he has died in there and the Seymours are concealing his death until they have made alliances strong enough to announce a Seymour regency to govern for their little prince. But I cannot see the Seymours; they are locked up like an enclosed silent order with the king. I cannot write to warn my uncle. I have to practise patience and hold Kitty in readiness for whatever is to come.

Dr Butts calls in other physicians from London, as if he has lost his famous certainty, and they come upriver in the royal barge, the ice cracking under the bow wave as the icy water washes down. I remember Dr Butts telling George to take off the king's helmet after the jousting accident – and all of us wondering if the head would come off, too. He was alone then; he did not need another opinion to bring the king to life. Can it be that the king is closer to death now than when his great horse rolled on him? Is Dr Butts more fearful now – is the king worse than when he lay like a dead man?

I walk, wrapped against the cold in my dark cape, hidden by the dusk, along the riverbank path, past the pier as the doctors board the barge back to London. One of them says quietly that cupping will never bring down a tertian fever as hot as this one. He lowers his voice: 'His heart can't stand it . . .'

Now everyone knows that the king has a tertian fever and that recurs and recurs till it kills the patient. Someone says that he was delirious with fever; they had to hold him to the bed to stop him throwing himself from the window, and now he has collapsed into a tranced silence, his glassy eyes on the ceiling, his mouth gaping in a silent scream of pain, while the poison in his leg runs through his body; and when it reaches his brain, he will die. His favourites never leave his rooms, as if they are to be buried with him, like pagan companions in a king's grave.

Once again, the court catches the king's terror of death. If he dies tonight, he has only a frail little boy to succeed him and a country divided against him. I should alert my uncle that his niece Kitty might be widowed; but he is travelling in the wild lands between England and Scotland. He has no messenger network as my spymaster did; we have no code, and in any case I cannot write that the king is dying – that is treason. I am the only person who can position Kitty for her future widowed state. I catch Thomas Seymour, as he runs up the stone stairs from the stables.

'Lady Rochford.' He bows.

'Sir Thomas,' I reply. 'Can you tell me: how is the king today?'

'Better,' he says, immediately deceitful. 'Better every day, I think.'

'I thank God for it,' I say, as dishonest as he. 'The queen will be happy to hear. And our prince, the queen's stepson, is well also at Hertford Castle?'

A sideways glance from his dark eyes tells me he has noted that I claim the little boy as Kitty's stepson. 'Yes, praise God.'

'The king always used to read the nursery reports to Queen Katheryn,' I remark. 'She has missed hearing of him. She's a very devoted stepmother.'

His smile tells me that he knows this is a lie. 'She is a young woman herself,' he says, as if to excuse her indifference.

'Old enough for motherhood,' I contradict him. 'The king thinks her old enough to be a mother and a stepmother. Old enough to supervise her stepchildren, our little kinswoman Lady Elizabeth and her stepson Prince Edward. When the weather is warmer, she will visit them both.'

He bows. 'I am sure they will be honoured,' he says. 'I will see that the queen gets reports from the Hertford nursery.'

'And she will send her advice through you, his uncles,' I say. 'Loving, motherly advice. You and she are the prince's only parents while the king is unwell.' I want him to understand that I'm not challenging their place as lords protector, but I expect a share of the power.

'We'll be glad to have her motherly advice,' he says. A direct glance from his dark eyes tells me that we understand each other, that when the king dies, there will be a Seymour regency and Kitty must be named as regent queen. He knows well enough that this is my idea and my plan, that he will have to deal with me and the Howards behind me. Kitty is our figurehead: I am the power.

He kisses my hand. 'I'm so glad we have had this talk.'

'I too.' I smile as he bows and goes up the stairs to the king's rooms, where the king is dying in secret as the fever heats his hurrying heart towards silence.

In the queen's rooms, we see no one. There is no singing or dancing or even playing cards. The young noblemen who ran in and out are now confined to the king's rooms, shuttered in silence. Only Katheryn's kinsmen visit her, and they are not of the king's inner circle and know nothing. Charles Howard comes to visit his sister and sips a glass of wine.

'Did you tell the king you were coming to my rooms?' Katheryn asks.

Her brother shakes his head.

'He didn't ask you to come to see me?'

'Alas,' he says insincerely.

'He sent no message?'

Charles looks across at me for help. 'No, he did not,' he says. 'He didn't, actually. No.'

Katheryn slips off her throne, so her brother has to rise to his feet. She puts her little hand on the richly embroidered sleeve of his jacket, and he awkwardly passes his glass to me so he can hold her hands.

She draws him away from the listening ladies. Only I can hear, as I follow behind them, her urgent whisper: 'Brother Charles, dear brother Charles, is the king my lord displeased with me?'

'Not at all not at all!' he shoots a glance at me imploring for help. 'His Majesty the king is in good health and thinks fondly of you, as ever. He is very well . . . he will do himself the pleasure, no doubt . . .' He detaches himself from Kitty's grasping hands, makes a low bow, throws a yearning glance to Margaret Douglas, and gets himself out of the room.

I catch him in the gallery outside. 'You do right not to alarm the queen, but you can tell me. Is the king thinking kindly of the queen? It's better if I know. It's better for all of us if I know how to advise the queen.'

My heart sinks as I recognise in him the alarm of a courtier who has lost control of his master. 'Nobody knows what he's thinking,' he whispers urgently. 'Because he's struck dumb: his face black as a chimney sweep, his breath coming in gasps. He sees no one but his doctor and his cook and two favourites. He does nothing but sleep and eat, except for when he raves like a madman for pain. God knows where this will end. I cannot say – you understand me – I cannot say.'

'But he has nothing against the queen?' I ask urgently, one hand on his arm. I dare not say: He has not sent for a lawyer? He has not changed his will? When he dies, she will be recognised as dowager queen? He has named no heir other than the little Seymour boy? He has not approved a regency council that excludes her? Anyone but a fool would know what I mean.

'He says nothing about her at all,' he explodes. 'I think he's forgotten all about her! When he's raving, he swears that he has no friend and no true advisor. His people are all rebels. He says he has no wife. He's dying as lonely and pained as she did. Nobody can take the place of Lord Cromwell.'

'He's missing Lord Cromwell?' I am aghast.

'He says he'll never forgive those who dragged him down – us Howards!'

'But Lord Cromwell made the Cleves wedding!'

'Now he says there was nothing wrong with the Cleves wedding! And nothing wrong with Anne of Cleves!'

'Does he think to recall her?' I am stunned. 'What's he thinking? Is he going back to the duchess?' This is like a nightmare. If he regrets the divorce of Anne of Cleves and the death of my friend Thomas Cromwell, and all the others: my husband, my sister-in-law, Henry Pole, Henry Courtenay, Sir Thomas More, Bishop Fisher ... then my whole life has been grief without reason, and I have lost my husband and my sister-in-law and the only friend I ever had to a madman.

My blank horror exasperates Charles. 'I told you! And I d-damned well should not tell you! He thinks he is d-d-dying . . . and he speaks only of . . .'

'Who?'

'The dowager princess,' he blurts out, and for a moment, I am so distressed that I do not know who he means. 'Who?' I demand. 'Who?'

'Katherine of Aragon,' he says. 'He is dreaming that he is a young man again and married to Queen Katherine. When he wakes, he cries for her and calls for Cardinal Wolsey and for his dear friend Thomas More and faithful Cromwell, and when we can't bring them, he says that nobody cares for him, for his true self, and we are all . . . all . . .'

'What?'

'Trai-trai—' He can't get the word: traitors out of his tight throat.

I grab his cold hands, and I force him to turn to look at me. 'You speak of her,' I command him. I hiss the words into his ear as if I would spit them into his stupid, handsome head. 'Put the queen, our queen, in his mind again. Say she is distraught with grief and worry for him.'

'How can I?' he says feebly. 'He's surrounded by Seymours, speaking of Jane and her son, their heir.'

'She has to be dowager queen!' My gripping hands are as cold as his. 'She has to be on the council of regency. You have to make sure he names her to the regency.'

'I tell you, he's going to die unshriven, without a will. He's going to die a madman.'

## HAMPTON COURT, MARCH

## 1541

Shrove Tuesday is the first of March this year, but I think Lent came earlier, heralded with drumbeats as the king's barge docked at the palace pier and brought us a Fisher king – a man who only wants a kingdom of silence and sorrow. There will be no masques or jousts or feasts. The master of revels orders no musicians; no scenery painted for the jousting arena and no costumes sewn for masques. We hardly know that it is Fat Tuesday at all – there is no special food at dinner; there is no lord of misrule. Will Somer the fool stays in the king's rooms and can raise no laughter: the muttered Lent prayers are like a spell that has spread a brooding silence, down quiet galleries, through echoing halls.

'This isn't like being queen at all,' Kitty whispers to me. 'It's worse than Lambeth. It's worse than Horsham! I might as well have stayed at home, a nobody and nothing; but free to do what I want.'

'Wait,' I tell her. 'These might be the most important days of your life.'

We observe Lent strictly in the queen's rooms, wearing modest clothes in dark colours, fasting at meatless dinners, and attending mass in the chapel, swept bare of any colour. We watch, in silent envy, as great mountains of food are marched into the king's rooms: meats and creams, butters and cheeses, puddings and rich morsels, flagons of deep red wines.

Kitty, on Lenten fare of fish and white meat, starts to lose weight; her round girlish face gets thinner, and never flushes with pleasure.

'You have to eat!' I urge her. 'You can order some game meat.'

She shakes her head. 'I don't feel like it,' she says. 'I don't feel like anything. When's the king going to come out, d'you think? Is he ever going to come out? Are the young men never going to be free again?'

The whole court starts to predict that the king will stay enclosed like the monster the pilgrims named him – the mouldwarp who lives feasting in dark tunnels underground. Will he hide in his rooms until Lent has ended and only come out at Easter? Can it be possible that he will sleep until the weather warms and not come out until Whitsun?

WITHOUT WARNING, THE guards are gone from the door to the king's rooms, the great doors to his presence chamber are swung open, and when we go to early mass in the chapel, there is the king, in his usual seat, with Sir Anthony Browne in Cromwell's place, bending over him and sliding letters before him, as if nothing has changed and he has never been away.

A giddy sense of relief sweeps through the court. People fall to their knees on the chapel floor for the first sincere prayer of thanksgiving in their lives. We courtiers, safe behind high walls, we landowners at war with our tenants – how would we survive if the king died? Who would keep us so richly, riding so high?

When the priest prays for the health of the king, everyone bows their heads; everyone is fervent in their prayers for his wellbeing, for his health and happiness, and for the life and fertility of his queen.

Katheryn glances across at him all through the service, her face pale behind the lace of her veil, and I know that she is afraid of this man who has come back from the dead, returned to us from his own earthly purgatory. It has been horrible to see the mountainous dinners going in and the dirty plates with bare bones and broken pastries coming out hours later. She feels like a bride in a fairy story, married to a monster.

The king does not take his eyes from the papers that are carefully placed, one after another, before him. But he does not sign them; he stamps each document, as if banging down an angry fist, and each paper is taken away for his signature to be inked-in later. Has he grown too lazy to even scrawl his name? Has he given away the sign that makes a whim into law? Who holds the stamp of his signature? Who is ruling the country if the king, who never read the decrees that he issued, does not even sign them now?

'Should I curtsey to him?' Kitty whispers to me as the mass ends with the bidding prayer.

'Yes,' I say. 'Curtsey and look up smiling with joy, and if he wants to speak to you, he will beckon you forward.'

She looks aghast.

'Smile,' I tell her. 'Look as if you are happy that he is well. Say something like God is merciful to us all, that you are well . . . something like that.'

She looks full of dread, but she rises to her feet, curtseys to the altar, and then turns and curtseys to the king. He waves a pudgy hand that she must come forward. She goes to him and, obedient to another wave, bends over him and kisses his cheek.

Without warning, he grabs the back of her head and pulls her mouth to his, kisses her wetly and lets her go.

Kitty straightens up as the court applauds. I can see she is shaking, but she manages a trembly smile. 'God is merciful . . .' she parrots. 'Merciful.'

'I am under His special protection,' the king tells her. 'God has restored my health and vigour.'

LONDON IS FREE from plague, and the king is well enough to be seen in public; he wants to enforce his recovery on us all. He demands a public ceremony to show he is as healthy and as fit as a man half his age, with a beautiful young queen at his side. At least Katheryn gets her ceremonial entry to her capital city. There will be no coronation until she is pregnant – never again is he going to be stuck with a childless queen – but he wants to show Kitty off to an admiring crowd and celebrate himself as the potent husband of a beautiful bride. He comes to her bed even though it is Lent, as if he does not care if it is a godly act or not, and he limps past me with a sly smile.

Katheryn blooms again at the attention and the promise of a public appearance. Over and over again, she asks me and her vice chamberlain, her brother-in-law Sir Edward, to describe the formalities and where she should sit and when she should move and the queenly gestures of acknowledgement for applause. Sir Edward, who has no patience with female vanity, begrudgingly tells her that she will be steered and guided throughout the day, and just to watch him and he will tell her what she would do.

Of course, this is no help to Kitty, who must be practice-perfect in every dance. So I put a chair in her privy chamber to serve as the throne of the barge, and the maids-of-honour walk past shouting: 'I am the guild of vintners!' and 'I am the guild of fishmongers!' and 'I am the lord mayor!' – and the ladies shout 'bang!' for the boom of the Tower guns, and some of them sit in the window seat and cheer to represent the people of the City on the riverbank to see their new queen.

The maids-of-honour turn this into a romp and throw strewing herbs at each other for river water and pretend to fall in the pretend river, overawed by Katheryn's beauty, and roll about miming drowning. In the old days, Kitty would have rolled on the floor with them; but today, she is very serious and tells them to do it properly or not at all and asks me the exact level of her seated bows to the lord mayor or to the guild of fishmongers. She orders all the gowns of cloth of silver brought from the royal wardrobe, and we send to the Tower for extra jewels. She is determined to dazzle the City that knows her only as an unimportant daughter of a disgraced nobleman, the lowly maid-of-honour to the former queen of royal blood.

'They loved Anne of Cleves, didn't they?' she demands nervously in the privacy of her bedchamber, as I hold one gown after another against her, while Catherine Tilney holds the long looking-glass and rolls her eyes.

'They didn't know her,' I reassure her. 'They'll love you. You just have to smile and wave.'

'And get into the barge without tripping,' she reminds me. 'And acknowledge the lord mayor and everyone at the Tower, and then do the river parade just right.'

'They'll love you,' I tell her again. 'And His Majesty will be at your side.'

'And he's had plenty of practice proclaiming queens,' Catherine Tilney says sourly.

But Kitty looks more anxious than ever at the thought of the king's brooding presence. 'Is he all right now?' she whispers.

'Am I to go on holding this mirror, because my arms are about to drop off?' Catherine Tilney demands rudely.

'Oh, don't be cross,' Katheryn pleads with her maid. 'Just hold it up. You'd be terrified if you were me.'

'I'll prop it.' The young woman leans it against the wall.

'Anyway, I'm as ready as I'll ever be,' Kitty says desperately, choosing a gown at random. 'I'll wear that one, with my pearls.'

PHILIPPA GREGORY

## THE TOWER OF LONDON, MARCH

## 1541

OF COURSE, SHE does not wear that gown – she changes her mind two or three times before her state entry to London. Overnight in the Tower, she changes her mind again, and then all progress grinds to a halt when she cannot decide on her shoes for the river parade from the Tower to Greenwich Palace.

'You'll be in the barge; no one will see your feet,' I say patiently.

'I shall know that they are hideous,' she says. 'And anyway, I can change my shoes a dozen times if I want to.'

'You can change as much as you like, but you can't keep the king waiting, and the council and the aldermen can't bob about on the river while you change your shoes,' I warn her.

The merest mention of the king throws her into a panic, and she is in the shoes she called hideous, out of the door of the royal rooms and down the stone stairs as the clock strikes the hour. She's so quick down the stairs that I cannot get beside her and guide her away from Tower Green.

She turns towards the Green; she walks past it – after all, it means nothing to her. I keep my eyes on the hem of her gown. I don't look up or look around me; I won't see Tower Green where they beheaded my sister-in-law, where the new grass grows fresh. I won't look up at the windows of the Tower where Thomas Wyatt – George's friend and fellow poet – may be looking down on me now, as he did on Anne on that day, looking out and wondering if he is to be freed as he was before, killed like so many of his friends, or just left here until he dies like Thom Howard.

I don't want to see his face. The ghost of my husband could be looking over his shoulder; these were his rooms, too. Francis Weston, Henry Norris, William Brereton, Thomas More, Bishop Fisher, and my spymaster Thomas Cromwell all gazed from these windows as they waited to die. I don't look for any of them; I don't want to see any ghosts.

I step forward to help the queen down the damp steps to the quay, where the royal barge is waiting, bobbing on the dark water, inside the water gate, which is lowered shut, a portcullis barring the light from the river. Her face is pale in the shadow of the archway. Housed in the rooms above us, on the south side of the Tower, is Lady Margaret Pole and the little Pole boy and his cousin, the Courtenay child. They will have heard the trumpets of the royal barge; they will hear the roar of the cannon to honour Katheryn Howard. I don't look up at their windows either; I don't want to see my old schoolmistress' face looking out.

The bargemaster helps Kitty up the gangplank of the barge and settles her in her throne at the back. The curtains are open so she can be seen by the waiting Londoners lining the riverbank and the gentry on their barges. The king comes down the steps leaning on Thomas Culpeper on one side and Edward Seymour on the other. Bishop Gardiner follows them as they load the king like cargo into his seat on the opposite side of the barge.

I think: if Margaret Pole sees Bishop Gardiner, an enemy of the reform of religion so favoured, she will think herself due for release. I think: how terrible to be inside these damp walls when outside the sun is shining on the river and the gulls are wheeling and crying over the water, and spring is coming, May Day is coming. Then I think again: May Day has never been a happy day of promise in the Tower.

'It is rather gloomy,' Katheryn remarks feebly as the rowers pull away from the dark water gate and it rolls down behind us, the mechanism rumbling in the tower above, the dark water washing between the grille of the gates and the seaweed trailing like drowned hair.

'It is,' I agree.

'Sort of sad,' she says. 'When you think of all the people who have been prisoners. And worse if you think of the ones who died.'

I really cannot chatter away about prisoners in the Tower and their execution.

'I suppose I could ask the king for mercy?' She glances uncertainly towards him. He is saying something to Thomas Culpeper; he pays no attention to her at all. 'I mean, asking for mercy is a good thing to do, isn't it?'

We pull into the centre of the river, where the London City barges are moored. The gun salute roars over our heads, and she waves and smiles at the City barges and the London merchants ships and the cheering people. The king has his back to us, waving to the other bank.

'Who's been talking to you?' I demand.

She owns up at once. 'Mary Howard,' she says. 'She says that Thomas Wyatt is a great poet and no traitor.'

'That may well be true,' I say. I wave to a couple of children leaning over the prow in an overloaded boat. 'So Mary Howard can ask for mercy, if she cares so much for him?'

'He wrote a beautiful poem about Anne Boleyn,' Kitty remarks, as if at random. 'He praised her for her beauty,'

'Yes, I know.' I think Mary Howard understands very well how to inspire Katheryn's vanity in one clever courtier's word.

'Mary Howard says that queens ask for mercy, and they let their hair down and kneel before the king, and it's a very pretty sight. People remember it and are grateful forever. If I did it now, then everyone in the river pageant would see that I'm a good queen.'

'Once,' I say dampeningly. 'Katherine of Aragon asked for mercy once for the apprentice boys, and it was all agreed beforehand: planned and designed and – yes – it was very pretty. But Jane Seymour asked for mercy for the pilgrims, the northern rebels, and the king left her kneeling on the floor with her hair down and only me to help her up. Can you imagine how foolish she looked?'

Kitty looks shocked at the prospect. 'Oh, I'd have to know he wanted to. He must want to pardon before I ask.'

'Then you're not begging for a man's life but putting on a masque,' I point out.

'Yes,' she says cheerfully. 'That's what I meant. Just like a masque. And me as *Mercy*. Can we do it now?'

'Now?' I glance over to the king's side of the barge. He is drinking wine and eating pastries, waving at the procession of ships that have come to celebrate the new queen.

'Now, where everyone can see me.'

'I'll ask if he wants to,' I say and beckon to Thomas Culpeper.

He comes at once, bows politely, and listens to my whispered question.

'Oh certainly,' he says. 'His Majesty thought fondly of Wyatt while we were overnight in the Tower. Asked if he had a good room and good cheer.'

I will not think about the king asking if a traitor has good cheer. I will not think about the monks who starved to death in their chains in these very rooms. 'Would His Majesty welcome a plea for mercy from the queen?' I ask.

'I'll make sure,' he smiles to himself. 'No man in the world could refuse her . . .'

I watch him cross the deck to the king, lean and whisper in his ear. The king's cheeks are swollen with food; he takes a gulp of wine before he answers. But then I see him beam, and he calls the bargemaster to halt, and the drum stops, and the rowers feather their oars to keep us steady in the water.

'Do it now,' I say to her.

'Now?' She is delighted. 'Right now? Can I?'

'You're very eager to get him pardoned.'

'No,' she says honestly. 'Just so that everyone sees me being a queen.'

Carefully, I untie the cape she has over her shoulders, take off her cap, take the priceless ivory pins out of her hair. The bronze mass of hair tumbles down over her shoulders, and I stroke it out.

'What do I do?'

'Just walk towards him, go down on your knees and put your hands together like you were praying and look up at him,' I say. 'If you can cry, that's good, too. But nothing to spoil your looks. Just a tear.'

'I don't say anything?' she demands.

'You say: "I cry mercy, mercy for Thomas Wyatt."'

She rises from her throne and throws a quick nervous look over at Henry. He is looking out at the river, waving at some people who are cheering from a fishing smack.

'What about his friend John Wallop?' I ask. 'And Lady Margaret Pole? She's still in the Tower, the king's own cousin. You could ask pardon for them, too? You should ask pardon for her first?'

'Oh no,' she says quickly. 'I can't go on and on. You know, I can't be boring. Besides, the people won't hear what I'm saying. It's just for show.'

She steps past me, steady on the gently rocking deck, up to the raised dais. In full view of the boats on the river, she kneels in her silver gown, raises her praying hands to the king and mimes – for everyone watching – the beautiful young queen begging for mercy. She does it beautifully, a single tear rolls down her cheek.

The king leans forward on his chair, puts his hands around hers, and raises her to her feet. She bends down, her hair tumbling forward, and she kisses him on his wine-stained lips.

## GREENWICH PALACE, MARCH

### 1541

MY FATHER GREETS us on the quay at Greenwich, kneeling to the king and queen, who process proudly past him. He rises to give me his blessing.

'I didn't know you were coming,' I say as I kiss his cheek. 'Is my lady mother well, and my sister and brother?'

'Yes, yes, all well,' he says. 'And before you ask, I'm here to ask the king for some lands at home – there's no inquiry.'

'Thomas Wyatt is to be released,' I tell him. 'The queen asked for pardon?'

'Lady Margaret Pole?' He raises an eyebrow.

I shake my head.

My father sighs. '*Circa Regna Tonat*,' he says, quoting a Wyatt poem. 'Thunder around the throne.'

I take his arm, and we follow the courtiers into the palace.

'And how is your new queen?'

'Young, but guided into her great calling,' I say.

He understands at once. 'Be modest, daughter,' he says gently. 'She should grow; but the greatest courtier never forgets he is in service. And you are on your own now you have no protector.'

'I have you,' I suggest.

He gives a little shrug. 'I could translate a text for you, but little more. I am an observer of the machinery behind the masque; I don't put my shoulder to the wheel.'

# GREENWICH PALACE, APRIL

## 1541

I COME INTO THE royal bedroom at Greenwich and find Katheryn is still in bed. She has a handful of counters from the gaming tables spread over her embroidered sheets, and a written calendar of dates.

'What's this?' I ask.

'I'm not quite sure,' she says. She is breathless; the calendar is scribbled over and corrected several times. She has marked question marks at the foot of the page and a week of bold ticks at the top. 'I'm not quite certain?'

'You're trying to calculate your courses?' I ask her.

She looks up with relief. 'Jane, d'you know if it's due? I think I am late?'

I have been a courtier to five queens. It is an essential tool of my trade. 'Yes,' I say. 'You're a few days late; but it could mean nothing.'

'But I could be with child?' She looks up from the counters and the calendar. 'I could be with child?'

'Only if you conceived as soon as the king came back to your bed. It's too early to say. Certainly, too early to tell anyone.'

'It must be then!' she agrees. 'He said God blessed him. I am with child; I know I am! I have a great desire for sugarplums.'

'You always do,' I point out.

'Far more than usual,' she says stubbornly. 'I shall tell the king.'

'No wait,' I say. 'We don't want to get his hopes up and then disappoint him.'

The look she turns on me is that of a far older wiser woman. 'Jane,' she says. 'Remember how he was before Lent? I have to get crowned.'

She is right: she must be crowned. We thought he would die then, and his illness is not cured but just in abeyance; it is a tertian fever it will flare up again and again. He could die before her baby quickens. A dowager queen veiled in black with a baby in her belly would be unbeatable. It's worth the risk.

'I'll tell him after mass,' she says, throwing back her fine linen sheets. 'I'll wear blue – get me my blue gown with blue sleeves, Jane. I'll wear blue like the Virgin Herself.'

'The *annuntiati*,' I agree, hearing the snort of laughter of a ghost.

S HE ASKS ME the correct way to inform a king that his queen is with child, and I tell her lord chamberlain, who informs the king's lord chamberlain. When mass is over, we ladies wait on our side of the chapel while the king gets Culpeper to haul him to his feet. I prompt her to curtsey very prettily, and step forward and whisper in his ear, blushing. Culpeper studies the floor.

The king takes her hand, kisses her on the mouth, turns her as if she were a little puppet, to face the altar and says: 'Rejoice, highly favoured one. The Lord is with you. Blessed are you among women!'

Everyone says 'Amen!' or 'Thanks be to God!' and gives a muted cheer. The Seymours look as if they have swallowed a furball and are going to have to go quietly into a corner to retch it up. But even they cross themselves and say: 'God bless you and keep you well!' to Kitty, who stands, flushed and so proud, among them all, with the king holding her hand and her eyes filled with tears, not crying so as not to spoil her looks – just tears of happiness.

## GREENWICH PALACE, SPY WEDNESDAY

### 1541

Spy Wednesday is the day before Maundy Thursday, named for Judas Iscariot, and I think of my master, the greatest spy in England, as if this were his memorial day – to honour spies. I think: what would he advise me – with the king disappearing from court? What would he do when the king came out, refusing to even remember that he nearly died? What would he do with a young queen who may have a royal heir in her belly? I think: he would have prepared for everything, for anything. That's what I must do.

Katheryn tries to escape the long masses and prayers in these final days of Lent, and I have to bribe her into church with beautiful black-lace Spanish mantillas that Queen Katherine of Aragon left in the royal wardrobe. But she refuses outright to wash the feet of seventeen poor women – one for each year of her life. 'It's far worse for the king; he has to do fifty,' I tell her. 'Old men, too.'

'It's worse for me because I have no need to humble myself,' she says. 'I wasn't born a queen. I am not an old king. Why do I have to wash their disgusting feet?'

'They're not disgusting; they're washed already,' I tell her. 'And every queen of England has done it.'

'I can't bear it!' she says with a little wail. 'Why do I have to?'

'Because Our Lord washed the feet of the disciples,' I said. 'The pope himself does it in Rome. The king does it. You can certainly do it.'

'Only if you show me exactly how, and if you promise me a favour after.'

'Oh, very well,' I say impatiently.

We set up a line of stools, and her young maids-of-honour throw themselves into the roles of being old and poor. They limp and cough and insist on being carried and seated. They roll down their stockings and slip off their satin shoes, screaming with laughter and accusing each other of having smelly feet.

'No laughing,' Kitty says crossly. 'The poor don't laugh, do they? Why do I have to do this properly if no one else does!'

I show her how each poor woman will have her feet in the bowl before her, and all Kitty has to do is pour a jug of water into the bowl and touch the top of the foot.

'Jane Seymour did it beautifully,' I prompt her. 'She saw it as part of queenly service.'

Down the line of seated giggling maids Katheryn goes, her face set and serious, pretending to pour from an empty jug, touching their feet with one extended fingertip. Margery Horsman takes the jug from her at the end of the line of stools, dries her hands, and hands her a purse. Kitty turns and walks back up the line, giving each woman a penny.

She stops at the end of the line and looks at me. 'Then, do I just walk away?'

'Bless them and wish them a Happy Easter.'

Katheryn turns back with the most angelic smile. 'God bless you, smelly old ladies, and Happy Easter,' she says.

The girls shriek with laughter. 'God bless you, Queen Katheryn!' they call. 'God bless your sweet face! God bless your goodly belly and the baby inside it! God save you get another the way you got that one! God hope you enjoy it next time!'

'Enough!' I say sternly. 'And put the stools straight.' I turn to Katheryn. 'That was well done. Do it just like that.'

'And now my favour!' She is suddenly bright with mischief; she draws me away from the noise of the girls taking the stools back to their rooms.

'What favour?'

'The favour you promised, if I do this?'

'What d'you want?' I ask uneasily.

'I have a craving,' she whispers.

'No more than ten sugarplums,' I rule.

She beams at me. 'It is a person, not a plum. But just as mouth-watering . . .'

'What person?'

'I wonder if you can guess? You who always know everything?'

'I won't guess a person,' I say unhelpfully.

'I'll tell you then! I want to see Thomas Culpeper, privately, in my rooms.'

'You can't,' I say at once. 'Your presence chamber is always filled with people, and your privy chamber with courtiers. You can't see a man in your bedroom. There is nowhere you can see him alone.'

'I want to give him a gift for Easter,' she says. 'No harm in that.'

'Depends on the gift,' I say warily.

'Just a cap – a velvet cap,' she whispers. 'Nothing special. The sort that the king gives his favourites at Easter. Just like that. To thank him for being so good to my husband when he was ill.'

'You needn't thank him; it's his duty. Are you going to see the Seymours and thank them?'

'Oh, don't be so dull, Jane! I've bought a cap for him, and I want to give it to him, and he'll think of me as he wears it.'

'This is nonsense,' I say.

'But there's no harm in it,' she pleads. 'I'm with child. I can't do wrong. Nobody could say anything against me, after all?'

'I don't even know where you could meet.'

'I've thought of that! Just outside my bedroom door! In the gallery. I could be coming out of my rooms with you. Catherine Tilney can walk past with him, and we meet by accident. Just for a moment.'

'What if someone else comes by?' I ask.

'Then I'll pass him with a bow,' she says. 'And you can give it to him later, instead. Go on, Jane – there's no harm in it.'

'There's no good either,' I say, unconvinced.

'Yes; but I want to!' she says, like the child she is. 'And I won't wash disgusting old feet unless you agree, and I won't even get up in the morning unless you agree.'

CATHERINE TILNEY HAS no objection to playing the part of *Bialacoil* – the welcoming friend in the stories of courtly love. Henry Webb, the queen's usher, fetches Thomas Culpeper to Catherine Tilney, who walks down the gallery arm in arm with him and then steps back as the queen comes out of her bedroom.

He stops still as he realises this is planned. He waits, like an experienced flirt, to see what she wants of him, how much she wants of him. Henry Webb goes to the other end of the gallery, looking down the stairs, ready to cough loudly if anyone comes up the staircase.

An accidental meeting between a queen and a courtier does not need guards. An Easter gift between queen and courtier does not need secrecy. But, equally, a secret meeting of lovers does not happen before three witnesses. This event is indefinable – on a border between one world and another, in a gateway. Culpeper may become known as the champion of the queen, her publicly acknowledged favourite, the king's deputy at dancing and hunting. His prestige will rise, and her reputation will be undamaged. Their hidden fascination might turn into public devotion of loyal courtier to beloved queen. Culpeper knows the rules of courtly love as well as Kitty. I am hoping this meeting – on the border of indiscretion – will move them both into the safe roles of humble lover and distant mistress. But it is all over in a moment.

I see her speak to him briefly and pass him something small, folded in her hands. He takes it and, obeying her hurried gesture, tucks it out of sight, under his cloak. He says something that he thinks is funny – I see the cock of his head and his laughing smile – but she takes it badly. She steps back, turns, looks at him sharply over her shoulder, says a few words, and comes away with a cross little swish of her gown.

I am hugely relieved. This is far better than him swearing a lover's fealty. He has offended her again, and she is no longer a half-lovesick girl, the youngest maid-of-honour, looking after him as he dances with his preferred flirt. Now, she is fully aware of her importance. Master Culpeper will discover that he cannot joke with Katheryn the queen as he did with Kitty the maid-of-honour; she will not forgive impertinence.

She says nothing until I am plaiting her hair for the night. 'That's a very stupid young man,' she remarks.

'I thought so,' I reply agreeably. 'He has facile charm.'

'He does!' she exclaims. 'That's just what he has.' She hesitates. 'What is that?'

'Easy,' I say. 'Light.' Now I am thinking of George and the cock of his head and his laugh. 'Easy,' I repeat, thinking of his smile. 'Light,' thinking George was always light-hearted, even in the worst of danger. 'Courtly love – all surface, no depth.' She catches my sadness. I meet her eyes in the mirror. 'Not lasting,' I say. 'Not real.'

'Yes,' she breathes. 'Courtly love, not real. D'you know? I gave him a cap of velvet with a gold brooch and a chain and gold-tipped laces – and he barely glanced at it! He laughed and said I should have been kind to him when I was a maid. As if I could have afforded such a thing then! After I had sent Webb for him and Catherine Tilney, and made you allow me, and gone out into the gallery to see him alone.'

'He's no lovesick troubadour,' I say, with quiet satisfaction. 'Not like a lover in a poem at all. Not worthy of the favour of a queen. Not good enough for you.'

'Not at all!' she says indignantly. 'And he can be very sure that if I had been dallying with him and given him a cap when I was a maid, it would have been no laughing matter for him. I would have made him fall in love with me and left him broken-hearted. But I'm queen now, and I have no time for vain young men. He can keep the stupid cap. He can wear it all the time, and I won't notice. I shan't bother about him again.'

I tie the ribbons of her white embroidered nightcap under her chin. She looks at her reflection with satisfaction. 'It's so lovely being with child, so the king doesn't come to bed me. My room smells so nice. You can sleep here tonight, Jane. We don't need men at all, not even young ones!'

## GREENWICH PALACE, GOOD FRIDAY

### 1541

We celebrate Good Friday in the old way. The reforms that my spymaster Cromwell won might never have been. He might as well never have been. The king goes on his knees around the stations of the cross in the royal chapel, praying and weeping at each point, in an orgy of holiness. He crawls to the altar, his huge arse moving ponderously and unevenly as he tries to keep his weight off his injured leg and then prostrates himself, arms outstretched, on the stone floor.

Kitty glances anxiously at me through her veil. 'Is he all right?' she mouths.

The king lies as still as a dead man in an ecstasy of religious fervour; Kitty fidgets on her prie-dieu, alarmed at first and then bored. Only after a good hour of lying on the cold stone floor, with all eyes upon him, does the king make a waving gesture with his outspread hands like a beached seal. His back has seized up, and now he can't get up. Thomas Culpeper, Thomas Seymour, and Gregory Cromwell haul him first to his knees, where he slumps like a dummy in the tiltyard. He is so heavy that they have to get Culpeper behind him, grasping him around the enormous belly, and Seymour and Gregory on either side, their shoulders under his arms. They have to count one-two-three before they can lever him to his feet. Astoundingly, he manages this with dignity, as if he is still rapt in prayer, his eyes tight shut, one hand clenching the Bible, the other a rosary. Only I see his grimace of pain as he has to bear weight on his bad leg. Only I guess this is a holy masque – a pretend saintly trance.

Katheryn's expression is hidden by her veil as she watches the three young men stagger under the weight of her husband and heave him back to his seat. The choir starts a low solemn chant; the service continues.

I think: God send us all eternal life – the king looks half-dead, and I've not yet got Kitty confirmed as regent queen. We're in no place for him to die yet.

## GREENWICH PALACE, EASTER SATURDAY

## 1541

On Saturday, we all go to chapel again to make our individual confessions to the priest in preparation for Easter Sunday. The king is at the altar again, in black velvet, a dark shapeless hulk in the dark chapel, blessing gold and silver rings at the altar, each one dipped in holy water from the font. Each ring goes on the tip of a fat finger and then into a tray as gifts for favourites as cramp rings: blessed by the king, they will ward off falling sickness and fits.

Katheryn is to make her confession first; even God listens in order of precedence. I kneel beside her as she buries her face in her hands to pray, preparing to sit beside the priest and whisper her sins into his ear.

'No need to say anything about Culpeper,' I say quietly.

She turns a pale face towards me. 'Isn't he a venial sin?'

'No need to mention him at all,' I tell her. 'Just say the sin of vanity.'

I see her lips tremble. 'It isn't vanity,' she whispers. 'It's not, Jane. It's not a little sin. It's a pain. I can't forget it.'

'It's not queenly,' I whisper urgently. 'Don't tell the priest that you're not a true queen. Don't tell God that. Not now!'

'God will forgive me,' she says certainly.

'You don't want the king to hear of it.'

This shakes her. She raises up her missal before her face, so we can whisper in the shelter of the prayer book. 'How would he know? If I say it in confession, only the priest and God hear?'

The priest will be in the pay of someone. Bishop Gardiner, a hard-bitten churchman, would give much to know that the new queen, a Howard queen, has met a young courtier in secret. Archbishop Cranmer, a reformer and friend of the Howards, would take an interest.

'The king's Head of the Church, isn't he?' I demand. 'So the priest works for him, doesn't he?'

She blanches white. 'I'll never confess another sin!' she swears. 'Not until I am on my deathbed and by the time anybody knows what I said I'd be dead.'

'You've got nothing serious to confess,' I assure her. 'Stick to vanity and gossip.'

She looks as if she might cry. 'I don't love my husband.' Her voice is a thread of sound, almost inaudible. 'Jane, I don't love my husband as I should.'

'That's all right,' I tell her. 'You obey him, don't you?'

'Oh yes!'

All childish rebellion was beaten out of her long ago.

'That's all that matters,' I tell her. 'Love isn't for queens.'

## GREENWICH PALACE, EASTER SUNDAY

### 1541

WE ARE AWAKENED by a choir singing hymns to the risen lord, and we get up at once and go to chapel. The place is blazing with light and colour again. All the painted saints are bright with new gilding; the holy statues are unveiled and have wax candles burning before them. The king is on his throne wearing cloth of gold; he beams at Katheryn as she takes a lower chair beside him.

There is a great Easter feast after the long church service and then walking in the garden, the birds are singing and singing, the Lenten lilies bobbing their heads in the cold wind. There is a sweet slight scent in the air from the tumbled mass of primrose banks. Every young courtier wants to stay out of doors and dance on the lawns which have been scythed for the first cut of the year and smell of new hay, every old one wants to get indoors, out of the chill.

Our Easter masque is the story of *Aphrodite*, the goddess of love. Of course, Kitty is desperate to be *Aphrodite* in a diaphanous robe, and the king as *Hephaestus* will rest his sore leg on an anvil and watch her dance. The story – that *Aphrodite* is unfaithful to *Hephaestus* with dozens of lovers – is tactfully ignored. Our *Aphrodite* is strewed with roses, and she loves her husband – and nobody else.

'It'll be just as it was,' Kitty says delightedly choosing the diamonds to pin in her hair. 'I look just the same. You'd never know I was with child. Perhaps I'll be perfect all the way through?'

'You had better hope that your looks change,' I say drily. 'Everyone wants to see you with a good belly.'

She makes a little face in the mirror. 'Well, at least there's to be an Easter joust,' she says. 'And I shall give my master of horse my favour and nothing to anybody else, even if someone goes down on his knees for it.'

Thomas Culpeper, unaware he has been snubbed, rides in the Easter joust, with Thomas Seymour, Gregory Cromwell, and the queen's brother George. But it is a lacklustre event, overshadowed by the memory of the great joust organised by Lord Lisle, who is still in the Tower. The king's great chair is placed in his viewing tower, but he does not watch; only a few of the old lords bother to attend, and we ladies walk through our parts at half-volume.

'I don't see the point of watching if nobody's watching me,' Kitty says disconsolately.

## GREENWICH PALACE, APRIL

## 1541

As soon as the joust and masque are finished, the king goes to Dover to inspect the defences, complaining bitterly that no one is capable of planning or building any more. He misses the masque for spring. Katheryn plays the part of incoming spring, in a green gown embroidered with daisies, who wakens all the ladies from their winter sleep by drawing off a white veil that stands for snow. Jane Seymour had the gown and the part before her; we all know our places, and it needs little practice and no scenery. The ladies choose their partners, and the whole court dances; Kitty goes down the line of bowing courtiers, and there is a moment – just a brief moment – when she and Thomas Culpeper are hand to hand and face to face, and everything seems to go very still and very quiet. They look at each other, as if seeing each other for the first time. They look wonderingly, as if recognising something in the other's awakened face – and then the musicians resume, and the dancers move on, and they are parted again.

The king comes back from Dover, exhausted by the journey and furious that the defences – thrown up in a hurry in terror of Spanish invasion – are already crumbling. Only Cromwell could have seen that they were properly built, the king declares. Only Cromwell could keep the kingdom safe.

Our safety is threatened from the north as well; my uncle the Duke of Norfolk bows his head beneath a storm from the king, who says that Cromwell would have held the north down as a Howard cannot. My uncle grits his teeth and endures the king's rage, secure in the knowledge that his niece is carrying a Tudor heir and she will be crowned, proud as a Seymour, as pregnant as a Seymour, at Whitsun.

It is not to be. That evening, when I go to her bedroom, she exclaims suddenly while the maids are undressing her and sends the maids and chamberers from the room. 'What can I do? What can I do?' she demands. 'Look!'

She shows me her white linen petticoat, stained with a scarlet ribbon of blood. 'My course! It's started again.'

She is astounded not to get her own way, but this is a drearily familiar scene for me. She bundles up the petticoat and stuffs it under her bed. 'Don't tell anyone,' she decides. 'We'll pretend it hasn't happened. You'll take away my clouts every morning and undress me at night. I'm always light. There won't be much to do; you can wash everything, and we can pretend it's all going on as it should be.'

For a moment, I calculate how many days until a Whitsun coronation and if we dare get the crown on her head and the oil on her breast, and tell the king afterwards. But then I remember his terrible coldness to Anne, after we had combed her hair and arranged her on pillows and she swore that next time she would have a boy and he would be stronger.

'No, we can't pretend. It makes it worse when you have to tell him.'

'After I'm crowned!' It comes out as a shriek, and she claps her hand over her mouth.

I shake my head. 'He'd think you'd lied from the very beginning. He's quick to see an enemy. He can turn in a moment. You can't risk it.'

She cries then, poor little queen, cries like a child with unstoppable tears and rushing choking sobs. 'But what can I do? What can I do? Jane, you have to help me! What can I do?'

I take her hands; I force her into a chair. I wipe the tears from her face. 'Be calm,' I tell her. 'It's too early. It wasn't a baby; it hardly started.'

'I don't care about a baby!' she hisses at me, in a whispered scream. 'Why would I want a baby to ruin my looks? I want my coronation!'

'I know. I know. But a baby's the only thing that'll get you a coronation. You have to tell him the truth this evening, tonight – you'll say it was a genuine mistake. As it was. The king's been married before—' I could laugh at this bitter truth. 'He knows that babies don't come easily. He knows you're only young, and you've never been with child before. He'll believe that you made a mistake.'

Inwardly, I think: can he even make a baby now? If he can do the act, is his seed not watery and weak? 'Flatter him. Tell him that you missed a course, and you thought it must be a baby, because he's so strong and potent that you're sure his lovemaking will give you a child at once.'

Her face convulses in a grimace of distaste. 'He hurts,' she says, in a tiny voice. 'And it takes ages. I don't believe you can get a baby like that.'

I hesitate. 'You have to pretend to pleasure,' I tell her. 'You have to tell him you love it.'

She sets her mouth in an ugly line. 'Larding it on like a spit boy,' she says resentfully.

'Larding it on,' I agree. 'You tell him that you were so eager to make him happy, to give him good news, you were too eager. Because all you want is his happiness.'

'I cry?' she suggests.

'You cry. But not like this. Not enough to spoil your face. And he loves you so much now that he's certain to be tender with you this time, this first time. You ask him for his favour; you get him back into bed, and next time, or the time after, it'll really happen. But never, never say that you were with child but you couldn't keep it. Never say "miscarry".'

'Another word he's not to hear? He's not to hear the word "death"? And now not "miscarry"?'

'Some words we never say in his hearing. You made a mistake with counting your courses, that's all.'

'Silly me,' she says bitterly. 'Stupid, stupid me.'

S HE HOPES THAT the king is so doting that he will crown her anyway. But he's not going to spend a fortune on a wife who has not earned her place as queen. Even in love, he guards his power. He comes to her bed every third night or so, and he asks me, quietly, one evening, when her next course is due.

'And how did you come to make such a mistake, even if she did?' he demands. 'You're not a silly girl, Jane. You're not a pretty fool.'

I scatter a treasury of words at his feet: her distress at his illness, her fears for him interrupted her courses, as can quite often happen. But her happiness at his returned health will make her fertile again, and his potency must make a child.

'How many in her family?' he asks. 'How many babies did her mother bear?'

'About ten,' I say, as if we are in a stable discussing a broodmare.

'Anne of Cleves was only one of four,' he says thoughtfully.

I catch my breath. 'The duchess, your sister?'

He gives me a sly little smile. 'Jane, you know I've got to have a second son and a third if I can. And six miles upriver, there is a beautiful, fertile, royal woman, eating up a fortune in my royal palace, while her brother befriends the French and marries into their royal family. She's more useful than ever, and she's costing me as much as a sister as she would as a wife.'

'Except that you love the queen so much,' I remind him. 'And she adores you. Nobody loves you more than she does. And she's so pretty. I think she could have married any king in Europe, but she only has eyes for you.'

'Oh, yes. Yes, I do.' It is as if I have reminded him of a detail which had slipped from his mind. 'And she's very young, and from fertile stock.'

## GREENWICH PALACE, MAY

## 1541

'Not whelping?' My uncle descends on me at the May Day festivities, which are subdued, since we have no Whitsun coronation ahead of us and nothing to celebrate.

'She made a mistake with her courses; she did not miscarry,' I specify.

'Aye, I know that's what you're all saying,' he says unpleasantly. 'That's what t'other one said, last time. I don't see why you women think it's better to say that she's a fool who can't count than a heifer who can't get in calf.'

I am silent.

'He goes to her bed?' he confirms.

'He does.'

'And does his business?'

I am not such a fool as to reply.

'So she should take?'

I nod.

'Make sure she does,' he says to me, as if I can summon a baby from the air that blows so sweetly off the river. 'I wouldn't give you three pence for her, if she does not.'

At once, the breeze feels cold. 'Why would you say that? He's not turning against her? She's done nothing wrong.'

'He married her to get another son; if she can't give him one, he'll find someone who can.'

'She's your niece,' I say desperately. 'You don't want him going back to Anne of Cleves or picking another maid-of-honour from another family. Where would you be, without a Howard girl on the throne?'

'Where I am now,' he says bluntly. 'I work like a dog for him in the north against the Papists, and all I hear is "Cromwell would have done it better. Cromwell would never have allowed this!" If she wants my support, she'd better get a baby in her belly and a crown on her head.'

I put my hand across my mouth to stop a rush of panic-stricken words. I don't want to gabble my fear that my uncle is demanding something that no woman can make happen. If we laid all the deadborns to the king's door, there would be more dead babies than live ones. He has sired a dozen ghosts. But it is against the law to even think this.

I REMEMBER THE OTHER May Day, when the king rode away after the joust, and nobody knew why. This time, he misses the masque for a meeting with his privy council. The whole court is on alert for Kitty's fall but it is the north of the country: in arms again, and the king furiously sending an army to put them down, blaming Reginald Pole in faraway Italy, and Reginald's mother Margaret Pole in the Tower. She was once the richest woman in England, but now she is so poor that the royal tailor sends her clothes. She was a princess but is now so powerless that she is not even allowed to claim her innocence. They will not bring her to trial; they will not let her speak.

The May Day masque was to be a celebration of the king's return to health, his restoration to virile youth, and the queen's pregnancy. But since he is not attending and she is not pregnant, the musicians play quietly, so as not to disturb the privy council, and we mark out the steps rather than putting on a show. We were going to do *Aphrodite*, goddess of love and fertility, again, but Kitty's heart is not in it, and she sits on her throne looking like a child left out of a game.

The young men of the court get drunk from boredom, and the older ladies-in-waiting leave early. I see how a court loses its ability to make magic – even when the machinery is still grinding away. Thomas Culpeper glances now and then towards Kitty, ignoring his lover Bess Harvey, but she does not even look at him. As the evening drags to a close, he works his way across the room towards me, with a word to one man and a pretty bow to a girl. I watch him coming.

'Lady Rochford.'

I cannot show a cold mask to this young man who bows and takes my hand as confidently as if he is about to draw me into an embrace. I know well enough that his charm is a habit, a courtier's mask; but there is something about Thomas Culpeper that is quite irresistible, almost like a perfume: the scent of desire.

'I so wish you were my friend, Lady Rochford.'

'Master Culpeper, I wish you nothing but well.'

'I want you to be my friend with the queen.'

'I've never said a word against you.'

He takes my hand, draws it under his arm, and leads me away from the dancers towards the open doors to the shadowy gallery where Kitty met him only a few weeks ago. I am standing where she stood when she gave him his Easter gift, but we are closer than they were, my hand held between his arm and his chest. I can feel the warmth of his body through his embroidered silk jacket and the hard sheath of the muscle over his ribs. I am vividly aware of his body under his clothes; I feel again the almost-forgotten sensation of desire for the scent of a man, for the touch of his skin, for the soft prickle of chest hair against my cheek.

'I am afraid I have offended Her Majesty,' he says, when we are far apart from everyone and cannot be overheard.

'I wouldn't know.'

He looks down at me, his brown eyes very warm. 'Ah, Jane, be my friend: you do know.'

Ridiculously, I feel the heat in my cheeks of a blush.

'She surprised me with kindness; she gave me a gift, a generous gift, and I was stupid when I should have been courtly. I was rude when I should have been loving.'

'I dare say she's forgotten all about it.'

'Oh, don't say that, Jane, dearest Jane. Speak for me – tell her that I am a fool. That I was hiding my true feelings. Tell her that I worship the ground she walks on. I will write her a poem . . .'

'Then write your poem,' I say coolly. 'Or a song, or ride in a joust for her. It is all courtly love, after all. It does not matter.'

He leans so close to me that I can feel the warmth of his breath on my cheek. If I turned, our lips would meet. 'It does matter,' he whispers. 'I will not lie. It is not courtly love: it is desire. How can I write a poem about that? I love her – not as a courtier, but as a man. I desire her – not as a queen, not as a lady far above me, but as a woman. Will you tell her that?'

I pull away from him. 'No, of course not,' I say coolly. 'It is not my place to speak to the king's wife like that. It's not your place either.'

His joyous shout of laughter turns heads. He snatches both my hands and kisses them. 'Ah, Jane, I love you, too!' But he cannot stop laughing. 'D'you think I don't know women?' he demands. 'You'll tell her what I've said, the first moment you're alone together. And she'll ask you for my exact words, and you'll remember them exactly! And I'll know that you have told her the first moment that I next see her. I'll see it in her face and in yours.'

I want to deny this; but I'm laughing like a girl at his knowingness, at his smiling confidence, and I push him away, back to the dancers. 'Go away, Master Culpeper; this is a May Day dance that you are leading me on, and I will not carry messages for you.'

He steps back and bows low to me, throws a quick, intense glance at Katheryn, who is pretending not to see us, but is head to head with Mary Howard, who really does seem to manage to then see nothing at all.

'WHAT DID HE want?' Kitty demands, the moment the last maid has left her bedroom. She drags me down to sit beside her on her bed. 'What did he say?'

'A lot of nonsense,' I say dampeningly.

'He's a very nonsensical young man,' she agrees eagerly. 'I'm surprised you even listened to him. What did he say that was such nonsense? Why were you laughing?'

I cannot resist the temptation to tell her. 'At any rate, you have your revenge. He says that he loves you.'

'Courtly love.'

'He says not. He says he loves you for real.'

She gives a little crow of delight and bounces to her knees on her bed. 'He does! Did he say he was sorry for being so rude about my gift?'

'Yes. He asked me if you were displeased with him.'

'Oh! Oh! And you said yes?'

'I did better than that. I said that I didn't think you even remembered it.'

She claps her hands. 'You are clever. That was best. And he is sorry?'

'Very sorry. He called himself stupid.'

She beams. 'Serves him right. He is stupid.'

I nod. 'And now you have your revenge.'

She sits back and holds her hands over her heart. 'When shall I see him?'

'No, you can't see him,' I correct her. 'I only told you because I knew it would delight you. This is where it ends: with your victory. You wanted him beneath your feet. You have him there. That's the end of the story.'

She widens her eyes at me; they have turned green with desire. 'Oh, but, Jane, I have to see him.'

'You can't,' I say simply. 'It was only once, when I was there, when you were carrying the king's child. Now you've got nothing to do, night or day, but conceive the king's child. Any other thought, any other action is a waste of your time. And a danger to your reputation. You can't be alone with any man until you have the king's baby in your belly.'

She closes her eyes for a moment, her hands still clasped over her heart. 'When I think of him, I just melt,' she whispers.

There is a loud bang of the outer door. Kitty's eyes fly open. 'Is that the king?'

It is his vice chamberlain, announcing that the king will come to Kitty's bed tonight. I hurry to tie her cap on her hair, to straighten her sheets. I see the joy drain from her face, her rosy cheeks go pale. I can almost see her grow dry and cold.

The double doors open, and the king limps in, Thomas Culpeper under his arm on his lame side. The king's page and Culpeper manhandle him to sit on the edge of the high bed beside her, then lift his legs and swing them up. The mattress sinks down on his side; the ropes of the bed creak. Kitty is thrown off balance and rights herself by holding to the bedpost.

They heave the king up to the pillows and pull the covers up to his fat chest. He lies like a rounded effigy, the bedclothes heaped over his stiffly upright feet, his thickly bandaged leg, and then the mountain of his enormous belly and his rolling chest. Beside him, Kitty looks tiny, like a kidnapped child. She does not look at Thomas Culpeper, nor at me. Her gaze is on her clasped hands, as if she is praying that none of this is happening.

'Goodnight, Your Majesties, God bless you.' Thomas Culpeper and the page bow out behind me.

I curtsey as I leave the room last. We walk backwards to the door so that I see – we all see – the old king turn his big fat moon face towards the girl who sits so still beside him, and we then see him lunge towards her.

T HE NEXT DAY, just as we are about to knock on the queen's door and go in to wake the king and queen, a weary messenger comes to the king's rooms with a letter from Scotland. Sir Anthony Browne has the authority to break the seal, and he tells us that the baby heir to the throne of Scotland has died, and – uncanny, unlucky, unbelievably – his newborn brother Robert has died, too.

This unbearable tragedy for the King of Scots is the happiest news anyone could have brought our king. Sir Anthony hands him the letter as he sits up in bed beside Kitty. The king reads it himself and then demands that Sir Anthony read it aloud to him as a satisfied smile spreads across his face. The king had wanted the tall, beautiful Queen of Scotland, Mary of Guise, as his own wife; Anne of Cleves was his second choice. Now, he sees this tragic loss of two baby boys as God's punishment for Mary of Guise, who preferred another man to him. Scotland – which had two little princes – now has no male heir; but England does! We have a prince, and they do not.

'That Mary of Guise made a great mistake when she refused my suit!' Henry says joyfully, reaching out both arms like a child for his men to pull him out of bed.

I wait at the door; but I can see from here that Henry was potent last night, and Kitty is fighting to hide her shame. Her nightcap has been pulled off and her blonde hair is a tangled mess. Her face is white, as if she is ill. She pulls the bedclothes up to her chin; she turns her face away. Thomas Culpeper and the king's page are courteously blind to her tumbled hair, the bite marks on her bruised neck. They heave the king to the side of the bed, get his fat feet in his slippers and his voluminous robe around his shoulders and tied around his swollen belly.

'Mary of Guise! Great mistake!' the king exults, but Kitty and Culpeper do not remember the many women that the king considered for his fourth wife. The king smiles at me, knowing that I will understand his joy.

'What's she got to show for it now?' he demands beaming at me. 'Married to a madman and two sons in the grave! She must be breaking her heart this morning. She must be crying her lovely grey eyes out!'

I curtsey. I imagine she is breaking her heart, but it will be for the loss of her two baby sons, not because she refused this selfish old man.

'You hear that, sweetheart?' The king, halfway to the door, pauses and turns back to bellow at Kitty.

She nods, her head bobbing like a doll.

'A great lady could 'ave been in your place; but she married another king,' he tells her. 'And now she's got nothing, because God did not bless the marriage. You get a son – you hear? And you will triumph over her as soon as you do, as I triumph over her now!'

Kitty nods. I know that she has no idea what he is talking about, but it doesn't matter. He is so delighted with himself, with the world, this morning, that he won't wait for a reply. The three of them – Thomas Culpeper, the king, and the page – their arms interlinked, stagger past me like drunks, followed by Sir Anthony and a few other young courtiers. Only the king is looking around, smiling. The rest look at their boots, as shamed as Kitty, who sits in bed in a crumpled nightgown, nodding and nodding while a crimson blush rises from her collar bones to her forehead.

'We'll go on progress,' the king decides at the threshold, bringing everyone to a stumbling halt. 'North. Triumphant progress. And we'll meet James of Scotland on the border. I'll commiserate with him for his loss, and we'll set a peace. He'll want a peaceful kingdom, now that he doesn't have a son. He can't risk his life fighting us, if he doesn't have an heir. But I do! I'll remind him that I do. This summer – we'll go this summer.'

THE GROOMS OF the household try to plan a route without Thomas Cromwell's expertise or his maps and eye for detail, then change it as the king demands different halts and visits on the way north. I, too, plan a progress which will show Kitty to the people of the northern lands, as a bringer of peace. I pick out coronets for her to wear to remind everyone that she is a king's wife now, blue gowns to remind everyone of the Holy Mother, dark-purple gowns to remind them she will be the king's widow. She will be dowager queen and – with luck – queen regent.

'You must visit the royal nurseries before we go,' I tell her. 'Establish yourself as stepmother to the prince and Lady Elizabeth.'

She makes a little grimace. 'Must I? Why do I have to?'

'It makes you stronger . . . If people see you as the prince's stepmother, taking an interest in his upbringing, being a mother to him – if the king sees you as mother to the prince, he'll crown you queen.'

'The Seymours are never going to let me near their precious boy. And besides, I don't like little children.'

'They will. I have agreed it. And when you see him, you must pet him, make much of him, put into his head that you're his new mother. He'll be king one day; and then your title will be in his gift – your pension, too.'

Kitty is never lazy when it comes to her own interests. Raised as the daughter of a poor relation in an ambitious house, she knows all about positioning in the family, at court, in the world.

'And Lady Elizabeth. Yes, her too,' I insist over her protest. 'You have to be stepmother to all of them. You've got to get on good terms with Lady Mary as well. You can't have her opposing you as regent.'

'I can't be her mother! She's years older than me! And she hates me!' Kitty protests.

'She's coming on progress with us,' I warn her. 'You'll ride before her as her stepmother. She'll be respectful to you, and you must look loving and kind to her. You have to look sure of yourself. You have to act like a queen crowned.'

'And if I do, will he crown me at York? He was going to crown Jane Seymour at York, wasn't he?'

'I think he will.' I cannot keep my own excitement from my voice. 'Especially now that it would be such a snub to James of Scotland and an insult to Mary of Guise who have lost both their sons. Yes. I think he will.'

PHILIPPA GREGORY

## HOLY CROSS, WALTHAM, ESSEX, MAY

## 1541

Kitty's visits to Lady Elizabeth and little Prince Edward are a triumph. The king is mawkish about the motherless three-year-old boy and weeps over him. Kitty is horrified by his tears, and the stilted wariness of the child. I put a firm hand in her back and push her towards the little boy. The king gives a gulping sob, and Kitty puts out a tentative hand, and the child bows. Realising how pretty they would look together, Kitty puts her arm around his shoulders and bends down to put her bronze head against his, her cheek to his round face. The child's staring eyes widen, but still he says nothing but the formal greeting that has been drilled into him. When I take him back to his nurse, I realise he has wet himself with fear.

Lady Elizabeth is presented to her father and has a poem to recite which she has translated from Latin. The king shows little interest in her, though she tries hard to gain his attention. I watch her dark eyes flick from him to Kitty, as she takes the measure of this new stepmother.

'My little kinswoman!' Kitty coos, stretching out her arms, and the seven-year-old girl curtseys and steps forward for a kiss, as if she does not much value the Howard connection or put much faith in a third stepmother.

Lady Mary is also visiting the royal nursery, and although Kitty makes a gallant attempt to be charming – the young woman is too experienced a courtier to show anything but false respectful affection. We meet in what were once Lady Mary's own rooms in a wealthy devout abbey, ruled by the king and queen, her mother and father. Not by a flicker of expression does she indicate that this rich centre of holiness is now an echoing shell, shrill with worldly ambition, where she visits occasionally, as an unwelcome guest.

'And where is Master Culpeper?' Kitty asks me, with an air of complete indifference. 'He wasn't at dinner last night?'

One of the pages of the king's chamber tells me that Master Culpeper is in bed.

'Ill?' Kitty asks the young man. 'Seriously ill?'

'Ill or injured, Your Grace. I just know he's taken to his bed.'

'Oh, send to his rooms and find out, Jane. Has he had a fall from his horse, or – God save him – an illness? Do find out if he has a fever – or – Jane, ask them if it is the Sweat?'

'I can't. It looks odd.'

'It looks like nothing,' she says impatiently. 'Send one of your maids to ask. There's no reason that you should not ask how he is? Or I'll send Catherine Tilney.'

'Don't send her!' I exclaim. It's better that I'm seen chasing after Master Culpeper than Catherine Tilney.

My maid comes back with the news that Master Culpeper is hot with a fever but expects to be well within the week.

Kitty sends one of the good dishes from her dinner table to the king's favourite. It's a gracious gesture, and nobody notices. Only I know that Master Culpeper – however ill – will laugh and take the dish as proof that I told Kitty that he was in love with her on the very day that he told me.

He sends a note to thank for the dish, and she replies to him. They make me their go-between, forgetting that in courtly love stories, there are two messengers – of two different natures: *Honte*, the prude who will prevent love and betray the lovers, and *Venus*, who helps them. But I am neither of these: I have no interest in helping a flirtation, and I would never betray Kitty. She trusts me as she trusts no one else. Every secret she tells is an extra thread to bind us. Like Francis Dereham, lounging around at Norfolk House, because of her girlhood indiscretions, I will be at her side, on her pay, and eating her bouche at her dining table, as long as I want. My future depends upon her being the greatest woman in the next reign: dowager queen, on the council of regency.

Far more powerful than *Honte*, far more than *Venus*, I am the watchman, the nightwatchman. I use the spy skills I learned from Thomas Cromwell to open, read, and reseal every note that passes between Kitty and Culpeper – banalities about the weather and the dances that Kitty would prefer. I know everything that happens, and I work in darkness. It's not hard for me to be completely discreet, to tell no one. Now that my spymaster is dead, I have no one to tell.

I THINK OF HIM – my friend, my only friend, Thomas Cromwell – at the end of May when his old enemy Lady Margaret Pole, the matriarch of the Spanish party and of the Papist family Pole, is finally released from her long, unjust imprisonment – not to freedom – which God knows she deserves; but to her death. The king, nagged by his conscience for keeping an innocent kinswoman in prison, relieves himself by having her beheaded. She goes to her death for no reason but the king's peace of mind.

It is a shock for me to realise that this is truly what has happened. This is the act of the king, the king himself: his free choice and his independent act. This is not a decision made by one of the many advisors that have guided him through his life: his grandmother, Queen Katherine, Cardinal Wolsey, Queen Anne, my uncle, or Thomas Cromwell. His advisors have always been blamed for past cruelties. I have blamed them myself. But this is his decision, his own: taken freely at a time of peace. Margaret Pole never raised a finger against her cousin the king. She never admitted guilt: not under torture, not even on the scaffold. She fought for her good name and her life until the last moment of it, demanding why should she walk to Tower Green, resisting the guards, even running away from the headsman's raised axe. She was a woman of nearly seventy, the king's mother's dearest friend, and he killed her without cause, without pity.

This is a revelation to me. As a courtier, I have thought of the king as a creature to be steered and managed and controlled – a creature that can be petted into docility or tempted into a new direction. All courtiers think like this. But now, for the first time I know different.

Nobody put the idea of killing Lady Margaret into the king's head; nobody persuaded him against his conscience. It was in no one's interest that she die; no one gained a position or earned a fortune at her death. It was a redundant death, a pointless death. This is not how a courtier thinks; this is not what an advisor plans; this is not what a good king orders. No person of any sense would have ordered the death of Margaret Pole. No one of any honour would have imagined it. It is madness, it is madman-thinking. Death on a madman's say-so, death as his mad choice, death only to show that he can cause death. Death as a comfort to him, to ease his mad mind.

The madman who decided this is the madman who rules us now without warders. All his advisors are dead, and they were all killed by him: men who he loved deeply, like Thomas More; men who were indispensable, like Thomas Cromwell; his spiritual father Bishop Fisher; the woman he adored, my sister-in-law Anne; my husband; their friends. The king kills those closest to him, because he cannot bear to need them. He cannot bear that they are wiser or better or even more beautiful than him. He loves them at first, calling them to his side to make himself shine, and then he cannot tolerate that they eclipse him. That, he cannot bear. The headsman is so overworked that he had to send out an apprentice who had not learned his trade to behead Margaret Pole. He hacks her to death in clumsy swipes as she screams defiance.

We dine in the great hall that evening, and after dinner, there is music and dancing. My smile is falser than ever before; there is a new joyless lightness in my voice. I have been afraid at court, constantly spying on the way that power moves from one lord or another, the rise and fall of one man or another, the favouring of one woman over another. I have been alert to the comings and goings of dozens of people. But now, I realise that it was all a waste of study. The court is an illusion of power, just as it is an illusion of happiness. There is no happiness at court, and there is no power here either.

It is all the king's. Power has always been in the hands of the king, and those of us who thought we were steering him or controlling him are victims in waiting. Only the king is in power: only he is happy; only he is unhappy. The rest of us are all pretending, and it does not matter what we feel.

There is no one left who dares to quarrel with him. There is no one who dares to contradict him. No one would ever suggest that he is wrong. We have guided his steps with our eyes on the path for so long that we have lost our way; only he is looking up and around. Only he has a destination in view. We have agreed to insane laws and now we find ourselves in a legal tyranny. We have winked at manic cruelty, and now we close our eyes in fear. We thought that we were steering a galloping horse, but we are tangled in the reins and being dragged to our deaths. We have birthed and dandled and fed a tyrant, and now we do not even mourn when our monstrous baby kills a woman that he once called the 'finest in England'.

She was a princess of the House of Plantagenet, the daughter of the Duke of Clarence, the greatest friend to the king's mother, advisor to his wife. She taught Lady Mary, Lady Margaret Douglas and me in the royal schoolroom, with the care that she lavished on her sons and daughter. We hear the news that she is dead without a break in our laughter, and the three of us, her beloved pupils, dance after dinner.

## ON PROGRESS, SUMMER

### 1541

WE DON'T LEAVE on progress until the end of June, and there are times when it seems impossible that we can ever start. Thousands of horses, an army with all the equipment ready for warfare, will march north with us. All the household furniture and goods – carpets, tapestries and furniture – will lumber behind us in a baggage train which will clog the roads for miles arriving hours after we get to our destination.

Lady Mary joins us with her household, servants, guards, and ladies-in-waiting. The surveyor of the king's buildings goes ahead of us to inspect and repair royal palaces at every stop, but he finds so much neglect and damage that he has no time to make good. We are bogged down in the muddy roads half an hour after leaving and have to give up on the journey for another week.

Kitty cries and says she is too ill to ride. She will not get up in the morning; her childish energy as a maid-of-honour has drained from her now she is the wife of the king. She has a pain in her belly, in her groin. She says she cannot sit on a horse nor lie in the mule litter. She swears she cannot go. The rain falls constantly, and they say on the North Road that there are puddles of standing water deeper than a man, and travellers drown when night falls.

We are staging a moving spectacle of power and authority, but when the wagons are stuck in the mud and the horses cannot get past, we betray ourselves. The people see we cannot even manage a simple journey. Our court is supposed to be a masque of infallible power and beauty, triumphing over distance and weather, weakness and old age. But here we are: stuck on a muddy road, trying to move an old angry man from one shabby palace to another.

Enraged at the delay, the king blames every parish for failing to maintain their roads, which are flooded by the early summer storms. He says – again and again – that nobody looks after details since Cromwell was taken from him and that people who don't help themselves can drown in their own puddles. The common people reply – in whispered songs and hidden poems – that God has cursed England with a king who has become a mouldwarp: an underground, underworld king, bringing death to his people under a sky that rains down tears of grief while he is dry-eyed.

We travel no more than eight miles that first day, and lodge in

Dunstable priory, speedily adapted from a great house of religion into a royal palace with adjoining king's and queen's rooms. We pray every morning in the chapel where the king's first marriage was annulled, but nobody remembers this; except the daughter who was bastardised on that day. Lady Mary exchanges a brief look with me as I walk into the church behind her, and I think: no wonder they say you are in constant pain – every time you visit a chapel or a palace, it must be an anniversary of loss. In a court that prides itself on forgetfulness, it feels as if only Lady Mary and I have survived five queens and remember every one of them.

Finally, the weather clears, and we can ride with our hoods down and look about us. Kitty has a new riding gown and matching jacket and her aches disappear. We go hunting and rein our horses in so that the king can get in front with the hounds and claim it is his arrow that brings down a great stag and two bucks. We cannot store or carry meat, so that evening, we dine well on venison at the long tables where the monks used to fast, and the king orders the spare joints taken to the Lord Mayor of London with the compliments of his sovereign.

After dinner, the great hall is cleared, the musicians play for dancing. The king orders Kitty to dance with her ladies, and she takes the centre of the floor. She is eating well again; I think she can tolerate the king's visits to her bedroom if he is not raging or coldly furious. When he has a good day – like today – she does not dread his company; when she has the court around her, she can face him.

She takes me by the hand, and I feel a folded note. 'Get it to him,' she whispers as the king waves the men forward to dance with the ladies, and Thomas Culpeper bows before me and takes me to lead the forming columns of dancers.

'Her Grace is happy tonight,' Thomas Culpeper observes, with a smile at me. 'Are you happy, dear Lady Rochford?'

'The queen's happiness is my own,' I observe primly.

'And do you love where she loves?' he teases me.

'Of course – we all love the king,' I say repressively, and I slide the note into his hand as the dance takes me away from him to another partner.

Slowly, the lumbering baggage train and army of guards wind their way northwards. We rest for a few days at the home of the king's grandmother, Margaret Beaufort, where the king becomes maudlin with grief and speaks of her devotion, without observing that he has destroyed her church. I think that he can only love people who have died. Only then is he released from envious comparing.

From Collyweston Palace, we go to stay with Catherine Brandon in her castle of Grimsthorpe. Of course, it is her husband the duke's castle now. The duke is excited to show off the prize he has won; but he is careful how much he boasts: this is a king capable of taking his host's property as a forced gift. Brandon has learned the courtier's trick of boasting with humility.

Catherine Brandon welcomes us into her castle. Everything is very fine and rebuilt with her money. As the maids make the rooms ready for the queen, I go to my own bedchamber. At once, Catherine Tilney taps on the door and says the queen wants to know if I have got the thing, a special thing that she wants. Tilney is bubbling with laughter, and I guess that Kitty has told her she is passing notes to Culpeper. The girl is bound in loyalty to the queen as a kinswoman and a fellow boarder at the dowager duchess' house at Lambeth; but Kitty is foolish to be indiscreet, especially with our uncle the Duke of Norfolk expected at any moment.

'Oh God, spare me my uncle!' Kitty says, although there are several courtiers in earshot.

'Amen,' Catherine Brandon whispers.

Thomas Howard arrives in a sour mood, to a scant welcome from the king, who is distracted by Charles Brandon and flirting with the young duchess.

'You all seem very merry,' my uncle says irritably when we meet in the queen's rooms before dinner.

'Yes, my lord,' I say pleasantly. 'Their Majesties are enjoying the progress.'

'And is he . . .' He need say no more. It is the only thing he ever asks me.

'Yes, my lord, as I say. We are enjoying the progress.'

He wants to know more; he wants guarantees that a man who everyone thought would die in Lent will have a son by next May.

'It is God's will,' I say repressively.

He puts a hand upon my arm, but he does not painfully grip as he sometimes does. I could almost think he was asking for help. 'Jane, if God does not favour us, then no one else will,' he says softly. The tip of his head towards the king makes it clear who he means. 'The king says he'll name Lady Mary as heir after Prince Edward. Our Lady Elizabeth is dropped.'

He lowers his voice. 'He's brought Lady Mary on progress to show that they are reconciled. He could give her the north – her own council in the north. What if he acknowledges it's a divided kingdom: north and south, Papist and Protestant? What will become of us if she has a council of the north and the Seymours a regency in the south?'

I shift, but he does not release me.

'D'you think he's standing up to the travel? If I can get my daughter Mary married to Thomas Seymour within a year – will that be soon enough? Or d'you think he might—' he does not dare say the word 'die'.

'He seems better,' I say carefully. 'Praise God.'

'Amen. But our future depends on Kitty getting with child and being crowned before he . . . before then! Does she use no potions or spells or witchcraft?' he asks, as if he hopes the answer is 'yes'. 'Can you do nothing more?'

I shake my head.

'Well, do what you can,' he says. 'Do whatever you can, Jane. You only have to look at him to see we don't have long.'

The Great North Road is in a terrible state and cannot bear the weight of our progress. If the king ever again needs an army in the north of England, they will never get there in time. I ride beside Kitty, following the mounted guards, avoiding the impassable road, going cross-country across fields and common land, planning our grand entry to Lincoln.

'And what am I to wear?' she asks.

'Cloth of silver, and the king is in cloth of gold.'

She giggles. 'We'll look like fairings,' she says.

'You'll look royal,' I say severely.

But she has already forgotten her costume. 'He says that if he can get away, he will come and see me at night,' she whispers.

'He can't,' I say flatly. I have already opened this twist of paper and read this promise, and I will insist it is refused. 'You said your notes would be safe to deliver – that you would just say how you were. You can't make secret meetings.'

'Just one,' she pleads. 'Just once, Jane. I have to see him alone, just once.'

I shake my head. 'No.'

'If you could find a little private gallery like we met before?' Kitty whispers. 'Please, Jane. I can't bear that every day he is one side of the king and I am the other, and some days I never even say one word to him.'

'I can't go wandering around the Bishop of Lincoln's palace, looking for a quiet corner! What explanation could I give?'

'You could say that you were meeting a lover!' she suggests, giggling. 'Go on, Jane. You're young enough and pretty enough. Why shouldn't you be sneaking out to meet someone? It could be Culpeper?'

'Because if the queen's chief lady-in-waiting is sneaking out to meet a lover, then it reflects badly on the queen!' I reprove her; but I can't help smiling.

'He says he'd meet you the moment you invited him. He says any of them would.'

I laugh. 'Oh, don't be so ridiculous, Kitty! I can't meet a young man any more than you can.'

'Just once. I swear, just this once.'

'It's not possible.'

The brightness drains from her face, and she brings her horse beside me and reaches out to clasp my hands on the reins. I have never seen her so serious. 'Jane, I am not laughing now. I really cannot bear . . .' She breaks off. 'It's hard for me to do what I have to . . .' She stops herself saying more. 'I don't see how to get through these days . . . these nights . . .'

She pauses for a moment and lets my hand go, takes up her own reins. Her face is grim; she looks like a woman in lifetime imprisonment. I think: we have driven her too hard; she cannot break down now.

'I have to have something, one thing that makes me happy!' she says piteously. 'If I am to smile all the time and dance every night . . . If I have to greet him when they roll him into my bed . . . if I have to let him . . . Jane, if I have to let him do what he must . . . and it's not like . . . it's not like lovemaking . . . I swear to God, I have to have some moment in the day when I am happy, when I am myself.'

There is such a bitter contrast between her fine gown, her bejewelled hat, and the deadness of her hazel eyes. I think: if I can just get her to York, he will crown her there, and then she is queen and we are halfway to the prize. I think: I have to get her through this year; he cannot last another winter. I think: I am a hardened courtier, but even I balk at forcing an unwilling young woman – really, a girl – into the bed of an old man for what is no better than a rape. This is brutal work; it is wicked work. If the price of her obedience is to see Thomas Culpeper once, I cannot refuse her. Better for me that I make the meeting safe than the two young lovers betray themselves. Better for me that I am *Venus* in this story of courtly love than that Catherine Tilney steps into my place and wins the power of a confidante.

'Very well – just this once, I'll see if there is a stair or a gallery or somewhere you can meet, but it can only be this once and only for a moment.'

'Just once, just for a moment,' she promises, and at once, childlike, she is transformed. Her face is radiant; the colour floods into her cheeks. 'Just once, Jane, and then I can face Lincoln and tonight. I swear I'll never ask you for anything again.'

WE MAKE A grand entry to Lincoln, the streets cleaned, ankle deep in silvery sand, the bells of the cathedral pealing, the citizens on their knees to beg pardon for the uprising, the clergy of the church and the officials of the town bringing gifts and reciting welcomes. Kitty is bored to tears by the Latin addresses, but her eyes are so wide, her mouth naturally upturned in a smile, that even when she is most sulky, she looks angelically beautiful.

We enter the cathedral for a long church service where Kitty kneels and stands and bows her head in prayer and kisses the crucifix and listens to a long welcome in Latin and a hymn in her praise without fidgeting. She does not glance towards Thomas Culpeper, who stands behind the king. She is as queenly as if she were born to it and not effortfully playacting.

The thanksgiving service lasts for hours; only Lady Mary pays attention all the way through, and when it is finally over, the royal couple leave the cathedral under the soaring west door and walk down the hill hand in hand over the swept paving stones to the bishop's palace. I can see from Kitty's awkward walk that he is leaning on her. The favourites close up, fearing that Kitty will stagger under his weight; but they don't dare to offer help.

He is flushed and sweaty by the time we get down the hill, dragging his foot over the hard cobbles of the entrance. As soon as the gates are closed on the gawping faces, he rounds furiously on Katheryn and sends her to her rooms. He beckons Culpeper and Seymour to either side, and they half-lift him indoors. As they manhandle him up the stairs, we hear a muffled groan of pain, and Kitty hurries out of earshot, with us running behind her.

She has a beautiful suite of rooms with large Venetian glass windows where she can see both cathedral and castle and the people still lingering in the streets below. My bedroom is the next floor up, adjoining her bathroom. It is the bedroom for the captain of the watch, and it guards a stair that runs directly to the rear of the palace, the stables, and the garden. I unpack my own things and then open the locked door and go down the little circular stone staircase to the inner ward, where the garden runs down the hill. It is perfect for a secret entrance.

The king has recovered his temper by dinnertime, and there are long speeches of praise that cheer him, but it is not going to be a late night. He eats hugely; every dish goes first to him and then to the queen and then out to the court in order of precedence. Nothing comes from the king's place untouched; he takes a spoon of everything and often double or even treble portions. Kitty beside him, pecking at her food, looks more and more birdlike, more and more ethereal. It seems quite impossible that she should be his wife. She looks as if she would break beneath his weight when he mounts her and be smothered by the fat of his chest.

But he will not get to her bed tonight. My uncle shoots me an angry look, but no one can stop the king eating himself into a torpor. By the time he is hauled to his feet and stands swaying, he is sodden with drink and flatulent with food. He thanks the bishop for good company, kisses Kitty's hand, and beckons his favourites to help him to his rooms. The young maids look hopefully at the queen, hoping for dancing and a merry night now that the old king is going to bed, but Kitty disappoints them by rising and going to her rooms.

We pretend to get ready for bed, dressing Kitty in her nightdress and ornate night robe, tying her nightcap on her head and ordering the maids to their beds. Kitty tells Catherine Tilney that she will sit with me for a while in my bedroom.

Catherine watches as I set the queen a chair and stoke up my little fire. 'Shall I wait?' she asks.

'No, I'll put the queen to bed,' I tell her, and close the door on her surprised face.

As soon as she is gone, Kitty leaps to her feet.

'Not yet,' I say. 'Not until they are all quiet and the lights are out all around the palace.'

'But he won't wait in the dark!'

'He has to wait,' I say firmly. 'We're not letting him in until I am sure that the whole palace is silent.'

She takes off her nightcap and frees her hair from the plait in a tumble of golden-brown waves. 'You're never meeting him like that,' I say flatly. 'Put your cap back on.'

Instead, she borrows a velvet hood of mine and puts a dark-velvet cape over her night robe. 'There.'

'Better,' I say. 'But we still have to wait.'

I let half an hour go by the cathedral bells, and then I open the stair door. With Kitty at my heels, I creep down the twisting stair, a hand on the cold walls on either side. I open the door at the foot, and suddenly, just across the gravel, there is the nightwatchman, making his rounds with a flaming torch in his hand.

I jump back into the shelter of the doorway and push Kitty back up the stairs. I close the door as we wait, trembling. I can hear his footsteps approaching the door, and we dash up the stairs, our slippered feet making no noise, until we are hidden by the curve of the staircase. Down below, I hear the creak of the lock as he turns the key on the outside and then takes the key away, leaving us locked in.

Above me, her face pale in the moonlight that filters through the arrow slit, Kitty is horrified. 'He's locked us in, and Thomas out!'

'You'll have to go back to bed,' I say quietly. 'We've lost our chance tonight.'

She looks as if someone has knifed her in the heart. 'I can't,' she says flatly. 'I can't not see him. Jane, you must run around, go to the garden and find . . .'

'No,' I say firmly. 'We'll just have to try again, later.'

'I've spent all day waiting for tonight.' Her voice trembles on the edge of tears. 'All day. He's the only thing that gets me through these days. I don't think I can bear—'

'I know,' I interrupt. 'We can try another night.'

'I don't want another night. I can't wait for another night. I want tonight!'

'We're locked in. The watchman has the key. There's nothing we can do.'

'Oh, Jane!' She gives a little shuddering sob. She is beyond argument.

'Kitty, be sensible. Go to bed now, and we'll try again tomorrow.'

She shakes her head. 'I can't stand another day without seeing him. What if the king comes to my bed tomorrow? I'd rather die than go another day. I tell you, I would rather die than have the king in my bed.'

'Stop. Stop this. Be calm – don't say such things. Think! You're the luckiest girl in—'

She catches my hand. 'Look at me!' she demands.

I look at her: her eyes are filled with tears, her face twisted with grief.

'I can't live like this,' she says.

She clutches my arm as we hear a noise on the door to the garden. It is not the watchman returning; it is a rhythmic little *rat-tat-tat*.

We creep down the stairs again. I go first, Kitty silent behind me.

'Who's there?' I whisper.

'Um . . . Sir Lancelot!' comes the laughing whisper.

'It's him!' Kitty breathes in my ear. 'He's come!' At once, she is restored, vibrant with desire. She would get past me to the door to whisper through the keyhole, but I hold her back.

'We're locked in,' I hiss. 'There's a nightwatchman. Take care he doesn't see you.'

'He's gone round the other side,' Culpeper says quietly. 'I think I can pick the lock.'

'He can pick a lock!' Kitty whispers adoringly.

We wait, listening to the sound of a thin blade being pushed into the barrel of the lock and the noise of metal against metal as it is jiggled into place. Then the lock yields, and it swings inwards, and he slips through. His servant, who picked the lock, steps discreetly back, but he has seen the two of us.

Kitty is in Culpeper's arms in a moment. I cannot stop her leaping forward or stop him wrapping his arms around her. They hold each other, her face buried into his shoulder and his brown head bent into her neck as he inhales her perfume.

'Get inside,' I say urgently. 'Come on. You can't stay here.'

In a moment, Kitty recovers herself. She steps back; he releases her. He bows; she bends her head.

'Forgive me,' he whispers, but his eyes are still dark with desire, and she is shaking. 'Forgive me.'

I lead the way up the winding stairs, through my bedroom to the queen's bathroom. The stool – a gloriously embroidered velvet throne with jugs of hot water and sponges and soaps – is in the corner of the room, hidden by a screen. In the main part of the room is a table holding a jug, an ewer for washing, drying sheets, a warm robe, two footstools before the little fire, banked in for the night, and a chair in the corner.

Kitty recoils. 'Not here!' she whispers. 'Not here!' Even in the most scandalous circumstances, she is still thinking about appearances.

'This is the safest place; nobody will disturb you here,' I point out. 'We can lock the door, and nobody can even knock. Nobody has the right to enter at all.'

'It doesn't matter,' he whispers. 'Anywhere, as long as we can be together.'

He draws her to the seats before the fire. I sit at a distance, in the chair. I watch them, silhouettes in the firelight. I see the absolute beauty of the two firelit profiles, the tenderness of the inclination of his head as she whispers and then her upward gaze to him as he replies.

I had thought, after that first plunge into each other's arms, that they would kiss; but they hold hands like betrothed children, and whisper for hours, so softly that they can only hear each other by putting their foreheads together, their cheeks touching, their lips to the other's neck. They speak of their childhoods, of their parents, of their families, of the lovers they have known, and for more than an hour, for more than two hours, they whisper when they first saw each other, when they knew that they were in love, how they have longed for this moment to be together. He begs her pardon for preferring another girl when she was a maid-of-honour to Anne of Cleves and confesses that he has been Bess Harvey's lover but that he will never be with another woman after this night. I hear her soft laugh. She says that the affair has not been of great profit to Bess, who is notorious for her shabby clothes. He says if Kitty had continued as a maid-of-honour, she would have been his mistress. She says not so – that she would have broken his heart in revenge, and he whispers that his heart is hers, so she has her revenge.

Like children, they plan nothing, they don't think of tomorrow, never mind the weeks ahead of us on progress, never mind what will happen when we all return to ordinary life in the royal castles and palaces and Culpeper must help the old king into the bed of the girl he loves. They do not speak of the king, not of his illness, not of his lust for Kitty; it is as if they are meeting in another world, where none of the cruelties of this world can hurt them.

They whisper, turn and turn about, like blackbirds settling at sunset – one speaking sweetly and the other softly replying – until I hear the nightwatchman shout the hour in the garden and the cathedral bell strikes three long notes, and I have to recall them to the real world: 'Your Grace, Master Culpeper, that's three in the morning – you have to go to your beds.'

They cannot bear to be parted. He goes to the door, then comes back for a kiss; she holds the ties of his cape and commands him to tell her that he loves her again. I have to order her to her bedroom and open the doorway to the garden stair and shoo him from my room.

I listen at the top of the stair to hear the door at the bottom open and close and know that he is safely out in the garden. Then I go back to the queen's bedroom and find Kitty in bed with her hair a tumble of bronze across the pillow, and she is already fast asleep.

A NYONE WHO CARED for her would see the next morning that she is transformed. The slight bruised violet colour under her clear eyes hints at lack of sleep, but the radiance of her face shows that she was sleepless with joy. The way she carries her head, the colour of her eyes, which shine today more green than hazel – something about her smile, which has a secret behind it . . . but no one in this whole court of people who depend upon her for their living – the servants who wear her livery, the ladies who dine at her table, even the criminal who goes free today because Kitty prettily asks the king for a pardon – no one cares for her at all. Among these thousands of men and women, only Thomas Culpeper and I love her for herself – my love is partly self-serving, and I don't know about his. Surrounded by an adoring court, just as she was surrounded by servants at Lambeth, she is still a lonely little girl neglected by those who should protect her.

Surprisingly, only our uncle Thomas Howard sees a change in her. 'Has she taken?' he asks me. 'She looks like a woman and not a starved waif for once.'

'Not yet,' I reply, but I think: he's right – loving Culpeper may make her fertile. Desiring him, she might conceive a child from the king. I think, for only a moment: Lord, what a beautiful child Kitty and Culpeper would make! – and then I think: too risky, unless we knew for sure that the king was in his last days, and then to make her a pregnant widow would be worth the risk and guarantee her title of dowager queen and her place in a regency council.

Kitty glows, a girl in love, in her first love, a sacred love. She can think of nothing but Thomas Culpeper. She gives Bess Harvey, his former mistress, a gown from the royal wardrobe as a private joke to him; but she makes no other public gesture. They get through the day with nothing more than a few exchanged glances.

The king goes to bed early again, and Kitty resists the temptation to stay up late and dance with Culpeper. Loving him has changed her; she does not want to flaunt him before her maids-of-honour, not even to triumph over Bess Harvey.

CULPEPER PALMS A note to me at dinner with one word – *midnight* – so I have no chance to refuse him. As the bell strikes twelve, Kitty waits for him before the fire in the stool room. Tonight, both my maid and Catherine Tilney insist on waiting up, thinking we are sitting before the fire in my bedroom again. I wish they would go to their own beds, but Catherine Tilney is a kinswoman and cannot be commanded. I make them both wait in an alcove outside my room.

I tell the lovers that the maids are outside my door and they cannot stay long; but no time would be enough for them. They repeat all that they said last night, and they speak of the events of the day that have kept them apart. He tells her that he cannot take his eyes from her when she and the king are at chapel; she tells him how she has to look at the ground when she makes her morning curtsey to the king. They don't complain that they are star-crossed; they don't wish that they had met before the king saw her, they don't even wish for more than they have now. They don't plan. They are entranced with the moment: the touch of a hand, the offer of a kiss, her finger on the dimple in his chin, his hand tracing the line of her slim neck.

While they court, blind to the dangers and consequences, I sit in my chair in the corner and wonder how to profit from this development. As a courtier, I should support my principal while turning this to my own advantage. I should guard us both from risk. I am not dizzy with love, blind to danger like her. Who knows better than I that evidence against a wife can be used to behead a queen? But the only man who could organise such a legal murder is dead, Kitty has no enemies like Anne, and her husband is blind with honeymoon love. She has no rival, as Anne did. No one has any reason to spy on her or lie about her. There is no powerful Spanish party planning to bring her down. I think, as I so often think: what would Thomas Cromwell advise me? What would he do if he were here?

While the two of them whisper sleepily to each other, I plot a course to keep Kitty safe through this love affair. A girl like Kitty was inevitably going to fall in love with someone, and I am lucky that it is an experienced courtier and a favourite of the king. My task is to keep my principal, a Howard queen, safe and smiling in her place, and Culpeper will help me. But, thank God, I don't have to do it for very long. Everyone who sees the king sick to his belly in the morning, exhausted at night, always in pain from a suppurating wound, knows that he cannot last long. If the king crowns Kitty at York and dies next Lent, then Culpeper could marry the dowager queen, both of them in my debt, and I could guide the regent queen into power.

THE PROGRESS MOVES northwards. Every village on the Great North Road is a witness to the power and wealth of the king. The cavalcade is preceded by his yeoman at arms. He rides beside Kitty in magnificent costume; he is followed by Lady Mary, his subservient daughter, and by ladies and noblemen of the court in order of precedence, then archers with bows on the string, and finally behind them, the household companions and their servants and then all the baggage and supply wagons. Troops of soldiers bring up the rear, as if they can protect us from the hatred that follows behind.

Whole villages turn out to play their part of loyal peasantry, cheering and bringing gifts and even throwing flowers down in the mud under the horses' hooves. It is a daily irony that they throw dog roses from the hedgerow, so the Tudor king is greeted everywhere with the white rose of York – the symbol of the earlier royal family. The very people who now throw white roses on the road had a white rose in their hatbands in the uprising. They know their parts in this masque of loyalty, where the king rides through lands that hate him, and villages still grieving for beloved kinsmen turn out to cheer.

Lincolnshire is boggy after the rains of this miserable summer, and we can only travel short distances before the king is exhausted and his beautiful costumes stained and sweaty. It is a relief to stay at Hatfield Chase for four days to rest the horses and brush the dried mud from cloth of gold capes. Local noblemen and gentry come to pay their compliments, and there is a feast every night. We put on the spring masque again, with reduced costumes but familiar dances, and Kitty and Culpeper go hand to hand in the chain dance and pass each other by as polite strangers.

'I will die,' she tells me in a thin little voice that evening, as I brush her hair before bed. 'I will die unless I see him.'

'It's too dangerous here,' I tell her. 'What with our uncle the Duke of Norfolk here and Charles Brandon the Duke of Suffolk in attendance? And all the other visitors? You're constantly watched. Kitty, you did very well at the dance; just keep being careful.'

'I'll hardly see him at all tomorrow.' She speaks as if it is a long sentence of exile. 'He's hunting all day with the king, and the next day they're going fishing. Even if I went, he couldn't speak more than a word to me. Every deer in the county has been driven into the park for the king to have an easy shot. I'm not going to see him for days, and I will die if I don't see him.'

I try to laugh it off as childish exaggeration, and I pat her shoulder. 'Hold on. And as soon as we get somewhere that is less public, I will bring him to you,' I promise. 'But not here – not while our uncle's rooms are just over the gallery.'

Kitty shudders and closes her eyes. 'I'd even risk him,' she says. 'I'd even face him for love, for true love.'

'No, you wouldn't,' I say firmly. 'Just wait until we move on. It's only four days.'

'Four days is like four years when you really love someone,' she says, and I try to laugh at her; but I know it is true.

'We'll try at Pontefract Castle,' I promise. 'It's a very grand castle, huge. There will be thousands of places where you can meet him.'

## PONTEFRACT CASTLE, SUMMER

# 1541

THE CASTLE THEY call Pomfret is an extraordinary old building, looming over the landscape, towers spiralling upwards, and the great gates thrown open to welcome us as we ride in. It's big enough to house everyone riding on the progress – a huge northern castle built long ago to host a fighting king, his court and army. The roof has holes where the rain blows in; the corners are shabby; there are whole floors with nothing but lumber stored in them, abandoned to rats and the birds that fly in and out of the unglazed windows. But the great hall is huge and brilliant with tapestries and painted beams, and warm with an old-fashioned fire on a huge hearth in the centre, smoke finding its way out through the hole in the roof high above it. The king's side is on the right of the great hall, the queen's side on the left. For the first time in my life, I am a creeping, watching spy, like the men my lord employed to break into houses and make *rendezvous* – I search for exits and entrances, hiding places and meeting places.

The maids-of-honour and the ladies-in-waiting are disappointed in their rooms – only Kitty's bedroom and stool room have been refurbished since the castle was built centuries ago, and everywhere is cold and dusty, and we are all tired of travelling and packing and unpacking every week. Only Lady Mary makes no complaint; but she has borne with uncomfortable castles for years. We cannot muster excitement at another poor town; we cannot even pretend we are interested in more rebels seeking pardons.

The queen herself has changed. She no longer romps with her ladies as she used to do, nor does she revel in their stories of flirtations and indiscretions. The love affair between one of the ladies-in-waiting, young Dorothy Bray, and William Parr, a married courtier, interests her only for a moment.

'Do you love him so much that you feel you would die without him?' she asks Dorothy.

'Gracious no!' Dorothy tosses her head. 'It is for him to die of love for me, I think.'

'Then you are a fool to be so indiscreet for nothing,' Kitty says, as stern as a queen. 'And I won't have my ladies behaving badly.'

Kitty tells her ladies that they cannot come to her privy chamber without invitation; she would prefer it if they did not even knock on her bedroom door. This upsets her old friends, who are used to running in and out of her rooms, and insults her sister Lady Isabel Baynton, who has a right to entry. The ladies mutter that they are supposed to provide good company in the queen's rooms – privy chamber and presence chamber – and if Kitty is too young and too ill-educated to appreciate good conversation, they are wasted here and would be happier at their homes. The maids say simply that she's got above herself and she's no fun any more.

Even worse, Francis Dereham chooses this very moment to arrive at Pontefract Castle to take up his post in the queen's household, as if we ever meant for him to actually work at court. All this time, he has taken a wage to stay away – living at Norfolk House in Lambeth – but now, without invitation, he arrives.

'What am I to do with him?' Kitty demands as Webb shows him into her privy chamber.

'I could be your secretary?' he suggests. 'Your personal and private secretary?' He is darkly handsome; he smiles at her, confident that he is attractive to women, knowing that she was once in love with him, dangerously sure of himself.

'You have no qualifications,' I say coldly. 'As we agreed. And the queen already has a talented and educated secretary. And why did you leave Norfolk House?'

'We had a falling out,' he says with a wink. 'She has a hot temper for a great lady. And it's too small a place and too old-fashioned for a young man like me.'

The queen says nothing to her former friend. I can see her holding her hands clasped tightly in her lap. I imagine she wants to jump off her chair and slap his smiling face.

'I was the duchess' personal secretary—' he begins, and then he sees my raised eyebrow. 'Well – gentleman usher,' he amends.

'Her Majesty could recommend you for service to another household,' I suggest. 'One more in the way and . . . more fashionable?'

He shakes his head decisively. 'Nothing's more fashionable than a young queen. I'm stopping here. But trust me, you'll be glad you hired me. And I won't go anywhere else.'

I lean towards Kitty so that he cannot hear our quick whispered consultation. 'We have to have him,' she says crossly. 'I can't let him gossip about what went on at Norfolk House. He can't say a word.'

'We can offer you a post, but it is for a discreet and quiet gentleman,' I tell him. 'You understand that you have to be sober, well-behaved, and respectful?'

He bows low to Kitty. 'I do know how to behave,' he says, with a rueful smile at her. 'You did like me once. Very much, if you remember?'

'I like you still,' Kitty says through her teeth. 'And I will like you again, if you cause no trouble. But the old days are long gone, and I have forgotten all about them.'

'Oh, then I've forgotten, too,' he says. He bows at me; he winks again. 'I promise you, Lady Rochford: nothing to fear from me! I have forgotten everything.'

As soon as he has smilingly bowed himself out of the room,

I round on Kitty. 'What did you do with him?' I hiss. 'Were you lovers? Were you full lovers? Did you promise marriage – was that why you held his savings?'

She is coldly furious. 'I did nothing with him,' she says. 'How dare you suggest such a thing? Look at him! I would never stoop so low.'

T HE COURT DINES together in the great hall, and now the king has rested, there is music and dancing after dinner and gaming tables set up and card games to entertain him. He waves his young companions to dance with the girls, and when Kitty sits beside him rather than dance with a young man, he laughs and pinches her cheek and says that she must take a whirl around the floor with a handsome young man, and who is her favourite?

She names Thomas Seymour, the court favourite; she chooses John Dudley; once, she makes the king laugh by naming her uncle Thomas Howard, who scowls at her and says that he is too old for dancing and if he was going to make a fool of himself, it would not be with his niece. She never so much as looks towards Thomas Culpeper, and he is never more to her than one of many courtiers, with a courtier's charm.

We dine in the thick woods that surround the castle after the hunts; we paddle like children in the river; we go out boating; we have a moonlight supper, and the king is so well entertained and so exhausted by the court merrymaking that he comes to the queen's bed only once, escorted by half a dozen companions. The clatter they make as they come through the hall early in the night gives us plenty of time to prepare, and Kitty is in her bed with her nightcap on, looking pretty by the time the king arrives.

All the other nights, Thomas Culpeper comes to her bedroom, up a little twisting stair that is used by the spit boy to bring firewood and take out the ashes. Sometimes, he even creeps into her room in the late afternoon, when Kitty is resting before dinner. They are never alone; they never ask me to leave. We lock the bedroom door, and I sit beside it on a footstool, and the two of them sit in the window seat, withdrawn a little so that no one glancing up at the queen's tower can see them. Sometimes, they have only a few minutes together; some days, he can stay for an hour. At night, when the castle is quiet but for the patrolling guards, they sit side by side before the dying fire and whisper together until the sky lightens with the early summer dawn and the birds begin to sing, and he whispers: 'I have to go . . .' and she says: 'Oh, don't . . . not yet . . .'

It is as if they are living two lives: the daytime one of show and noise and parade of wit and manners, and this inner hushed secret life where they never speak above a whisper and they never touch more than the gentlest kiss on her hand, or her fingers to his cheek, or her hand on his heart.

One evening, someone turns the latch on her bolted bedroom door and Thomas leaps onto the bed, grasps the bedpost, and hides himself in the curtains. I fling open the door, and it is one of the maids, Lucy Luffkyn, bowling in, uninvited with a pile of newly ironed linen.

'How dare you?' Kitty demands, and the girl looks at her, open-mouthed.

'I just brought your shifts for tomorrow? Same as always?'

'The door was locked. You shouldn't have tried it. I've gone to bed; I'm not to be disturbed just because the laundress has finished ironing!'

'But you're not in bed,' the girl says stupidly. 'I could see the light from under your door. I could hear voices.'

'I'm in bed if I say I am! Go at once! And never disturb me at night again, and never try the door. I won't be woken up by the likes of you!'

I hustle the girl from the room and take the shifts from her.

'What's wrong with her?' she demands rudely. 'She wasn't asleep. I could see the light. Why would she lock the two of you in together? What's she so upset about?'

'She's tired,' I say quickly. 'We're all tired. It's been a long day, and she's upset that her course has come. Don't pay any attention to it. Just don't come in without being told to.'

The young woman, who learned her court manners when Kitty was a playmate with her ladies, is offended. 'And why are you the only one she sees now?' she demands.

'I'm her kinswoman,' I say flatly. 'I do as I am bid, and so should you. Don't come without invitation, don't try the door without knocking, and don't question your betters.'

She gives a little flounce off to her own bedroom. When I go back into the room, Kitty is unwrapping Thomas from the bed curtain, hopelessly giggling, clinging to each other, muffling their laughter.

'What a virago you are!' Thomas exclaims, and Kitty puts her face against his jacket to silence her scream of laughter. 'I shall never dare to offend you, I swear. What a raking!'

'You'll never offend me.' She lifts her face to his, flushed with laughter. 'You never could.'

'I wish to God I could come into your bedroom without knocking,' he says, suddenly serious, as if shocked by the rush of his own desire. He puts his hands on her waist; he draws her closer. 'I wish to God we could tell everyone we were locking the door and not to be disturbed until morning.'

Pontefract Castle is a long pause in this progress, which is starting to feel interminable, and now Sir Edward Baynton tells me that the court is to go to York, where the King of Scotland will meet us for talks to bring peace to the border regions and an alliance between the two kingdoms.

'Any special ceremony?' I ask, my heart in my mouth, not daring to say the word 'coronation'.

For once he is smiling. 'A ceremony in front of King James? With Mary of Guise watching? He's having half the town rebuilt for something . . . I would think you could brush off the ermine and send a message to the jewel house.'

He means a coronation, but I only tell Kitty that we are to meet James of Scotland, and every afternoon for a week, we practise the exact depth of curtsey suitable for a neighbouring king.

'At York?' she asks.

'At York,' I confirm.

The king goes to Hull to inspect the defences with Thomas Culpeper and his riding court. At once, there is a holiday atmosphere for those of us left behind, and we dance for pleasure, not for appearance, and hunt at a full gallop behind hounds giving tongue; we don't have to wait for driven game. Kitty is playful with her ladies in her rooms again, and everyone knows – but nobody says – that the court is a happier place without the king. Even Lady Mary breathes more easily when her father is not staring at her, wondering whether she is of most use to him in England, paraded as a captured trophy, or whether he should marry her to a foreign prince and send her far away.

Francis Dereham takes the new freedoms too far and sits over his wine after dinner with the senior gentlemen of the queen's household, as if he were one of them. Of course, they tell him to leave with the other ushers, and madly, in a drunken rush of temper, he claims that he has his place by special favour, and that he will outstay them all.

'We'll have to see him and order him to be more discreet,' I tell the queen. 'Or we'll have to dismiss him. We can't have him speaking of you and talking about special favour.'

'We can't dismiss him,' she says, her eyes dark with apprehension. 'What about the letters?'

'Your grandmother said she had them all?' I check at her aghast expression. 'Don't tell me there are others? Oh Kitty! Nothing written by you?'

'No, and anyway, Grandmother has them all?'

'Then we deny them and we can dismiss him.'

She orders Francis to her presence chamber, though by rights Sir Edward should dismiss him.

'You have upset the gentlemen of the queen's household,' I accuse him, quietly. 'We had an agreement – Master Dereham – that you would keep to your place. You are not at Norfolk House now.'

'I know it,' he says, with a bow to Kitty and a sugary smile to me. 'We were merry company there. But here Master Johns and Sir Edward are such pompous old—'

'Their place is above you,' I interrupt. 'You may not even comment. You were told to keep to your place and show respect. In the circumstances I have no choice . . .'

'I think you do have a choice,' he interrupts me. 'I won my place as an old friend of the queen. I've never failed in my friendship to her, even though certain honourable promises were made that were not honourably kept.'

'Oh, Francis, stop it!' Kitty says irritably. 'I can't have you being rude to Master Johns, and you know very well you can't say anything about old friendships. Grandmother gave you back your money – and you probably stole it from her in the first place. Here—' She pushes a little purse into his hands. 'Take that, and stop causing trouble.'

I am horrified that she is bribing him. He weighs it in his hand as if he might ask for more. He bows to us both; he looks as if he is biting his cheek to keep from laughing in our faces. 'Why, Your Majesty, Lady Rochford, I thank you for this charming gift. You'll have no more trouble from me, I promise you.' He goes to the door, opens it himself, and steps out. 'Unless I need more money!' he laughs, popping his head back in, and then he is gone.

'Why give him money?' I demand. 'We were going to dismiss him, and the moment he said—'

'I'm queen, aren't I?' she returns. 'I'm the richest woman in England, aren't I?'

'Well, not really . . .'

'I'm rich enough to buy a fool like Francis Dereham a hundred times over,' she says irritably. 'And neither you nor anyone else can tell me what to do with my money.'

## ST MARY'S, YORK, AUTUMN

## 1541

WE ENTER YORK as a punitive force in September. The journey north from Pontefract is erratic – constantly stopping for gentry and local people to come and prostrate themselves before the king to atone for their part in the Pilgrimage of Grace. In some villages, the bodies of fathers and brothers are still rotting in metal cages hanging from roadside gallows. Their sons and brothers kneel at the crossroads for forgiveness as we go by.

When we enter the city of York, the archbishop himself, with three hundred priests, kneels to the king and offers a treasure chest of money, asking pardon. Lady Mary watches the king harangue them, knowing they were trusting her to come to their aid, knowing they hoped to put her and Reginald Pole on the throne in place of her father. She sits completely still on her horse, her face as blank as a painted saint on a plastered wall; her guilt and grief only shows in convulsive swallowing as she fights the desire to vomit.

We stay at the empty abbey of St Mary, half of the buildings tumbled down by the storm of destruction which is called the king's reformation. But the abbot's house has been repaired in a hurry for this visit, and there is a great stone-floored hall where most of the court can be seated to dine; the queen has the rooms for honoured guests, and the king has the abbot's rooms. There is a charming little parlour room on the ground floor where the abbess used to speak to visitors through a grille. Thomas can enter, unnoticed, from a courtyard and Kitty can slip down a private stair from the abbess' bedroom when the court has closed for the night.

I go with her, in case there is any trouble, and sit at the back of the room while the two of them play *Pyramus* and *Thisbe* speaking through the grille for the first hour, until their lips come closer and closer to the metal lattice, and then Kitty opens the little door, and she is in his arms.

'You're hot,' she leans back to look into his face.

'I have a slight fever,' he smiles. 'My heart beats faster when you are against it.'

She puts her hand on his forehead. 'Thomas, you must take a draught and go to bed. I am sure you're feverish, and how shall I see you, if you're ill?'

'I'm not ill.' He takes her hand from his forehead and kisses it. 'Dying of love, of course.'

'Jane!' She summons me. 'Feel his forehead – isn't he hot?'

He certainly has a fever. His eyes are bright, and his cheeks flushed; his forehead is burning hot and dry.

'You'd better put yourself to bed and let the queen go,' I tell him.

It would be disastrous for her to be ill now, when her coronation might be announced any day. All the king's pleasure in his pretty bride will not keep him in the same palace if she has sweating sickness. He is more afraid of illness than anything in the world.

Reluctantly, Culpeper releases her.

'But who will look after you?' she asks him, as I draw her away.

'I've got good servants,' he assures her. 'And the king will send Dr Butts if he thinks I'm ill.'

'Don't say a word about us,' she reminds him. 'Not to the doctor. Don't say about late nights and no sleep.'

'Never,' he says simply. 'Never. You know I would die rather than betray you.'

She looks aghast. 'Don't say die! Don't speak of it. If you . . . if you . . .'

Gently, I push her towards the door. 'He has a slight fever,' I say, very matter-of-fact. 'He'll be well by next week.'

'Send me word how you are,' she says as I get her to the foot of the stair. 'I won't be able to sleep unless I know you're getting better.'

'Let him go to bed now,' I interrupt. 'Master Culpeper, send your page in the morning and tell me how you are. But don't write anything.'

'No, write to me!' Kitty begs. 'Write to me every day.'

One passionate kiss on Kitty's hand and he slips out of the door.

Kitty's green eyes are tragic. 'What if he were to be very ill?' she asks. 'What if he were to . . .'

'He's a strong, healthy young man,' I say to her. 'He's not old, he's not fat, and he's not poisoned by an ulcer and broken by old injuries. He can have a fever and jump out of bed in two days, none the worse for wear. There's nothing for you to fear.'

I N THE MORNING, we enter the chapel and there is no curly brown head bowed behind the king.

'Can I write to him?' she whispers. 'I have to, Jane. I will.'

'You can tell me what to write, so it's not in your hand,' I say. 'And nothing but what anyone could read.'

She nods and dictates it to me in a whisper, while the long service goes on. I write a passionless *précis* – not at all what she wanted to say – and I palm it and pass it to Webb as we leave the chapel and tell him to give it to Culpeper's servant. If he reads the brief words, he will think that it is from me – fool enough to pursue a younger man. But I have outlived far worse scandals than this.

The page sends word that Thomas Culpeper is very ill, with a burning fever, and is to be cupped later today. Kitty can barely endure the long ceremonies of the day and the many changes of dress: the procession to the cathedral, the presentation of loyal wishes, the submission of former rebels. She does it by rote, with an empty smile. The king beside her sees only her obedience to the order of the service; he has no idea that she is sick with longing for another man.

After dinner, the king sits beside Kitty to watch the dancing and tells her, with a pleased smile, that she is to prepare for a great event. It is a sign of how her marriage has schooled her that she does not leap to her feet with excitement about her coronation. She bows her head and says that she will do whatever he wishes.

Equally, she shows no disappointment when the king adds that it is to be a royal visit: his sister's son, his rival, his neighbouring monarch, King James of Scotland, is coming to York to meet the greater King of England. If he brings his queen, the famously beautiful Mary of Guise, who preferred the lesser king to the greater one, Kitty will have to show herself as the younger, more beautiful, and certainly more fertile woman. Queen Mary must regret her choice of husband, and King James must see that our English king has the better wife. We are to send to London for extra jewels and gowns, and the queen's household must have the best tapestries and glassware – all this must come north at once, and it is Kitty's task to see that the English court and the English queen outshine the Scots.

Kitty's eyes widen at the enormity of the task. 'But I don't know how . . .' she starts, and the king laughs at her and gestures to me: 'Jane will know what to do,' he says. 'How many kings have we bested, Jane? How many royal shows have we dazzled with?'

'And we have the most beautiful queen ever.' I smile and curtsey. 'When do they arrive, Your Majesty?' I ask. 'How long do we have to make York into a little Hampton Court?'

It is the wrong thing to say – the king's face darkens with sudden anger. 'He'll come when he's bidden,' he says furiously. 'He'll come when he's ordered!' He rounds on Kitty. 'Do you question me?'

'No! No!' Kitty gasps. 'And nor did Jane!'

She is brave to try to defend me, but we are in for one of his sudden, inexplicable storms, and nothing will restore his good temper.

I drop into a curtsey and keep my head down as he roars over both of us to Thomas Howard the Duke of Norfolk: 'When d'you think the King of Scots will arrive? Eh? You're so pressing for this meeting, and here's a lady of your house questioning me! Me!'

Our uncle, taking in my bowed head and Kitty's white face in one swift glance, says smoothly: 'For certain, he'll be scrambling to meet you as soon as he can get here, I should think. But he's at Falkland Palace now – did he not write to Your Majesty? A pretty humble letter: he knows his place. I'll give him safe conduct through the borders. I think he fears your stout English borderers!'

'What sort of king is frightened by border reivers?' the king asks contemptuously.

The duke laughs. 'He is!' he says. 'He doesn't have the grip on his people that you do, Your Majesty. But how can he? So young a man, in thrall to the Church and to his advisors, commanded by your sister his mother! Give him time, and he'll learn from you how to govern.'

I rise up from my curtsey, and the duke shows Kitty and me a loveless smile. 'And he'll envy your bride. He should have thought of our English beauties before he tied himself up in a barren alliance with France.'

The king cracks a laugh. 'He should!' he says triumphantly. He turns to Kitty and to me; his ill temper is all forgotten. 'He married a Frenchwoman and her babies died!' he says triumphantly. 'He should have tried fertile English stock.'

Kitty manages a smile, but she can barely stand as the rage passes over us.

'Dance!' the king says suddenly. 'You should be practising your dances. And we will have to put on a masque. What would be a good one? What would show the Scots that we are as far above them as the angels above men?'

Kitty waves to the musicians to play a circle dance and escapes to the dance floor.

My uncle rolls his eyes towards me; he has no idea what to suggest for a masque. '*Spring*?' he suggests stupidly, remembering the last masque we did.

At once, the king's smile dies. 'What's spring got to do with it?' he demands.

The music strikes up. Kitty glances across at me anxiously and starts the dance, but the whole court can see the king is falling into ill temper, again.

'*Aurelian?*' I snatch at an old, half-forgotten lesson. '*Aurelian*, the Emperor – conqueror of the German barbarians?'

The king scowls, racking his drink-fuddled brain. 'I've never . . .'

'Your Majesty will remember from your extensive reading – Emperor *Aurelian* saved Rome from the barbarians. Famously saved them! And – Your Majesty will remember – he built the Aurelian Walls to keep the barbarians from Rome. How is that as a slight to the Scots?'

'Just like Hadrian's Wall!' the king crows, finally getting the point. 'That says everything! Of course. That's my choice. Tell the master of revels that I command a masque based on the building of the Aurelian Walls. He won't know anything about it, but he can ask Jane. Don't trouble me. I'm busy enough with ordering repairs to these buildings to house them all.'

'Would Your Majesty play the part of *Aurelian?*' I ask, sweet as honey. 'In a toga – a long toga – and crowned with laurel.' He will look more like *Nero* than *Aurelian*, but he still loves to dress up and disguise, and a long robe will hide his rotting leg. 'You could be carried in on a throne at the end in triumph, when the masque wall has been built by the dancers and the choristers. The queen could be *Peace*?'

'Yes,' he says, pleased. 'That's very good, Jane.' He turns to my uncle. 'What a scholar your niece is, Howard! You'd never have thought of *Aurelian* – I doubt you've even heard of him!'

'Indeed,' my uncle says, the falsest of smiles glozing his face. 'She is such a treasure.'

THE KING, THE whole court, and the city of York throw themselves into frantic preparation for the visit of the Scots king; but first, the city must be cleared of the private armies of the border lords who have fought the Scots for generations and are more likely to dig in for a siege than prepare a peaceful welcome. Orders stream from the court that buildings shall be prepared, that great tents and pavilions shall come from London, that furniture, carpets, tapestries must come north, labouring up the muddy Great North Road, and must not be delayed.

Everyone knows there is to be a great event at York; but no one knows what it is. Of course, given that Jane Seymour was to be crowned at York after the birth of her child, everyone assumes that all this fuss is for Kitty. Everyone thinks that she is secretly with child and the coronation is to be her reward.

'What am I to do?' she asks me, blank-faced. 'I don't want to deny it!' She flushes with annoyance. 'And I should be crowned! Why can't the king just say he's crowning me? So everyone stops talking?'

'I'm hoping he will do it during the visit of the King of Scots.'

'Then why not say that the King of Scots is coming?'

'He doesn't want the embarrassment of waiting for a less important man.'

'He's embarrassing me!'

We both know that Kitty's embarrassment does not matter to King Henry, who – however much he pets her – will always put himself first.

'I have to tell Thomas that it's not true,' Kitty frets. 'I must tell him I am not with child. What would he think of me?'

'You can't: he's still in his bed with fever.'

'Then I'll have to write,' she says, as if it is a mighty undertaking.

'You can't write anything like that.'

'But I have to tell him.' She turns to me, her eyes filling with tears. 'Jane, you don't know what it's like, day after day not seeing him, and only hearing that he is getting better but never seeing him. I can't live like this. I can't be fitted with dresses and practise dances and listen to the king going on and on about the King of Scots if I never see Thomas.'

'Be calm.' I try to soothe her. 'Be calm, Kitty. This is just ordinary courtier work: dancing and rehearsing and being seen by the people. You can do this, even without Thomas, and, anyway, you have no choice.'

'But let me write to him!'

I am afraid that she is going to start crying, and we have to rehearse the masque in just a few minutes.

'Jane, I swear to you, I won't dance, I'll say I am ill, and I'll go to bed and not get up again, unless I can write to him.'

'Yes, yes, you can write,' I surrender. 'Shall you dictate, and I write it for you?'

'No,' she says. 'I want to write to him myself, in my own hand. I don't care if it's dangerous. I want him to know what he is to me.'

I won't let her start until she has practised her part and is released from the rehearsal. Then she sends for a quill and a ream of paper. She asks me to comb the paper to give her invisible lines to follow, she asks me to mend the pen and get her a pot of the best ink from her secretary. Then she insists on writing the letter herself.

Her education has been completely neglected. This is a great effort for her to write even in English. She works as hard as any spy transcribing into code, she asks me how to spell 'recommend'. Despite the guide-lines drawn across the page, her words waver hopelessly, and there is a blot from a tear. It is a letter that a schoolgirl would write – aspiring to formality but shot through with a childish longing. It is a letter that should never be written by a queen – not even if she were writing to a king, a beloved husband. It is too revealing; it is suffused with her love. I cannot bring myself to tell her she may not write this; it is far too late to tell her not to feel like this. This is the passion of a young untutored woman who has lived all her life in a heartless family, commanded by her husband, and now she has someone who cherishes her for the very first time. I could as easily repress this, spoil it, censor it, as I could slap a trusting child.

*Master Culpeper,*
*I never longed so much . . . to see you and to speak with you . . . it makes my heart die to think . . . that I cannot be always in your*

*company. Yet my trust is always in you that you will be as you have promised me . . . praying you that you will come when my Lady Rochford is here . . . and thus I take my leave of you, trusting to see you shortly again, and I would you was with me now that you might see what pain I take in writing to you.*

*Yours as long as life endures,*
*Katheryn*

KITTY CANNOT SLEEP or eat while Thomas Culpeper fights his fever. A dozen times a day, she asks me how he is, and will I send to ask? I order the queen's usher, Henry Webb, to leave his post and go into Master Culpeper's service so that he can come and go between the queen's household and the king's side. All the other servants think he has been unfairly dismissed, and Lucy Luffkynn swears darkly that the Dowager Duchess of Norfolk will send another favourite into the queen's service and that new servants will come up with the baggage train from London and replace everyone.

There are long days while Kitty goes hunting beside the king and walking with him in the garden, sits beside him through interminable dinners, and dances after dinner, going hand to hand with his handsome young companions, but never sees Thomas. The king is preoccupied with his building works, every day he goes out into the city, changing his mind on the rebuilding of the abbey, shouting for the master builder, demanding a tower be restored which is to be called Henry's Tower and will be a lookout over the great walls of York for a thousand years, posting a man on it to warn of the arrival of the Scots king.

Kitty bears the boasting and the outbursts of complaining very patiently; but tells me that she has a pain in her belly that comes on at dinnertime, when she sits down to eat beside the king. Sometimes, she cannot swallow when he puts a great haunch of meat on her plate; she pretends she is eating for hour after hour of dining, as he calls for another dish and another to be brought to the table.

We assume that King James will come with a riding court of some hundreds, but we have to be ready to house a thousand courtiers – the English cannot look unprepared or too poor to pay for rebuilding. The old tents from the Field of the Cloth of Gold are pulled out of storage, reburnished, and sent on their way up the North Road too. They will be set up on the meadows outside the walls, to house the Scots court overflowing from the rebuilt abbey and castle.

While the king redraws plans and spurs on the builders to throw up halls and rooms and kitchens and stables, he dreams of dominating the younger man. He will resolve the constant border warfare; he will separate the king from his alliance with France. He will win Scotland to peace. More than anything else, he will make Mary of Guise regret her choice of James of Scotland over Henry of England. This visit to York – originally just one of the many stops on the progress around the north – has become the centre of his plans, the legacy of his reign.

Every day, we rehearse the new masque. Dressmakers work on togas, and all the artists in the north of England are summoned to York to make masks, headdresses, scenery, and to build the Aurelian walls of plaster. They have to design and build pretend siege engines; this Roman army is to have cannon and thunderflashes. *Aurelian*, the king himself, swathed in a toga of cloth of gold with a crown of gold laurel, is to enter on a throne of gold pulled by the white mules of the queen's litter. Stands are built for an audience of thousands.

The grander the plans, the greater the work, the more certain I am that he will announce Kitty's coronation at the end of the masque, when he is in his golden pomp as *Caesar Aurelian*. I commission a masquing crown of painted gold for her, ready for his command. I keep her to the rigid schedule of rehearsals, entertaining the king, praying beside him, dining beside him, and even smiling with pretend pleasure as he comes barging into her rooms at night and is heaved up into her bed. In just a month's time, she will be crowned

Queen of England, I promise her – just endure another day. In a year's time, she will be dowager queen, with a massive fortune, and a place on the council of regency for seventeen years until little Prince Edward comes of age – just endure another night.

'It's worth it!' I tell her in the morning.

She turns her face from the stinking sheets. 'Is it?'

WE ARE STILL preparing for King James' arrival when a letter comes from Falkland Palace to say that he has not even started his journey. This is an insult that Thomas Cromwell would never have allowed. We would never have gone near the border until we knew that the Scots king had started on his journey. The king blusters that it gives us more time to prepare, that he is glad. He is not waiting on his nephew but taking his own time on his works. He hides his anger and is more terrifying, seething in silence, than when he is ranting. Nothing can divert him from his silent fury: his daughter Lady Mary fades from sight – she is always at her prayers. The queen is like the kitten of her nickname – she slinks off to a corner whenever she can. The courtiers cannot escape. We have to walk with him, kneel beside him in prayer, try to divert his brooding inattention, we are all afraid of him.

One morning, very subdued, we process into the chapel and see Thomas Culpeper in his place behind the king. I am proud of Kitty; she does not betray herself for a moment. She curtseys to the king to the right depth of reverence and calmly walks to her place in the church. She kneels and closes her eyes in prayer. Only then do I see her sway on her knees, and her lips move to bless his name, but she does not glance towards Thomas until breakfast, when he bows to her as we all walk into the hall.

'Master Culpeper, I am pleased to see you are well again,' she says lightly, and no one can hear the longing in her voice.

'I thank you for your kind wishes.' He bows and goes to his place.

She watches him go.

'Kitty,' I say very quietly, and she turns to me with her face closed and calm.

'I know,' she says, and I think: we are teaching her to be a courtier. We are teaching her to be a liar.

THE KING SENDS Thomas Culpeper as his deputy to bring us ladies into dinner. As he takes my hand, I feel him slip a little ring into my palm. It is a cramp ring, blessed by the king at Easter.

I look up at him and see his dark eyes are bright with laughter. 'This is a kind gift,' I say.

'It's a crime,' he says. 'I've incriminated you, Jane. I stole it from the king's collection last Easter, and I swear it brought my fever down. I thought you might like it, in case you are ever ill.'

'You shouldn't have taken it,' I scold him. 'The queen would have given you one if she had known that you wanted it.'

'I do want one from her,' he says earnestly. 'Think of it as an exchange. I want hers in return for this one.'

'You shouldn't ask,' I say, then I see his mock-penitent face. 'Oh, very well.'

'And she must give it me herself,' he insists. 'This evening.'

'If it's safe,' I say.

I THINK NOTHING WOULD have prevented him coming; nothing could have made her refuse him. He walks through the abbess' little conversation room, up the stairs to her bedroom, and the moment he is in the door, they are in each other's arms, enwrapped in the huge vaulted room, young lovers on a bench before the fire. She sits on his knees; she winds her arms around his neck. She buries her face in his shoulder; he grips her as if he would never let her go. They are entwined. She whispers to him that life is unbearable without him; he says that he had passionate dreams of her, that he was delirious and thought that she came for him in a beautiful barge that sailed through his bedroom window.

But still, they do not plan beyond the next night, when they can only be together if Thomas is not called to sleep in the king's chamber. They don't speak of her coronation, about the presentation to King James. They don't think about the journey back to London; they don't even think of this coming autumn or winter, nor how they will bear to be parted in the court's daily routine when we are living in the London palaces again. They take all their joy in the present moment; they want nothing more than this now: this fierce grip of passion, the whisper of desire.

To my absolute horror, I suddenly hear the noise of several men crossing the hall outside the bedroom door and then a loud knock on the door. The couple at the fireplace freeze for a moment, and this time, they don't leap apart; he does not run to hide, leaving her alone to face whoever is at the door. They rise to their feet; they turn towards the door. He puts his hand around her waist. They look like two beautiful lovers facing a wicked enchanter: they are poised together, confronting danger, as if ready to be turned into stone together.

'Are you mad? Fssst!' I wave him to the doorway, and unwillingly, he goes towards it. 'Don't go down the stair!' I hiss. 'There may be someone at the bottom, guarding the parlour door!' I close the door on him, and turn to Kitty. 'Ready?'

She is blanched with shock. Wordlessly, she nods. I go to the main door that leads to the hall.

'Who is it?'

'Anthony Denny. Is that you, Lady Rochford? Is the queen still awake? Will she receive His Majesty?'

I don't need to glance back at Katheryn to see that she cannot be forced into bed with the king tonight. She is shaking from head to foot as if she has the ague. Even he would notice.

I press her into a chair so that she does not fall to the stone floor in a faint.

'Her Majesty is asleep,' I call. 'Shall I wake her?'

Anthony Denny, outside the door with a couple of companions, pauses for a moment. He will be thinking, as we all think, what an ordeal this marriage is for the queen. He may be thinking that the king is drunk and probably incapable.

'No, don't wake her,' he decides. 'I'll tell the king she is already abed. It's all right, Lady Rochford. Let her have her sleep.'

'Thank you,' I say. 'Goodnight.'

Kitty and I freeze, listening to the steps of half a dozen men going back across the stone-floored hall to the king's side. The little staircase door swings open, and Culpeper comes out, as pale as if he were still sick.

'I'd better go,' he says shortly. 'If he's staying up, he'll ask for me.'

Slowly, they reach for each other, as if they are wading through deep water. She slides into his arms; she lifts her face for his kiss. She clings to him as he wraps his arms around her and kisses her deeply, passionately, wordlessly. She takes a cramp ring off her finger; he holds out his hand, and she puts it on the wedding-ring finger of his left hand. He bends his head and kisses it and her lips. Then he steps back and plunges through the door and down the little staircase, and we hear the door shut at the bottom, and he is gone.

THE WORK GOES on wearily. We are step-perfect in our masque, and all the costumes have been made, and the elaborate machinery of pretend cannon and walls and miniature siege engines is ready. New buildings in the city are topped off by the exhausted workmen with a branch of a tree in the chimney and an allowance of ale, but as soon as they are finished on one building, they are sent to another site. The tents and pavilions arrive on lumbering wagons drawn by oxen up the ruined road from London, and the ground is cleared in the scythed meadows; but still, we wait to hear from King James.

One of the English border lords writes to say that he has heard that James of Scotland has not left Falkland Palace and has no intention of coming south. My uncle the Duke of Norfolk, who urged this meeting as the only way to tame these warring lands, has to face the king with the news that the king of Scots does not trust our guarantees; he will not risk himself so far into English lands. He does not even decline the honour of our invitation; he claims that he never accepted it in the first place. He pretends that he did not promise to attend; he pretends he said nothing. It hardly matters what he says to add insult – he is not coming.

He makes all of us look like fools – all our rehearsals and rebuilding, and the lumbering wagons clogging the roads with our ostentatious treasure. To prepare so richly for a visit and have a guest simply snub us, is worse than if he had refused at the start. By claiming he is unsafe in English lands, he accuses the king of dishonour: putting a fellow monarch at risk, offering a safe passage that he is too weak to deliver.

The worst thing for the king's men is that they know that James' belief that the king is dishonourable, and these lands are unsafe, is true. Even though the king did not plan an entrapment he would have been amused if James had been jeered and jostled in the English border lands, and would not have protected him from angry borderers. The entertainments – our masque – were deliberately choreographed to insult James as the weaker king of a smaller kingdom. The grand hospitality was to humiliate him as a poorer king of a poor kingdom. There would have been nothing for him to enjoy, and every agreement – peace on the border or safe passage for merchants – would have come at a high price. King James was wise to refuse, his wife was right to avoid her former suitor, and their insulting absence shows King Henry not only that he cannot command his nephew, but that many believe he has lost control of the north of England, too.

Worse for me, for Kitty, for all of us on the queen's side, is that there will be no coronation if it does not distress Mary of Guise. Sweating with offence, the king cancels everything. He demands that we go home, and it is as if York's reconciliation, the peace talks with Scotland, even the queen's coronation, are of no more value than the painted canvas Aurelian walls, which are torn down and burned.

WE HAVE A week of rain, and although nobody wants to travel for long days, soaking wet on muddy roads, we might as well go back to London as sulk in York. The king sinks into an angry torpor, and no one can please him: not even Kitty; not even his fool, who has too many topics to avoid; not even my uncle, who is given the impossible task of expelling every single Scotsman from English lands – however valuable his trade, however long his family has settled with us. The king will do anything, however petty, to revenge himself on his nephew, and he only speaks to my uncle to sponsor vindictive raids by English reivers on Scots lands. The young men of the court, Thomas Culpeper among them, are mustered to make an army for surprise attack on isolated Scots' castles. My uncle advises against deploying jousters against fortifications, so the king now thinks his young companions are of no more threat than painted cannon, and he is furious with them too.

It is not until late September that we turn the weary cavalcade and ride down the roads we took before. It was raining when we left, and it is raining now, and the king is in a worse mood than ever. Nothing is well done, nobody can speak without offending him, nothing is organised as Thomas Cromwell would have done it, and nobody understands the pain that he is in. He sends Kitty from dinner to her rooms as if she were a daughter, not a wife; and he stops coming to her bed. He keeps his young men up all night to gamble with him, and they all learn to lose as he cannot tolerate anyone else winning. Night after night, Thomas cannot get to Kitty's rooms as he has to play with the king, lose a small fortune, and then sit with him late into the night as he complains of perfidy, and smoulders, like a wet peat fire banked down with hatred.

## COLLYWESTON PALACE, AUTUMN

## 1541

THE KING WAKES later and later every day, as he stays up all night gambling and drinking and he rarely comes out of his rooms before midday. So on our first morning at Collyweston Palace, Thomas Culpeper and half a dozen of the young companions come on their own to sing under the windows of the queen's ladies, and the girls and Kitty throw on gowns and run down into the garden for the sunrise as if it were a May Day for young lovers. Unnoticed by the ladies and young companions, Culpeper wraps a cape around Kitty's shoulders. For just a moment, he holds her, and then stands beside her to face east, where a rosy sun is rising through wispy clouds. They stand quite still, the sunlight on their rapt faces, as if this moment of stillness and silence at sunrise is a spell which will hold them entranced all through the rest of the day.

Someone laughs and makes a joke, and the magic is broken, and I sweep the ladies back up the stairs and bundle Kitty back into bed and stoke the fire in her bedroom.

'That's the last time you'll be able to run out this season,' I warn her. 'You'll have to take more care when we get home. Has he said anything?'

Her eyes are shining green with happiness at being with Culpeper for one moment. 'No? What should he say?'

He must know as well as I that they cannot meet at Windsor Castle or Hampton Court or Westminster Palace as they have done on progress. The routines are too fixed, the king more regular in his habits. He will come to Kitty's bedroom once or twice a week, but always without notice, and we cannot turn his groom of the chamber from her bedroom door ever again. Besides, there are more ladies at court when we are near London; the great ladies of the kingdom who have served other queens expect entrance to the queen's bedroom. The wives of the lords have nothing to do but watch and gossip. The spy networks of ambassadors, the council, the churches and the advisors have been absent on progress but they will all be watching in London. Kitty cannot meet Thomas in her bedroom in any of the royal palaces, there is nowhere that they can meet secretly and they cannot even speak together for very long.

'Thomas says the ulcer on the king's leg is getting worse,' she whispers. She glances to the door, which is shut and locked; she glances at the curtained windows. 'He says it's down to the bone, like a dog bite, and running wet as if it was a rabid dog that bit. Dr Butts has warned the king that he can't eat and drink as he does. He says he is gambling with his health. He says he might . . .' She breaks off.

'He's an old man,' I say cautiously.

'Thomas says the Seymours are preparing a regency for next spring,' she says. She puts her hand half over her mouth, as if her pillows cannot be trusted with these treasonous words.

'Next spring?' They think as I do that winters are hard on old men; the king nearly died last Lent, and he is heavier and sicker now than he was last year. He can't live for much longer, and then Kitty will be free – we will all be free of him.

'Next spring.' She nods. She taps the wooden headboard of the bed; it makes a hollow knocking sound, as if on a coffin lid. At once, she looks aghast. 'I meant to touch wood for good luck,' she says, 'only good luck.'

'We won't speak of this,' I say. 'But I wish us good luck, too.'

She holds out her hands. 'And you'll stay with me, Jane? When I am dowager queen? And then . . . when . . . I remarry?'

I think: yes, I will stay with the dowager queen. If we could get the prince into our keeping, we could have a household which was a royal court. Who could be a better governess for the young prince than me? Who in this court is better read? Where might this life take me? Dear to the dowager queen, the keeper of her secrets, and she the stepmother of the next King of England. My face does not show my leap of excitement, my soaring ambition.

'I will stay with you,' I say sweetly. 'I will stay with you always.'

## CHENIES MANOR, BUCKINGHAMSHIRE, AUTUMN

## 1541

Our route home takes us to the country house of Lord Russell – a firm favourite of the king, one of the old lords who has served the Tudors since their arrival, one of the old lords who has taken my Lord Cromwell's fall as his own advantage. He was made a baron at the last round of ennoblements, and he is Lord High Admiral.

His house, Chenies Manor, is much changed from when I was here before. Then, I was with my sister-in-law Anne, on the progress we made to celebrate the arrest of Sir Thomas More, when Anne was at her greatest peak of success. If I believed in ghosts, I would be haunted by my younger self and by Anne and George – all three of us supremely confident in our looks, our charm, our wit, and our future. Now, a fifth queen and I ride under the great red-brick archway to the inner courtyard, and there is no Queen Anne waiting for me on the great stone steps before the open double doors, but Lady Russell, beaming with pride, richly dressed waiting to welcome us.

She is rightly proud of her house, built in the modern fashion with soaring gables and high chimneys. I take it that Lord Russell has been given a brickyard among his other rewards, for the house is a palace with great gable ends of red-brick triangles without windows, like a fairytale castle. She takes us to the beautiful pavilion in the garden, where we have views over the parkland, newly enclosed for hunting and stuffed with deer, should the king choose to shoot at them as they are driven towards him. While the king rests in his rooms and complains to Lord Russell about the Scots king, who is poisoning his mind as his ulcer poisons his body, Lady Russell has wine and sugarplums served to Kitty and tells us the gossip from London.

The Ottoman army has reached Budapest, and I think this must be a benefit to England, as the Christian princes will want England to join a war against the infidel at the very gates of Christendom. An appeal from Spain and France will take the king's mind off the insult from the Scots. But I have no one to discuss this with, my thinking hobbled by the company of ladies whose only concern is what this invasion will do to the price of soaps and silks. The only other person who might think strategically – Lady Mary – will not hear a word of criticism against Spain. She greets Lady Russell with particular affection. Her ladyship was in her Lady Mary's household when she was a princess, before it was diminished. They are both extremely careful to show the greatest respect to Kitty.

Lady Russell takes us up to our rooms, and I see that the royal guest rooms have a picture gallery running between the king's side and the queen's rooms, where the lovers might meet. We dine in the great hall, and there is music after dinner, conversation and singing; but the king orders there is to be no dancing. He sits with his leg propped on a stool, and even from a distance, we can smell the oozing ulcer, which has opened up again. He is a man rotting before he is in the grave, and when he calls for more wine and more pastries, I think he is a man knowingly destroying his own body, as he destroys everything around him.

Lord Russell makes the mistake of telling the king that thieves have been caught at Windsor Castle. The king bursts out in an extraordinary fury that the two poor men must be charged with treason and hanged for treason, because stealing from a king is an attack on his greatness. This is not thieving, this is treason, high treason, the men must be hanged, cut down while they are alive, their bellies slit and their guts drawn out. Lord Russell – who has sat on more than one treason trial, including the death of my husband – is not a squeamish man; but even he murmurs that since the king was at York at the time of the burglary, it was no attack on him personally, nor on His Majesty.

'Don't speak to me of York!' the king screams. 'Don't you dare speak to me of York! It's treason, too! That's treason to say it!'

All the musicians fall silent; the chorister warbles a note and then waits, open-mouthed. For a moment, I think: this is it! He has gone full-moon mad, and what are we going to do? We cannot overthrow him; we cannot disobey him. We have raised him all-powerful, and now he is beyond restraint, and none of us are safe. If you make a madman a despot, what are you to do when he goes insane?

'Your Majesty . . .' Lord Russell says helplessly.

The king waves furiously at Thomas Culpeper and Thomas Seymour, and they rush to his side, haul him to his feet and, half-dragging, half-lifting, get him out of the room.

Lord Russell, white with shock, turns to Kitty. 'I am so sorry, I did not mean to offend . . .' he starts.

Kitty is as frightened as a choirboy; she is open-mouthed like him.

'No offence was intended,' Lady Russell intervenes, smiling at the queen and at Lady Mary. 'No doubt the king is weary from his long ride. Shall we all take our leave, Your Majesty? Shall we say goodnight? And I shall see that the king has a late supper; some good food and wine will restore him.'

'Yes . . .' Kitty stammers. 'Goodnight, Lady Russell, Lord Russell. Thank you for your hospitality.'

WE THINK THAT Thomas will not be able to get away, that the king will gorge himself in his bedroom and want Thomas as a bedfellow to listen to his ranting before he sleeps. But at midnight, there is a light tap on the door from the gallery, and Thomas slips into the room.

He looks grim, and she is pale and strained. They cling together like children escaping a terrifying ordeal. They say nothing for long moments, and then he pulls back and looks at her face.

'Is he asleep?' she asks.

'Dead drunk,' he replies.

They do not speak another word. He leads her to the bed, and I turn my chair so that the high back shields them and I am facing the locked bedroom door. They are quiet, a few whispered words and warm kisses; I hear her sigh with pleasure and the susurration of her nightgown being raised. I hear him make a little wordless exclamation of longing and then delight, and then I hear him sigh. They don't swive so much as melt together, and I find that I am breathless as they are, my cheeks burning, my body yearning. It is five years since I felt a man's touch, since I heard the quiet whisper of words of love breathed against naked skin. Five years, but even before then, I was never touched as Thomas Culpeper silently touches Kitty, and I never sighed as she does, against his shoulder, muffling a cry – just one – as she finds ecstasy.

In silence, I wait for the chime of midnight from the clock on the red-brick tower before I whisper, without rising from my chair: 'It's time to go.'

I hear them breathe together, as if awakened from dreaming, and when I turn my chair around they are like creatures entranced; she is tying the cords of his cape, he has his hands on her waist, drawing her to him. Her hair is tumbled down, her nightgown pulled from her shoulders, her neck rosy with the flush of desire, her eyes green as a cat's.

'He has to go,' I remind them.

They are far beyond words; they cannot even say goodnight. She lifts her face to him, and he kisses her softened mouth. She clings to him as he holds her. I think I will have to peel them off each other, one tendril after another, like bindweed.

'You really have to go,' I tell him.

Gently, he puts her from him. 'Perhaps tomorrow,' he whispers. It is the first time I have ever heard him think beyond the present moment. They are starting to want more than the intensity of now, than the moment of intimacy – they are starting to want a future.

'Yes, yes, I have to see you tomorrow,' she tells him.

'If it is safe, if it is possible,' I say.

I take hold of his hand and draw him away. She leans back against the wooden bedpost, as if she cannot stand if he is gone. Gently, I push him out of the door and lock it behind him.

'I love him so,' she says simply.

Gently, I guide her back to her bed, and put her between the rumpled sheets. She turns her head till she finds the place where he laid his head and she puts her face beside it, as if to inhale the scent of him as she sleeps.

'Goodnight,' I say.

She cannot speak, she smiles as if she hears his voice, sees his face. I take her candle and I sit by the fire until she sleeps.

I never thought I would see a true love, a love as green as a willow, in this arid court. I thought I would steer her through the hazard of courtly life and bring her safely to widowhood, bitter, wiser, and richer. I thought that court would spoil her and enrich her. I never dreamed it might transform her into a creature as beautiful as a swan, paired for life.

I, too, am changing. I never dreamed that I would come through this cold-hearted court, through the valley of the shadow of death, to believe that love matters more than power. The love that we offer to the king is false coin. The love that he promises to one favourite after another is worthless, too. The king only loves himself, and he loves himself madly, without restraint. The court is a flock of starlings, stripping everything it can peck. But I walk through this battlefield of warring desires as if spring is greening all around me. I have lived in a deception all my life; I have never had a mouth clean of lies – but now, I believe truly. I believe in something that rings true: I believe in the redeeming power of love.

Francis Dereham, having been quiet and at peace, a discreet beggar for occasional purses, now strolls into the queen's room while she is sitting with Lady Russell and the ladies after breakfast. The king is in too much pain to hunt, but he is taking a ride around Lord Russell's new park on a steady horse.

'Your Majesty,' Francis Dereham says, with his oily smile. 'I bring you a friend from our happy childhood, a friend from Norfolk House!'

I rise to my feet, dreading the introduction of one of the tutors, schoolmasters, or pages who seemed to have spent their time flirting with the girls, or one of the indiscreet cousins that litter Norfolk House. Kitty is watching him like a bird watches an approaching snake.

'Oh Alice!' she says in relief as a young woman comes in and makes a demure curtsey. 'Alice Restwold!' She leaps to her feet and kisses her on both cheeks. 'How glad I am to see you! What a long time it's been!'

She turns, smiling and pretty. 'Lady Russell, may I introduce my friend Mistress Alice Restwold. We were brought up almost as sisters in my grandmother's house, and I've not seen Alice since I left for the court!'

Yes, I think at once. So why are we seeing her now?

Lady Russell greets the young woman, who curtseys politely to her and then to the rest of us. Her manners are elegant, there is no reason to refuse her a place. I would just rather not add another pupil from that school of vanity at Lambeth.

'You can lodge with Catherine Tilney,' Kitty says. She looks at me. 'She can come to London with us, can't she, Lady Rochford?'

'Of course,' I say, feigning a welcome. Since the girl is introduced by Francis Dereham, he is sure to have told her that childhood friends are welcomed and will be well provisioned if they play their cards right.

Catherine Tilney takes Alice off to her room, and before dinner,

Kitty gives her a pair of gowns and a couple of hoods. They are the same height and build.

'We used to be bedfellows,' Alice says, admiring her reflection in the queen's long looking-glass. 'Together night and day.'

'That was a long time ago,' I say repressively. 'And Her Majesty is called to a different station now.'

'Oh, of course,' she says quickly, her gaze going from the new gown to my grave face, reflected over her shoulder. 'Her secrets are safe with me!'

'I should hope there are no secrets,' I say firmly. 'Nothing can be said in the king's court that cannot be said to the king himself. And nothing can be said that would displease the king.'

'No, no,' she says again. 'You can rely on me, Lady Rochford. I'm very glad to be here.'

'You're very welcome,' I lie.

WE STAY AT Chenies for several days, and though Lord and Lady Russell are extravagantly generous hosts, the king's temper scarcely improves. He is a *Zeus Xenia* who demands godlike hospitality for merely arriving at their door. They lay on hunting and fishing, and they lose money to him playing cards every evening; but the insult at York burns in his belly and makes him belch after every enormous meal. I can see the same strain in Lady Russell's face that I see in my mirror every morning.

I have some sympathy for her. For her husband, Lord Russell, a couple of days of feasting and driving deer towards the king is amply rewarded by the wealth that he will skim from England as a trusted favourite. But Lady Russell, who has to supervise the household, provide the entertainment, simulate admiration and even desire for an impossible guest, it is thankless work. I see her glance at Kitty with genuine pity: she knows that to be a queen to a sick and dying king is no way to spend young womanhood.

'D'you think she might get with child?' she asks me. My heart plunges at the thought that for the first time, I think the answer might be 'yes'.

'There's no reason why not,' I say firmly, denying the reality of an ill-tempered, sick man who wants to be a father at fifty.

'It's the only thing that would make him happy,' Lady Russell says ambiguously.

This is a woman who reported to Thomas Cromwell just as I did. She learned spy-craft from him, as I did. She knows how to hear meaning in silences, what words would fill the gaps in conversation. She can make a casual comment and note the reply – just as I do.

'Yes, she delights him.'

'And in the future – would she be kind to Lady Mary . . .?' She lets the question trail off.

I could smile that we once thought the Spanish party was defeated and Lady Mary's last defender dead. Yet here is another, quietly working for her. 'The queen loves all her stepchildren,' I lie.

'Would she speak against a French marriage for Lady Mary?' she whispers. 'I know Lady Mary would rather stay in England than be sent abroad. And she would be a good stepdaughter to the queen if she could stay?'

I see, this is how it will be for me; I will be the advisor behind the throne of the widowed queen. I will keep the balance between the Spanish party for the old faith and the reform party for the new. Kitty – who could not care less either way – will be guided by me, so that we gain the most power and benefit from whichever party is on the rise.

'Are you sure that is Lady Mary's wish?' I ask. 'Did she ask you?'

She is far too well trained to name her principal. 'We who love her must wish for her to stay in England,' she says carefully. 'We would not want her to go to a country like France, without friends. But I fear that some of the king's advisors do not think of her happiness.'

'Oh we do,' I say reassuringly, wondering how long it will take for my words to reach Toledo. 'The queen is the best stepmother that Lady Mary could have. If she were crowned queen, she would take Lady Mary as her first lady and most beloved daughter.'

And that's our price for Lady Mary to stay in England! – I could almost laugh aloud. That's your stake in this gamble! You support Kitty's coronation, and her inheritance as dowager queen and her position as queen regent, and in return we will prevent Lady Mary's exile now and we will see her restored to the line of succession after the prince.

Cromwell-trained, Lady Russell betrays no pleasure that we have made an agreement.

'I am so glad the weather has been so fine for your visit,' she says.

'The queen has enjoyed your gardens and parkland,' I say. 'A most beautiful setting for a beautiful house.'

Kitty impresses me in these last days of the progress at Chenies. I start to imagine her as a young dowager queen. Exquisitely dressed in her hunting costume, she stands beside the king as he sits on his bowman chair and shoots deer that are driven towards him, and her pity for the terrified creatures and her disgust at their agonising deaths never crosses her pretty face. She does not mount her horse until the king has been hauled into his saddle, so that she is never above him, looking down, so that he never feels that he is old and slow. She never shows a moment's impatience when the horse staggers under his weight, when he is pale and bad-tempered, she says that she is tired, how exhausting the day has been! She only dances when he asks her to lead out the dancers, and even when the music sets everyone's feet tapping and the man she adores is on the floor with another girl, she sits beside the king and tilts her head to hear his new complaint over the poor quality of the music, and how he was the best dancer in England.

When he comes to her bed, dragging his stinking leg, she smiles in welcome and ignores the men who help him mount into the high bed. She looks straight past Thomas Culpeper as he gently lifts the king's bandaged leg, and she smooths the richly embroidered coverlet over the mountain of the king's belly and does not turn her head, not even by a fraction of an inch, from the stink of his rasping breath.

She knows as well as I do, that if she and Culpeper happened to make a child on that one, irresistible time, then she has to bed the king for the rest of this month, so that he thinks it is his. Culpeper's seed has to be followed by whatever the king can squeeze out, so that any baby can be named as royal. I don't have to tell her this. These are the politics of the stable-yard, of the hound kennel. This is about breeding, not love. It is dirty and ordinary and unconcealed, and we set to it like kennel masters.

As we call at Windsor on the way to Hampton Court, I think: we won't have to do this for long; the king is dying by inches. Every day, he does less; all he maintains is his enormous appetite, and as he belches and farts and sweats from every pore, it looks as if his digestion is breaking down, too, and foul juices and stinking gas are oozing out of his skin.

I think of the Seymour expectation of a regency in the spring, my alliance with Thomas Seymour, of the promise from Lady Mary's supporters and the Spanish party to support Kitty, of the Howard army that is quietly mustering more men, and I know I am prepared. I really doubt that the king will get through Christmas. Kitty will be widowed in the new year.

## HAMPTON COURT, AUTUMN

### 1541

WHEN WE HEAR of the death of the king's sister, Margaret Tudor the Dowager Queen of Scotland, I think it is an omen for her brother, our king. Margaret was his senior by only two years, the nearest in age of the family of four, the one most like him in her impulsive defiance and relentless optimism. Now, he is the only one left of the four Tudor children – the last living child of Henry Tudor, the self-made king.

Surely, he must feel this! He must have a sense of his generation passing, of his own mortality. But he does not even order the court into mourning; we do not wear black for the last Tudor princess of her generation. He hugs his anger to himself and denies death, as he always does. He cannot forgive her son's snub at York, or that she kept Scotland proud and independent when she was queen regent. He blames her for dying – for bringing the thought of death into his mind where even to speak of his death is illegal. In life, he envied her as a rival Tudor. In death, she is immediately forgotten. Nobody even remarks on the loss of Princess Margaret Queen of Scotland; except her daughter, poor Lady Margaret Douglas, trapped at the court of a vindictive uncle, still unmarried, still courting Charles Howard in secret in hidden corners.

She will get little comfort from him. Charles Howard is a young man with a light heart and a lighter understanding. In her secret grief for her mother, Lady Margaret turns to her friends, the princess Lady Mary, and Mary Howard; and the three of them refuse to dance for a week and absent themselves from hunting to pray for the soul of the Tudor queen. The ladies of the queen's room wordlessly give Lady Margaret field forget-me-nots, stems of rue, and little silver crosses. We all know that there is to be no word spoken at the Tudor court; but we sorrow with her.

Nobody even asks why the death of a royal queen should go unmourned, unrecognised by her home court. Nobody asks why we cannot speak of death. But I believe it is the conundrum that my father identified: how shall a man completely absorbed in himself ever imagine that he could be no more? How can a man who imagines himself as half a god think of his own mortality? How can a man, so vested in his material life, so heavily corporeal, imagine the death of that thick body?

The king cannot grieve for his sister; he cannot even acknowledge that she is gone. When someone he loves has died, they have – for him – abandoned and betrayed him, and the only way he can bear their loss is to persuade himself that they were never really there at all.

As if to insist that he is a young man, not an old one and the last of his generation, as if to be as young as his child bride, the king declares that instead of a service of mourning for his dead sister, we will hold a service of thanksgiving for his young wife. To make it blindingly clear that he is not thinking of the sister he has lost, he chooses All Hallows' Eve to celebrate his young queen – as if her youth and beauty can exorcise ghosts.

'Is he going to announce my coronation?' Kitty asks me urgently, as she dresses in one of her progress gowns of cloth of silver. She will wear the gown with Tudor green sleeves and a green hood. 'Is he? And what should I do? What do I do when people give thanks for me? Is it like a toast – do I return it and say a prayer to reply to them?'

'I don't think so,' I say, smiling at the thought. 'No, it's not like a toast. I think you should lower your head and close your eyes as if you were praying, too.'

'Are you sure?' she asks earnestly. 'You know I like to do things exactly right. What did any of the others do? What did Jane Seymour do?'

'He never held a service for thanksgiving for Jane Seymour,' I say and watch her face light up at a greater honour than a queen who went before her.

'He didn't? Not for sainted Jane?'

'No. This is special for you. You will pray when everyone prays, and at the end of the prayer, rise up and curtsey to him. Very low.'

At once, she calls for a chair, and I have to be the king in his gallery, and she is the queen, with her maids-of-honour and the ladies-in-waiting as congregation. 'No giggling,' Kitty says sternly. 'We have to get this right.'

Alice Restwold is the priest, and she says: 'La la la,' for the prayers and the end blessing, and then Kitty rises and turns to the gallery, where I am the king. She curtseys to the ground before me.

'Quite right,' I say. 'And watch for him beckoning you to his gallery. He might want you to kneel before him in fealty or kiss his cheek.'

'But which?' she demands. 'How do I know which?'

I show her the gesture with his hands out that will cue her to kneel and put her hands together in prayer before him, and the outstretched gesture that invites her to kiss his cheek.

'Shall I wear my hair down?'

'She always wants to wear her hair down – ready for bed,' Alice Restwold jokes, and everyone laughs but Kitty, who waits solemnly for my decision.

'Yes,' I decide, thinking that it will look like a coronation. 'Coronet on and hair down.'

'Is it going to take very long?' she asks. 'Is it instead of usual mass or as well as it?'

'Probably as well,' I say. 'But no worse than Good Friday or the Easter services. No longer than that. You'll be seated, not kneeling. It can't go on too long, because the king . . .' I break off. There is no need to say that the king's attention span has shortened and he cannot bear to spend too long anywhere but the dining table. His bowels move unexpectedly; he sometimes farts loudly and has to be hurried to the stool room. Nobody needs to tell the preacher or the celebrant when the king is getting bored; they keep a wary eye on him and speed up the service or cut the sermon at the first sign of restlessness.

'And you all wear my badge.' Kitty turns to her maids-of-honour. 'And pray in thanksgiving for me.' She looks sternly at Catherine Tilney, who looks ready to giggle with Alice Restwold. 'You will give thanks for me! You of all people should be glad I'm queen. Nobody else would employ you – God knows.'

## HAMPTON COURT, ALL HALLOWS' EVE

## 1541

WE WAKE EARLY, and Kitty has a bath in the great royal bath in Bayne Tower. The tub is big enough for the king, huge for a slip of a girl like Kitty, and she allows her favourites, Alice Restwold and Catherine Tilney, to plunge in with her in their bathing shifts. The three romp in the hot scented water, splashing each other and holding their breath and going under the water, until I insist they come out and wrap up warmly to run back to the queen's rooms and help Kitty to dress in her cloth of silver gown.

When we have her sleeves laced on and her green silk shoes on her stockinged feet, we stand her before the mirror and comb the waves of her bronze hair over her shoulders and put her little coronet on her head.

'Should be a crown,' she whispers to me.

'Perhaps he'll announce it today.'

We line up. In strict order of precedence, Lady Mary will go behind her stepmother, Lady Margaret Douglas behind her, and then all the ladies-in-waiting in order behind them. We file to the Chapel Royal, and Kitty curtseys to the king in his gallery, and we sit before the altar, and the service begins.

The Bishop of Lincoln leads the service and prays for all the departed and all saints and especially gives thanks for the good life that His Majesty the king leads with the queen . . . and hopes to lead, he adds sonorously, in case All Hallows' Eve makes us think that the king might be mortal. I am hoping that the herald will announce the coronation; but the service goes on through the usual collects for the day, and though the sermon praises the king and queen as peace-bringers to the north of England, the king's confessor does not seem to have been instructed to hint at a coronation for Kitty.

Of course, it suits the Seymours if she is not crowned, especially if the king dies soon. Easier for them to create a Seymour regency if there is no crowned Howard queen. It suits the Spanish party, too – a blood royal princess outranks an uncrowned commoner wife. All of them must hope that the king dies before Kitty conceives and is crowned.

If I could be sure that the king would not see another Easter, I would even think it worth the risk for Kitty to pretend to a pregnancy to win herself a coronation. Anne would have dared to do such a thing – but Anne had courage that none of us know. Anne could have sworn she was pregnant and wept at the deathbed with a pillow strapped inside her gown. Even Jane Seymour would have done it, if she had been ordered. But Kitty is too young and has none of the steely Howard ambition, nor clever brothers. She would betray herself; she is not yet fully a courtier with two faces.

Finally, the service is over, and Kitty turns to the king's gallery and sweeps a deep graceful curtsey to show her gratitude for the honour. He kisses his hand to her, a pretty gesture, and she smiles radiantly. Then she leads the way from the chapel back to her rooms. We will change our clothes and wrap up to walk in the autumn gardens and beside the river before dinner.

We celebrate All Hallows' Eve with a little masque of the boggarts, black dominos over our usual gowns and monster masks. Thomas and Kitty manage to steal a dance together; he holds her closely, and her eyes behind her mask are green with desire, and nobody notices them among the bobbing heads of deer and cuckold horns and antlers.

The king's pain is eased with a constant supply of tumblers of wine, and at unmasking, when Kitty is discovered dancing with Alice Restwold, he exclaims that he had no idea who was who, and that it reminds him of just last year or the year before, when he danced with all the ladies and no one would ever have known him; but that he was the best dancer, and the only one who danced all night.

He says that next year, we shall have a grander masque, and he will lead Kitty out to dance in a minotaur mask. She holds her shoulders very still so that she does not shudder at the thought of her monstrous husband in a monster mask. Edward Seymour catches the mood before the king gets maudlin over previous glories, by telling him that his son the prince has recovered from a fever, and the king goes to bed happy, with one arm on Seymour's shoulders and one leaning on Culpeper, and I think: and there is our regency council: the dowager queen's husband, Thomas Culpeper; the prince's uncle, Edward Seymour; the dowager queen's uncle, Thomas Howard; and the queen regent herself.

# HAMPTON COURT, ALL SOULS' DAY

## 1541

THE NEXT DAY is All Souls' Day and another long church service in the morning. The king is inattentive, reading papers and muttering with the old lords, Audley and Russell, over court business. He barely looks up when we curtsey and leave. We expect the king and the young men to come to the queen's rooms for an archery competition at noon, but only the young men come in, smiling and joking, with their bows on their backs. Thomas Culpeper and Kitty exchange a quick intense glance before looking away and talking vivaciously to other people. He makes his way over to my side.

'I couldn't come last night – tell her I would have been with her if I could.'

'I'll tell her.'

We are experienced courtiers; we speak of Kitty, but our eyes are fixed on Alice Restwold, who is miming a parody of an archer and making a circle of friends laugh at her closed eye and grimace as she aims the arrow.

'Is the king coming?' I ask him. 'Should we go to the butts ahead of him?'

'Something's happened. He's in a huddle with the old lords and Cranmer.'

'Not another rebellion?'

'Something bad. They're not happy. But they're very secretive.' His young face is gloomy. 'They flock round the king like hungry chicks around a poultry woman. Nobody under the age of ninety is allowed in. And they tell him only what he wants to hear.'

I don't laugh. 'We all flock,' I say wryly. 'Scratting and pecking in dirt.'

'Then how will anything change?' Culpeper demands.

We are both silent; we know the only way that there will be a change. And it is illegal to say it.

There is a knock at the door, and the king's vice chamberlain is announced. He bows to Kitty and tells her that the king is detained with business and will not come to the archery.

Kitty glances uncertainly at me. I give a little shake of my head, and she says: 'Then we'll wait till His Majesty can come. There's no competition without the greatest champion.'

'For sure, he is certain to win!' someone says, in the hopes that his comment will be repeated to the king.

The young men hand their bows to their servants, throw off their hats, and Kitty says that everyone may sit or stand as they wish. Thomas Culpeper goes casually across the room to her side and sits on a stool beside her great chair. Lady Mary takes a seat nearby with Mary Howard. Someone starts a riddle, and then someone enacts a charade for us to guess, and soon the young people are shouting with laughter. Nobody wonders what business has delayed the king but Thomas Culpeper and I – for everyone else, it is a holiday without the old men watching.

The archery contest is delayed this day and the next as it is so wet and cold. The king's business – whatever it is – continues to absorb him, and we see him only at chapel in the morning. He does not come to Kitty's bed, and he does not dine in the hall. His place is set at the high table, and the servants bow to an empty throne as if he were there, but his pages take dish after dish into his privy chamber, as if he were feasting in secret.

'Is he ill?' Kitty asks Thomas quietly on the fourth day of the month, when the king has not been seen since All Saints' Day.

'The doctor's not been called,' he says cautiously. 'I think it must be bad news from Scotland or the north. Two lords left court after All Saints', and Thomas Wriothesley went away today.'

'Have they summoned the Duke of Norfolk from his home?' I ask. 'If they need an army against an uprising, it'll be his.'

'Not that I know,' Thomas says.

'Will you put him to bed tonight?' Kitty whispers. 'Or . . .'

'I can't come,' he tells her. 'Don't look at me, Kitty. I can't say no to you when you look at me.'

'Look at Alice doing a mime!' I prompt her.

Obediently, she looks away from Culpeper's handsome face. He speaks to her profile, as clear as a cameo.

'I won't come to you until we know what's happening,' he says. 'It might be that he's ill again but denying it, and then he'll send for me in the night. Or it might be that he'll tell me what's happening. With the lords away from court, he might speak to me – I'll go to him now.'

'Oh, stay . . .' she whispers, looking away from him.

In reply, he takes her hand and kisses her cold fingers and goes from the room. Carefully, she does not look after him.

## BOLEYN TRAITOR

## HAMPTON COURT, NOVEMBER

## 1541

Something is wrong at court. I can feel the heavy air of a coming thunderstorm. It is not something in Scotland, nor far away on the northern borders. But there is something very wrong at court. I have lived my life here, and I can smell it, like the first hint of smoke in a burning building. I wonder: did Lady Mary use the progress to meet with northern Papists, and are the king's advisors following a trail that will lead to her door? Archbishop Cranmer is seen going in and out of the king's privy chamber – would he lead an investigation against the king's own daughter? Or is she so determined against the marriage with France that she was planning to run away again, and have they sighted a Spanish ship riding at anchor off the north coast? Or now that his sister is dead, is the king planning a war with Scotland to teach King James greater respect for his uncle?

But none of these plans would send the old lords away from court; they would come together with the king, to plan an invasion or a new plot or a cruel punishment; they would not go individually, one by one, to wherever it is that they have gone. And where have they gone? And why does nobody know?

Only I am uneasy. Everyone else continues as usual, which makes me think that I am mistaken; I have been thrown back to the time when I held a vigil for my missing husband, going round and round a quiet palace, opening doors on empty rooms.

I use my traitor skills, I see what horses are in the stable-yard, what lords have places set at dinner. I walk slowly past Dr Butts' chamber hoping to see visiting doctors, come to consult with him. I watch for royal messengers riding north with muster papers – but there is nothing that I can see out of the ordinary – but that the king will not eat or be merry with the queen he called his 'rose'.

I persuade myself I am worrying about nothing, but then, Lady Isabel Baynton, Kitty's sister, comes on the fifth day of November to complain that Francis Dereham has disappeared.

'Just left as rudely as he arrived,' she complains.

'Gone?' I ask her. 'Or just drunk in a whorehouse somewhere?'

'All his things are gone from his room,' she says. 'My husband says he took his pay for the quarter on Michaelmas Day so ungraciously that he half-thought he would leave then. He's not made himself popular.' She lowers her voice. 'It's not as if we'll miss him.'

'I'll tell the queen,' I say.

'I doubt she'll care,' Isabel observes.

I fold my lips on an angry retort. Is the woman so stupid that she has forgotten how he got his place, why we endure his company? Does she not remember that her own family forced him into Kitty's service, introduced as an old friend, because he had a cache of secret letters in the keeping of the dowager duchess? Where would he go which is a better place than this? Where else could he use the currency of indiscreet letters?

Francis Dereham's absence is barely noticed by anyone but me, but then Catherine Tilney and her friend Alice Restwold leave court suddenly, without notice to anyone. I stand in the doorway of their shared bedchamber, as if a precipice has opened up under my feet, I have such a vertiginous sense of the past. I open the chest for their gowns. It is empty but for a little scrap of ribbon. I smell the sandalwood of the chest, and I recognise this feeling of falling. This is the feeling of being powerless, of things coming undone, of a bobbin rolling along the floor, unspooling. This is the tug of a single thread that unravels the whole picture of a tapestry.

I dare not say anything to Kitty. There is no one I can speak to; there is no one I can trust with my fear that something is happening at court, something is happening again. I would talk with Thomas Culpeper, but I don't want to be seen on the king's side, where messengers come and go and the privy council seems to be meeting daily, at odd times of day, with the king attending as if it is a matter if great importance to him.

Every day, one of the old lords rides into the beautiful stables at Hampton Court and goes straight to the king's rooms without speaking to anyone else, without calling in courtesy to the queen. Every day, another man rides out. Thomas Wriothesley, who served under my Lord Cromwell and knows how to interrogate a suspect, is still absent, but Archbishop Cranmer, Edward Seymour, and William Fitzwilliam come and then go again.

ALICE RESTWOLD DOES not come back, and Catherine Tilney sends no word from wherever she is. I think I can safely send a note complaining of their rudeness to the Dowager Duchess of Norfolk. It will alert her to their disappearance, and maybe she will reply and tell me that she needed them for some reason, so urgently that they had no time to tell me they were leaving.

It is a sign of how anxious I am becoming that I am relieved to see the red flag with the white crosses of the Howard standard at the head of an armed troop clattering into the yard.

I run down the stairs to the inner court and greet my uncle as he is dismounting.

'What the hell is happening here?' he demands.

'Why have you come?'

He scowls at me. 'Summoned. Urgent. No idea.'

He throws his reins to his groom and strips off his leather gloves.

'I don't know what's happening. Something's wrong,' I tell him. 'But I don't know what.'

'Must be very secret if you've not managed to stick your nose in it,' he says rudely.

I break into a half-run to keep up with him as he strides towards the archway towards the main hall. 'Have you ever heard of a rogue called Francis Dereham?' he stops and suddenly demands.

My face is expressionless. 'Francis Dereham?'

'Some kind of usher or rogue or pimp at Norfolk House.'

'I've never been to Norfolk House.'

'A madhouse,' he says bitterly. 'Anyway, he's been arrested.'

'What for?' my mouth is dry with fear.

'Piracy,' he says. 'In Ireland. Months ago. They say he was bedding half the girls at Lambeth.'

'Surely not,' I say. 'Not under the dowager duchess' supervision.'

'Aye that's what we'll say,' he strides towards the stair leading to the privy chamber.

'I'll come to the Howard rooms later,' I say to his retreating back.

WHEN I GET back to the queen's rooms, they are empty of company. None of the young men are visiting us. Isabel Baynton, seated with her back to the window with the light on her work, is frantically sewing, setting stitches at random. She looks up when I come in, her mouth pinched and her eyes darting to the guard on the door behind me. The women sit beside her, all of them heads down, bending over their work. It is shirts for the poor, always a bad sign. Isabel nods towards the closed door of Kitty's bedchamber. I tap on the door and go in.

She is very still in the window seat, looking down into the garden where she played at a snowball fight and the yew-tree allée where Thomas Culpeper kissed her wrist nearly a year ago.

When she hears the door, she slowly turns her head, as if she does not want to see who is entering. When she sees it is me, she barely moves. 'I thought you were gone, too!'

I come slowly into the room. 'No. I'm here. What's happened?'

'I've been told to stay in my rooms. The privy council sent a message asking me to stay here. No company. No music. No dancing. Just wait. They didn't say why. They just said stay indoors. No company. No music. No dancing.'

I'm thinking furiously. 'They can't know anything,' I say. 'If they knew anything for sure, they'd be making arrests. They always make arrests quickly. So, they can't know anything for sure.'

'What could they know?' Her eyes are tragic. 'I've done nothing.'

In her loving heart, of course, she has done nothing. Over and over again, she has looked away from the man she adores; she has avoided his company. She has danced attendance on a man old enough to be her grandfather and never given him the slightest moment of unease. She has lived her life to please him; she has never said a word to contradict him. Since that one day of the snowball fight, she has been completely discreet, never showing her passionate longing for another man. She has laid with him only once, and that was in complete secrecy. She was praised in church as the comfort of the king's life, just last week.

'Is Thomas safe?' she whispers.

'I think so,' I say. 'Nobody's missing from the king's rooms. But Francis Dereham's been arrested for piracy.'

'Piracy?'

'From when he was in Ireland,' I say.

'That's nothing to do with me.'

'I know, I know. But suppose he talks about the money he left with you, about his promises to return?'

She shakes her head violently. 'No, no, no, no, no, the money was for safekeeping – it was not a dower. There were no promises to marry. I just held some money for a friend.'

'Not a dower?' I demand. I cross the rooms so we can whisper, head to head. 'Dower? Francis Dereham's money? You never said it was a dower before?'

'He asked me to marry him; but I never said yes,' she says quickly. 'We courted – I didn't know what I was doing. I was so young! It wasn't love – I know that now. It was nothing. When he went away, he asked me to wait for him and marry him properly when he came back.'

'Marry him properly?' I would scream if I had not locked myself to a whisper.

'In church. We weren't in church the first time.'

'But you made a promise? You were betrothed?'

She shakes her head. 'No, it was nothing. It was love-talk. Lies.'

'Did the dowager duchess know that you were courting? That you promised?'

'Yes,' she says miserably. 'But she slapped my face and told me to forget all about it, so I did.'

I think furiously: whatever she says now, there's evidence enough here to prove a precontract. Any fool could get Dereham to say that they spoke of marriage, they were courting, he gave her his savings to keep for him while he went to win his fortune, and he expected to come back to marry her. Enough there – plenty there – if the king wants evidence of a precontract to say that Kitty was handfasted and married. If the king wants the marriage annulled, he can put her aside and say she was married before, and this time, it will be true. You don't need to be a Cromwell to turn this into an annulment.

She's no duchess; she won't get a palace to buy her off, but it need not be a complete disaster. Kitty could come out of this quite well. She'll have to return her queen's fortune to the king, but she'll get a nice little house in the country; she could live secretly with Culpeper in half-disgrace until the king dies, and then they could marry. Nobody would care if they married then; she could even come back to court as Prince Edward's former stepmother with her new husband.

I won't even have to retire with her. The scandal took place before I was her lady-in-waiting, and I did nothing but keep Dereham's purse until they gave it back to him. If the king lives long enough to get this marriage annulled and marries another woman, he will ask me to be her chief lady-in-waiting. Who knows what he likes better than me? Who better to train a sixth wife?

'This could be worse,' I tell her. 'It's a pity that it comes out now.' I don't have to say: the secret nearly outlived the king. 'But it's still your word against Francis Dereham's. At the very worse, you can admit you were handfasted and accept an annulment. It's what Anne of Cleves had to do.'

'No!' She gives a little scream. 'I was not married to that . . . that . . . stock fish! I will not have people say that I married him! He was never of my quality, and I won't go from being Queen of England to Kitty Dereham!'

'You wouldn't have to live as his wife . . .' I start to explain but she can hear nothing.

'We weren't lovers!' she shrieks. 'Anyone who says it is a liar. Let me see the king! Let me go to the king! I will tell him there was nothing! It was nothing! I was a child playing at weddings. It was nothing!'

I grab her hands. 'Quiet,' I say sternly. 'Quiet, Kitty. You can't go to the king like this. You can't go out of your rooms like this. We'll get through this, and we'll get clean away with the other . . . we'll get away with everything; but you have to be quiet and clever and calm.'

'I'm not!' She shakes her head wildly. 'I'm not clever and quiet!'

'No. Not clever. But you can be steady and queenly. You know how to act queenly. You do it beautifully. Be a queen who has been insulted. A little bit hurt and a little bit proud and very dignified.'

I can feel the hammering pulse in her wrists slow to the forceful rhythm of my words. 'You will see the king,' I promise. 'You're right. You need to see him to explain. But not like this. He hates a scene when someone else does the talking. Just wait. Dry your eyes and wash your face and wait. When you look beautiful, when you can kneel in front of him and ask for a pardon; you can wear your hair down and ask for pardon. He loves you – it's not like getting rid of Anne of Cleves. He wants you as his wife. He loves you as much as he can love anyone. If everyone stays very calm and says nothing, then it might be that nothing is proved and we can go on as we are.'

I think: I calculate like a philosopher working on a theorem. This may work. Kitty will not face an investigation organised by my spymaster; it will be the slower wits of the old lords: Audley, Southampton, Russell, and the gentle archbishop Thomas Cranmer.

Someone like Thomas Wriothesley will invent whatever evidence the king wants, but the king will want evidence of innocence – he will have told them to disprove the allegations against his rose of England, the love of his life. We can trust to his hounds not to riot; they are well-schooled, they will follow the line of what he wants to hunt. They're not going to dig up something he doesn't want to see. All Kitty has to do is wait quietly, and this will blow over, like the fright we had last Lent that blew over by Easter, that the king would go back to Anne of Cleves.

'Where is my brother Charles? Is he with the king?' she demands. 'And has my uncle come? He'll speak for me!'

'Yes, he's here,' I say. 'Your family are all in the right place.'

'Tell him we will deny everything.'

I nod and leave her in her window seat.

I walk through the silent presence chamber. The yeoman on the door lets me pass without comment, and I stroll down to the stable-yard to see what horses are in the stalls.

'Where's Charles Howard's horse?' I ask one of the Howard grooms.

'Gone to Lambeth,' the man says.

Charles must have ridden home to tell the dowager duchess what is happening here at the palace.

I don't dare ask more. I look around; the stables are half empty.

'Where is everyone?' I gesture to the empty horse stalls.

'They've all gone to Lambeth,' he says helpfully.

My face does not change, but my heart skips a beat. 'To Norfolk House?' This can only be an inquiry into Kitty's childhood and a search of her grandmother's papers. I only pray that the dowager duchess had the sense to burn them.

'Nay – Lambeth Palace. Privy council is meeting there.'

I breathe again; I want to laugh and clap him on the back and give him a shilling. The privy council can meet at the archbishop's home and discuss anything they like. It makes no difference to me.

I nod and I walk round the empty yard and pat my own horse,

idle in his stable, and I think I will just stay here for a moment, to see if anyone else is coming or going. I have sunk to being the sort of spy that lingers in kitchens and stable-yards and eavesdrops: a common sort of gossip. I no longer have a patron to tell me which way the light breeze of royal favour might blow today; I no longer have the greatest lawyer in England to ask me to find the evidence he wants. I have to sieve the grist for any goodness and scan the midden for worthwhile scraps.

I can hear the wolfhounds baying with excitement and the huntsmen blowing their horns. A royal groom leads the king's horse out of the stable, and I step back into the shadow of the doorway as the king himself comes out, leaning on his master of horse, Anthony Browne. His great, broad-chested, big-boned warhorse comes up to the mounting block, and the king hangs on to the saddle and swings his good leg over his horse, Anthony Browne and a page pushing him upwards.

He is going hunting, but there is none of the usual bluster and boasting of men ready to enjoy a day's sport, and they're going out late in the day. Hardly anyone is riding with him, though the hounds are here, the huntsman here, the bugle for the hounds rings out in the cold air; but there is no bustle and excitement, no courtiers jockeying for precedence, no flirtations as ladies are lifted into the saddle.

The king is certainly not going out after deer; he can't ride to hounds as he used to do, he is using his hounds as cover for something else: a secret meeting in the woods. This can be nothing to do with the queen; it must be something else altogether. An inquiry about Kitty would be made by the privy council, in a formal meeting with a clerk taking notes. So something else is drawing the king out into the woods of Hampton Chase. Is he meeting the Spanish ambassador, pleading for Lady Mary to be spared marriage to France, or the Scots ambassador, pleading for forgiveness for his king, or some other secret that I can't even imagine? Kitty and her trivial childhood errors might be quite forgotten, we could be home and dry, while the king goes out into the drizzling rain to hunt other prey.

Sir Anthony goes ahead to the gateway to give the signal to the hounds. I watch the king follow them out of the yard, remembering him riding away from the May Day joust with his greatest friend Henry Norris at his side, and my husband George racing after them to his own death, Anne telling him to say she was innocent, innocent of everything, and I think: no, this is different. It is odd, but it is different. I must not panic; I must not let myself be haunted; I must not frighten myself with memories. These are different times; the king loves Kitty, and no one would care about a whispered promise to a fool like Dereham. They will hang him for piracy and forget him. The king does not want to expose anything about his young wife, and these are not the men to uncover well-hidden kitchen gossip. It is a different queen. These are different times, and I am different, too.

I go back indoors to tell Kitty the good news that the king has gone hunting for the day, that nothing is serious enough to keep him home. But as I climb the great stairs, I hear a bubbling cry and the noise of running feet. It is Kitty, crying and running along the gallery, hair down over her shoulders, blinded with tears, hands holding her gown out of the way, feet pounding. Isabel and a couple of fools are dashing after her and the guard on her door starting after them, uncertain what he should do.

I step out and catch her, as if we were playing a game.

She pulls away from me. 'No! You shan't stop me! I must see him! I must see him! He can't go! I can make it all right if I can see him.'

'He's fine,' I say. 'There's nothing wrong. Hush, Kitty. He's gone out hunting.'

Wildly, she turns to me. 'Gone hunting?'

'Yes! So, see, there's nothing wrong! He went with just a few friends and his master of horse. He looked well. There's no need for you to be distressed, Kitty. He wouldn't have gone hunting if he was upset.'

She stumbles. 'He's going!' she screams at me. 'Not hunting! He's going! He's left me like he left her – Anne! Like he left Jane!

Like he sent Queen Anne away! Like he left Queen Katherine! He's going, and I have to catch him before he leaves, or I'll never see him again! Like them! Like all of them!'

I feel an icy sweat prickle in my armpits and down my back. 'Hunting,' I repeat faintly.

Isabel Baynton shakes her head at me. 'Gone to Whitehall,' she mouths.

I wish I could think quicker. I know that my face is as blank as my mind when I look from Isabel's hopeless face to the distraught young woman. 'Well, anyway,' I say, 'you wouldn't want to be seen like this. No hood, and your hair a mess.'

'I have to ask for pardon.' It comes out as a sob. 'I let my hair down to ask for pardon. That's how it's done.'

'Yes, but not like this. And you've done nothing that needs a pardon. Let's go back, get properly dressed, and when he comes home after hunting or back from Whitehall, if that's where he's gone, you can see him.'

Isabel and I walk Kitty slowly back to her rooms, between us like our prisoner. I think that those in service to a tyrant are called to strange and dark work. I want to think that I am a master courtier, steering her through a crisis in her marriage, and this will all blow over. But right now, I don't feel like a master courtier at all; I feel like her gaoler, and I think that when you enter the service of a tyrant, you never know what work you will sink to.

We consider her gowns for the day ahead. I braid her hair into a neat coiled plait under her hood. She chooses a dark-blue gown with dark-blue sleeves and an overdress of bright blue: saints' colours. She wears her French hood of blue pulled forward to hide her hair, as modest as a maid.

As she is fitting the hood, I go out to the gallery where the windows face towards Hampton Chase. I see my uncle's standard, and he at the head of his men, riding out, as if they are going hunting, riding out after the king, and I think: there he goes, the old rat, saving his own skin, whatever else he is doing.

But what is the king doing? He does not come back that afternoon, and his horse is not in the stable next day, when Sir Edward Baynton, now silently regretting his marriage to Kitty's sister, tells me that the lords of the privy council are coming to see her at noon.

'I thought they were at Lambeth?'

'Their lordships meet where they please,' he tells me pompously, as if being a Baynton and not a Howard will save him from disaster if the king has turned against us.

'What am I to do?' Kitty asks me. 'What should I wear?'

'You'll wear your dark-blue gown with the sleeves,' I say. 'And you'll sit on your chair in your presence chamber.'

'I'll have all my ladies there,' she says. 'Standing behind me.'

'There are one or two missing,' I warn her. 'Lady Mary has gone to join the household of Prince Edward.'

She looks aghast. 'She's run away from me?'

'Just a visit to her brother,' I say. 'And it's not as if you like her. You wouldn't have wanted her in your rooms, with the privy council coming in. And she'd be no use – she'd be scared to death of them. Remember, they nearly arrested her for not signing the oath, and your uncle said he would bang her head against the wall.'

She brightens. 'Oh, did he? How funny! My uncle will come with them?'

I think of him, bent over his hunter's neck, riding out to meet the king somewhere in the forest. 'I don't know exactly who's coming,' I say cautiously.

'Do I curtsey?'

'They bow to you; you don't get up.'

She nods her head repeatedly, like it is on a spring: nod, nod, nod. 'I don't get up,' she repeats.

As soon as I have Kitty on her throne in her presence chamber, I glance out of the window. There is no black barge without a standard on the flagpole, waiting in silence, with the gangplank run ashore. It is different this time. They are not going to tell me to fetch Kitty's cape as she will feel the cold on the water. She is not going to be taken from her palace. It is different this time.

When they come, our uncle is among them, and I think this will help our case: the last thing the old duke wants is another Howard girl accused of unchastity – especially lovemaking under the beaky nose of his own stepmother in the family home. And Charles Brandon Duke of Suffolk has married a young woman who was betrothed to his son: he is predisposed to dismiss scandal, having been alongside it all his life. Bishop Gardiner, the churchman who hates reform, will be in favour of Kitty, who has no interest in religion; Thomas Audley, the lord chancellor, is a clever lawyer who will argue whatever the king wants as if it was Bible truth; and Archbishop Cranmer is a gentle reformer who would have saved Anne if he could. No one here can be thought of as a friend, but none of them are our enemies.

Kitty sits in her chair under the canopy with us ladies on either side, in her blue gown, looking very young and small but on her dignity. Always conscious of her appearance, she has taken my hint to be queenly, and her head is poised under her jewelled hood.

Thomas Cranmer speaks to her gently, respectfully. He says that Francis Dereham has made allegations which suggest that he behaved to her as a husband – did they exchange promises and court, when she was a girl?

'No,' Kitty says, widening her eyes. 'No. That's not true.'

Cranmer ignores this flat denial, so he must have evidence against her word. I am standing in frozen silence; but I listen intently to Cranmer's questions, like a scholar tracing the source of a quotation. I am the daughter of a translator: I think about sources, I am a spy; I can hear a voice behind the words, and identify him.

Clearly, they have interviewed Dereham himself, but also, I think I hear the echo of gossip from some maid in the old duchess' household. I am sure it is a woman who has told them the detail of kissing and late-night parties in the maids' rooms. Francis Dereham, boasting or fearful, would have forgotten strawberries and midnight feasts, but this girl remembers it vividly.

They say nothing about the damning evidence of the purse of a hundred pounds, and – absurdly, incompetently – they don't seem to realise that Dereham has been working in the queen's household under their noble noses, for the last month. This sounds like an old song, half-forgotten, that someone has sung to the archbishop in late-blooming autumn malice. He says nothing about Kitty's behaviour as queen. There's nothing against Dereham after he left for Ireland; there's nothing against Kitty since her marriage. Best of all, there is no suggestion of adultery against the king.

Standing impassively at her shoulder, I keep an expression of attentive concern on my face; but inwardly, I am grinning like a mask of *Thalia*. All they have is spiteful old gossip, nothing to set in the scale against the king's massive vanity. He will have told them to make a proper inquiry and clear Kitty's name. This is what they are doing. We are safe. This is going to be all right.

'None of this is true at all,' Kitty says clearly. 'And besides, my grandmother is very strict, and she agreed to my marriage to the king. How could such a thing be true?'

I note my uncle grimace as Kitty invokes the dowager duchess and drags in our family dignity; but none of them have any appetite to pursue the question or answer it.

'And where is my husband?' Kitty demands indignantly. 'Is he back from hunting? Does he know that you are asking these questions of me?'

'His Majesty has gone to Whitehall,' Thomas Cranmer says gently. 'He asked us to inquire.'

'He will have asked you to inquire into the wicked people who are making up these lies!' Kitty says, brilliant in her indignation. 'He would never have asked you to say them as true! What d'you think he will say when I tell him that you have brought these lies to me, said them to my face, in front of my ladies-in-waiting? That you have upset me? That you made me cry? Don't you think he will be angry?'

I see from the hidden anguish on Thomas Cranmer's face that he is very sure that the king will be angry, and whether or not they find any mud that sticks, the king won't thank them for this work. He has not told them – as he twice told Lord Cromwell – to get a marriage dissolved at any price and get rid of the unwanted wife.

I imagine they've had very ambivalent instructions: he will have told them to leave no stone unturned to find the truth; but they know well enough that the only truth the king wants to hear, is the one he believes already. Their task is to find out what he believes, and prove it as incontrovertible fact.

They mutter urgently among themselves, and then they apologise to the queen for disturbing her in her rooms, and they bow themselves out.

Kitty, flushed with triumph, turns to her ladies. 'They're shitting themselves,' she says, and the young maids scream with laughter.

THE NEXT DAY, Thomas Cranmer comes back again after breakfast to speak to Kitty and takes a seat beside her at the head of the table, like the father of a family, while the rest of us nibble sweetmeats at the far end and pretend we are not straining to listen. He does not look much like a man who is shitting himself: he looks like a kind old grandfather who is ready to hear a confession. I cannot think how to signal to Kitty that she should trust this kindness no more than the most frightening men of the kingdom who tried to bully her yesterday; but then I see her talking earnestly to him, and his whispered replies, and I think: not to worry – she will wrap him around her little finger.

At first, she has him dancing to her tune; but then I see him get graver and quieter, and now Kitty seems to be stumbling as she speaks, and now she is more and more distressed, and I can tell that she is frightened. I beckon to one of the youngest maids-of-honour.

'Go ask the queen if she wants some wine and water,' I tell her.

She looks across the room. 'I don't dare, Lady Rochford,' she says. 'He's raking her over.'

She's right. Thomas Cranmer is no longer grandfatherly; but has become the terror he can be in the pulpit. His fluffy white hair is standing on end, his bright-brown eyes never leave her face, and I can see him speaking urgently, insisting, overbearing.

Kitty blushes hot scarlet, and then she bursts into tears.

It is agony watching her being bullied into saying things that might damage her. She cries more and more, mopping her flushed face on her priceless sleeves and on her table handkerchief, and he does not give her a moment's pause but still goes on speaking, low-voiced, until she slides from her chair at the head of the table and collapses onto the floor in floods of tears.

Now I can interrupt, and I go forward to help her up, and he stops, gets to his feet, puts his hand with the great ruby signet ring on her head, and he blesses her and leaves her, the Queen of England, on the floor of her own presence chamber.

I had hoped that she was playacting despair; but even when he has gone, she continues to cry bitterly, her breath catching, her sobs getting louder. Her wet face is in the strewing rushes; she throws off her cream and pearl hood and spreads herself on the floor in a frenzy of distress.

She is not pretending. Over and over again, she says: 'My husband the king!' but nothing else is clear. At any rate, I think, nobody can say that she has confessed anything, for she is quite beyond speech.

I take her head onto my lap to let her have her cry, and I see, from the corner of my eye, the door close behind the skirt of a gown. Someone has gone running to tell their spymaster that the queen has collapsed in tears.

Isabel Baynton, her sister, gets awkwardly gets to her feet. 'I'd better tell my husband.'

'Tell him that she will die of grief if they try rough handling,' I say over her weeping. 'Who could doubt her innocence? Her heart is breaking at these questions. Tell him that they will have her death on their conscience. She is too fine and too pure to be accused of anything base. Ask him how they will answer to the king if they kill her?'

I see the tiny gleam of understanding, and she nods and goes out. I think – they'll never dare to push the king's little sweetheart into collapse. They have had a denial to their faces. Cranmer has frightened her into uncontrollable weeping, and none of this is evidence.

I raise her from the floor, still crying, and take her to her bedroom, sit her in a chair by the fire and dry her face and pat her hands with lavender water, as if she has fallen from a horse and is still shaken.

After about an hour of this quiet petting, there is a knock at the door, and it is Archbishop Cranmer again.

I try to refuse him, saying she is too distressed, but he insists on coming in, and Sir Edward Baynton is nowhere to be found to refuse him. So Kitty emerges from her bedroom, her hair tumbled down, still weeping, and Cranmer sits beside her, at the fireside in her privy chamber, and whispers in her ear.

I try to intercept, but he looks mildly at me with his gentle smile and says: 'I will not distress your royal mistress again, Lady Rochford. I am come to bring her comfort and promise that His Majesty will be graciously kind to her if she confesses the truth. Please leave us.'

With no support from her sister and no senior ladies-in-waiting to refuse him, I have to wait with her ladies in her presence chamber, hearing sounds of comfort and reassurance. But I think: nobody could accuse her; nobody who sees her in this despair could doubt her innocence. Even I believe in her innocence, and I held the purse that Dereham gave her in my safekeeping!

They stay together for the rest of the day, though the archbishop goes to the great hall for his dinner, and Kitty takes a little meat and some wine in her bedroom and lets us wash her face and hands and change her gown.

'You're doing very well,' I whisper to her, plaiting her hair and putting on her hood.

A sudden chill clutches me when I meet her gaze in her looking-glass and see the despair in her eyes. They really are going to kill this child if they continue hounding her. I warned them not to distress her, and I spoke more truly than I knew. She is too young and too fearful of the infinite power of the king to be able to bear this interrogation from his archbishop. She feels that she is under the eye of God and Man. She is not on a rack, but they are pulling her apart all the same.

Cranmer returns with a fresh ream of papers in his arms and a pot of ink and a sharpened quill and sealing wax and a candle. Surely, he cannot hope that she can speak coherently enough for a statement of innocence? And then I think: of course he does not! He will have it already composed in his own mind. This is him, wrapping it up neatly: a confession of small sins in girlhood and a general plea for mercy. I am so happy that I help him with the ink and the candle, and settle the two of them at the table in the privy chamber and order the ladies to bed, except for Isabel and I, who wait in the presence chamber.

It goes very quiet behind the great doors to the privy chamber, and I know, as surely as if I were a spy at the keyhole, that he is writing down an account, a completely fictional version of Kitty's petty misdeeds at Norfolk House, Lambeth, forgivingly transcribed.

At midnight, the archbishop comes out with a sheaf of papers, heavy with seals.

'Watch her,' he says to me, as if it was not him who drove her to hysterical crying. 'She is much distressed; but she will feel better for her confession.'

I dare not say: she has confessed to nothing but what you have named to her – this is a *quaesita* – an inquiry by torture. My spymaster Thomas Cromwell would have had every scrap of evidence from everyone else before he even spoke to her; and then he would only have allowed her to confirm what the king wanted to know. Thomas Cromwell knew every word of evidence that he wanted before he looked for it. But you – prurient as any old midwife – will have been raking through her linen and asking her about privy marks and hot breaths and dirty sheets, and now she is crying for shame at your disrespect in naming such things to her. You are a fool as my spymaster was not: you don't know what you want to know, and you don't know what to do with what you've found.

THE NEXT MORNING, the archbishop comes to our rooms and says that although she may not meet with the king today, she may write him a letter. She is to explain all that she has done and explain everything that has been said against her. This will serve as confession, vindication, and plea for pardon, and her husband the king will read it and forgive her.

Of course, she should have a clerk or secretary to write for her, and she ought to have a lawyer to warn her what not to say. But I remember Sir Thomas More warning Bishop Fisher to write nothing, to say nothing, and then Sir Thomas More was executed for saying nothing and the bishop was executed, too. So it makes little difference what she writes, as the archbishop has already heard the confession, set a penance, and is about to deliver the king's pardon. I carry sharpened quills and pots of ink behind the two of them, and I lay them on the table before her, as tidily as I used to prepare the writing table in my father's library.

I rest a hand on her trembling shoulder, and I say to Archbishop Cranmer: 'Would you like me to write for the queen, as her secretary, Your Grace?'

And the old fraud says: 'No, no, she shall write it herself.'

I think of her misspelled love letter to Culpeper and how she told him that she had taken such pains to write in her own hand. She is incapable of assembling her distress into coherent sentences; she cannot even form legible letters. If a fluent statement of confession comes out of this morning's work, we will all know that the author is the Cambridge University educated archbishop and not the girl who was taught nothing more than flirtation and dancing at Norfolk House.

It takes him the full day, but in the dusk of the early evening, the father of the church comes out smiling, with three pages of beautifully written narrative, and says to me: 'She will be easier in her mind now that she has made a full confession and asked the king for pardon.'

One glance at her anguished exhaustion tells me that she is not easier in her mind, and I am very sure she has not made a full confession; but I curtsey very low, bowing my head, and he gives me his signet ring to kiss.

'God's will be done,' I whisper, knowing that it is the king's will that is done and that Kitty's confession is whatever Cranmer thinks that the king wants to hear. He has the pages in his hand; I can see the writing as I curtsey. It is a work of art in the *cursive antiquior* – court hand – of official documents, elaborate and complicated.

I glimpse a sentence: *My sorrow I can by no writing express. Nevertheless, I trust your most benign nature will have some respect unto my youth* . . .

I could almost laugh. Kitty Howard never used a word like 'benign' in her life and would have no idea of how to spell it; she would make many attempts and certainly never imagine a 'g'. But the main thing – really the only thing – is that the Archbishop of Canterbury has turned this farrago of tears and confessions and downright lies into a plea of pardon to an old husband quite besotted with his younger wife. She can say that she is a sinner; she can say that she was misled and misguided; she can say that she was ignorant of the glorious destiny before her. She can even admit to a pretend betrothal, while he was marrying his third wife before this very archbishop; she can humble herself and say she is worthy of the most extreme punishment – and he will forgive her.

Francis Dereham has done the only good act in all his worthless life: diverted everyone from Culpeper. Since everyone has been looking at the windy braggart Dereham, with his loud assertions of intimacy with the queen when she was a girl, nobody has noticed the infinitely more desirable Thomas Culpeper who is her lover now she is a wife and a queen. The girl will not be blamed for being coerced by a rogue whose greatest ambition was to be a pirate. She will be accused of childhood folly, and they will completely miss the great love of her life.

I put her to bed with a bowl of soup and a glass of wine, and I tell her that it is all over. Tomorrow, she will be restored, and everything will be well. I speak to her gently, reassuring her as if she were a little girl frightened by a nightmare. In truth, we are all frightened by a nightmare, and none of us have the courage to name the monster that comes after us in our dreams. But tonight, I tell her that we are through the worst of it and that we will survive and be happy. I am certain that if we can only get through the next six months, it will be May Day and the king – the monster in the maze – will be long dead and gone.

She is paler than her fine linen sheets, the shadows under her eyes as dark as if they were bruises from a husband's fists. 'It's over?' she whispers.

'I think so. Two signed confessions – and best of all: no mention of Lincoln or Pontefract or York.'

She reaches up and puts her cold little hands over my mouth. 'We never speak of it.'

'Never,' I assure her.

'Is he all right?' she asks. 'No one has questioned him?'

'He won't speak of it, and no one is even thinking of him.'

Her eyes warm at the thought of him. 'As long as he's all right,' she says. 'As long as he's safe, I don't fear anything.'

IN THE MORNING, she is weeping again, asking why the king went to Whitehall without a word to her, and when will he return? I put her back to bed after mass in her chapel and breakfast and use this new burst of weeping as proof that they are driving her too hard. I tell Isabel Baynton that her feeble husband must do his duty as the queen's vice chamberlain and protect her. He must take sharp knives out of the presence chamber where we dine; he must keep her away from the high windows; someone must sit with her in the day and sleep with her at night. When they tell king of this, it will turn him to forgiveness at once. He will like to hear that she is losing her mind with grief, it gives him a wonderful part in a drama. He can come and forgive her when she is dying for his forgiveness in the greatest masque we have ever staged – this is *Cleopatra* and *Ariadne* and *Dido* but with a happy ending. I also remember Thomas Cromwell telling me when Lady Margaret Douglas was questioned: a woman cannot be questioned or even arrested if she is out of her wits.

'Everyone is saying that the king believes the marriage is not blessed by God,' Isabel says – reliably repeating and embroidering the most damaging thing for us. 'Invalid from the start, and will never be blessed with children. They say that Anne of Cleves should be restored as queen.'

'How invalid?' I ask Isabel, gambling that not even her sister knows if Kitty went through a betrothal with the fool Francis Dereham.

'How should I know?' she says irritably. 'I don't know anything. I wasn't even home at the time . . . and she wasn't under my control . . . or anyone's really.' Her voice dies away. 'I was only telling you a silly rumour. Of course, Anne of Cleves would never come back as queen.' She pauses. 'Would she?'

Even though Kitty has now made two written confessions and been promised forgiveness, we still are all but confined to the queen's side. We attend mass in her chapel, and we dine in her presence chamber and sit in the privy chamber. The yeomen are guarding the door as usual, but it feels that they are keeping us in. Nobody wants to test this and I use the fire boys' stairs to the stable-yard, which has been left unguarded.

I am hidden in the little doorway, hoping to see the king's big hunter nodding over his door, and everything back to normal, when I see Thomas Culpeper, high on his beautiful horse with a couple of the king's companions mounted and ready for hawking. He has his saker falcon on his glove: a beautiful creature with her breast mottled in pure black and white, her back as sleek and dark as black velvet. She wears a black hood of best leather, with a red feather on top, and the bells on her jesses ring softly as she shifts her bright yellow feet to grip tightly. His happy smile, the casual tilt of his cap on his curly head, his ringing laugh at something someone says to him, the bright colours of the autumn trees of the chase make the scene look like a tapestry of happiness named: *The Lover Goes a-Hawking*.

Nobody seeing Thomas Culpeper could think of him as anything but blithely light-hearted. His casual pleasure is a greater witness to his innocence than any evidence could be. As he rides out, he gives a casual greeting to the incoming horseman, Thomas Wriothesley, riding in with his clerk and groom. Wriothesley dismounts, throws his reins to his groom, and goes heavily up the stone stairs to the great hall.

I whisk around and up the fire boys' stairs, and I am seated in the queen's rooms, sewing in the presence chamber with the other ladies, before we hear his tread on the wooden floor outside the double doors. I rise and curtsey with the others when he is announced.

Thomas Wriothesley tells us he has come to speak with the queen alone, but I stay beside her and say very respectfully: 'Oh no, my lord.'

He checks. 'The archbishop met with Her Grace alone?'

So he knows about the archbishop's interrogation, so he may have read the first confession and then the second, which was half retraction and throwing all the blame on Dereham. He may have seen the letter to the king, begging for mercy, and he may know about the hysterical tears.

I smile at him as I curtsey, and I think – you've always been the vanguard, never in the front of the charge. You were the clerk my Lord Cromwell would send to double-check – never a lead inquisitor, but useful in support. Heavy-handed, a bully, the very man for the day after a confession, to make a guilty person vomit the rest, just when they think it has finished. Well, you're not doing that now.

'The archbishop is the queen's confessor . . .' I point out.

Kitty takes the hint. 'The ladies can wait in the presence chamber, but Jane will stay with me.'

I see by his quick surrender that he is not authorised to bully her. I guess from this that he thinks she could reconcile with the king and punish anyone who offends her now. He bows obedience, he smiles tentatively. Inwardly, I laugh inside at his cowardice as Kitty leads the way into her privy chamber and sits in the chair.

'Yes?' she says. The tears are in her eyes already. I hand her a handkerchief; she dabs at her eyelashes.

'I am tasked by the privy council with an unpleasant duty,' he says, falling into pomposity as men do when they are on weak ground.

'Yes?' she says, her face hidden in the fine linen.

'It is to inquire into your, er – your – er – it is to inquire, in short, into Thomas Culpeper?'

Thomas Culpeper, who just rode out hawking, as happy as his falcon?

I see the pearls on Kitty's hood tremble slightly as she flinches. 'Yes?'

'You know Thomas Culpeper?'

'Of course.'

'You and he were courting when you were a maid-of-honour to the former . . . to the king's sister Lady Anne of Cleves?'

'No.'

'People said that you were going to marry?'

'Who said?' she demands coming out of the handkerchief with sudden irritation. 'Because if it is Bess Harvey, it is because she was in love with him herself, and if you listen to gossip, you will hear no good of yourself.'

He is shaken by her burst of temper.

'Of course, it is the duty of the maids-of-honour and the king's companions to create good company,' I explain, as if he is so new to court and so ill-bred and ill-educated that he does not know this.

He flushes at the snub. 'And after your marriage to the king? Master Culpeper was a regular visitor to your rooms?'

'Of course,' she says grandly. 'The king visits me every day. His companions come too.'

'And during the progress . . .?'

I drop my hand to her shoulder. She feels like carved stone; she is stiff with fear. There is no way to tell her that nobody knows anything – they cannot know anything. If they knew about Lincoln and Pontefract and York, they would have sent a black barge from the Tower. This is an arrow shot into darkness by an archer of the second rank.

'What?' she shrieks. She leaps from the chair before I can stop her and stands before him, a diminutive beauty, puffed up like an angry goldfinch. 'What?' she demands.

'You locked your door,' he stammers.

As if I can see the privy council inquiry papers in my inner eye, I imagine Anthony Denny's carefully worded submission: that he tapped on the door of the queen's bedroom, and I told him that she was asleep, and he went away again.

'Of course we did!' I interrupt. 'In strange houses? In the north of the kingdom? We locked it every night.'

'At York?' he remarks.

I know from this that the council has not spoken to our chamberers or maids-of-honour. Lucy Luffkyn has not told that she tried the locked door at Pontefract with an armful of clean linen and was scolded.

'Of course,' I repeat. 'Do you not remember the confusion? The border lords? The pilgrims seeking pardon?'

'But when Anthony Denny came to announce the king's coming, the door was locked against him and the lights were out . . .' he says.

'He never told me!' Kitty counters.

'No, Your Majesty, you were asleep,' I tell her. 'I answered the knock and he told me to let you sleep.'

Kitty turns to Sir Thomas, her eyebrows raised. She lets the silence hang.

'Very well,' he says and bows low and goes from the room.

The door closes, we hear the sound of his riding boots on the stone pavers as he retreats.

Kitty falls into my arms and I hug her. 'And that's all he's got,' I say triumphantly. 'You did that beautifully. Just right. They've got nothing on Culpeper. They've got nothing more than that one night when Denny came to your door. Never confess anything. Never say anything about Thomas. They have no evidence. You did very well – but if they come back, and I cannot be with you, never say a word.'

'Nor you,' her joy at besting Wriothesley dies away. Her eyes darken with fear and her face pales. 'Nor you, Jane. Swear you will never say anything. Swear on your life that wild horses won't drag it from you.'

Even in our danger, I laugh at the exaggerated language of children's tales. 'My dear, "wild horses" have nothing to do with it. But I swear. We will never admit to anything, and Thomas won't either. We are safe.'

We spend the rest of the morning with one of the maids reading from the great Bible while we sew shirts for the poor. Kitty's needlework has been as neglected as her scholarly education, and the shirt she is hemming will have to be laundered before it is given to an almsman – it is stained with her blood from pinpricks. I am at peace; I have no objection to sitting here sewing. I think we have won and are certain to be released from the rooms tomorrow. The king will come back and command that no one is to ever speak of this time – his terrible ordeal – and it will be as if it never was.

Sir Edward Baynton is announced before dinner, and I glance at Kitty's sister Isabel and see from her guilty expression that this was planned, that she knew her husband was coming. I will get hold of her before dinner and remind her of where their interest lies: with

Kitty, not with the old lords who have failed in their conspiracy against her.

'Your Grace, your household is to move in a few days,' he says, bowing.

Kitty's face lights up. 'Are we going to Whitehall to join the king?'

'No,' he says steadily, with the air of a man getting through a speech he has rehearsed. 'Your Grace is to go to Syon Abbey, and there is no room at the abbey for all your ladies. You are to take my lady wife, your sister Isabel, and three other ladies-in-waiting.'

'I don't want to go to Syon,' Kitty says, like a disappointed child. 'I don't want to go there.'

Syon Abbey seems to have become the resort for royal ladies under a cloud. It's where Lady Margaret Douglas was sent when she was in disgrace; it signals the king's disapproval – but not condemnation. It is a discreet place for a punitive visit – but not a prison for interrogation. Royal ladies are detained – but not under arrest. Lady Margaret Douglas came back to court from Syon Abbey without a mark on her reputation. They must be pursuing a signed denial of the precontract and not simply forgetting all about it if they send us to wait at Syon.

'It is His Majesty's will,' Sir Edward says heavily. I can almost see him cranking open the doors of a heavy and obvious trap. 'Are you refusing to obey your husband?'

'Of course not.' She slips into a pretty curtsey at the mention of his name. 'Please tell His Majesty that whatever he wishes, I will do, of course, and that I will not know an hour of happiness until I see him again.'

Sir Edward's disappointment at his inability to entrap his own sister-in-law is embarrassingly evident to everyone, including his quicker-witted wife.

'Well, we shall have to pack,' she interrupts him, as if this is an ordinary movement of the court from one palace to another.

'Yes, indeed,' I say, to support the lie. 'Did you say in a few days?'

'No hurry,' he says feebly.

KITTY GOES TO bed saying she cannot understand that the king should turn so hard-hearted. Can he want to put her away as he did Anne of Cleves? Can he blame her for what happened in her childhood, when she was – in any case – forced against her will by an older man, in a house that allowed all sorts of unholy licence?

'You were forced?' This is a disagreeable new turn of the story.

'Yes,' she says. 'Francis Dereham persuaded and prevailed upon me and overcame me. I was nothing worse than a young and silly girl.'

'Did you tell the archbishop that Dereham forced you into a promise of marriage? You never told me?'

'You never asked me. But the archbishop asked me over and over. I said I couldn't remember.'

'This really matters Kitty,' I tell her. 'Is the archbishop saying that you were betrothed, against your will? But betrothed?'

She turns a mutinous pale face to me. 'I don't know! How should I know what he is saying? He just went on and on!'

'Because a forced betrothal is a way out,' I say. 'It's not forgiveness. But there are worse things that could be said against you. A forced betrothal is not your fault.'

'I wasn't betrothed!' she insists.

'The king's marriage to you would be bigamous, and set aside but no fault of yours and no insult to him. You get away with it. They dissolve your marriage and you retire to the country.'

'That would be dreadful,' she says flatly. 'My uncle would never forgive me, and my grandmother would beat me.'

'She couldn't beat you; you wouldn't have to live with her,' I start.

'No, no. That would be awful,' she insists. 'What's a precontract?'

It has been more than a week of interrogation, and she does not understand the accusation. I feel something like despair. How is she ever going to plead innocent when she does not understand the words they use? How is she going to manage a vulgar bully like Wriothesley if he speaks the language of the law courts to a girl who knows little more than the language of the nursery?

'When they say things you don't understand you should stop them. You don't want to agree to something by accident.'

She shrugs. 'So what is it?'

'A precontract is why the king put Anne of Cleves aside,' I say very carefully.

'She made him impotent,' she says firmly. 'That's why.'

'No, no, don't ever say that! They said that she had been married before – d'you remember? That her first marriage contract was not properly cancelled. So, she could not marry the king because she was married already?'

It is no good. I can see that the most simple words pass her by, as if I were explaining in Greek.

'They may be trying to prove that you were married, or at least betrothed, that you made promises to Francis Dereham to marry. If so, your marriage to the king was invalid and he will set you aside. But that's not treason. That's not adultery. He could put you aside, and you might get a nice house like Anne of Cleves and later . . . later . . . you could . . .'

'I wasn't married to Francis Dereham,' she says fiercely. 'I told the archbishop: Francis persuaded and forced me – I was unwilling. I was too young to know what to do, and he threatened me.'

'But obviously they've questioned him, and he's not going to admit to rape. He will say you were willing. And you kept his money safe for him as if you were a wife.'

'I didn't keep his money safe,' she says triumphantly. 'You did! If that's proof, then you were his wife, not me!' She shoots a sly little look at me. 'You needn't think I'm going to take all the blame! I'll tell them you kept Francis' money safe for him and then you got him a job!'

'Don't try to threaten me,' I say steadily. 'Your only hope is that I stay loyal to you and to Thomas Culpeper, too.'

At his name, her face crumples, and she pitches forward into my arms. 'Oh, Jane! How am I ever going to see him again?'

'If you get through this, you can see him,' I promise her. 'If you agree you were married to Dereham, then your marriage to the king will be annulled and you will be released. You could be free, Kitty!'

'I'd rather die than be Francis Dereham's wife!' she declares. 'Thomas would never look twice at me. A gentleman like him doesn't want Francis Dereham's leavings! He loves me as his queen. I'd rather die than say I was Mistress Dereham.'

WHEN I SPY on the stable-yard next day, I see my uncle's horse, and I go to the Howard rooms as they are taking his breakfast in.

'Sit,' he says shortly and waves me to a place at his table.

I am served eggs and beef and small ale. I find I have no appetite.

'Has she been swiving that mincing puppy who was so great with the king?' he asks me shortly. 'Have you been such a fool as to let her meet him?'

'What?'

'Spare me the May Day games. Just answer the question.'

'Who says so?'

'Answer.'

'No,' I say flatly.

'What's she been doing then? Snowball fights and dancing?'

'Yes. Snowball fights and dancing. Courtly love.'

'Again?' He scowls at me over a trencher of meat.

'It's a young court. Young men play at love. Yes.'

'Will she stick to that? Will you?'

I nod. 'Because it is true.'

'We're coming to see her after breakfast. The whole privy council. She'd better deny it and go on denying it in front of me, or I'll take her head off myself.'

'She will,' I say. 'If you stand by her, you'll see a Howard queen by Easter and one day a Howard-Seymour regency.'

He looks thoughtful. 'Not hungry?' he asks, with a glance at the crumbled bread on my plate. 'Go then.'

I GET OVER TO the queen's side unnoticed by going down the main stairs to the stable-yard and then crossing the yard to the fire boys' stairs. Culpeper's horse is in its stall.

'Not hawking today?' I say cheerily to the groom.

'He's meeting with the privy council,' he says proudly.

I keep my smile on my face as I run silently up the little stone stairs and through the presence chamber, the queen's privy chamber, and then into her bedroom, where they are clearing breakfast. She is dressed beautifully in a gown of dark-green velvet with a dark-green silk hood sewn with emeralds. It brings out the colour of her eyes.

'Good,' I say. 'You look well. The privy council are coming at any moment.' I lean towards her to whisper. 'They might ask about Thomas Culpeper.'

The colour drains from her face. 'But I thought it was all about Francis?'

'They know nothing for sure,' I say. 'You can say there were snowball fights and dancing, everything that everybody saw. Admit everything that everybody saw, but it was all – always – courtly love. They can know nothing that was secret. Just deny all that. He will. And I will, too, if they ask me.'

'They'll ask you,' she says suddenly. 'It was all your doing. You stood guard for us; you let him in.'

'No, I did not,' I say fiercely, wanting to shake her answers into her silly head. 'Because nobody let anyone in. He was not there. Nothing happened.'

'Oh! Will they question him?' she demands, suddenly agonised.

'They're bound to, but you can keep him safe. The king might forgive you, but he would never forgive Culpeper. You must deny everything.'

'I would die to keep him safe,' she swears. 'I must warn him. I must tell him to get away.'

'It's too late,' I say. 'The only way to keep him safe is by denying it all, completely.'

'I will,' she says. 'They know nothing. They can know nothing.'

THEY COME IN their pomp, with their staves of office and their regalia, a masque of authority in the pretty rooms. I make sure she has all her queenly trappings: seated on her great chair under the canopy, and we ladies are ranged on each side of her. In comes Archbishop Cranmer, half the House of Lords with him. My uncle the duke is there, William Fitzwilliam, Robert Radcliffe, Edward and Thomas Seymour, inscrutable, Lord Russell – who was our host at Chenies and now seems to tag on the end of everything – and Thomas Wriothesley, with four other lesser lords. They announce that they will meet the queen alone, and though she shoots me an imploring look, they do not allow me to stay with her.

Her ladies and I hover, uncertainly, in the gallery outside the door, where two yeomen of the guard stand with crossed pikes. I look out of the window at the royal pier and the barges. They are turned around against the tide, pulling on their ropes, facing downstream to the city, ready for a prompt departure. So perhaps this is to be brief and formal, certainly they have enough evidence to prove she was precontracted – whatever she says – perhaps they have come to formally tell her that the king is releasing her from their mistaken marriage.

If they agree that her intimacies and oaths with Francis Dereham amount to a marriage, then it really does not matter if she met Thomas Culpeper or not. If she was married to Dereham, she was not married to the king, so she did not betray him. If the inquiry is heading towards Culpeper, she will admit marriage to Dereham to save him. If I can explain this to her, she can confess to the lesser crime of precontract. She can confess to the marriage with Dereham, the dowager duchess can produce the letters that passed between them, I can witness to the purse of gold he gave her for her dowry, and we can all create evidence, as we did with Anne of Cleves, to prove a precontract. Then there was no royal marriage. Then there was no adultery. Then there is no wound to the king's vanity and no treason trial.

This is not the trial of Anne Boleyn – where one accusation was loaded on another to destroy her. This is the divorce of Anne of Cleves, where the offence was kept to the minimum necessary to release the king from marriage.

I cannot hear what is going on behind the barred doors, but it is not the simple denial that I promised my uncle, as it lasts all day. This is a bad sign; either they have put new reports to her – gossip from the maids or chamberers, which she must steadily deny – or, more dangerously, she is embroidering her simple denial with assurances of how she did not meet Culpeper, barely knows him, hardly saw him, that she did not give him a cap one Easter, that she gave him a cap but it meant nothing, he was not at all grateful.

All day, from breakfast, they are behind the barred door, and at dusk, my uncle comes out, his face twisted with fury, and says shortly to me: 'Go to the Howard rooms and wait for me there.'

I take one look at his face and I dare not ask to see the queen. A man in Howard livery is waiting to escort me, and my uncle's lord chamberlain admits me to the Howard privy chamber and fetches me a glass of wine and some sops. The servant stands by the door, apparently to serve me – but really so that I cannot slip out to check on the horses in the stable-yard or see if any barges have caught the turning tide downstream.

The duke comes in at supper time and says that I will stay in his rooms for the time being; the queen will be served by her sister. My clothes have been brought from the queen's side.

'I should be with her,' I try to say. 'I have work to do. I have to pack for her to go to Syon.'

'Others can pack,' he says dourly. 'You stay here.'

'But her jewels?'

'Anne Herbert has the care of them.'

'Has someone said something against me?' I ask, wide-eyed.

'Not much!' he says, with a bark of sudden harsh laughter. 'Not much at all!'

I look at him warily. 'Anything against me is against a Howard,' I say. 'Anything against the queen is against our house.'

He snarls like a dog. 'I don't need you to remind me of that,' he says. 'I have Edward Seymour to tell me that, or that hypocrite Gardiner, or that snake Wriothesley or any of the reformers, or Lady Mary's friends, or rival lords. There are many, many men ready to tell me that if the queen falls, we all do.'

'My reputation is as good as yours,' I say. 'Unsullied.'

He gets hold of both my shoulders in a hard grip, and he brings his face very close to mine. 'I asked you did she swive Thomas Culpeper and you told me "no".'

'I did. I will always say so,' I promise.

'Her grandmother says that she was free with that dog Dereham and with another poxed fool, Manox.'

'I don't know anything about that. It was before—'

'Exactly. It was before she ever met the king. So anything she did then does not hurt him.'

'It's better than that!' I tell him eagerly. 'If she was married to Dereham, then her marriage to the king is invalid and there is no adultery!'

'Tells me everything that this is the best outcome you can think of,' he says, his bitterness dripping from his words. 'Our second queen, for Christ's sake. Tells me everything that this is the best we can hope for.' He pushes me away from him. 'Tells me everything that you, the clever one, could not convince her, the pretty one, to admit to that one thing in time.' He steps back and slams the door.

I face the wooden panels and hear the key turn in the lock.

It is like the time before, but this time, it is different, I tell myself. This time, the duke my uncle is desperate to clear our names – all of us. He cannot throw the blame on Boleyns, who were Howards only by marriage. His own stepmother, Agnes, the dowager duchess, will be examined, his brothers and sisters, his nieces, his cousins, his nephews – his entire family have ridden on Kitty's train into places of power and sucked up great fees. All of us will be questioned as to how much we knew; all of us have to be exonerated and freed.

I spend an uncomfortable day in the Howard rooms. I cannot believe it is two weeks since we thanked God for the blessing of Kitty as queen. Now I am all but under arrest, and my uncle goes out early in the morning and comes back with Thomas Wriothesley. I am to meet them in the Howard presence chamber; Wriothesley has a paper and pen before him, as if I can be tricked into saying anything by a brute like him.

'It's about the queen meeting Culpeper,' my uncle says abruptly. 'You'd better tell us what happened. And tell us the truth. Everything you know.'

'I don't know anything about it,' I start. 'Of course, she met him in the ordinary way.'

'We're way beyond that,' my uncle spits. 'You can tell us about the cramp rings, about the cap and the backstairs and the secret meetings on progress. And you can tell us if you saw them swive in the stool room, for God's sake!'

I am stunned with shock at this terrible list. It takes me a moment to realise that there is too much detail for it to have come from malicious gossips such as Catherine Tilney or Alice Restwold. These are meetings that only Thomas, Kitty, and I know about. Nobody was there but us three in the stool room. Nobody but me saw her put her cramp ring on his finger like a wedding ring, I saw him kiss it.

My uncle must see these thoughts on my face; my courtier mask has slipped.

'Yes, we know it all,' he says coldly. 'Both of them have confessed – sung like blinded thrushes. You're the last one to hold out. Bit of a forlorn hope, Jane. Both of them have blamed you, for it all. They blamed you before each other. They both say that it was you who made the meetings, found the backstairs, urged Culpeper to come, and persuaded her to love him.'

'No!' I say, shocked out of silence. 'No, it was not like that.'

'So, what was it like?' Wriothesley asks me. 'Because it sounds very like treason, and it sounds very like adultery, and it sounds like you were pimping her out, the Queen of England in the royal stool room! So, if you want to get out of this, with your head on your shoulders, you'd better tell us what it was like.' He lifts the pen and dips it in the ink and bares his teeth in a smile at me.

'For Christ's sake, Jane,' my uncle says quietly. 'Let this start and stop with the queen and Culpeper. None of the rest of us need to be blamed for their mistake. Your loyalty is first to your family.'

'Kitty is family.'

'Not any more.'

I take a breath. I turn to Wriothesley, knowing that he will grasp this quicker than my angry uncle. 'If she is precontracted to Francis Dereham, as you have proved, then as his wife, as Mistress Dereham, she's not the wife of the king. Whatever she did with Culpeper – *whatever* she has confessed – it's not adultery against the king.'

His smile never wavers. 'Oh, we're not bothering with the precontract now,' he says. 'Why should we try to get her off? We won't even try to get you off. You'll have to save yourself.' He gestures to the blank sheet of paper. 'Save yourself,' he recommends to me. 'When did the queen first tell you to fetch Thomas Culpeper to her?'

I speak slowly, so that he can write it down word by word, and when I hesitate, once I am choked with tears, my uncle turns on me and says: 'Get on, get on,' as if I were an unwilling horse checking and shying away, a warhorse tearing up the tiltyard ground, backing away from a joust.

I get on. I tell them of the snow princess; I tell them of the little gifts. I tell them how she sent dinners to Thomas Culpeper when he was ill, how he came to her when he was well again. I tell them how we all three found ways around the court and ways around the palaces on the progress north and back again, so that they could meet, so that he could kiss her hand, so that she could tell him that she loved him.

'And did he swive her?' my uncle demands. 'Yes or no?'

'I sat at a distance,' I say. 'I had my back to them. One night, I fell asleep. I can't say.'

'Are you telling me that the young sod picked a lock, climbed the stair, got into her stool room, and then spent the night talking?' he jeers.

I can't say it; I can't bear for him to speak of it. I think of it as it was: love, true love, the ideal of courtly love. Culpeper loved the young queen, as *Lancelot* loved *Guinevere*, with a passion that took them outside the normal rules, with a love that few people ever know. But they had it – they risked their lives to be together. I risked my life to see them together. It was love. It was true love.

'Shall I put down that they fucked or not?' Wriothesley asks, bored.

I nod. Put it down. It doesn't seem to matter.

I CAN SEE FROM my window the royal barge that is to take Kitty to Syon Abbey. They have shuttered the sides so that no one can see her, so whatever gown she has chosen is wasted. I hear the slam of the guard presenting arms and the opening of the garden door, and then I see her. From my window, high above, I know it is her. They hurry her down the path and down the pier under a muffling cape so that I cannot see what she is wearing. But despite their hurry, she is doing her queenly walk – I have seen her practise it a dozen times. I imagine she has practised this exact walk: from the garden stairs, through the garden where she played at snowball fights only last winter, to the pier where she took the barge for her triumphant entry to London in the spring.

They try to rush her on board, but she does her queenly walk all the way up the gangplank, and then they cast off, and I can hear, even through the window, the beat of the drummer making the time for the rowers, and they lean on their oars and pull the barge into the centre of the river, where the current picks up and takes them downstream, and she has gone.

The wake from the barge ripples away to nothingness among the swaying reeds of the bank; the waters close over her passing. A heron flaps on broad wings across the river and lands, knee deep in still water and looks down at its own reflection.

An hour or so passes. I find a book on heraldry – my uncle's library of books are all about his own importance – and I am seated in the window, turning the pages, when I see that the Howard barge has come to the pier and swung round, to face downstream.

The double doors of the room are thrown open, and my uncle comes in. 'Get your cape,' he says. 'They'll send your things on.'

I rise to my feet. 'Am I going to Syon with Kitty?' I ask. I think: now that we have both confessed, we will live in disgrace together, and I can write the script of our recovery.

'Yes,' he says. 'Hurry up.'

We will have to hurry, for it must be near slack water now. I get my cape and draw it around me because it is a cold November day and I can see the surface of the river is ruffled by wintry winds.

He gives me his arm, and we walk side by side through the garden, the dead leaves skittering away from our feet. We reach the pier, and he walks me up the gangplank to the back of the barge. The gangplank is run ashore, the lines cast off. The rowers raise their blades in salute, and then the bargemaster pushes us off and steps on board, and the rowers dip their oars.

I am surprised he is coming with me, I would have expected him to distance himself from Kitty, from me too. 'You're accompanying me?' I ask him. 'Are you joining us at Syon?'

'You're not going to Syon,' he says grimly. 'You're going to the Tower. This is an arrest. I am arresting you for treason. Another Boleyn traitor.'

# THE TOWER OF LONDON, NOVEMBER

## 1541

ONCE AGAIN, I watch the metal grille of the Tower water gate rise up and hear the clanking of the chains and see the water swirl. The barge glides in, and the new constable of the Tower, Sir John Gage, is here to greet me. He takes my hand as respectfully as if I am stepping out of the royal barge behind the queens I have served: Katherine of Aragon, my sister-in-law Anne, Jane Seymour, Anne of Cleves, Kitty in her pomp, on her entry to London. His face is grave, and he tucks my hand in his arm, as he walks me to the White Tower, up the outer steps, up the inner stair, and then we turn right and go to one of the good rooms, with a fireplace, a window overlooking the green, a privy chamber and, beyond that, a bedchamber, and a little room off for a servant.

I pause on the threshold, but I don't have to ask: I know this was George's room. This is the room where my husband waited for his trial, waited for his pardon, and then waited for his execution.

I stand for a moment in the doorway, and I can almost see him. I can almost see Anne, the woman he died for. I think how incredible it is that I should have been spared arrest then, that the two of them should have died together then, leaving me utterly bereft without them – and now I am here anyway!

Aghast, I turn to Sir John and see nothing but compassion in his face.

'Could I not have another room?' I whisper.

'We're full up,' he says grimly. 'And expecting more. This is the best room available. The dowager duchess and her daughter are to have the royal rooms . . .' He breaks off in embarrassment.

Agnes Howard the Dowager Duchess of Norfolk is arrested? And her daughter the Countess of Bridgewater? This makes no sense: the two of them knew nothing of Culpeper; but everything about Dereham. This changes everything again! The privy council must be charging Kitty with precontract, after all. The Tower is filled with Howards and their servants who know about Kitty's childhood – they will all offer evidence and we will all come out again! There is no law against Mistress Kitty Dereham taking Culpeper as her lover, the king has chosen the most merciful route, the one that shows him in the best light. They will release Kitty from Syon; they will release us all from the Tower.

All I have to do, for the next few days, is keep my wits about me when I sleep in my husband's bed and search the stone walls for the carving of his name among the many others imprisoned in this room. I trace it with my fingers as if it was a message for me. All I have to do is stay very calm. I am going to be released. I will stay calm and wait.

MY MAID SERVES my dinner in my privy chamber, but I find that it tastes of nothing. The maid is a spy, of course – not the spy that I was, in my heyday, when I was taught and mentored by the greatest spymaster in England. She is a conniving, snivelling, poor thing, the sort that we employed to listen at keyholes. I know she lingers at my bedroom door, hoping for heartbroken prayers of confession. But I have nothing to confess.

The queen is being investigated about her childhood, long before I knew her. Her guardian, her step-grandmother, will have to answer for that. As soon as this dawns on the slow intelligence of Thomas Audley, I will be released. As soon as he realises that the queen is guilty of nothing but marrying the king while married to Dereham, he will order the release of everyone but Kitty, who will probably stay at Syon in disgrace, for the rest of the king's life. If the doctor is right, that will be in the spring. At the very worst, we all have to get through the next six months.

I ask for books to study and papers to write, but they say I can only have paper and ink to write my confession. I am so furious at this that I scream at my maid that I am the best-educated woman in England – except for Margaret Roper, daughter of Sir Thomas More – and she curtseys and dashes out of the room. The next thing I know, in comes Sir Thomas Wriothesley with a writing desk and pen and ink and papers, to ask me what part Margaret Roper played in this adultery.

'She is as guilty as me of being a clever woman,' I snap.

'What do you know of her?' he asks keenly.

'You will drive me quite mad!' I say unguardedly. 'Margaret did nothing. The dinner is ill-cooked so I cannot eat, and you have lodged me in my husband's rooms – I sleep in my husband's bed . . .'

He looks quite shocked, and then he makes a note on the paper. 'D'you speak of Margaret Howard? And George Boleyn – you know that he is dead? D'you remember that you are a widow, Lady Rochford?'

We look blankly at each other. For once in my life, I cannot think. What is this fool asking me? Why drag Margaret Howard into it – who never did anything in her life but what her mother-in-law ordered? I never saw her in Kitty's rooms after she presented Francis Dereham.

'Margaret?' I ask him, buying time, but really, I cannot think what he wants of me. 'Which Margaret?'

'Do you know the name of the king?'

'I should think I do,' I say bitterly. 'And the queen's name is Katheryn.' I cannot hold back a bitter laugh. 'Katheryn again. Katheryn the second.'

He makes another note; his breath is coming faster. I see him glance to the door. 'I am going to send a kind gentleman to talk to you,' he says. 'Do you understand me, Lady Rochford?'

'I don't want to talk to a kind gentleman. I don't want to talk to anybody. I can't eat the dinner here. I can't sleep in my husband's bed. I can't stay here. I can't stay here for six months. I want to go home.'

'Why six months?' he asks quickly.

I look at him mutinously. 'Why not?'

'Where is your home?' he asks, as if he does not know what I did to win the ownership of Blickling Hall.

'You know as well as I do!' I exclaim. I think of my house and lands at Blickling and that they were given to me by Lord Cromwell in return for saying nothing. But I chose to live in palaces, I have spent more time at Greenwich Palace than anywhere else. My certainty dies away.

'Here,' I say desolately, thinking that this is my family vault; my husband and sister-in-law are buried in the Tower chapel. 'This is my family home, don't you think? I am in the Boleyn rooms? Isn't it our name on the wall? Isn't it our family vault across the green?'

He is stuffing papers and inkpot into his neat little writing desk and cramming down the lid on them. 'I will send Dr Butts,' he tells me. 'For your appetite and sleep. You can tell him. He is the one to judge . . . I will ask him to attend you . . .'

Holding his writing desk, asking for no help from his spy, my maid, he kicks his booted heel to hammer against the door, and the guard throws it open. I think I have never seen him so flustered. I laugh out loud; it is something to see Thomas Wriothesley running from my room like a scolded girl. I cannot think what is wrong with him.

I turn to my maid, the spy, and I see she has the same look as Wriothesley. She is terrified. She is terrified of being alone with me.

Then it comes to me. I give a little *tut* at my slowness and stupidity. Wriothesley thinks that they have driven me mad, that I am mad. This girl thinks I am mad, and she is locked up with a madwoman who might turn violent. And I – fool that I am – should have played mad as my last great performance the moment I arrived. A madman cannot be interrogated; a madman cannot be accused; a madman cannot be executed. How could I have forgotten this? I should have told Kitty, who is half-mad with natural silliness anyway. But I shall be mad until the king dies, and no one will accuse me of anything, and they will send me somewhere pleasant to stay, and I will slowly – very slowly – recover my senses.

I wear the mask of *Dionysus* – god of ecstasy and madness – and slowly, I let myself slide into fantasy. At once, my appetite returns, and I drink wine, mulled ale, and twice-brewed beer. I honour *Dionysus* by being drunk from the moment that I rise to loudly say my prayers in the morning until bedtime, when I sometimes forget to get undressed.

I feel my own imagination spinning loose, and for the first time in my life, I am not a courtier. I do not say what the king wants to hear – I speak for my own ears – I say what I like. Inside this prison, I am free for the first time. My room gets brighter and darker through the day; it is the only way I know the passing of time, because I cannot seem to keep up with the chimes of the Tower bells. Facing north, overlooking the green, it is always cold. I insist that the fire is lit in the grate before I will get up in the morning. 'I'm cold,' I say. 'Cold.' It is dark. Sometimes, I see a sunset in the evening sky, but it is dark when I wake in the morning. 'I'm dark,' I say. 'Dark.'

I am not quite sure who lives here with me and who is passing through as a visitor. No one is ever properly announced. George, my husband, is here most evenings; he's always looking out of the window for someone to come with a pardon. 'I will come,' I tell him. 'I will see the king. I will tell Jane Seymour to take off her hood and let down her hair and ask for pardon, for you and for Anne.'

Sir Thomas More usually comes around dawn and wakes me to

the cold room and the striking of the clock at six or nine, or it might be midnight – I can't count the chimes all the way through. 'How come you're so clever and yet you didn't say "no" to the king?' I ask him. 'Why does nobody ever say "no" to him?' That defeats him. 'Silence won't save you,' I tell him. 'I am silence.'

Dr Butts comes, as someone promised me he would. He asks me very dull questions about the date, as if I would know, living here in dark and light as I do! He asks me the name of my father and where is my house? I say: if he does not know that, he must be as mad as I am. Surely he knows I have no father? I am an orphan. Who has ever come to court to see me for fatherly love? My father only ever comes to behead someone. As for my house – I tell him the little joke that this must be my house, since my family vault is across the green, and my family crest on the wall; but he does not laugh. He looks at me very gravely, and when I go, he presses my hand. 'I will say you are unfit to testify,' he promises. 'But take care of yourself, Lady Rochford. Do not melt into your mask.'

He is not my only visitor. My Lord Cromwell never comes, and yet I would like to see him. I don't like to meet the others. So many others troop through my rooms and through my dreams at night: the Carthusians, Bishop Fisher, Geoffrey Pole with a bread knife in his fat chest, his mother Lady Margaret Pole, with her old neck hacked to pieces. No one said 'no' for her, and we all should have 'no' when they came for Lady Margaret.

'I'm not "no",' I tell my maid. 'I am silence. But silence doesn't save you, either.'

I catch her writing down declensions of Latin verbs, which I recite to show I remember everything. She mistakes Latin for the raving of a madwoman – she is such a fool.

'I am mad,' I say, to reassure her. 'Quite mad.'

Of course I am mad. I cannot comprehend that I am here, in my dead husband's bedroom, wrongly accused as he was, threatened with execution as he was, hoping for mercy from a merciless tyrant, as he did. Of course I am mad. Nobody could be at the court of this king unless they were out of their wits. We are all far from our humble beginnings; we are all out of our sphere; we are all masked, disguised, tutored, and tortured into insane shapes to make him look handsome, powerful, loveable. We all practise carols of praise to him, telling him over and over again, repeating like madmen and madwomen: what a great king he is, how wise, how gifted, how loveable.

Dawns come and go with Sir Thomas More. Two of them? Perhaps three?

'Who is the King of England?' my maid asks me. 'Who is the King of France?'

'Don't say he's been arrested, too?' I am staggered. 'On what charge?'

She shakes her head, angry with me as a keeper is angry with his madman, and she goes out of the room to tell someone that I am no better, that it is as Dr Butts says, that I cannot be questioned and I cannot be accused.

THIS MORNING – I know it is morning, because Anne walked under my window out to the scaffold on Tower Green at nine of the clock – the girl comes to me and says very loudly, as if I am deaf: 'Get your cape on. Put on your boots. Pull up the hood.'

'Am I going home?' I ask, in my new courtier voice, very high and pleasing. 'To Blickling?'

'Yes, yes,' she says, so readily that I know that she is lying.

She pushes my two gowns and my linen into a sack with my Bible and my hoods and my shoes. All jumbled, and the gowns will crease.

'I don't want to go without George,' I say.

'Oh, he'll come later,' she assures me. 'You come now, and he'll be along later.'

It is comical how courtiers will agree with anything. George my husband has been dead for five and a half years. I laugh at her folly, and she looks at me oddly.

I say: 'You know, when you see a madman, you should just say "no",' and she hustles me out of the door, where a guard leads the way, and one comes behind. I don't really want to walk past Tower Green, but there is no scaffold built for any execution, and there are no ghosts, just the grass growing, winter sere.

We go down the stone steps to the water gate; the tide is low, slack, and the plain barge without a standard bobs at its mooring. The maid hurries me on board, and the guard comes with us. I pull up the hood of my cape; it is bitterly cold, and the mist lies along the river like a wraith. I think it is very remiss of them not to send the Howard barge.

'Very discourteous,' I say to the girl, and she says 'Yes, m'lady,' and takes a stool beside my chair.

The water gate rolls up, creaking on its green wet chains and dripping from its points. The barge pushes off, and the rowers take us out into the river, where the tide is turning to take us upstream. They close the shutters so that no one can see me, but there is no need for them to take such care. It's not as if I am Lady Margaret Pole. She was of the old royal family, and governess to Lady Mary, mother to a cardinal – and still nobody said 'no' to her shipping and arrest and death. Nobody will say 'no' for me.

'Nobody ever says "no",' I tell the girl.

I think we are going upstream to Windsor Castle or perhaps Hampton Court. Perhaps the court is spending Christmas at Hampton Court, and they need me to plan the masquing. I am not sure how my mask of *Dionysus*-madness will fit a Christmas masque, but then I realise that everyone is mad at court anyway. The mask they wear is one of sanity, so that no one can ever mirror to the king his own mad face, his own mad will.

But we are not going to court. We pull into the north bank at the water stairs of a private house, and as I climb up from the river, I recognise the long garden and the handsome face of Russell House, and there is Lady Russell, who I last saw at Chenies, welcoming me to her London house.

She leads the way up through the hall, up the stairs, to my own rooms: a bedroom and a privy chamber that overlooks the garden and the busy sunlit river, and I realise, with a dawning sense of unreality, that I have done it! I have pulled off the greatest performance of my life. This was my finest dance, my wittiest script, my greatest masque. I am to be free; I am forgiven. I am officially mad, and as a madwoman, I am safe.

The only disadvantage with this part is that I cannot seem to stop playing it. Like all courtiers, I become what I was pretending to be. I spent my life pretending to be a loyal servant to an ideal king. I pretended I did not notice as he grew to be a monster. Now he is a monster, and I am madly loyal still.

## RUSSELL HOUSE, LONDON, DECEMBER

## 1541

I LIVE A SOLITARY life in Russell House. I only see his lordship at midday on Sunday when we all attend chapel, and he comes to my rooms after divine service and asks me: am I well?

'Yes, I thank you,' I say cautiously, for I think it safest to be mad until I receive a written pardon or the king is dead – whichever comes sooner.

'Can you tell me any more about the queen?' he asks.

'I can tell you about all of them. There have been many, and I have served them all.'

He looks at me, his brow a little furrowed. 'Be careful what you say,' he warns me.

'Superfluous,' I remark. 'We are always careful what we say.'

'Tell me about Katheryn Howard? Did she plan the death of the king?'

It is against the law to speak of the death of the king. 'Shush,' I say to him. 'Don't say that. Remember – never say that.'

He flinches. 'Jane, if you would hold on to what is real and give evidence against her, you would be pardoned,' he says. 'Do you understand that, Jane? Say that she was adulterous and hoping for the king's death, and you can go free.'

'Oh, certainly!' I say helpfully. 'Tell me! I will say anything! Anything the king wants me to say. I cannot imagine my own death, you know. It is impossible to imagine your own death.'

'You must tell the truth,' he says. 'A lie won't save you. You must tell me truly – did she bed Thomas Culpeper?'

'I don't know,' I say simply. 'They kissed and said they would die for love of each other.' I smile at him. 'Are they going to die for love?' I ask. 'Can I go to court for Christmas now?'

CHRISTMAS IS AT Greenwich this year, but although I told Lord Russell what he said he wanted, I am not invited. Nor are Lady Russell and her husband, and she tells me that the king wants no company and no celebrations of the season.

'But he will want gifts,' I caution her. 'He can live without dancing but not without gifts. He needs sacrifices. Human sacrifice.'

She looks oddly at me and says: 'Thomas Culpeper and Francis Dereham have been executed.'

'See?' I say.

She says gently: 'Jane, if you are pretending madness to escape trial and execution, it's doing you no good. Come back to your wits if you can.'

I laugh. 'I am the best educated woman in England but for Thomas More's daughter,' I tell her. 'I could not lose my wits; they are all I am. I could not be a courtier without them, and if I were not a courtier, I would be nothing at all.'

'Jane, I must warn you, we won't house you forever. You don't want to be begged as a fool, and go and live in a strange household as their idiot, do you?'

'No,' I agree. 'But I was sent to live in a strange household as an idiot when I was a little girl of just eleven. It's all I know, really.'

She shakes her head, and I think: but I know, and you do not, that the king will die in four and a half months' time. 'Will you keep me until May Day? I think I will be well by May Day.'

'I don't know,' she says. 'It's not my choice. Go to chapel and pray for your wits to come back to you, Jane.'

'I am pretending nothing,' I assure her. 'For the first time in my life, I have stopped pretending. I am in my right mind for the first time ever.'

She shakes her head. 'He won't let you stay with us, Jane, mad or not.'

'Oh no,' I assure her. 'I shall be back at court when he chooses his next wife. I always serve the Queen of England. He's never had a queen but I've been her lady, teaching her never to say "no" – whether it's a baby that he wants, or a divorce. He will choose another wife, and when he wants her to confess to a precontract or accuses her of treason or heresy, I will make up the evidence against her. Do you know yet who it will be?'

She looks deeply shocked. 'Silence! Madness does not excuse you! Go to your rooms!'

I really don't know what has upset her – the certainty of my return to court, or the certainty of another queen.

'I'm not mad to say the king will marry again,' I say quietly, as I go. 'I know his mind as well as I know my own. He cannot live without a woman far superior to him, a woman to humiliate. He cannot bear his impotence without a beautiful woman to blame. He cannot bear his own rot without a healthy body beside him.'

She claps her hands over her ears and shouts at her lady-in-waiting: 'See Lady Rochford back to her room! I won't hear this.'

I curtsey to her and smile at them all. 'Good day,' I say.

## PHILIPPA GREGORY

### RUSSELL HOUSE, LONDON, JANUARY

## 1542

I RECEIVE NO NEW translation from my father in the new year, and I see that he does not set his hand to the machinery of court, not even when it is his daughter caught in the gears. Nothing from any of the Howards. Not so much as a ribbon from Mary Boleyn – 'it's Mrs Stafford now!' – my sister-in-law. I conclude that I am cast off, declared mad, and quite forgotten. Dr Butts, the king's own physician, comes to visit and asks me what season it is, and what time of day, if I am a married woman or a widow, if I know the King of England?

I laugh and tell him that it is cold winter, Tudor winter, and there will never be a May Day for Henry again. The summer will bring the Sweat – the disease that came in with the Tudors. The winter will bring floods – we have not had good weather since King Richard was ridden down into mud. I tell him that once I was a wife – does he not remember my wedding? But now I am a widow, my husband killed by the king. The king is Henry – I know this well enough, because I am a widow thanks to him. I know him better than anyone in England knows him. I was raised to serve him, swore to die for him, and everyone I love has been killed by him. He only spares me because I am mad – he has driven all his courtiers quite out of our wits, and I am the only one who knows this.

Dr Butts takes my hand and speaks very quietly and quickly, almost as if he were hiding what he is saying from my maid who stands at the door, and the guard who stands outside it and perhaps another watcher who is in my bedroom at the half-closed door, straining to hear. 'Jane, I am trying to tell you something. Blink your eyes if you understand me.'

I am not such a fool. I stare at him with my eyes goggling wide.

'There is a law come before the new session on parliament which will be passed and turned into law without even the king's signature, just on his nod.'

I am as unblinking as an owl at dusk.

'It says there is a new treason: no woman may marry the king if she has had a lover or a husband before.'

'Katherine of Aragon, Anne Boleyn, Anne of Cleves, Katheryn Howard,' I say – naming four of five queens, divorced by the king for that very reason. 'He'll find that inconvenient.'

'It is to be applied retrospectively,' he says urgently. 'Do you understand? Backdated. Katheryn Howard will go on trial for marrying the king when she was betrothed to Francis Dereham. And she will be accused of foreseeing the king's death with Thomas Culpeper.'

Finally, they understand the contradiction in accusing her of adultery. I smile in my pleasure at the logic. 'It's tyranny, of course. But at last, it makes sense.'

'Listen,' is all he says. 'There is another clause to this new law. Anyone who is insane can now be interrogated – contrary to the previous law. Anyone insane can now be accused of a crime. Anyone insane can now be executed – contrary to the previous law. A madman can be executed even if he does not understand why.' He looks into my face. 'Or a madwoman.'

'No, no, madness is a complete defence under the law,' I tell him.

'Not any more. The king has ordered the law to be changed. Madness is no defence. A madwoman can be executed.'

His words pierce my indifference. 'He has changed the law on precontract, just to kill Kitty?' I whisper. 'He has changed the law on madness just to kill me?'

He nods.

'He is determined that she shall die because she is young and pretty and preferred a young handsome man to him?'

He nods again.

'And I am to die for knowing this?'
The spies strain their ears in the silence.
'Will no one say "no" to him?'

# THE TOWER OF LONDON, FEBRUARY

# 1542

I DO NOT NEED to pretend to madness in the world we live in. We are ruled by a madman, and we are all so bereft of our wits that, having started by obeying him, we have gone on to do what he wants before he even asks for it, and now we are all as mad as him. When he was young, he was fair and handsome, and we admired him, loved him, and thought he would go on to do great things. Now that he is tyrant, we go on saying he is fair and handsome and we admire, love, and expect much of him. He threatens war with his neighbours, he destroys the Church, he rewrites laws, murders his friends, and destroys his wives, and we are as mad as March hares – we never ever say 'no'.

The dark barge comes for me in February, and I don't bother to caper or sing. Whether I am mad or sane, the king is going to kill me, as he has killed hundreds of others: from the pilgrims, starved to death in their metal cages hanging at crossroads in Yorkshire, to those that waited obediently for their deaths in the Tower, as I do.

I am not alone in here. Sir John Gage could not give me my old room when I came again to the water gate. The place is as busy as an inn; he could not reserve my usual rooms for me. Kitty's step-grandmother the dowager duchess is in my old room, her daughter the countess with her. Kitty herself is in the rooms where Anne waited for her death. Others of her family and her maids-of-honour are in cells in the White Tower and in the nearby buildings. Dozens of us are charged with treason, because the king cannot bear to think that a wife nearly young enough to be his granddaughter might have fallen in love with a young man who was deeply in love with her.

We are not waiting for trial. The lords will use the device of my spymaster, the writ of attainder, so we can be proclaimed guilty without being heard. It is – as he told me – so much more efficient than a public trial. Kitty chooses not to defend herself – how could she? She would have had no idea that there was anything to say in her own defence. She would not play *Guinevere* – but she will play the dying queen – *Polyxena* – and they tell me she has the block brought to her chamber so she can practise kneeling and laying down her head. It gives me a little shock to think that I will have to kneel where she knelt just minutes before, lay down my cheek on the block where she laid hers. They'll never clean it properly; I will die with Kitty's blood on my cheek.

Or perhaps we will just wait in the Tower, wait for years, like Margaret Pole, like Lord Lisle, as the king's fickle attention scampers elsewhere – war with France, the marriage of Lady Mary, an alliance with Scotland, the return of the Church? He could be thinking of anything but us. I doubt he will kill Kitty until he wants a new wife, as he usually does. The longer that we wait – all the first week of February and into the second – the more sure I am that he has forgotten about us.

'The king dined with some ladies,' my maid tells me one cold grey morning. 'He held a great dinner, and sixty-one ladies attended.'

Choose your partner – I would have foreseen this if I had been still mad. But it is the ladies who paraded themselves at dinner for the king to choose who are the mad ones.

'Was the king happy?' It's all that ever matters. 'Was he happy? Was he pleased? Did he favour anyone? Is he well?'

'They say he was pleased with Lady Cobham, Elizabeth Basset, and she who was the wife of Sir Thomas Wyatt, Elizabeth Brooke, oh – and Kateryn Parr.'

'Old friends,' I say, smiling at the revival of the ambition of

Elizabeth Basset and the return to court of the others. Three of them were fellow spies with me for my Lord Cromwell. 'Dear old friends.'

It is now a race, and if I were a gambling woman, I should put money on the king becoming urgent in his desire for a new wife before the ulcer on his leg kills him. If he wants to clear the Tower of the friends and kinsmen and -women of his fifth wife before his wedding to the sixth, then the executioner will be busy. But if he tries to dance on his one leg, in his one-sided courtship, then he may kill himself before he can kill us. It is a race, and my life is the stake.

I think I am amused by this until I hear the noise of hammering wood, and I look from my window. Just out of the corner of the window, only visible if I press my face to the cold little panes of old glass, I can see Tower Green, and they are building a scaffold, and I know I have lost my bet, and little Kitty Howard has lost hers. The tyrant is clearing the way for another wife. Whoever she is, she will have to keep her wits about her.

We should have said 'no'. We should have said 'no' at the first sign of madness – the dismissal of Queen Katherine of Aragon. We should have said 'no' to the deaths that followed. All that is needed to defeat a tyrant is the courage to say 'no'.

I see little Kitty, head bowed, walk under my window to the green. It is a new walk for her; she will have rehearsed it. Her head droops like a tired lily on its stem; she sways a little, as if she is hearing the music of a dance in her head. Her new walk is a slow lilting pace, like the *Volta*, her scaffold walk.

Even pressed against the window, I can only see the ladder up to the platform and the waiting headsman. But I hear the silence fall on the small invited crowd as she climbs the steps, and the silence as she speaks – she will have rehearsed her speech but it will be quite nonsensical – then the silence as they wait for her eyes to be masked and for her to kneel before the block, and then the roll of the drums, and the thud of the axe and the 'oh' as the crowd witnesses a death prettily done, well done by Kitty who liked to do things well. But they should have said 'no'.

There is a knock at my door, and Sir John Gage comes in, his face grave, his eyes on the ground. 'Are you ready, Lady Rochford?' he asks.

'I'm ready,' I say.

But I should have said 'no'.

# AFTERWORD

Anyone might think that there has been enough written about the Tudors! I, too, have made a contribution to this huge library. But there are still characters never explained or understood, and one of the greatest is Jane Boleyn, Lady Rochford.

There are good reasons for this – she was a minor Tudor woman, and, like all Tudor women, not much was recorded about her in her own time. We don't know the date of her birth, we don't have any lengthy letters, we don't even have a portrait of her, though Hans Holbein sketched many of her friends.

She was not named as a witness in the trials of her husband and sister-in-law, and George Boleyn's complaint that he was being convicted on the evidence of a woman did not identify that woman as Jane. Research now suggests that she was not one of those who gave evidence against him and his sister, and we have a letter from her to George, promising to speak to the king for him.

And yet she is blamed. Years after the trial, after her own disgrace and death, her reputation was destroyed by the accounts that she had betrayed her husband and her sister-in-law. These were not unbiased new findings, but part of the rehabilitation of Anne Boleyn's reputation when her daughter, Elizabeth, took the throne. The new queen's mother had to be exonerated, without blaming the queen's father, Henry VIII. The building of the Tudor story, supporting their right to rule, was the start of the whitewashing of Henry VIII's reputation. The price was the vilification of Jane.

This is my first novel since writing *Normal Women: 900 Years of Making History*, an exploration of how women's history is missing from what we read as complete history books. It became clear that the unstated, often unconscious, biases of historians have skewed the history of what women actually did. Even when there was evidence before them of independence, agency, and logical action, historians have still reported dependence, weakness, and even madness. Jane Boleyn's history is a striking example of this.

Even though she was hardly mentioned in the first accounts of the trial, Jane was later blamed for a murderous plot against her husband, and then for going on to pimp her kinswoman, Katheryn Howard, into an affair with a courtier which led to their deaths. Why – the all-male historians of the Victorian period asked themselves – why would a woman do that? Their only answer was that she must have been profoundly wicked – and terribly unladylike. 'Jane Boleyn the monster' was born out of widely held Victorian beliefs that women are naturally sexually frigid, naturally domesticated, and naturally lacking in ambition. Thus, any successful woman courtier tainted by sexual scandal cannot be a lady, cannot be a heroine. Indeed, she is so unwomanly, she is barely human. She is a monster.

This image of the monster-Jane was revised by new attitudes to women from the 1960s onwards, though a more liberal view of female sexuality has done her no favours, but instead has created a new lens of shame. The new, sexually liberated imagined Jane is driven by perverse desires as a voyeur. This Jane takes sexual pleasure from watching: first her husband with his sister, and then her young cousin with her lover.

And there her reputation was fixed, until more recent publications began to assert the common-sense view that Jane Boleyn could not have been a successful courtier, holding down a highly desirable post through five reigns, in the grip of an uncontrollable sex addiction or murderous spite.

Of course, Jane is not the only historical character to be written and rewritten according to the changing views of historians.

In time, everyone is revised. I, too, have been part of that re-imagining. I wrote of Katherine of Aragon as she was when she first came to England – not the tragic, old, defeated woman of most of the histories we read. Anne Boleyn's public reputation has gone from an imaginary, murderous, incestuous, adulterous villain, to Protestant heroine, and even martyr, as each different generation of historians has sought and found a different Anne Boleyn. My first Tudor novel, *The Other Boleyn Girl*, was written from the point of view of Anne's sister, Mary Boleyn, who (I think) could have been deeply afraid that what was being said of her sister was true; my novel describes her worst fears. Jane Seymour was the great favourite of Victorian historians, a quiet wife who had the grace to die in childbirth, and there are not many records of her short, married life for recent historians to revise. Nobody looking seriously at Anne of Cleves' enchanting portrait could believe Henry VIII's report that she made him impotent – but Team-Henry historians supported that story for five hundred years, until more forensic analyses of Henry focused on his accidents and illness. And Katheryn Howard's reputation has risen since her disgrace, with the increased understanding and sympathy towards young, sexually active women.

Katheryn claimed in her confession that she was sexually abused, and this has led to a rewriting of her history as a victim, rather than a thoughtless nymphomaniac. Alas, there are still some determined dinosaurs, but most people see that Katheryn did not give full consent to the two so-called lovers of her childhood and cannot be seen of as knowingly, consciously, consenting to her marriage with the king. The disparity of power was so great that the seventeen-year-old niece of a highly ambitious uncle could not have refused the King of England. Gareth Russell's recent biography of Katheryn Howard emphasises her youth and inexperience as well as her flirtatious nature.

Recent historians have pulled back from the view of a hyper-sexual Jane Boleyn as well. Julia Fox's thoughtful biography offers us a portrait of a loving wife and loyal sister, neither accusing her husband nor relishing his adultery. But Jane cannot simply have been in the wrong time and place – a key witness at two trials for royal adultery, and two royal divorces.

I think the answer to the mystery of her career is to be found in the turning point for the Boleyn family. When they were disgraced in a show trial against a flirtatious queen who had lost her husband's love, failed to give him a son, and had no powerful supporters, Jane did not share their disgrace. The Boleyn sister and brother and their supporters died on the scaffold, and the Boleyn parents retired to the country, but Jane sailed on into the next reign – well paid, promoted, and respected. She was appointed almost at once to serve the new queen, Jane Seymour.

She even benefited from a law, passed in Parliament, that gave her an improved widow's dower. How did she get this? Neither the Boleyns nor their great family, the Howards, could, or would, have done this for the widow of a traitor. I think it can only have been Thomas Cromwell, at the peak of his success, building a spy and management network throughout the court and country. I think Cromwell brought her back from temporary disgrace and then used her as one of his many lady-spies in the queen's rooms, through three reigns.

When Jane Seymour died and Anne of Cleves arrived, it was Jane Boleyn who was her chief lady-in-waiting, but not even her warnings of the failure of the marriage could save Cromwell from the plotting of his great rivals and enemies, the Spanish party, who continued to support their heir, the Roman Catholic princess Lady Mary.

Cromwell did not survive the divorce of his candidate, Anne of Cleves, though I think he and Jane created the evidence for the divorce; and his death left Jane without a spymaster and patron. But she still had the fortune that he had won for her – the magnificent Blickling Hall in Norfolk was hers for life, with other lands that paid rent. She could have retired from court and lived on her lands as a wealthy widow. She was rich enough to be an attractive wife and could have married again. But she did not.

You don't have to be a Victorian historian to imagine that Jane was ambitious. The court life was all she had known from girlhood, and the arrival of young Katheryn Howard at court was a wonderful opportunity for Jane to advise and guide another queen, especially as this one might outlive her husband. There is no historical evidence that Jane was hoping to be lady-in-waiting to a queen regent – that part is my fiction. But 'my' Jane – the Jane of this novel – has studied Henry VIII all her life, and sees, as everyone saw in real life, his deterioration in these years.

We know that she helped Katheryn and Thomas Culpeper to meet, fully aware of the danger. The great question about Jane is why would she do this? The outdated answers – firstly that she was murderously wicked, then that she was sexually perverse – are, I think, very unlikely. If Jane's was jealous of her queens, why did she help Anne of Cleves to safety and prosperity? If she was compelled by voyeurism, she could have satisfied it without fatal danger to herself, her young kinswoman, and her family. The fact that she was in the room when the lovers met – even when they were sexually active – is not proof of her perversity, nor of theirs, but of an attempt by all three to cling to a sort of respectability. And though shocking to the Victorians, and perhaps to us, we must remember that in medieval England people often had sex in crowded rooms with others watching or hearing; privacy is a modern invention.

Jane cannot be accused of being a pimp in the Howard–Culpeper affair, even though they both blamed her once they were caught. Nobody reading Katheryn's letter to Thomas could think that this was a girl tricked into meeting an unwanted suitor. Her letter – which I quote in the novel – are the words of a young woman deeply in love. She wrote,

> *'I never longed so muche for [a] thynge as I do to se you and to speke wyth you, the wyche I trust shal be shortely now, the wyche dothe comforthe me verie much whan I thynk of ett and wan I thynke agan that you shall departe from me agayne ytt makes my harte to dye to thynke what fortune I have that I cannot be always yn your company.'*

I think Jane helped the lovers because she saw the opportunity for herself. I believe that she looked at Katheryn Howard, nearly thirty years younger than her injured, overweight, deteriorating husband, and thought: this could be a dowager queen of England. If Katheryn could get pregnant and crowned before the king's death, she would have a good chance of being on a regency council ruling England. If she gave birth to a royal son, her importance was guaranteed – and so was Jane's. But how was Katheryn Howard to conceive?

Jane knew that the king was frequently impotent and had been so for years. He had been occasionally impotent with her sister-in-law, Anne Boleyn, he conceived a son with Jane Seymour; but complained that he could not consummate his marriage Anne of Cleves – Jane was even commissioned to state this as evidence for the divorce. Jane may have thought that the only way Katheryn Howard was going to get pregnant was by another man: Thomas Culpeper.

Jane had good reasons to help the lovers meet: their dangerous bond linked them forever in a treasonous conspiracy that guaranteed her future, either as trusted ally or a blackmailer. But in the novel, as fiction, I suggest that this woman, who had never been in love, whose life was always dedicated to ambition and the hard-hearted flirtations of a court, saw a real love, a tender love between two young people, and was inspired to help them.

Unspoken thoughts and unwritten emotions are always the material of fiction, and not of history, which cannot see or record them. So, this part of my novel is all fiction. But it is based – as my fiction always is – on the facts that history does know and report. We know that Jane took a fatal risk to help Katheryn and

Culpeper be together, and that she played the part of chaperone at the meetings where he did no more than kiss Katheryn's hand. Far from throwing them into bed together, she helped them meet and talk. The two never confessed to doing more than falling in love and meeting in secret. Jane never confessed to more than helping them to do that. What they seem to have wanted was to be together, to court like young lovers, and what Jane seems to have done is help them do that.

We know nothing about Jane's education, except that her father was a famous scholar, specialising in translations from Greek and Latin to English. He gave his works as New Year's gifts to the king and to Lady Mary – as I describe in the novel. David Starkey's work on Jane's father, Lord Morley, even tells us the titles of his works, and it is from that research that I discovered that Jane's father gave Thomas Cromwell a gift of the works of Niccolò Machiavelli – the famously cynical description of power and tyranny. Whether Jane was trained as a Machiavellian courtier, we do not know – but the connection between her father and Thomas Cromwell is deeply intriguing.

One of the metaphors used throughout the book is the two-faced nature of the Tudor court: the costumes and disguises of the masques reflect the dishonesty of the court of a tyrant. This view of Henry VIII has evolved from the first, Elizabethan view of him as the founder of a nation, and from a post-war view of him as a jolly eccentric. Now, there is a growing understanding of him as a dangerous man: an abuser of women, a false friend, and a tyrant. Like modern tyrants, Henry used the institutions and traditions against his society, he used the law to unlawfully persecute his victims. Advised by Thomas Cromwell, he used the writ of attainder to sidestep treason trials and execute men and women on his word alone. Even more complex: he ordered a new law to execute Thomas More, Bishop Fisher, and many others. He even changed the law which excluded the insane from execution, solely to behead Jane Boleyn, who was either mad or pretending to be mad hoping for asylum under the law's protection. Tyrants corrupt good institutions against their people; Henry VIII did this five centuries ago.

Tyranny is the theme of this novel, written in difficult times when so-called 'strong men' (or those who posture as strong), are in power. All of us have to decide what offence against our institutions, against our traditions, against our liberties, or against the liberties and lives of others, is our sticking point: the point where we say 'no'. History tells us that we must find the courage to defend others, and our country's institutions and traditions before the danger is immediate and personal. By the time the tyrant comes for us – it is too late. We must not be like Jane Boleyn, recognising the dangers too late to say 'no', or we will be silenced like her, and the tyrant will write our history, too.

# BIBLIOGRAPHY

Adams, Beverley, *The Forgotten Tudor Royal: Margaret Douglas, Grandmother to King James VI and I*, Pen & Sword, 2023

Akkerman, Nadine and Langman, Pete, *Spycraft: Tricks and Tools of the Dangerous Trade from Elizabeth I to the Restoration*, YUP, 2024

Baldwin Smith, Lacey, *Catherine Howard: The Queen Whose Adulteries Made a Fool of Henry VIII*, Amberley, 2009

Bapst, Edmond, *Two Gentleman Poets at the Court of Henry VIII: George Boleyn and Henry Howard*, translated by J. A. Macfarlane and Claire Ridgway, Independently Published, 2013. Originally published in French by Librarie Plon

Bernard, G. W., *Anne Boleyn: Fatal Attractions*, YUP, 2010

Bezio, Kristin, *The Eye of the Crown: The Development and Evolution of the Elizabethan Secret Service*, Routledge, 2022

Borman, Tracy, *Thomas Cromwell: The Untold Story of Henry VIII's Most Faithful Servant*, Hodder & Stoughton, 2014

Borman, Tracy, *Henry VIII and the Men Who Made Him*, Hodder & Stoughton, 2018

Brigden, Susan, *Thomas Wyatt: The Heart's Forest*, Faber and Faber, 2012

Bruce, Marie Louise, *Anne Boleyn*, Collins, 1972

Byrne, Conor, *Katherine Howard: Henry VIII's Slandered Queen*, History Press, 2019

Castiglione, Baldesar, *The Book of the Courtier*, translated by George Bull, Penguin, 1976

Chambers, R. W., *Thomas More*, Harcourt Brace & Co, 1935
Cherry, Clare and Ridgway, Claire, *George Boleyn: Tudor Poet, Courtier and Diplomat*, MadeGlobal, 2014
Childs, Jessie, *Henry VIII's Last Victim*, Jonathan Cape, 2006
Claiden-Yardley, Kirsten, *The Man Behind the Tudors: Thomas Howard 2nd Duke of Norfolk*, Pen & Sword, 2020
Clark, Nicola, *The Waiting Game: The Untold Story of the Women Who Served the Tudor Queens*, W&N, 2024
Denny, Joanna, *Katherine Howard: A Tudor Conspiracy*, Portrait, 2005
Dodds, Madeleine Hope and Dodds, Ruth, *The Pilgrimage of Grace, 1536–1537 and The Exeter Conspiracy, 1538*, vol. 2, CUP, 1915
Fletcher, Anthony and MacCulloch, Diarmaid, *Tudor Rebellions*, Longman, 1997
Fox, Julia, *Jane Boleyn: The Infamous Lady Rochford*, W&N, 2007
Fraser, Antonia, *The Six Wives of Henry VIII*, Phoenix, 2012
Grueninger, Natalie, *The Final Year of Anne Boleyn*, Pen & Sword, 2022
Gunn, Steven, *Charles Brandon: Henry VIII's Closest Friend*, Amberley, 2015
Guy, John, *A Daughter's Love: Thomas and Margaret More – The Family Who Dared to Defy Henry VIII*, Penguin, 2012
Hart, Kelly, *The Mistresses of Henry VIII*, History Press, 2009
Hershman, D. Jablow and Lieb, Julian M. D., *A Brotherhood of Tyrants: Manic Depression and Absolute Power*, Prometheus, 1994
Howard, Maurice, *The Tudor Image*, Tate Gallery, 1995
Hutchinson, Robert, *Thomas Cromwell: The Rise and Fall of Henry VIII's Most Notorious Minister*, W&N, 2009
Kesselring, K. J., *Mercy and Authority in the Tudor State*, CUP, 2003
Lee, Frederick George, *Reginald Pole, Cardinal Archbishop of Canterbury: An Historical Sketch*, Wentworth Press, 2019
Lipscomb, Suzannah, *1536: The Year that Changed Henry VIII*, Lion, 2009
Loades, David, *Henry VIII and His Queens*, Bramley Books, 1997
Loades, David, *The Boleyns: The Rise and Fall of a Tudor Family*, Amberley, 2012

Loades, David, *Jane Seymour: Henry VIII's Favourite Wife*, Amberley, 2013

Locke, A. Audrey, *The Seymour Family*, Houghton Mifflin, 1914

Machiavelli, Niccolò, *The Prince*, translated by George Bull, Penguin, 2003

Mackay, Lauren, *Among the Wolves of Court: The Untold Story of Thomas and George Boleyn*, Bloomsbury, 2020

Mackay, Lauren, *Inside the Tudor Court*, Amberley, 2014

Matusiak, John, *Wolsey: The Life of King Henry VIII's Cardinal*, History Press, 2014

Mayer, Thomas, F., *Reginald Pole: Prince and Prophet*, CUP, 2000

Nelson-Campbell, Deborah and Cholakian, Rouben, *The Legacy of Courtly Literature: From Medieval to Contemporary Culture*, Palgrave Macmillan, 2017

Newcombe, D. G., *Henry VIII and the English Reformation*, Routledge, 1995

Randell, Keith, *Henry VIII and the Reformation in England*, Hodder Education, 2001

Rees, Laurence, *The Dark Charisma of Adolf Hitler: Leading Millions into the Abyss*, Ebury, 2012

Russell, Gareth, *Young and Damned and Fair: The Life of Catherine Howard, Fifth Wife of King Henry VIII*, Simon & Schuster, 2017

Scarisbrick, J. J., *Henry VIII*, YUP, 1968

Schofield, John, *The Rise and Fall of Thomas Cromwell: Henry VIII's Most Faithful Servant*, History Press, 2011

Soberton, Sylvia Barbara, *The Forgotten Tudor Women: Margaret Douglas, Mary Howard and Mary Shelton*, Independently Published, 2015

Soberton, Sylvia Barbara, *Ladies-in-Waiting: Women Who Served Anne Boleyn*, Independently Published, 2022

Starkey, David, 'An Attendant Lord? Henry Parker, Lord Morley,' in Marie Axton and James P. Carley, eds., *'Triumphs of English': Henry Parker, Lord Morley, Translator to the Court: New Essays in Interpretation*, The British Library, 2000

Starkey, David, *Six Wives: The Queens of Henry VIII*, Vintage, 2004

Taffe, James, *Courting Scandal: The Rise and Fall of Jane Boleyn, Lady Rochford*, Independently Published, 2023

Twycross, Meg and Carpenter, Sarah, *Masks and Masking in Medieval and Eary Tudor England*, Routledge, 2002

Warnicke, Retha M., *The Rise and Fall of Anne Boleyn*, CUP, 1989

Warnicke, Retha M., *The Marrying of Anne of Cleves: Royal Protocol in Tudor England*, CUP, 2000

Weir, Alison, *Henry VIII: King and Court*, Pimlico, 2002

Williamson, Hugh Ross, *The Cardinal in Exile*, Michael Joseph, 1969

Wilson, Derek, *In the Lion's Court: Power, Ambition, and Sudden Death in the Reign of Henry VIII*, Hutchinson, 2001